Love Against the Autumn Sky

Love Against the Autumn Sky is published under Reverie, a sectionalized division under Di Angelo Publications, Inc.

Reverie is an imprint of Di Angelo Publications.
Copyright 2021.

This book is a work of fiction. Names, characters, places, and incidents are either the products of the author's imagination or used fictionally, and any resemblace to actual persons, living or dead, business establishments, events, or locales, is entirely coincidental.

Di Angelo Publications
4265 San Felipe #1100
Houston, Texas 77027

Library of Congress
Love Against the Autumn Sky
Second Edition
ISBN: 978-1-955690-04-1

Words: Willa Frederic
Cover Design: Savina Deianova
Interior Design: Kimberly James
Editors: Ashley Crantas, Stephanie Yoxen

Downloadable via Kindle, Nook, and Google Play.

For educational, business, and bulk orders, contact sales@diangelopublications.com.

1. Fiction --- Romance --- Contemporary
2. Fiction --- Romance --- Western
3. Fiction --- Small Town & Rural

Printed in the United States of America with int. distribution.

Love Against the Autumn Sky

WILLA FREDERIC

One

"Ma'am? We're here."

Ava MacDaniel glanced out the rain-streaked window of the Escalade. Sure enough—twenty-nine blocks had blurred by in what felt like seconds. She had been so wrapped up in her pie charts and spreadsheets that they could have been in Africa instead of the Upper East Side and she wouldn't have noticed.

"Thanks, Andy," she said to her driver, tucking the folder into her red Hermès handbag. She reached for the door handle and saw Andy's smile tighten in the rearview mirror. Ava had made it clear she was perfectly capable of climbing out of a car on her own, but Andy was old-fashioned, and habits die hard. Ava stepped onto the wet sidewalk and smoothed her dress. . .Everything needed to be perfect today.

The air felt unusually sticky for early autumn. She looked up and saw heavy clouds gathering and growing darker by the second. What was it people always said about New York? *If you don't like the weather, wait ten minutes.* Good thing she was already at her building. As she hurried towards the massive revolving doors, she checked her bag once more: phone, files, binder, wallet. She still felt like she was missing something. Ava yelped and shuffled back as a motorcycle ripped down the narrow alley to her right, echoing its roaring exhaust up the skyscraper walls on either side.

Someone shouted her name. She turned and saw Andy, his hand raised in her direction.

"I'm sorry, what was that?" she called.

"I said good luck, ma'am! I don't know what you're walking into today, but I can tell it's important to you. You're gonna be great."

Ava grinned, waving as he pulled away from the curb. Andy was right. She *was* going to be great. True, she was exhausted from staying up until four a.m. going over every sum and punctuation mark, but it was nothing a little under-eye concealer couldn't handle. She checked her watch: ten minutes to spare. With her plan sketched out to the penny, this should be a piece of cake.

Cake.

Oh, no. The pastries! She had forgotten to ask Andy to stop on the way. She stuck out her hand, but she knew it was no use; she'd never get a cab at this hour. Ava twisted her long auburn hair into a topknot and tied the belt on her Burberry trench snugly around her waist. She glanced up once more and noticed that the clouds had knit together into a steely blanket that stretched across the whole sky. It was four blocks to Wrobleski's Bakery... She'd better run.

Breathless, Ava watched the red number change as the elevator beeped at each level. Finally, the doors opened as an irritatingly calm voice cooed, "Fortieth floor."

She rushed off the elevator, turning her face away from each office door as she hurried along the spotless marble tile. She didn't have time to make small talk.

Mode Capital Enterprise occupied the entire level, but the art deco building lacked the open floor plan of newer skyscrapers. To her left, empty glass conference rooms opened to a wall of windows. Ava's own office was tucked into the large suite at the very end of the hall.

Outside the frosted door, she wiped the sweat off her neck and checked her reflection in the glass: not her finest, but it could be worse. As she wiggled her cramped toes, wincing at the bruises forming on the balls of her feet, she heard a sudden roar of rushing water. The floor-to-ceiling window in the nearest conference room looked as if it was behind a waterfall, the rain pouring so hard that she couldn't even see the next building. Her eyes widened; it could definitely be worse. She took a deep breath and swung open the heavy door, the echo of her footsteps announcing her arrival.

It was chilly outside as winter crept closer by the day, but the fortieth floor always felt at least ten degrees colder. The building might be a hundred years old, but MC Enterprise existed squarely in the twenty-first century. Despite the best efforts of a few green houseplants, the interior was intentionally angular and bare, a palette of gray and white. *An aesthetic*, her mother might call it.

Immediately, a hand snatched Ava's trench coat from her arm and grabbed the white pastry box. Margo was like a ninja.

"Morning, Ava!" she chirped, her wide grin lighting up her round face. With one swift movement, Margo flipped open the pastry box and set it on the coffee counter. "I'm so glad to see you. I've been calling you nonstop for the last fifteen minutes! Did you get my texts?!"

Ava's assistant Margo had graduated from Wharton the year before. Neat, enthusiastic, and a hyper-organized art fan, she'd probably take over a Fortune 500 company by twenty-five if she didn't have a nervous breakdown first.

"Sorry, Margo, I was running late—that's the order from Wrobleski's."

"I'm your assistant!" Margo protested. "You should have let me get it, especially today."

Ava shrugged. "Normally, it wouldn't have been a big deal. . .I just kind of forgot with everything going on. You said you were calling me?"

"Oh, right!" Margo's face lit up. "You'll never believe it: *DAR #5* just sold for fifty-thousand dollars—less than twenty-four hours after listing!"

Ava looked at her, drawing a blank. "*DAR #5*?"

"Yes!" Margo shrieked. "We've been getting calls all morning. Practically everyone in town wants to meet with you!"

Margo passed an iPad to Ava as they hurried through the lobby. Ava glanced at it and recognized several of the names: some of the most notable agents and gallery owners in town. Her eyes widened as she scrolled to a second full page. As they passed the reception desk, she gave a little wave to Roger, which he returned with the same warm nod he'd been giving her every morning since she'd first walked into MC Enterprise several years earlier.

Suddenly, it hit Ava. "Oh! *DAR #5*! That's the blue one, right? *Dolphin at Rest?*"

"Wow," Margo said, her eyes shining with admiration as she followed Ava into her snug corner office. "I can't imagine being such a prolific painter that I forget my own work. People are saying you might be the next Rothko!"

Ava flashed what she hoped passed as a flattered smile. Rothko was known for being horribly difficult to work with, but she could tell Margo meant it as a compliment.

Ava set her handbag on her desk and glanced at her watch: 9:10. *Yikes.*

"Hey, Margo, is Carla in? I'm a little late and we're supposed to have that meeting."

"Oh my gosh, yes, of course! I'm sorry to slow you down! She told me to send you in the minute you arrived."

"Thanks," Ava said. "Please let everyone know the pastries are here."

She wiped her palms on her dress before clutching her folder to her stomach. *Here goes nothing.*

"About damn time."

Good morning to you, too, Ava thought, forcing a smile as she closed the heavy walnut door behind her. "Hi, Mom."

Carla MacDaniel always looked taller than her five-and-a-half feet, but especially when she was perched behind her massive mahogany desk. Today, she wore a crisp white blouse and red lipstick. She patted her perfectly coifed blonde hair that added another two inches to her height before fixing her catlike eyes on Ava.

"You're late," Carla said, dryly.

"I know, I'm so sorry. . .It was my turn to get the pastries," Ava said, pressing herself against the door. "And you know how Lola Wrobleski always talks. She said she's knitting you a scarf for Christmas and wanted to know how you feel about wool? Oh, should I get you a croissant? I didn't think to ask."

"You're nervous," said Carla.

"Right. Yes. Sorry," Ava said, taking a few awkward steps toward the desk. "I just—well. . .I'm really excited is all."

"Well, let's see it then," Carla said. She sipped her tea and waited.

Ava took a deep breath. She could feel her heart pounding in her ears. She pulled out her folder and carefully spread four brightly-printed charts on the desk in front of Carla.

Game time.

"Mom, I know you have concerns about the feasibility of an artists' live-in workshop, at least financially—and I get it. I know what it looks like from the outside."

"It looks like charity," Carla interrupted. "And, darling, we can't afford charity on that scale."

"I hear you," Ava said, smiling forcefully as she straightened her shoulders. "And *that's* why I asked for this meeting. Take a look at the bar graph."

Carla slipped her tortoiseshell bifocals onto her nose and yanked one of the papers closer. She stared at the figures for several seconds, her expression unchanging.

Ava swallowed. "Recognize those names?" she asked.

"Of course," Carla said, tossing her an impatient glance.

"I thought you might," Ava said. "Those are some of the most famous breakout artists of the last few years. Now look *under* each name. That's the country each artist came from. . .Not your usual hotspots, are they?"

Carla eyed Ava's annotations. "What's your point?"

"If the only artist you know from that country is a huge trailblazer, imagine how much undiscovered talent is still there! Talent without a mentor. No one in New York is looking for artists in Sri Lanka or Honduras or Tibet. But I just know the talent in those places must be incredible. We can give them a space to learn and create, and then introduce them to the art world."

Carla looked hard at Ava. She glanced at the graph again. Ava stuck her trembling hands behind her back. Finally, Carla spoke:

"It's noble, I'll give you that, but it's not business. You're an artist, but I'm a venture capitalist. This just isn't a good investment."

Ava's throat tightened. She knew she'd been lucky when it came to her career. She'd always had her mother's support—well, financially, anyway. If Carla hadn't taken her to Paris, gotten her into the best programs, introduced her to the who's who of the art world. . .Ava doubted she'd have anyone referring to her as the next Rothko. So many artists never got a chance at the opportunities Ava had been handed.

"I'm sorry to burst your bubble, Ava," Carla continued,

stacking the other charts into a neat pile. "But you haven't exactly presented a business plan."

Ava lifted her chin. "I had a feeling you were going to say that."

She slapped down a bound, professionally-printed file, with pages of profit estimates, long-term gains, and any comps she could find. She'd had it printed as an afterthought at Kinko's at two in the morning, but Carla didn't need to know that.

She eyed Ava with curiosity as she began thumbing through the pages. She scanned one page, then another. It felt like decades were passing. Finally, Carla looked up.

"What exactly am I supposed to do with this, Ava?"

"You wanted to see profits, Mom. Here they are. We create a brick-and-mortar gallery. Every artist we mentor sells through us, and the contract would stipulate a five-year exclusive sales agreement. Not only that, but we can use the gallery to sell my paintings without a middleman. I'm sure you heard about *DAR #5*."

Carla almost smiled. "I'm told it might be a new gallery record."

"Exactly!" Ava said. "And how much of that sale is ending up in Eduardo Alvarez's pocket? You fund this project and MacDaniel Fine Art Residence and Gallery—working title, of course—keeps a hundred percent in-house."

Ava knew all the sleepless nights and stolen hours of research had given her a sound plan. Carla may not be particularly sentimental, but she could smell a great investment across the Atlantic. How could she possibly say no?

Carla studied Ava. "I have to say, I'm impressed. I had no idea you were such a shrewd businesswoman. Must be genetic."

Ava's heart was a kick drum now.

"This has potential to be a moneymaker," Carla continued, tapping the booklet against her desk, "and that's not even considering the residual benefits from all the good publicity."

"Oh my gosh, thank you, Mom," Ava gushed. "You have no idea what this means to me. You won't regret it—"

Carla raised her hand to silence Ava. "But I'm not ready to jump."

Ava's stomach lurched. Of course it wasn't going to be that easy. It never was with her mother.

"Take all the time you need, Mom," she said, doing her best to stay composed. "I know it's a big decision."

"I don't need more time, Ava. I need you to do something for me."

"Anything!" Ava said. "Name it."

Carla looked over her bifocals at Ava for a long beat. "Harris called me today."

Ava drew a blank. "Harris who?"

Carla looked up. Her usually steely eyes had taken on a tired glaze. "Harris, my brother."

"Uncle Harris called you? But you haven't spoken in, what. . .ten years?"

Carla nodded. "About that long, I'd guess. We don't exactly see eye-to-eye on many things. But that's not what I want to discuss."

Ava waited.

"Harris mentioned what a shame it was that you and your cousin lost touch all those years ago. I have to say, I agree."

None of this was making any sense. "What does Macy have to do with my gallery?" Ava asked.

"It's simple," Carla said. "I want you to go to Utah. Fix things with Macy. Then, and only then, I will fund your little art project. Not only that, but it won't even be a loan; you'll own the gallery free and clear. Consider it an early inheritance."

Ava was stunned. "You want me to go make nice with Macy? After all these years. . .that's what you care about?"

Carla simply nodded.

Ava shook her head. "I can't, Mom. No. Macy doesn't like me—I think that's been made pretty clear. I don't know if this is some kind of weird game to you or something, but I can't go back there."

Ava grabbed her papers and headed for the door. She knew she'd get no further with Carla today.

"Thanks anyway, Mom. I guess I'll see you at the lunch meeting."

"Ben is missing."

Carla had spoken so quietly that Ava almost thought she imagined it. She turned back to Carla.

"What. . .? Ben?"

"Yes," Carla said, rubbing her temples. "Macy's husband."

Ava's chest clenched. "How could Ben be missing? Have the police been notified?"

"I imagine they have, considering it's been nearly two years."

Ava steadied herself on the wingback chair in front of Carla's desk. How could something like this have happened without her knowing? For two years, she'd been working and traveling and celebrating birthdays and art sales. . .and all the while, Ben had been missing?

"It seems that Harris couldn't reach me at the time," Carla continued. "It'd been so long since we last spoke. But he saw a write-up on you in *The Wall Street Journal* and contacted the editors. They gave him my information, and here we are."

"Poor Macy," Ava said, feeling numb as she sank into the leather chair. "Does anyone know what happened?"

"Apparently, Ben was on some Special Forces mission in a mountain range—undisclosed location, of course—when an avalanche knocked his entire team out of communication. Weeks later, everyone except Ben and another soldier was found. Dead."

Ava gasped and sat down. She'd never met Ben. She had no connection to any part of her Utah family's life, not since she'd left a decade earlier. She tried to picture Macy as the woman she must have grown into, but all she could see was the leggy blonde teenager she remembered.

"Harris tells me it's common knowledge that Ben's body will never be found. Everyone has accepted his passing. . .everyone except Macy. She's closed herself off from all her friends and poured herself into work. Harris is worried about her. I know it took a lot for him to call and ask me for help."

Ava swallowed. "I feel terrible," she said, finally. "I truly do. But what does any of this have to do with me?"

"I'm no good for Utah," Carla said, daintily grabbing a tissue from her desk drawer and dabbing her nose. "That place was as glad to see the back of me, as I was of it. But I have you. And I have money. I stand by what I said: if you go to Utah and help Macy move on. . .I can make this vision of yours come to life. And I will."

"How long are we talking about, Mom?"

"A week; maybe ten days," Carla said. "I certainly can't spare you for longer."

"You expect me to make a difference in a week?" Ava asked.

Carla shrugged. "I'm offering you a big incentive. I'm sure you can figure out the details." She neatly folded her tissue before sliding it into her breast pocket. She crossed her arms over her chest and watched Ava expectantly.

What could Ava say? Her life was in New York now, and had been for most of her adult life. And who knew if Macy would even speak to her after all this time. But how else could she get her artists' residence? The world needed something like this place. *She* needed it.

Before she could form a response, Lucas burst through the door. "How's our favorite girl, Carla? Heard *DAR #5* has the whole town talking!"

He kissed Ava softly on her forehead and perched on the corner of Carla's desk. As MC Enterprise's PR wunderkind, Lucas could get away with just about anything. Add in dark Italian features and a lean, muscular, former-soccer star frame, and it was easy to see why he was rarely met with anything less than an adoring smile—especially from women. Luckily for Ava, she was the only one who ever got that same look from him.

He was unusually buoyant this morning. "I've got reporters begging for interviews, ladies. Ava: first stop, a photoshoot at noon. I've got the style team already preparing for your arrival. I'm sure Carla can spare you from the lunch meeting?"

Neither Carla nor Ava spoke. He cocked an eyebrow.

"Okay. . .What did I miss?" he asked.

Ava stood, her legs a bit wobbly. "Come on. I'll fill you in on the way to the shoot."

As she turned toward the door, Ava felt Lucas wrap his arm tightly around her waist.

"Ava, wait."

Ava looked over her shoulder at the sound of her mother's voice. She looked smaller than she had just a few minutes earlier.

"I'm grabbing dinner with Paul at eight," Carla said. "Will you join us?"

"I have a lot to think about, Mom. What if I stop by for dessert?"

Carla smiled. "Perfect. We'll be at Uva. Come around nine thirty?"

"I'll be there," Ava said, suddenly very tired. She wondered if there'd be any bear claws left in the lobby. Sugar and coffee were definitely needed, especially if she had to go smile into a camera for the next few hours.

"I know you'll do the right thing," Carla said, softly.

Ava felt a rush of nausea as she left her mother's office. Lucas seemed to sense her mood and tightened his grip as he guided her through the lobby. As she looked into his long-lashed brown eyes, he flashed her that special Ava-only smile. Those dimples could melt her every time. Everything would be okay. Wouldn't it?

Two

Ooph. Ava sucked her stomach in as her favorite stylist, Leo, zipped her into a hand-beaded emerald Givenchy gown. Zarah, the makeup artist, expertly shifted around Leo as she clamped down on a second set of false lashes.

Ava gazed up at the gold mid-century chandelier that hung from the thirty-foot ceilings. Had she been in this studio before? Every room at Cream Studios looked the same: polished concrete floor, glitzy chandelier, immaculate white walls. The only difference was the number on the door.

"Hold still!" Zarah scolded.

"Sorry," Ava mumbled.

Zarah stepped back, assessing her work. She dabbed a concealer brush against a pimple on Ava's chin.

"Are we back on milk?" Zarah asked. "This looks like a dairy zit."

"Spanx to the rescue!" Leo said before playfully kissing

Ava's cheek. The dress did fit—well, as long as she didn't need to breathe. Leo tapped Ava's calf, signaling her to step into one Manolo, then the other. She stared out the giant picture window, watching a pigeon balance on the outside sill as Leo fastened the straps around her ankles. He stood, surveyed her from head to toe, then nodded.

"I'm happy!" Leo proclaimed before turning to Zarah. "You happy?"

Zarah nodded and stuck a hand mirror in front of Ava. "Anything you want different, sweetie?"

Ava shook her head.

"I'll go let them know she's ready," Zarah said before ducking around the canvas backdrop.

Ava stepped back and stared at her reflection in the long mirror attached to the wardrobe cart. The dress was like something from the Oscars' red carpet, with a mermaid skirt and sweetheart neckline. Her auburn hair had been curled into perfect flowing waves that cascaded over one shoulder and framed the gigantic diamond studs that were on loan from some famous jeweler whose name she'd already forgotten. High cheekbones, smoky eyeshadow. . .She had to admit she looked glamorous, but hardly like herself. Her eyelids felt heavy under the weight of all the lashes.

Lucas walked up behind her, whistling approvingly. "I am speechless," he said. "You're absolutely stunning."

"I'm an artist," Ava said, turning to face him. "Does this ever seem like a bit of a circus to you? Who really cares how I clean up?"

"The world cares," said Lucas, gently turning her back toward the mirror. "You act like you've never done this before. What's gotten into you? You're a brand now, remember?"

He rested his chin on her shoulder, then wrapped his arms around her waist. Their eyes met in the reflection.

"I've been thinking about everything you told me," he said, his voice husky in her ear. "It's just crazy that your mother would suggest you leave *now*. We've been working for ages to get you to this place in your career. . .You're on fire by anyone's standard."

Ava had to agree. It had taken her years to get noticed by the art world. She'd sometimes sell a painting at a student show or an art walk, but more often ended up donating her work to charity auctions to try to get her name out. Then suddenly, in the last six months, her face was everywhere. It was hard to point to what had seemingly changed overnight, but changed it had. Once, they were begging for people to take meetings with her. Now, she had a waitlist for her work, not to mention the recent auction sale with record-breaking numbers.

Carla had fueled all of it. Anytime Ava was ready to give up, Carla had anecdotes ready about the obstacles the Old Masters had faced before taking their places in the galleries of history. With every sale, she devoted more of her time to managing Ava's career. No auction price, press release, or collaboration escaped Carla's watchful eye. The investment arm of MC Enterprise was as lucrative as ever, but Carla now delegated much of the work to her team so she could focus on Ava.

That's what felt so confusing. Sure, Carla was Macy's aunt, but Ava had never known her mother to make a decision based on emotion. Her focus was business, profit, and making a name for her company. She might have expected Carla to send an expensive fruit basket, but to bribe Ava into going back to Utah? She took a shallow breath—the dress's corset was beginning to feel like a straitjacket.

Lucas shook his head. "How can our future be decided by some heartbroken redneck who might decide she hates you no matter what you do? That's just unfair."

Ava pulled herself free of his embrace. "I need to go find the photographer," she said. "They're probably waiting on me."

"I'm sorry, that was harsh," Lucas said, gently gripping her arm. "I'm just frustrated. But you have to admit, Carla *is* putting your future in the hands of someone who might as well be a stranger. A stranger in the middle of nowhere. These meetings next week— magazines, galleries. . .They're contacts we've been hounding for years. I don't know if they will wait."

Ava gave him a small nod before she tugged her arm away and walked to set. The photographer impatiently glanced up from his phone.

"We ready, Ava?"

She nodded and stood squarely on the taped mark in front of a huge white canvas backdrop. Before she could even settle in, the flashbulbs began blinding her.

She needed to make a choice. How was she supposed to think about this, here? As much as the thought of returning to Utah terrified her, Ava couldn't just pretend she didn't know about Ben's disappearance. Lucas stood off to the side, watching her thoughtfully.

"Is it really that bad of an idea to go?" Ava asked, fixing her eyes toward Lucas as she tried to keep her face toward the lens. "It's not like it would be for that long."

"If I'm being honest, I'm a bit conflicted," he said. "I can't believe Carla would suggest you step foot outside the city right now, especially with your momentum. But on the other hand, that amount of money is hard to ignore. Financially, this could be the opportunity you've been fighting for ever since I met you."

Ava opened her mouth to speak, but Lucas continued. He was used to talking for both of them.

"You know, the more I think about it?" he continued. "I think a double investment in our plan could mean the fast track. Every milestone we hoped to reach in five years, we could hit in three. We could market our gallery to all the big publications, staff ten assistants—not just one Margo. We could be huge, and we could do it fast."

Ava stared at the gray Manhattan skyline through the window. Her thoughts swirled as the photographer clicked around her.

"With that kind of cash," Lucas said, more to himself than to her, "we could fill our stables with some proven ponies, not just a bunch of pitiful starving artists barely getting their footing."

"Did you just call them 'ponies'?" Ava asked.

Lucas smiled, chastened. "Sorry. Again, poor taste. I know you're sensitive to these people. But artists aren't that different from racehorses: it's all about betting on who will pay off in the end."

Ava whirled around to face Lucas. "You do realize you're dating an artist, right?"

"As your boyfriend, I can see all the passion and creativity you put into your work," Lucas said, impatiently running his fingers through his coal-colored waves. "As a businessman, I'm just pointing out that the bottom-line number showing up in black is all that really matters. Part of my job should be to make sure that your good idea actually makes money."

Ava bit her cheek. She might be an artist, but that didn't make her incompetent. They'd been over the numbers she'd come up with dozens of times. Sometimes, it felt like Lucas saw her as a child when it came to anything related to business.

The photographer heaved a pointed sigh and rested the camera on his hip. Ava avoided his stare; she knew she wasn't exactly being an ideal subject at the moment.

"The whole point is to make this place specifically *for* new artists," Ava said. "The ones who never got the opportunities I did. Artists that the world needs to see; artists that might make *history*. That's the whole point!"

Lucas smiled at her patiently. That smile always had a way of softening Ava, no matter how angry she got with him.

"That is the perfect sound bite for our first interview, my dear," Lucas said. "Absolutely adorable. You're the heart; I'm the drive."

The camera shutter clicked, the flash startling Ava. She turned and the photographer pointedly held the camera in her direction. She couldn't blame him for being impatient. She forced a smile in his direction and hurried back to the masking tape "X" she had apparently wandered several inches away from.

As much as she'd prefer to have this conversation in private, she couldn't wait for alone time. Their schedules had been jam-packed for months. Her birthday dinner weeks ago was the last time she could remember a night with just the two of them. Ava glanced towards the makeup chair. Thankfully, her style team was busy scrolling through their phones.

"So, what do we think?" Lucas said. "You go to Utah, win over that cousin of yours, and we take the art market by storm in three years, tops?"

Ava smiled weakly. If only it was that simple. "Lucas, there's more to the family drama than you know. I can't just go back to Utah. It's complicated."

Lucas studied her. "So. . .explain it to me."

Ava sighed, trying to keep her face camera-ready as she spoke. "When I was little, I spent a good chunk of my life in Utah. I mean, it was always just Carla and me. . .And this was before she really made a name for herself. So anytime she had to travel for work, she dumped me on the ranch so her brother Harris could keep an eye on me."

"That sounds rustic," Lucas said with a grimace. He wasn't exactly outdoorsy.

Ava smiled. It had been rustic. It had also been full of skinned knees, shared secrets, and adventure. Melted popsicles, backyard campfires, and so many other moments she couldn't put it into words.

"I loved that ranch. We rode horses every day, no matter the weather. We fished, hiked, camped... It was a whole different world for me, coming from the city. But when I was thirteen, Mom *really* left me there. That time was different. She got a job in Paris and said there wasn't room for a teenage girl."

Ava swallowed, then took a deep breath. "My mom never came back for more than short visits for four years." She looked down, angry at the hot tears that filled her eyes after all this time. Lucas was silent for a moment. Then he reached out and squeezed her hand. The photographer sighed in resignation as he plopped onto a stool.

"I'm so sorry," Lucas said.

She looked at him. His face was so familiar and warm. She knew that perpetually stubbled jaw and those tanned, freckled cheeks better than she knew her own face. Her throat relaxed a bit.

"It was hard for me," she said, taking a deep breath. "It took me years to really get over it."

Ava remembered those first, dark months in Utah. She had barely left her room, and hardly spoken to anyone. She just filled one sketchpad after another and locked herself away from the world, confused and abandoned.

"Eventually," Ava continued, "I let some of that anger go. . .or, I don't know, maybe it was fear? I wasn't sure if Carla was ever coming back for me. The few times she visited, she never stayed longer than a weekend and never mentioned taking me with her. Uncle Harris and Macy became my family. And after a while, believe it or not, I became a farm girl. I came to love my life with them."

She smiled, remembering countless family dinners in the wallpapered dining room of the ranch house, passing notes with Macy in the halls of the county school, and the day-to-day simplicity of rural life.

"Then. . .one day, Mom came back," she said, with a shrug. "She told me she had this important new job and a place for both of us in Paris. By that point, I was obsessed with drawing and painting, and she had somehow secured a spot for me at the Parisian Art Institute. I loved my life on the ranch, but it wasn't really my home. And I just wanted my mom, you know? So, I left."

Lucas studied her. "I know you'd mentioned growing up with

a cousin, but I had no idea you had this entire other life. You should have told me."

Ava tipped her head back and sighed. "I guess I tried really hard not to think about that time. Considering how I left things." She rubbed her fist against her eye, leaving a black smear of mascara on the back of her hand. Zarah would likely rush over any minute to scold her and touch up her makeup, but the flash kept right on blinding Ava. The photographer must have accepted that this was the best he was going to get. Hopefully, he'd get at least one shot they could use.

"So, how did you leave things?" Lucas asked.

"Well, Macy was devastated. I mean, I left with no warning. My mom maybe gave me an hour heads-up to pack and get out the door. Before I left, Macy told me that if I went with Carla, she'd never forgive me. She said that Carla would never be there for me like she and Harris were. She couldn't believe I would walk away from them—from her—after what Carla had done. She had a good point, but what could I do? Carla's my mother. My *mom*. And now, looking back, she never did leave me again."

"Did you ever go back and visit?" Lucas asked quietly.

"I meant to go back. I really did. But it was a long, expensive flight, and life got busy. I've told you how intense art school was, and taking time off was a big deal," Ava sighed. "But when it comes down to it, none of those things were really stopping me; I just couldn't face Macy."

Suddenly, Zarah popped onto the set, wielding a wet wipe. She said nothing, just tenderly wiped away the trails of black makeup that stained Ava's cheeks before quickly reapplying foundation, powder, and blush. She squeezed Ava's shoulder and gave her a little smile before hurrying off the backdrop to watch.

"Ms. MacDaniel!" the photographer called to her, agitation dripping from his voice. "You look great, but I don't think we have it quite yet. Some of these shots are tear-streaked, some blurry from talking, and well. . .all have this *distracted* look." His face was pursed as if he'd smelled something foul, and Ava got the impression his inner monologue included expletives. She had to admire his tact, all things considered.

"Of course she's distracted, she's an artist!" Lucas exclaimed. "What are we paying you for?!"

He laughed and winked at Ava, and despite her mood, she began to laugh, too. Lucas raised an eyebrow as if to say, *You got this now?* She nodded and mustered a reassuring smile. He pressed his phone to his ear and wandered to the other end of the airy loft.

Ava could only imagine what she must look like to this photographer—some high-maintenance drama queen too wrapped up in herself to appreciate what a charmed life she led. This wasn't the time. She shoved her shoulders back and smoothed her hair, connecting her gaze straight into the camera lens. She was no model, but she'd done enough of these shoots to know her good side, how to cross her legs, and to stand at just the right angle. She flashed her most practiced grin. The photographer's scowl melted, and the rapid-fire clicking of the shutter told Ava he was much happier.

A few minutes later, the shoot was wrapped. Ava felt wobbly and raw, but she knew they had gotten some good photos. She wished she'd brought jeans; at least her dress from work allowed her to breathe.

Zarah tenderly wiped the last of the heavy makeup from Ava's skin as she leaned back in the director's chair. Ava sat up and smiled when she caught a glimpse of her clean face in the vanity mirror. Much better. She thanked Zarah and Leo and politely refused their invitation to grab drinks with them before she wandered back onto the darkened empty set. What a day. She looked at her phone: it was only 3:30.

Ava heard footsteps behind her. She turned as Lucas walked over to her, smiling as he draped Ava's trench coat around her shoulders. He tipped her chin towards his face.

"You okay, babe?" he asked.

Ava pressed her face against his hand.

"Lucas, if I do this—if I go to Utah and somehow find a way to help Macy—when I get back, why don't we go away together? We could take a cruise or something and just reconnect. I feel like we're always running and I just, well, I miss *us*. A little break wouldn't set us back much. It would recharge us, even. Not forever; just maybe two or three weeks?"

She laced her fingers through his. He looked thoughtfully at her.

"I can't give you three weeks," he said. "Let's be real. I haven't been on a vacation like that since I was a kid." He glanced at his phone. "But what about the next three hours?"

Ava smiled. "I suppose I better take what I can get."

She squealed as he suddenly scooped her into his arms as if she weighed nothing. She wrapped her arms around his neck and leaned her head against his chest.

"Where to, my lady?"

"The zoo," she replied, nonchalantly.

If he was surprised, he gave no indication. "The zoo it is."

He turned and carried her out of the warehouse, only stopping to bend down so Ava could scoop up her handbag.

Ava's cheeks hurt from smiling so much. She hadn't had this much mindless fun in. . .Well, definitely not in recent memory. Going to the Central Park Zoo during a weekday afternoon meant that they had the place nearly to themselves. It was warm for early October, and most of the animals lounged about in the late sun, likely recovering from entertaining the crush of students and young families that packed the zoo each morning.

Lucas and Ava spent the afternoon visiting each and every exhibit, from the chubby manatees to the Godzilla-like Komodo dragon. They hammed it up for the zoo photographer and paid ten dollars to feed the giraffe a handful of iceberg lettuce. It was a great date, and it was so much more than that. They really talked, for the first time in what felt like years. Lucas kept his phone silenced with the vibration off the entire time—a rare gesture for him—and he seemed to hang on her every word. He never stopped touching her, walking with his hand protectively against her lower back and stealing a kiss any time they found themselves alone. Lately, Ava often found herself craving his rough fingers against her skin; craving the feel of his lips murmuring against her ear. So much of their relationship unfolded in a professional setting that they hardly had time to act like a real couple. Today, she was reminded why she was still head-over-heels in love with

Lucas.

For a short time, they were lost in each other, only realizing the zoo was closed when a plump man swinging a giant ring of keys cleared his throat and politely tapped his watch. After the man locked the iron gates behind them, they passed beneath the brick archway onto the crowded city sidewalk. The air was crisp, and the musty scent of damp leaves permeated the air as Ava chewed on leftover under-salted popcorn. She noticed Lucas seemed lighter than he had before they came. They both were. She smiled as she tossed a kernel into the air and caught it in her mouth on the first try.

Lucas applauded. "I can't believe I've never actually gone into the zoo," he said with a chuckle. "Ten years in the city. . .I guess I've never really taken time to explore."

"I told you you'd love it," Ava said. "From the minute you walked in, you were like a little kid—mouth open at everything! And then, the ape house?"

They both laughed.

"That monkey had it out for me!" Lucas protested.

"The way he pointed that finger at the glass when you came in? You clearly had some kind of history I don't know about."

They walked on in happy silence for a few moments, his hand warm and rough against her own. It felt to Ava as if time had paused just for them. If only they kept walking, they could push off the e-mails, the meetings, the expectations. The city was sparkling at night, noisy and bright. Ava loved it so much for what it was—alive.

She realized that before today, she'd always come to the zoo alone. As a kid, Carla had often dragged her along to meetings in the city. Ava would dread these trips that meant a long car ride and then an hour or so in a lobby with nothing but a coloring book. By the time she was nine or ten, she'd convinced Carla to drop her at the zoo before her appointments. It was a small zoo, only six or so acres, but that only added to its appeal for Ava. She never got lost, and for a few hours, the zoo felt like it was hers. From the animal-themed clock that played music every half hour to the adorably rambunctious seals, it may as well have been Disneyland in Ava's eyes.

"I really needed that," she said. "Things have been so insanely busy lately. I'm obviously grateful that my art is finally taking off, and I know how important all the press is. . .but for a few hours, all of that faded and it felt like it was just you and me."

Lucas stopped her, pulling her arm around his waist. She relaxed into him, feeling his torso press against hers as she leaned her head against his chest. He always smelled like Bvlgari Extreme, the musky cologne she had bought him for their first Christmas together. He wrapped his fingers through hers and rubbed her palm with his thumb, their own secret little gesture.

"Don't get me wrong," he said into her hair. "I had the best time with you today. We needed this. But you have to be careful when you take your foot off the gas. This isn't who we are; not now, when we're so close to getting everything we've worked so hard for. We have to focus on what's really important—our brand. I think you know the right move, Ava."

She looked up at him and nodded slightly. His brown eyes were intense. "I better go meet my mom and Paul," Ava said.

"You sure you don't want to come over for a nightcap instead?" Lucas asked, brushing his lips against her ear. "I haven't been able to get the image of you in that green dress out of my head."

"As much as I'd love to, you know Carla will be waiting for an answer," Ava said. "Walk me?"

Lucas smiled and tucked a stray wisp of her hair behind her ear. "I'd love to."

Three

Ava checked her packing list for the umpteenth time as her mother droned on over speakerphone. OK, enough art supplies to tide her over until she could find a good store. . .her laptop. . .but did she have enough clothes? She didn't even know what she'd be doing while she was in Utah. And did it snow in October? She couldn't remember. She stuffed her puffy parka into her now bulging suitcase.

She offered the occasional "mmhmm" and "yeah, for sure" as Carla talked about all the galas and openings she and Lucas would attend in Ava's place. At least there was one perk to this trip: Ava had never felt comfortable in a Manhattan gallery with a bunch of rich strangers. All those empty conversations with "people of status." People whose gazes inevitably shifted around the room while she spoke, making sure they weren't missing someone more interesting. She always felt like an imposter in those rooms, even as her work became more well-known. Despite the blown-out hair and couture outfits loaned by the hottest designers, she was still just trying to prove she belonged.

Oh! She had almost forgotten her new boots.

She dragged a long Bloomingdale's box from beneath her bed and opened it to reveal chestnut Italian leather riding boots. These definitely weren't fitting in her suitcase. She yanked out the parka and tucked the boots in their place. She had a wool peacoat; surely that would be plenty for October.

Carla was now droning on about some gallery director she suspected of undercutting them.

"Thanks for the first-class upgrade, Mom," Ava interrupted.

Carla laughed. "You're my daughter, but you're also a very valuable investment. Only the best for our star."

Ava was looking forward to the silence of the flight. Maybe in those five hours she could figure out what to say to Macy after all these years.

All week, Ava had been so busy with interviews, she'd barely had time to paint, let alone think. Her heart started racing every time she pictured stepping foot onto the old farm.

"Has Margo arrived yet?" Carla asked.

"Yep, you know Margo. She was here waiting in the lobby when I got home from yoga this morning."

Ava tucked her list into her carry-on and knelt on her suitcase, relieved when it zipped without much force.

"So, will Uncle Harris be at the airport, or should I get an Uber? Does Utah even have Uber?" Her face felt clammy. "Did we talk about this already?"

The line was quiet. "Mom?"

"I'm here, dear," Carla said after a moment. "About Harris. .

.Well, I didn't exactly tell him you were coming."

Ava's stomach plummeted. "When you say you didn't *exactly* tell him. . ."

"I didn't tell him at all," Carla said.

This was not good.

"Do you expect me to just show up unannounced?" asked Ava. "What if they're not even there?"

"They run a farm, Ava, they won't be on vacation. It's just, Harris never could keep a secret. And besides, I was worried you'd change your mind."

She *had* almost changed her mind dozens of times since that meeting in her mother's office last week. But the dream of her own artists' residence was finally within reach. Not to mention, Lucas was now enthusiastically parroting Carla's plan and Ava couldn't bear to let them both down. And there was something else. . .She felt a quiet tug from within—a little nudge from the past. Something about Utah was drawing her back.

"So, where exactly will I be staying, Mom?"

"They're family and they have a giant farm; you'll stay with them, of course. If for some reason that's not an option, I'll reimburse you for an Airbnb in town."

Ava sighed. Her stomach was officially in knots.

"Look, it's going to be an uphill battle whether they know you're coming or not," Carla continued. "But it's only a week. I admire you for this, Ava. I couldn't bring myself to go back. I never figured out that place. But if anyone can, it's you."

"I'm sure it will be fine." Ava's voice sounded more confident than she felt.

"Great!" Carla said, sounding relieved. "I've arranged for car service once you land. Keep all your receipts so the company can reimburse. And Ava?" Carla's voice hitched, a momentary gap in her armor. "Thank you."

Ava heard a soft knock on the bedroom door. "Ava?" Margo called. "Are you about ready? Your flight's in two hours."

"Just about!" Ava replied. "I gotta go, Mom. I'll call you when I'm there."

As Ava hung up, she glanced around her nondescript bedroom one last time. It looked empty, but then it practically *was* empty. She'd planned to decorate her Carnegie Hill apartment with boho touches from the flea market, but she hadn't gotten around to it. She spent so little time at home that when she finally had the chance to decorate, she was usually too exhausted to care. She flung open her wardrobe doors and stared at the rows of blouses and dresses. It was no use. . .There was nothing she could pack that would magically ease her anxiety.

She crossed the room and opened the door, finding Margo standing at attention. "Sorry, Carla wouldn't stop talking," Ava said, stepping aside. "Come on in."

Margo had generously offered to water Ava's plants and keep an eye on the place while she was gone. Ava made a mental note to bring her back a nice gift.

A nice Utah gift. Ava felt the panic begin to rise again.

"Are you OK, Ava?" Margo asked.

"Yeah, I'm absolutely fine," Ava said firmly. "Good day for travel, huh?"

Margo eyed her with concern. "Alright, then," she said. "Why don't I take whatever bags are ready to go and pull the car around?"

"Sure. Thanks, Margo."

Margo grabbed the handle of Ava's rolling suitcase, suppressing a grunt as she hauled it across the silk rug.

"Hey, Margo?"

Margo looked back at her over her shoulder.

"Do you think I'm doing the right thing?" Ava asked. "Leaving all this behind, just when my career is really taking off?"

Margo shifted awkwardly from one foot to the other. Ava couldn't blame her hesitation to answer. . .She was Margo's boss, after all.

"Well. . .What do *you* think?" Margo finally asked. "Does it feel like the right thing?"

Ava considered. "According to Carla, my uncle thinks I can actually help my cousin. And it seems really important to my mom that I go. . .Plus, there's the money, right? I mean, Lucas said it best: if this goes well, I could have my gallery *and* my artists' residence in a matter of years, not decades."

"You didn't exactly answer my question," Margo said, a soft caution in her voice. "I hope you don't take this the wrong way, but if I had half the talent you have, I'd be doing whatever the heck I wanted to do. Maybe. . ." She hesitated, then snuck a glance at Ava before continuing. "Maybe you should listen to yourself for a change?"

Ava opened her mouth, then closed it again. Margo gave her a little nod before yanking the suitcase through the doorway and disappearing down the hall.

"I'll be right there!" Ava called after her.

She braced her hands on either side of her vanity table and stared at her reflection. Her wide green eyes blinked back, looking like a deer in headlights. She took a deep breath.

She could do this. She *had* to do this. She didn't need to be reminded that everyone was counting on her—it was all she could think about. From the corner of her eye, she saw the little silver-framed photo of her and Lucas, horseback in Central Park on their first date. They looked so happy and so hopeful in that picture. If he believed in her, surely she could find a way to believe in herself.

Four

Ava's grip tightened on the wheel of the Chevy Malibu she'd been driving for the last three and a half hours. Her back was stiff. The jagged mountains that ran parallel to the road were now casting long shadows across the landscape as the sun sank behind them. She needed more coffee.

It seemed Carla had been rich for just long enough that she'd forgotten that "car service" and "economy rental car" weren't quite the same thing. Still, Ava was grateful for the solitude. Living in New York, she hadn't been alone in a car for as long as she could remember. In fact, it felt like the only time she'd had to herself in the past year or so was when she was asleep. No wonder she had a hard time painting lately.

Ava didn't remember the ranch being this far from the airport, but she'd only had her license for a few months before leaving Utah for the last time. She rolled her windows down the second she pulled out of the rental lot, the smell of crisp leaves and clean air overwhelming her senses. Everything smelled so fresh and so faded at the same time, as only autumn in the country could.

She'd forgotten how different Utah looked from anywhere in the northeast. Its boulders and gritty sand looked like the desert, but it was awash in lush trees and bushes. The road could twist up and down through miles of red canyons and gorges, then suddenly run flat all the way to the horizon.

She yawned. She needed to do something if she was going to make it the rest of the drive, and there wasn't a Starbucks in sight.

"Hey, Siri, call Lucas."

He answered on the first ring.

"She lives!" Lucas teased. "I was getting worried about you."

"I'm nearly there, I think. It's hard to tell. Everything out my window looks identical. . .golden and red and absolutely gorgeous."

"Don't fall in love with it too much," Lucas said. "I'm counting on you running back to me as soon as the mission is completed."

"That almost sounds scandalous," she said, grinning. "Hey, Lucas, I was thinking... Why don't you come visit for the weekend? You could meet my uncle, meet Macy too, if she's speaking to me by then. We could hike or kayak or take a horseback tour. It's so different than New York. I think you'd love it if you could see it for yourself."

"Ava, that's sweet, but you don't know what you're saying," Lucas said with a laugh. "Can you really picture me on a hike with one of those sticks? I know you remember what happened when we went on that walking tour of Brooklyn."

How could she forget? It had involved a single bee and a lot of hypochondria. "Well, then, maybe more of an indoor getaway," she said. "They have beautiful lodges here. It would be so nice to spend some time together, without all the pressure of work."

Lucas was silent for a moment.

"Ava," he said, his voice gentle. "You know how I was before I met you. I'd never had a relationship longer than a month, if you could even call that a relationship. And then you walked into my office, with your big green eyes and that incredible talent. . .and I was a goner. But that doesn't change who I am. You know I don't do relaxing well. Besides, we spend plenty of time together. I love my work and I need to be here. For us."

Before Ava could argue, a familiar sign caught her eye on the side of the narrow country highway: *Cobalt, Utah – 1 Mile.*

"Hey, Lucas? I'm close to the turnoff. I better go. I'll call you soon, OK?"

"Be careful, Ava. And come back to me as soon as you can."

Ava took a deep breath. "I will."

Ava slowed the car to crawl as she bumped down the mile-long gravel drive to the heart of the ranch twenty minutes later. The land looked exactly as she remembered. Century-old trees fanned a canopy over her car, and a few hundred feet to the left, a clear, roaring creek raced along the road. She saw a patch of dirt just big enough to park a car. She knew if she walked from that point straight into the tree line, she'd find the old tree house.

She saw an unfamiliar steel sign curving over the road where it forked ahead.

"Autumn Lantern Riding Academy," she read aloud. She followed the road to the right, driving under the massive arch. A riding academy? She smiled. Macy had done it after all.

Soon, the trees gave way to a gravel parking lot. A massive stable towered ahead where Ava remembered a weathered wooden barn. To the left, she saw a low metal building she didn't recognize.

She parked in the nearly empty lot. She took a sip from her water bottle, then closed her eyes and pressed her forehead against the wheel. She needed to gather her thoughts.

Thump, thump, thump! Ava yelped as the pert rapping snatched her from the solitude. She looked out the drivers-side window. A square, eager face looked back.

"Hello, and welcome to Autumn Lantern Riding Academy!" the muffled voice called through the glass. The woman was plump and appeared to be in her mid-50s or so. Based on how she expectantly shifted from one foot to the other, Ava thought she might be related to the Energizer Bunny.

Well, no time like the present.

She popped a piece of gum into her dry mouth, grabbed her purse, and stepped out of the car. It felt good to stretch her legs after the long drive.

"Hi! I'm Lizzie," the woman said. "And you are?"

"Ava."

"Welcome, Ava!" Lizzie chirped. "First time at our stables?"

Technically. "Yep!" Ava said.

"Fantastic!"

Ava got the impression she meant it. This woman clearly liked her job.

"Any previous riding experience?" Lizzie asked.

"A bit," Ava said. "But it's been years."

"No problem. We have riders of all levels. Macy MacDaniel-Paxton will turn ya into a high point champion in no time. You from around here, dear?"

Lizzie seemed genuinely interested and Ava was delighted by her enthusiasm. New York had plenty of kindness if you knew where to look, but overall, the people Ava met on a daily basis lived up to the city's reputation of being gruff, cold, and in a hurry.

"I'm from New York, actually," Ava said.

"Wow, New York?!" Lizzie exclaimed. "Was there in '96 for New Years. Neat town, but it moved a bit fast for me."

Ava found it hard to believe that anywhere moved too fast for such an enthusiastic woman.

"Well, let's get you the full rundown, then," Lizzie continued. "The MacDaniels and their ancestors ran Autumn Lantern Ranch as a cattle operation for more than a century, up until about five years ago when the riding academy opened. I'm told it's one of the oldest ranches in the state, from way back when Utah was still a wide-open frontier. In fact, legend has it that a band of outlaws who hijacked the Pony Express hid out with stolen gold in the fields for over a month before the lawmen found them. Of course, I'm sure the MacDaniels had no idea—angels, those people—but where are my manners?! Come right this way! Let's give you a proper tour."

Lizzie motioned for her to follow as she headed briskly toward the stable. Ava clutched her purse tighter. It didn't seem right to tell Lizzie that *she* was a Utah MacDaniel. . . After all, she wasn't sure she really qualified anymore. Still, she felt a little guilty. She hurried to catch up to Lizzie, who was beaming as she held open the stable door.

Ava took a deep steadying breath. A tour seemed like a great way to get reacquainted with the old ranch. . .and bought her a few minutes to ready herself to face Macy.

Five

Though the ranch was achingly familiar, it had changed so much. The wind whistling through the leaves and the guttural songs of the birds matched the soundtrack of her memories. . .Even the creak of the old pasture gate hadn't changed. But for everything Ava recognized, she discovered something new.

The low metal building turned out to be an indoor arena, complete with bleacher seats and an announcer's booth. Lizzie told her that Macy hoped to host AQHA shows—short for American Quarter Horse Association—but that was still a long way off. It sounded like Macy's riding academy had been gaining students steadily, but as a new barn, it was still building a reputation in the horse show world.

The stable was unlike any Ava had ever seen—not that she'd seen many. Each stall had an automatic watering system, and the place was spotless. She looked up at the huge sloping skylights. When they were kids, this had been nothing more than a cobwebbed drafty barn that housed rusty farm equipment.

Ava remembered hours spent in the wooden loft, which had groaned under every step. The girls had made it their unofficial headquarters when it had been too cold or wet to hang out in the treehouse. Ava would draw or paint, sometimes alone, and sometimes as Macy watched.

Once, on a rainy afternoon when they were around ten years old, Macy had snatched a feather boa from the dress-up trunk. She'd stood on a bale of straw, wrapped the boa around her neck, and announced that one day she would be a championship rider with her own riding school and a gorgeous husband. It was funny how dreams shifted and evolved with age for some kids, and for others, they stuck. It seemed that Macy's dream had come true. . . .though parts of it had fallen away, just like the old barn. *Poor Macy.*

Ava noticed Lizzie had stopped walking and was watching her expectantly.

"I'm sorry. . .Did you say something?" Ava asked.

Lizzie laughed. "It's a lot to take in at once, I know. I said, if you'd like to follow me outside, you can see the outdoor arena where you'll take classes! Well, as long as the weather holds up."

Ava smiled. "Sure."

Lizzie slid back the massive door, and Ava followed her into the dwindling sunlight, wobbling a bit as she navigated the gravel path in her stilettos. At first glance, the pastures and riding ring were just as Ava remembered. But then, she noticed the fencing was a bright white vinyl, not peeling painted wood. A low stone wall curved behind an iron patio set, and red landscaping rocks and neat bushes framed the entire area. The last time Ava had been back here, this area had been a barren patch of dust and weeds. Harris had maintained the ranch, but with an eye for function more than appearance. Now, everything looked pristine and manicured.

Ava had ridden her first horse in that long arena. How old had she been? Six? Seven? Back then, they rode in dusty sunshine and muddy rain, sticky summers and blistering winters. Until they earned the privileges that came with adolescence, the arena was the only place Ava and Macy were allowed to ride without Harris supervising. The girls' imaginations had run wild within that oval as they pushed their old geldings to run and jump, sometimes bareback, often with costumes. Ava remembered pretending to be barrel racers at the rodeo, princess pirates on a desert island. . .all with Macy by her side.

"Just lovely, isn't it?" Lizzie asked as she watched Ava absorb the view.

"It really is," Ava replied.

"It makes it real easy to come into work every day," Lizzie said, chuckling.

Ava followed her around the edge of the barn. Everything felt bigger than she remembered. Lizzie pointed out a couple of concrete wash stalls and a long low fence with water troughs. Two teenage girls, their sweaty hair plastered to their forehead, led their equally sweaty horses past them.

"Hey, Lizzie!" the shorter one called.

"Looks like you two had a good lesson," Lizzie said. "I've got some cold waters in the office; help yourselves. Just be sure you don't put Coda and Toby back covered in sweat."

"You know we would never!" the taller one said. "We'll hose them off inside."

"Becca, Kat—this is Ava," Lizzie said. "She's thinking of taking lessons here."

"Nice to meet you both," Ava said.

"You'll love it here," Becca said enthusiastically, wiping her face with her sleeve. "Macy can be strict, but she's super supportive."

"This is my fourth barn, and she's by far the best instructor," Kat added as Becca nodded in agreement.

"My mom's waiting," Becca said apologetically, "but I hope we see you around!"

"Me too," Ava said, and she realized she meant it.

As she watched the girls walk side-by-side toward the stable, Ava remembered two different teenage girls leading their horses home after a long afternoon ride. Of course, there had only been an ancient barn back then.

Lizzie continued the tour, showing Ava a storage shed where they kept buckets and horse shampoo, then a stone firepit with wooden Adirondack chairs all around where Lizzie said students and parents chatted between lessons.

"Have you worked here long?" Ava asked.

"Four years, come January," Lizzie said. "I retired from an ag career and lost my mind after about two months of watching Netflix. I was not designed to sit still. Macy had a flyer in town for a barn manager, and I've been here ever since."

"What's 'ag'?" Ava asked.

"Agriculture," Lizzie said. "I worked for the Department of Agriculture. Federal job. Good honest living, but the hours sucked it out of me. So, I did my twenty years and clocked out for the last time! Now, Autumn Lantern is the perfect office; I can work outside and talk to people, and Macy's real flexible with vacation time. My boys are grown now and doing grown things, so it's on me to visit them most of the time—one on each coast."

"What an office," Ava said. After years of painting to the soundtrack of cars blasting music and helicopters circling overhead, she could see the appeal.

"I feel blessed I found this place," Lizzie said simply.

"Sounds to me like Macy's the one who was blessed," Ava said.

"That's sweet of you to say," Lizzie said, beaming. "Well, that's just about everything she wrote, except the trails out there." She gestured to the forested hillside in the distance, awash in orange and red. "Once you get some of the basics down, you can join our monthly trail rides. We have over twenty miles of trails back there, if you ever untangled them to measure."

Ava was pretty sure she'd once spent time on every inch of those trails. She felt a throbbing ache of nostalgia in her chest; back then, this ranch had been as good as hers.

Suddenly, Ava wanted nothing more than to rediscover this place. But she hadn't been in a saddle for over a decade. . .and she wasn't sure if Macy would even want her on the property, let alone anywhere near a horse. The ache in her chest became a pounding.

"It's hard to picture it now," Lizzie said, seemingly oblivious to Ava's distress, "but until recently, this ranch had more cows than horses. Macy's dad was the last cattleman here and he retired."

"Does he still live here?" Ava asked hopefully. "Her dad?"

"Nope," Lizzie said. "He bought himself a little place in town. But you'll see him around most days. I know as well as any retiree: old habits die hard."

Ava followed Lizzie off the gravel path, doing her best to keep her weight in the balls of her feet so her three-inch heels wouldn't sink into the soft dirt.

"What's that field used for?" Ava asked, pointing to a pasture far off in the distance. Vegetation had grown to half the fence height, giving it a wild look. Ava could make out toppled tomato cages and trellises swallowed by brown vines. Raised wooden garden beds had weeds poking through the boards. The field stood in stark contrast to the tidiness of the rest of the ranch.

"Those fields *were* used for crops," Lizzie said. "But now that Ben—er, Mr. Paxton. . .Well, no one has grown much of anything over there in a couple seasons now."

Ava studied the field again, trying to imagine what it must have looked like when it was alive with carefully tended plants. She pictured a strong man around her own age piling ears of corn into an overflowing basket but couldn't quite imagine his face. She realized she'd never seen a picture of Ben.

"So, do you have any questions, Ava?" Lizzie asked.

"You know, I think you covered everything," she said. "This was great. Thank you."

"How about we head to the office and take a look at the class schedule?" Lizzie suggested. "Not to bribe you, but I have a fresh pot of coffee waiting for us. Half-caff, given the hour."

Ava smiled. She could definitely use some caffeine. Just as she was about to reply, she heard the clank of the gate opening. She turned and saw a petite woman leading a leggy bay horse into the arena.

Ava watched as the woman attached a long nylon tie to the horse's halter and clicked her teeth, urging him forward in a big, slow circle. She gently tapped the ground behind the horse with a long whip until he settled into an easy lope. Ava remembered her uncle calling this "lunging", and he'd often do it when a horse needed training or more exercise. A cream-colored cowboy hat hid the woman's face, but a familiar blonde braid stretched down her back. Ava's throat tightened.

"Actually," Ava said, turning back to Lizzie, "I'd love to just take in the view for a minute, if that's OK? It's so beautiful, and I've been in the car for a long time."

Lizzie smiled and nodded. "I know that feeling," she said. "This place fills my soul. Take your time. I'll be in the office when ya need me."

"Thanks," Ava said.

Her smile faded as she watched Lizzie disappear inside the stable. Ava wrapped her wool jacket tighter around herself. Was it colder in Utah? It was hard to say. She spent so little time outdoors these days. She sighed and straightened her shoulders. There was no more avoiding it... It was time to face the past.

Six

Ava wavered just the outside the arena, waiting for Macy to see her. After five minutes or so, it became clear that wasn't going to happen. Her cousin had always been laser-focused when it came to horses, and that hadn't seemed to change.

Ava glanced down at her tan suede Louboutins, now caked in dusty dirt. She sighed. At least she had her new riding boots for the rest of the trip.

She climbed clumsily through the fence slats, but Macy gave no indication she noticed. Now only fifteen feet or so away, Ava could see tiny headphone pods in Macy's ears. She wore an oversized blue plaid flannel shirt with fitted bootcut Wranglers, snug on her trim, muscular frame. Even at a distance, Ava could see the sun-freckled skin and sharp blue eyes she remembered so well.

Ava loudly cleared her throat. Macy threw a glance over her shoulder as she continued to lunge the tall gelding.

"Oh! Hello, ma'am!" Macy called politely. "I'm working Astro here, but if you head inside, you'll find my office manager Lizzie. She'd be more than happy to help you."

"Macy!" Ava said loudly. "It's me! It's. . .Ava."

Macy continued tapping the crop on the ground behind Astro as he circled her again. Only a stiffening in her posture told Ava that she had heard her.

Ava's ears began to ring. This was a horrible idea. If Macy had wanted to see her, she'd had a decade to reach out. She'd lost her husband, who Ava had never even met. What could she possibly do for Macy?

"Whoa," Macy finally called to Astro in a low voice. He immediately stopped. She tapped her headphones, then walked over to the horse and unfastened the lunge line. He wandered a few feet away as he sniffed the ground, and Macy turned to Ava, winding the line around her arm into a loop.

"What are you doing here?" Macy asked evenly.

Ava forced a smile. "The ranch looks amazing! And a riding academy?! I can't believe you actually made it happen! Well, I mean, I *can* believe it, of course, it's just—you did it, Macy!"

Macy planted her fists on her hips but said nothing. Astro snorted, oblivious to the tension as he chewed grass under the fence.

"Lizzie is great, by the way," Ava continued. "I think she mentioned she's from town? Oh, and speaking of town, Harris lives there now? That's hard for me to picture."

Ava forced a laughed. She knew she was rambling. She rubbed her palms together, suddenly unsure where to put her hands.

"So, listen," she said, trying to sound light. "Since I'm here, I thought I might stick around for a bit." She shoved her hands into her pockets. "Do you think maybe I could stay here?"

After what felt like an eternity, Macy looked at her.

As their eyes met, Ava's stomach clenched. She could see a weariness in those blue eyes she hadn't noticed before... Or maybe she had caused it.

"You didn't answer my question," Macy said, finally. "What are you doing here, Ava?"

Ava hesitated. That was the million-dollar question, wasn't it? She could have said she was there to make her mom happy. To please Lucas. To make her dream a reality. To help Macy. To fix the past. Ava wasn't sure what the truth was anymore.

"I missed you, Macy," Ava blurted. "It's been too long and I'm sorry. I really want to catch up with you and just. . .see you."

Yet another truth. A half-truth, maybe, but was any single truth the whole story? She couldn't read Macy's expression.

"Or maybe you know of an Airbnb nearby? A bed and breakfast or something?" Ava added quickly. "I shouldn't assume you have extra space here. I have money."

After another infinite pause, Macy nodded toward the forest. "At the edge of that tree line is a cabin. You can't see it from here, but it's behind those rocks. You may as well use it."

"Thanks," Ava said, letting out a breath she'd didn't realize she'd been holding. "Is the cabin new? I don't remember anything being over there."

Macy nodded tightly. "We had it built for my mother-in-law. She'd visit from California. It's been mostly empty, ever since. . .Well. I assume you know." Ava watched Macy's face darken, something shuttering behind her eyes. She couldn't fathom what it must be like to lose someone like that, never even getting the closure of knowing where his life had ended. She wondered if it had been like in the movies, with a stone-faced man in uniform coming to the door of the old ranch house.

"Macy, I'm so sorry about what happened to your husband," Ava said. "I'm sure he was an amazing man. Are you. . .Are you OK?"

Ava swallowed, cringing inwardly. What a stupid question. After all those hours ruminating on the plane, she had hoped she'd handle this conversation with a bit more grace.

"Listen, Ava, I'm fine, OK?" Macy said. "You're welcome to the cabin. Have at it."

"Thank you," Ava said, mustering a smile.

"Well, there you are, Miss Ava!" Lizzie called, approaching from the stable. "I see you two have already met!"

Macy looked curiously from Lizzie to Ava, but said nothing.

"I'm off in ten minutes," Lizzie continued brightly. "Let's get you squared away before I head home. I checked and we have room in tomorrow's ten a.m., semi-private. That's a lesson with just you and one other person. He's an adult student too and a really nice fella. . .Could be a good place to start. What do you think?"

Ava turned to Lizzie, avoiding Macy's stare.

"Sure, let's do it," Ava said.

"Well, come on to the office and we can get you in the system," Lizzie said. "Becca's mom just left some cookies, and they've been staring at me, so you'd be doing me a favor by taking a couple."

"I've never needed coffee and cookies more than right now," Ava said with a laugh.

"Well, then, follow me!" Lizzie called, heading back inside.

Ava finally met Macy's stare. Ava waited for her to ask about the lessons, but Macy said nothing.

"Can I buy you dinner tonight?" Ava asked. "Wherever you want."

"I have plans," Macy said sharply.

"Sure," Ava said. "No worries. . .Maybe another time."

Chastened, Ava walked to the stable. Her back ached and she could feel the heel of her left stiletto coming loose. She couldn't wait to change.

"How about Friday?" Macy called.

Ava turned back. "Friday would be just lovely. It's really good to see you, Macy."

Macy gave a curt nod and turned back to Astro. Well, it wasn't exactly the warm welcome Ava had hoped for, but it was a start.

Ava unrolled the well-worn leather case that held her brushes. She'd need to pick up canvases somewhere, but she never painted without her lucky set. Carla had pushed her to work as much as possible while in Utah, and Margo had sent her the info for a local company that specialized in shipping valuable items. Even here, Ava couldn't truly clock out.

After getting the cabin keys from Macy, she had driven to the Quik Pik off Route 92 for a few essentials, hoping to get enough to tide her over until she could do a proper grocery trip. By the time she returned to the ranch, it was too late to get a feel for how much sunlight entered the cabin throughout the day, but based on the large east- and west-facing windows, Ava suspected it would be perfect for painting. She gazed out the small bay window, but it was too dark to make out anything other than the star-filled sky.

The cabin was charming and surprisingly chic. From the outside, it looked like a rustic log home, but the inside was straight out of a West Elm catalog. Stainless steel appliances and gray tile floors below, and above, a cozy loft with a queen platform bed. The little living area had a small sofa, a tiny electric fireplace, and built-in shelves packed with paperback books. Apparently, Ben's mother was a big fan of James Patterson and Nicholas Sparks.

Ava's phone vibrated from the kitchen counter. She picked it up: Lucas. Her heart warmed at the sight of his name.

"Hey you," she said, putting the phone on speaker.

"I miss you already," Lucas said. "Are you miserable yet?"

Ava laughed. "Actually, it's kind of great here," she said. "You should see this place. From my window, I can see the mountains. When we were little, we'd try to run fast enough to catch the sun before it disappeared behind them. Spoiler: we never did."

"While that's kind of adorable," Lucas said, "Just think of all the ticks and mosquitos that must be out there at that hour."

"It must have been my uncle's way to get the last bit of energy out of us," Ava said, ignoring the bug comment. "I can't help but picture doing that with my kids one day."

"Huh," Lucas said, his voice detached. She'd gotten used to his distance whenever she talked about kids. He told her once that he didn't picture children in his future. His own father had worked all the time, and Lucas still didn't have much of a relationship with him. Ava had a hunch that when Lucas got to a place in his career where he was satisfied, he'd slow down enough to change his mind. It wasn't that he hated kids, he just didn't think he could be a good dad. But Ava believed, between his calm patience and habit of giving his all to everything she'd ever seen him try, that he'd be a great dad.

"I'm staying in the cutest little cabin," Ava said, "right here on the ranch. It's so homey and quiet. I think they built it four or five years ago. So much has changed since I was here last."

"You're staying on the property after all," Lucas said. "Macy must have been happy to see you."

"Well. . .'Happy' wouldn't be the word I would use. But she didn't scream and run away. I think it's gonna take some time."

"Ah," said Lucas.

"Not what you were hoping to hear?" Ava asked.

"Your life is here, Ava, and even a week is really pushing it. I just don't want you to miss too much. You know how fast things move in the art world."

"Well, art imitates life, right? Maybe I'll get some new ideas."

"Just don't go tapping into High School Ava," Lucas said with a chuckle. "Remember when you showed me your first portfolio? Your paintings looked like those calendars they used to pass out at gas stations."

Ava's jaw tightened. She'd learned that those picturesque landscapes didn't sell as well as the abstract figures she'd become known for, but they were still a part of her journey.

"Listen, Lucas, I'm wiped and I have a riding lesson in the morning. Can I call you tomorrow?"

"*You* have a riding lesson?" Lucas asked incredulously. "I can't picture you on a horse."

"Hey!" Ava protested. "I was pretty decent once upon a time. Also, our first date was literally on horseback. Have you forgotten?"

"Of course not," Lucas said, a smile in his voice. "I guess I didn't realize that riding through Central Park with a bunch of tourists hinted at some former life as a cowgirl. Either way, I find it adorable. I feel like I'll never know all the sides of you. Maybe one day."

Ava smiled. "One day," she said.

When she hung up, she saw a text from Carla: Make it OK?

Ava: Yep, staying on the ranch.

Carla: Great. See? Easy.

Ava snorted.

Ava: Settling in. Seeing Harris tomorrow—he lives in town now.

Carla: Give him my regards—and keep me updated on your plans for Macy.

Ava: Will do. Night. XOXO.

Ava plugged her phone into the charger and switched it to silent. She knew she needed a plan if she was going to make any real difference during her short visit, but it could wait until tomorrow. It had been a long day.

She walked to the bookshelf and scanned the titles until her eyes rested on a tall, familiar spine amidst the mass-marketed paperbacks: *The Complete Works of Thomas Cole*. Cole was the first painter Ava could remember learning about. She opened the front cover. In childlike scrawl, it read, "Property of Ava MacDaniel." She must have left it behind all those years ago.

She lugged the large book up the narrow staircase to her bed. She flipped through the first few pages but set it aside before she'd finished the introduction. Her eyelids felt like they weighed fifty pounds. She climbed under the down comforter and switched off the light, but the loft was still illuminated by the glow of the night sky. Ava felt a sense of peace wash over her as she fell into a dreamless sleep.

Seven

The next morning, Ava felt light as she walked across the dewy grass outside her cabin. She'd slept well, and things always felt more hopeful in the morning. She'd taken her time getting out of bed, luxuriating in the freedom of waking up without an alarm.

Ava was glad she'd packed for riding. She had a stylist at Bloomingdale's who could always fill even the most specific requests. Ava thought she looked sharp, even as she felt the early twinges of a blister forming on her right heel. These boots were gorgeous, but they definitely needed some breaking in. She wore a navy crushed-velvet blazer over a silk tank, a pair of ivory jodhpurs tucked inside her boots. The black cashmere beret wasn't exactly a hunt cap, but it would conceal her future helmet hair.

Ava followed the sounds of voices through the open stable door to the office, where she found Lizzie and Macy sipping coffee. Lizzie gave Ava a cheerful wave. Macy looked at Ava, then burst into laughter.

"What?" Ava asked.

"You look like an American Girl doll," said Macy. "Did you join a runway hunt club?"

Ava's cheeks grew hot.

Macy wore a faded pink flannel open over a blue tank, flared jeans and lace-up boots. Is that what she had always worn riding? Ava couldn't remember. She crossed her arms over her chest as sweat began to stick to her back.

"Should I—" Ava began. "I mean. . .Do I need to change?"

Macy smirked. "The boots look sturdy enough," she said. "But just so you know, those pants will probably be brown in an hour from the dust alone. You remember we ride Western, not English, right?"

Ava nodded but could no longer recall the difference. "I remember plenty of things," she said, her jaw tightening.

"Great," Macy said, a twinkle in her eye. "Then why don't you go saddle up Gunner? He's the third or fourth horse around the corner. Help yourself to the tack room and meet me outside in twenty."

"I'll see you there," Ava said, as brightly as possible.

But as she left the office, her smile faded. Based on her outfit choice alone she was in over her head, but she'd never give Macy the satisfaction of admitting it. She'd just have to figure it out.

Ava wandered the aisle until she found the open tack room. She wished she'd paid closer attention during the tour. She studied the wall-mounted saddle racks, perplexed. Some were plain; some had lots of elaborately carved silver plates fastened all around the edges. Several had small seats, others much wider.

She vaguely remembered a pad that needed to go underneath the saddle. . .and then she'd need a bridle with the right kind of bit. She took a deep breath and tried to steady herself. *One thing at a time.* She grabbed a plastic caddy full of grooming supplies and headed down the stable aisle.

Thankfully, the stalls were labeled. Midnight, Coda, Bella. . .and finally, Gunner. Whiskery gray nostrils sniffed at the stall bars.

"Hey, Gunner," she said softly. "I'm your new friend, Ava. Please go easy on me."

She opened the heavy metal latch and slid back the stall door. Where to start? Gunner already wore a halter, that was good. Thankfully, someone had left a lead line tied in a quick release knot to the bars. Ava remembered that this kind of knot was important in case a horse needed to be untied quickly in an emergency, but she had no idea how to tie one herself. Gunner nuzzled his soft nose against her back as she set the grooming bucket on the floor. She scratched him behind his ears before hooking the lead to his halter.

Ava picked up a rubber curry comb as long-buried muscle memory began to surface. Starting at Gunner's neck, she moved the comb in circles, breaking up dried sweat and dirt. Once she'd combed both sides, she began to smooth his coat with a wood-handled brush. Gunner seemed to enjoy the grooming, closing his eyes as Ava worked.

Now, it was on to the hoof pick. Ava knew she had to pick out any rocks with the hook side and then brush out the loose dirt, but how was she supposed get Gunner to lift up his hoof?

She twisted her hair into a quick braid. She leaned forward and grabbed Gunner's hoof tightly. She pulled. Gunner stood firm. Ava grabbed the hoof again, this time with two hands, pulling harder. Gunner eyed her with mild interest, but didn't move.

"Gunner, I'm trying to help you," Ava whispered. "Can you please just lift up your foot?"

Gunner licked his lips and began to doze again. Ava sighed. Sweat began to bead on her forehead and her throat tightened.

"Gunner—*hoof*!" she said desperately. "*HOOF!*"

It was no use.

She heard a snort from the stable aisle. Great. All she needed was an audience.

"I can hear you, you know," she snapped.

"I'm sorry, I didn't mean to eavesdrop," said a male voice. "I heard we had a new student today and I thought I should stop by and see if you needed help."

Ava wiped her forehead with the back of her hand and sighed. She didn't really have a choice. "I can't remember how to make him pick up his hoof," she said. "Horses 101, I know."

The man stepped into the light and leaned against the open stall door. Ava's breath caught in her throat. He was fairly tall, at least six feet, his baby blue polo shirt pulled snug over a muscular build. His hazel eyes glittered with humor, brilliant against the leftovers of a summer tan. Deeply carved smile lines creased his angular jaw. By any standard, he was gorgeous.

Most of the men Ava had known from this part of Utah wore work clothes: flannel tops, Wranglers, and Carhartt jackets. But other than a sturdy pair of cowboy boots, this guy looked like he could have stepped out of a J.Crew ad. Ava suddenly realized she'd been staring too long.

"I'm Ethan," he said, looking amused.

"Ava."

"May I?" Ethan asked, extending his hand. She reluctantly gave him the hoof pick, then stepped back as Ethan entered the stall. He leaned his shoulder against Gunner's flank, then ran his hand down the horse's leg. Gunner immediately lifted his hoof. Ethan picked out a few clumps of dirt and gently set it back down, then did the same to the other three hooves. He made it look easy.

"Now I remember," said Ava, feeling small as he handed her back the pick. "Thank you."

"Just a little lean and a little squeeze and old Gunner here will do the rest," he said, patting Gunner's neck affectionately. "Have you tacked up before?"

"Yep. Many, many times."

"Okay, well, then I guess I'll see you out there," he said, giving her a little nod before leaving the stall.

"Wait," said Ava. "You're sharing the lesson with me?! Lizzie made it sound like you were a beginner. You don't act like a newbie."

"You haven't seen me ride yet," he said, smiling. "Trust me, you'll feel better. In the interest of full disclosure, I was a bit nervous around horses not long ago. I spent the better part of a year helping out around here and getting comfortable before I had enough courage to actually get on a horse. I've only been riding for a few months."

Ava noticed he said all this without a hint of embarrassment.

Most guys she knew would never admit to being afraid of anything, let alone a horse.

"Well, then, also in the interest of full disclosure," she said, "I would love help tacking up. I was telling the truth; I have done it many times. Just not in at least ten years."

Ethan laughed. "Come with me," he said. "I've ridden Gunner before, so I know what bit he does best with..." He matter-of-factly surveyed her body, and Ava felt her stomach tighten. "You're tiny," he continued. "I'll grab you Macy's old saddle. How about we let Gunner relax for a minute while we go figure it out?"

She felt her panic begin to subside as she unfastened the lead line from Gunner's halter. He nickered as he found a stray bunch of hay in the corner. Ava tucked a loose wave behind her ear and headed out of the stall. Ethan flashed her another smile before gesturing for her to follow him down the aisle. She couldn't help but notice he looked just as good from behind.

Suddenly, he turned to her, an expectant look on his face, and Ava realized he'd asked her something.

"I'm sorry, what was that?" she asked, her ears burning.

"I asked if you brought a padlock. For the lockers?"

She shook her head.

"Well, I doubt anyone here will mess with your stuff, but maybe it's best if you share mine just in case."

"Thanks," she said quickly as she followed him into the tack room.

Ava gripped the reins in her right hand and led Gunner into the aisle. She felt a little nervous being alone with this giant animal, but Ethan had gone to tack up his own mount. She wondered if she was supposed to close the stall door behind her, but noticed several other empty stalls standing open. She pulled Gunner toward the exit, accidentally yanking on his bit in the process. He tossed his head in protest before settling beside her with a patient snort. Under the circumstances, Ava was a little surprised that Macy had chosen an easygoing horse for her, but she was grateful nonetheless. She patted Gunner apologetically as they continued down the aisle in jerky starts and stops. She was relieved to find the stable door already wide open. As they finally made their way outdoors, she spotted Ethan just ahead, leading a massive paint horse.

Ava slowed her pace, trying to mirror the way Ethan confidently walked at his horse's shoulder. She was so glad he had offered to help her. He had shown her where the students' equipment was kept and stashed her keys and phone with his own. It wasn't like she'd need her phone; Ava had learned there was no cell reception out here. According to Ethan, everything was a dead zone except for the main house and cabin, which were on WiFi.

Ava had forgotten how heavy a saddle actually was, but she'd managed to heft one onto Gunner's back by herself. Ethan showed her how to see if the girth was tight enough around a horse's belly by sticking her hand under the cinch, and how to poke her fingers in the gap between Gunner's teeth to get him to open his mouth for the bit. Though parts of it felt familiar, she never could have done it all on her own.

Macy stood with her arms crossed in the center of the arena. She looked annoyed as she glanced pointedly at her watch.

"Sorry!" Ava said. "I had trouble finding everything, but Ethan helped me. It's my fault we're late."

"Well, let's get to it," Macy said coolly. "Go ahead and start warming up at a good walk."

Ethan mounted his horse and led her to the rail. She was beautiful, with big black-and-white spots all over her giant frame. Ava thought most riders would look like children on Nikita, but Ethan looked distinguished and powerful on her back.

Ava looked at Gunner. He swished his tail at a fly and blinked. He was tall, at least compared to her. How was she supposed get her foot into the stirrup? She lifted her left leg as high as she could but still couldn't reach. She gripped the saddle horn and tried again. This time she managed to hook the stirrup with her toe, but her stiff boot wouldn't bend at all. She had no idea how she was going to lever herself into the seat. She tightened her grip on the saddle horn with one hand and braced herself on the girth strap around his belly with the other. Suddenly, Gunner hopped sideways, taking her boot with him, and Ava nearly toppled over as her foot jerked back to the ground. She realized she must have been accidentally pressing her fist into his stomach.

"Sorry, Gunner," she whispered, shoving her sand-covered foot back into the boot. He snorted again, and Ava thought that this was what horses must sound like when they laughed.

She shot a glance toward Macy, who mercifully had her attention on Ethan.

"Your posture looks much better, Ethan, but let's work on getting your heels down," Macy said. "And try to give Nikita a little more rein."

She turned to Ava. "Were you just going to stand there all day or did you want to actually ride?"

"I, uh. . .Well, I just—" Ava stammered. She took a deep breath. "I can't remember how to get up there."

Macy sighed. She grabbed a large bucket from outside the arena, then turned it upside down on Gunner's left before taking the reins from Ava.

"Put your left hand on the horn, right on the back of the saddle," Macy said. "When you do this on your own, the reins will go in your left hand. Left foot in the stirrup, then swing the right foot over."

Ava nodded. She climbed onto the bucket and put her weight in the stirrup. She braced herself on the horn with both hands and jerked her right knee up to her armpit before awkwardly slipping it over the saddle. She grabbed the reins, hoping Macy didn't notice her trembling hands. How she would ever get up there without the bucket was beyond her.

"Thanks," Ava said, but Macy was already walking away with the bucket tucked under one arm.

Ava squeezed her heels against Gunner's sides, and he jolted forward. Okay, that was clearly too much. She pulled back on the reins and he stopped abruptly, then began to back up.

"Ava!" Macy called from the other side of the arena. "You're right-handed, correct?"

Ava nodded.

"Both reins loosely in your left hand," Macy said. "Gunner knows what to do. Try offering a suggestion instead of a command. Relax."

Ava didn't realize how rigid her body was until she released the breath she'd been holding. Was she this tense in her everyday life?

She loosened the reins like she'd watched Ethan do, then gently leaned them against Gunner's neck. She squeezed her left leg and Gunner turned toward the rail. Slowly, she felt her body began to ease into the rhythm.

She laughed as she rested her right hand on her thigh. "I think I'm getting it!"

Something seemed to click as her heels eased down. She sat tall in the saddle, her legs hanging long. She surrendered to the rocking motion of Gunner's walk as they circled the arena.

"Looking good, Ava!" Ethan called.

Ava smiled.

"Ethan, why don't you go ahead and jog?" Macy said.

Ethan made a clicking sound with his teeth, and Nikita picked up speed. He bumped up and down, gripping the saddle horn with his free hand.

After watching for a few minutes, Ava eased the reins forward and tightened her legs. She imitated Ethan's clicking until Gunner began to jog. Her hips rocked side to side with the horse, almost as if they were one unit. She felt a flood of exhilaration; she had forgotten how much fun this was.

Ava circled the arena a few more times. She kept glancing at Macy who was watching her, but calling out no instructions.

Ava moved her right heel back and squeezed lightly. She made a single kissing sound and Gunner moved into an easy lope. They passed Ethan and Nikita and continued around the arena. The wind brushed her face as she gave Gunner even more rein. Eventually, she called out a low "*Whoa!*" Gunner stopped before she could even pull back on the reins.

"Good boy," she said, grinning as she leaned forward and

patted his neck.

"Ethan, go ahead and lope Nikita when you feel ready," Macy said.

"What do you want me to do now, Macy?" asked Ava.

"It looks to me like you're doing just fine on your own today," Macy said, her lips curling into a small smile. "It's amazing how much you remember. Maybe you should trust yourself more."

After the first half hour, Macy guided them through some basic drills: backing, pivoting, and side-stepping. Ethan's attempts were mostly a bit clumsy, but he laughed at himself and seemed to be having a good time. Ava, on the other hand, performed each task with ease. It was as if all this knowledge had been stored in a little box inside her and she only had to get back in the saddle to unlock it. The rest of the lesson flew by, and before she knew it, she saw two preteen boys waiting with their horses outside the arena.

"Okay, guys!" Macy called. "Let's bring 'em in, dismount, and head inside. Ava, you need a hand?"

Ava shook her head; she remembered it was always much easier getting down than climbing up. She felt like a whole different horsewoman from an hour ago. They walked their horses to the center of the arena. Ava swung her right leg over Gunner's back and slid gracefully to the ground, her left leg following. As soon as her feet hit the ground, however, her knees buckled, pitching her sideways into the sandy dirt.

She groaned, her legs feeling like pudding as she pushed herself up to sit. Macy laughed and took Gunner's reins. Ethan walked over with Nikita and extended his hand. Ava took it, trying to remain composed as she struggled to her feet.

"You OK, Ava?" he asked.

"Yeah. Totally fine!" Ava said as she forced a smile. She braced her hands on her knees and saw Ethan and Macy share an amused glance, the look seeming to linger between them.

"I can take it from here," Ava said, holding out her hand for the reins.

"You sure?" Macy asked.

"Positive," Ava said, with as much confidence as she could muster.

Her hips ached as she led Gunner back to the stable. She had embarrassed herself, and yet, she felt a glowing wave of pride. It seemed her mind remembered what to do on a horse. It was just going to take some time before her muscles got the memo, as well.

Eight

Ava parked her rental car behind a dark blue pickup and glanced at the small white cottage on her right: 510 Clark Street. Yep, this was the one. Her leg muscles protested as she climbed out of the car and swung her handbag onto her shoulder. After the lesson that morning, she had done some stretching and popped a few Advil, but she had a feeling tomorrow would be even worse. Thankfully, her next lesson was still a few days away.

As Ava approached the front door, she noticed several lawn gnomes around the perfectly trimmed front yard. She smiled. She was definitely at the right place.

She knocked and waited, but no one came. She peeked through the window, and although the gauzy curtains hid the room, she could see the lights were on. She knocked again and rang the doorbell. After another minute, she turned to leave.

"I'm in the back! Come on around!"

Ava passed through a tall wooden gate around the side of the house. A compact white-haired man raked leaves into a giant black trash bag. He turned and gave a little wave, leaning against the rake as he watched her approach.

The last time Ava had seen her uncle, his black hair was just beginning to gray. Otherwise, he looked the same: strong and spry with a twinkle in his eye, as if he already knew the punchline to every joke.

"Ava! Come here, girl!" he exclaimed, extending his arms. Ava met his embrace, smiling to herself as she registered the sweet scent of butterscotch she remembered. She winced as he squeezed her even tighter.

"It's so good to see you, Uncle Harris," Ava said when he'd finally released her. "You don't seem surprised to see me."

"Macy called me when you showed up," he said, then laughed. "Sounds like your big entrance really threw her for a loop. After all this time, I know it couldn't have been easy to come back, but it sure does mean a lot. I know you've got that big art career waiting for ya, too."

Ava smiled but looked away. Harris gently grabbed her arm.

"I hope you know how proud I am," he said, beaming. "I follow everything you do. All my buddies at the lodge know to keep an eye out for articles about you. I even have a scrapbook. . .Wanna see it?"

Ava smiled. Carla had always been a bit apathetic when it came to mementos, never even bothering with a baby book. It was sweet to think of Harris with a glue stick in one hand and a newspaper write-up about Ava in the other. She'd really missed him.

"Maybe another time," she said. "I'd rather hear about you. I never thought I'd see the day you retired!"

"Yep, well, for everything there is a season," he said. "I sold off the cattle years ago and just rented out the fields to other folks. Once Ben joined the family, the ranch ran just fine without me. I was tired, if I'm being honest, and I welcomed their offer to buy me out. But as you can see. . .I'm still farming."

He gestured to the raised garden beds and a small wooden chicken coop. Ava laughed.

"Well, the house is adorable," Ava said. "I'm glad you stayed close by."

"'Adorable,' she calls it!" Harris said, throwing his head back and roaring with laughter. "I prefer 'majestic,' personally. But why don't you come inside for some iced tea and decide for yourself?"

Ava followed Harris toward the house, noticing more lawn decorations along the way: a little Dutch windmill, a carved stone birdbath, and a sea glass wind chime hanging from the maple tree in the corner. A black yard sign caught her eye: *POW-MIA: Prisoners of War – Missing in Action. You Are Not Forgotten.*

Ava stepped into the kitchen and closed the screen door behind her. Harris filled a tray with crackers, cheese, and little Chips Ahoy! cookies.

"I thought you said iced tea," Ava said.

"Well, I like to think of tea like the English do. . .An excuse to have snacks," he said, his eyes shining with glee as he added a pitcher of tea and two glasses to the tray.

"I won't say no to snacks," said Ava.

"You never did," Harris said.

Ava smiled. She had loved her time in Cobalt, and loved this man like the father she never knew. It was clear to her that Harris held no grudge against her for leaving, and for that, she was grateful.

She followed him to a little breakfast nook and sat across from him. A giant picture window overlooked the backyard. Harris had been right to be proud of his house; it was small, but tastefully decorated and updated with modern appliances.

"OK, you win," said Ava as she made a little cheese-and-cracker sandwich. "I'd definitely call this place 'majestic.'"

Harris smiled. "I knew you'd agree. I remodeled the kitchen myself. I even built this nook."

"It's perfect," said Ava. She sipped her tea and gazed out over the yard, watching a chicken hop from its perch inside the open coop to the straw below. She noticed the raised garden beds were full of leafy green vegetables.

"I don't remember you growing crops at the farm," she said. "When did you start gardening?"

"That's actually a newer hobby for me," Harris said. "Ben was a big gardener, and when I expressed some interest, he took me under his wing. You should have seen all the heirloom tomatoes I grew this past summer. . .Cherokee Purple, Brandywine, Black Krim. Some weighed in over two pounds! Delicious, too."

"Ben sounds like he was a pretty special guy," Ava said. "I wish I had gotten a chance to meet him."

"He truly was," Harris said, nodding. "I was honored to be his father-in-law. He was good people."

"And Macy got that riding academy she always wanted," said Ava. "It's pretty amazing."

"Did you know Macy went to business school?" Harris asked.

Ava shook her head. "She never talked about college to me."

"When Macy gets her mind to something, she's relentless," Harris said. "She knew she needed more knowledge to get that place off the ground, so she worked during the day and took class at night. She even graduated a year early."

"Wow," Ava said. "That's great."

"It is. . .and it isn't," Harris said. "That same relentless streak can often rear its head as plain old stubbornness. And that's where we've got ourselves a problem."

"You mean about Ben?" Ava asked.

"I do," Harris said. "Now, I don't mean she needs to go out and find herself a new husband. Macy can certainly take care of herself, and I can't imagine how hard it would be to find someone as well matched for her as that man. It's something—I don't know—deeper. . .Macy just won't accept that's he's—well, that he's passed."

"I see," Ava said. "And there's been no sign of him?"

"Oh no, and there won't be," Harris said. "For security reasons, the military never disclosed the exact location Ben disappeared, but I do know it's a very remote mountain range. And the avalanche was massive. No way anyone could survive that. I just wish they had found all the boys. Ben and one other Green Beret were never found. I hate to say it like this, but it would have been easier on everyone if they had."

"Macy hasn't said much to me, but she doesn't seem like a woman who is falling apart," Ava said.

"Well, she poured herself into the stable," Harris said. "And she's a tough cookie. But I can see it. She doesn't see her friends anymore, doesn't go out. And she let Ben's field just die and fill with weeds."

So that explained the overgrown pasture Ava had seen on her tour.

"Ben must have been quite a gardener," she said.

"I'm a gardener," Harris said. "Ben was a master. He worked on it while he was home for long spells, and Macy would keep up with it when he was gone. He grew organic heirloom vegetables, mostly. No one had a greener thumb. Farmers' markets started to request him, and his booth sold out in hours every time. The lantern festival still offers Macy a booth each year in his place, but she keeps turning them down."

"Lantern festival?" Ava asked.

Harris laughed. "You *have* been gone a long time. Guess it's going on nine or ten years now. It's a huge harvest festival, really. The town wanted to turn the county fair into something that might bring in some tourists. Our mayor, Wang Lei, grew up in China and told a bunch of us on the city council about the lantern tradition. We loved the idea and now here we are."

"So, you now have an autumn lantern festival near Autumn Lantern Ranch?" Ava asked, raising an eyebrow.

"The irony wasn't lost on me!" Harris chuckled. "Though we call it 'The Sky of Embers Festival.' But you know how the ranch got its name, right?"

Ava nodded. Harris had told her and Macy the story countless times.

"Your ancestors bought the property and couldn't decide on a name," Ava said. "Their first night there, the harvest moon shone bright orange through the trees, looking like a giant lantern in the forest."

"Your ancestors, too," Harris said gently.

Ava smiled. "I like that story."

A comfortable silence stretched between them, Ava nibbling her snacks while Harris sipped his tea and looked thoughtfully out the window.

"So. . ." Ava said finally. "I was a bit surprised to hear you wanted me to come. I'm sure you know Macy and I don't talk; haven't in a decade now. I barely know her anymore. . .What could I possibly do to help her?"

"If I'm being honest, Ava, I don't really know," Harris said, looking evenly at her as if he'd been waiting for the question. "But I do know my Macy is lost. And she was never more herself than when you girls were together. . .not until Ben came along. I'm hoping—well, I thought. . .maybe you could find her. And bring her back to me."

He cleared his throat and blinked a few times. Ava reached out and placed her hand over his.

"I'll do my best," she said, giving his hand a gentle squeeze.

Harris nodded, dabbing the corner of his eye with his cuff.

"I should probably get going," Ava said. "I should paint today, and I need to pick up a few things first."

Harris nodded and stood, loading the tray before carrying it to the counter. Ava followed and set their empty glasses in the sink.

They walked through the living room to the front door. Recessed lighting brightened the snug space, and Ava guessed that was Harris' handiwork. That and the giant flat-screen TV on one wall. Ava could remember many Sunday football games on the big screen in the ranch's living room, Harris explaining every call and flag to her as Macy roared when the other team scored.

"Pretty great, huh?" Harris said. "It's an eighty-two inch. You've never seen *Indiana Jones* until you've seen it on that baby."

"You did an awesome job on this place," Ava said. "It's funny; so much is different since I was here last, but in some ways, it feels just the same."

Harris smiled. "I was thinking the same thing about you," he said. He pulled her into another bear hug, then held open the storm door before following her onto the porch.

"Lizzie said something about an art store in town," Ava said. "Do you know of it?"

"Just turn left onto State Street and you'll see it about three blocks down on the right. Oakenwood and Sons. I know we're a small town, but I hear it can compete with the best."

"Great. Thank you." She smiled and nudged Harris with her elbow before adding, "And thanks for the fancy English tea."

"I'm sure I'll see ya at the ranch, but come by anytime, Ava. It sure is good to have you back."

"Macy and I are grabbing dinner tomorrow night at the Timber Café," Ava said. "Why don't you meet us after for a drink?"

"I would love to," Harris said.

"Great. Let's say around seven-thirty?"

"I'll count down the hours," Harris said. "Thank you for coming, Ava. It truly means the world."

Ava smiled, turning her head as tears blurred her vision. She gave him a little wave before climbing into her car, wiping her eyes as she saw the sign for State Street at the end of the block.

A bell jingled on the door as Ava stepped inside Oakenwood & Sons Fine Art Supplies. Despite the cheap seventies wood paneling and worn carpet, Ava could immediately see that the store was well stocked. She spotted her favorite Terry Ludwig pastels and found a container full of Progresso pencils on the counter. It was clear Oakenwood—or at least his sons—knew art.

Though no employee was in sight, Ava could hear movement in the back. She hadn't brought anything to mix colors with to Utah, so she browsed the palettes and grabbed a small wooden one.

Ava saw a corkboard near the register full of flyers. One advertised a wine-and-painting night at the shop, another, a quilting class at the senior center. The others all showcased the comings and goings of small-town life: babysitters for hire, a pancake breakfast at the fire station, a church food drive. Then Ava saw a bright orange paper with an illustrated lantern across the top: *Sky of Embers Fall Festival – October 20th*. Too bad she'd be long gone by then.

To the right of the checkout was a wall with a long wooden shelf and gallery lighting. Several paintings were mounted with price tags beside them. Numerous artists were showcased here, each specializing in a different style. The shelf held a few sculptures and mixed media pieces. One small piece caught Ava's eye.

She stepped closer, fascinated by the little wooden boy sitting on the side of a bridge with a fishing pole cast into the river below. The detail was so specific that Ava could almost see his legs swinging back and forth as the water roared past. Astonishingly, it appeared to be carved from a single piece of wood. This one had no price next to it.

"Can I help you, ma'am?"

Ava jumped, then turned to find a tall ponytailed young woman, probably in her late teens, wearing a green polo shirt embroidered with the store name.

"Hi, yes. . .I'm looking for some canvases," Ava said. "Do you carry linen?"

"Yeah, for sure," said the girl. "Do you have a size in mind?"

"Twelve by sixteen would be great," said Ava. "How many do you have?"

"I can check," the girl said, heading for the back. She paused and turned to Ava. "Just to make sure—you know the linen is gonna be pricier? In that size, they run ya about seventy bucks each."

"That's no problem," Ava said. "I'd love ten, oil-primed if you have them."

The girl's eyes widened. Ava knew she wondered what on Earth this lady needed with ten professional-grade canvases. But the girl said nothing—just nodded and disappeared into the storeroom.

She returned with two stacks. Ava felt a familiar thrill as she saw the blank surfaces, full of nothing but possibility. The girl rang up the order, then looked at her apologetically when the total came close to $800.

Ava handed over her credit card and the girl was just about to swipe it when her mouth fell open. Wide-eyed, she gawked at Ava.

"You're Ava MacDaniel?" she squeaked. "*The* Ava MacDaniel?!"

Ava laughed. "I guess that depends on what you mean. Are you familiar with my art?"

"Familiar is, like, an understatement," said the girl, her eyes shining. "I did a whole presentation on your abstract style for my modern art class last spring."

"So, you're an artist too?" Ava asked.

The girl's neck flushed red. "No, not really. This was just for my high school class. But I'm a huge fan, and you're amazing."

"Thank you," Ava said. "What's your name?"

"Oh, duh, I'm sorry," the girl said, smacking her forehead with the palm of her hand. "I'm Kelly. I'm supposed to wear a name tag."

"Do you always run the store by yourself?" Ava asked.

Kelly shook her head. "Just when my dad's off," she said. "He's at a convention this weekend."

"Your dad is Oakenwood?" Ava asked. "But you're not a son. . .at least, as far as I can tell."

Kelly laughed. "One-hundred-percent female," she said. "Dad opened this place in the late eighties and already had four boys. They all worked here at some point. I was a surprise baby. By the time I was born, my brothers had all already moved out." She shrugged. "No one ever thought to change the name."

"Well, it's nice to meet you, Kelly Oakenwood," Ava said. "Your store is great."

"Come in anytime," Kelly said. "I'm here after school and on weekends."

"I definitely will," Ava said, stacking the canvases into a tall pile.

Kelly stepped around the counter and took half the stack. "Here, let me help," she said. "Where's your car?"

Ava led her straight across the sidewalk, where she'd secured a spot right in front of the shop. As they loaded the back of the rental, Kelly chattered on about life in Cobalt, sharing her favorite restaurant and coffee shop recommendations. She told Ava all about the art walk in the town square and the famous iron sculptor who kept a retreat in the nearby mountains. After Ava thanked her and drove away, she glanced into the rearview to see Kelly waving and smiling enthusiastically. *They really ought to change that name to Oakenwood and Daughter*, she thought as she turned back onto State Street and headed toward the highway.

Nine

The sun was past the line of midday as Ava balanced a blank canvas on the folding wooden easel she'd packed. She still had an hour and a half or so of decent light before she'd have to rely on the harsh track lighting in the cabin ceiling. Like many artists, Ava rarely painted at night.

She swirled some steely blue paint onto her brush and dragged it across the untouched white. Sometimes, especially for commissions, Ava spent weeks sketching plans before finally creating her first lines with pencil. Other times, when she painted for practice, she tried to leave her brain out of it and didn't sketch at all. She followed her intuition...or at least her *trained* intuition. She had become exceptionally skilled at delivering what people wanted from her work. First at art school, then for the critics. Sometimes, for her mother, sometimes for a buyer. The work was always hers, but like the lighting board used in a stage play, some levels were turned up higher, and some were turned down. She knew how to shape her artistic voice to make people happy. As often happened, Ava quickly fell into a flow. Before she knew it, the room had grown dim. She glanced at her watch: almost five p.m.

Ava stepped back and surveyed her work. It had promise, the angular lines and smooth curves arching across the empty expanse. Not a bad start. Often, Ava liked to work on several paintings at a time, switching back and forth between them depending on her mood. She would often add crushed eggshells or gritty sand to the oil paint to create texture and make parts of the image rise off the canvas. Each piece took weeks to layer and get the exact gradation of color she wanted, but the basic design of curves and lines would be the same. As she smudged the border between a pearly silver and a deeper metallic gray, blurring the still-drying paint with the edge of her brush, she realized these would be her first pieces to be created in two different states. There was no way she'd have time to finish them before she had to go back to New York.

Ava loved when fans told her all the meaning they found in her work. . .symbols of triumph and loss, representations of life itself. She usually just smiled and nodded, thanking them for spending so much time and thought with her pieces.

She couldn't remember the last time she'd painted something as an expression of her own feelings or as a symbol of something more complex; she'd simply learned to create pieces that got people excited. Sometimes, she wondered if that made her work dishonest. But when she saw the delighted faces in the gallery, she could see the meaning was very real in their eyes. Maybe that was the burden of the artist—to bear work to the world while only ever being able to enjoy it filtered through the reactions of other people. Perhaps so.

After she washed her brushes and tidied the cabin, Ava grabbed her sketchbook and a pencil and curled up in the window seat. Here, enough October sunlight still splayed through the window to be able to see. She flipped to a clean page and wrote:

<u>The Macy Challenge</u>

She chewed her eraser. She thought of her conversation with Harris earlier, of all the things Carla had told her, of all the things she'd noticed in Macy since she'd arrived yesterday. This wasn't going to be easy; she needed a plan. Plus, Carla had demanded she send one. And so she wrote:

1. Find Macy a date.

In Ava's romantic experience, the best way to move on was to find a cute distraction. She had no intention of trying to get Macy to forget Ben, or even find a new husband, but a little fun certainly couldn't hurt her healing.

2. Take back the field.

It was clear now that those gnarled weeds and rusted tomato cages were more than just careless neglect. For Macy, that field was a part of losing Ben she hadn't yet faced.

3. Get Macy to have fun with friends again.

Macy had always been more serious than Ava, but even old Macy enjoyed a night on the town. If Harris was right and Macy had let all her close friendships fade away, she must be lonelier than Ava could see.

4. Help Macy accept that Ben is gone.

Ava stared at what she had just written. It was why she had come, after all, but she still felt guilt slosh in her stomach as she read the words back. She knew Macy needed to acknowledge the permanence of his absence, needed to face forward again. But Ava also knew that meant pain. Still, it had to be for the best.

She took out her phone, snapped a photo of the list, and texted it to Carla.

Ava: As requested. Anything you want to add?

Carla: Looks good to me!

A sharp knock startled Ava, her pencil rattling to the floor. She hopped off the window seat and peeked through the front window. There, hands in his pockets, stood Ethan.

She opened the door. He had to bend down slightly to be seen through the tiny house's doorframe.

"Hi there!" he said with a grin. He nodded to the sketchpad still in her hand. "Sorry if I'm disturbing you."

She closed the book and pressed it against her chest.

"I just finished working, actually," Ava said. "What's up?"

"I was helping Lizzie muck stalls, and I thought I'd come by and see how you're settling in," he said. "Don't worry, I changed after."

Ava smiled. "Do you muck stalls for fun?"

Ethan shrugged. "I used to do it just to get out of the office, but eventually I noticed Macy had stopped charging me for lessons. Now the joke's on me; I think I'm an indentured servant."

They both laughed. His optimistic energy was contagious.

"I work in an office all day," he continued. "It's nice to do something with my hands." He lifted his arms and spread his fingers wide. "Speaking of," he added, "there's no soap in the barn.

Mind if I use your sink?"

Ava scrunched her nose. "You brought your horse poo hands all the way to my house?!"

Ethan simply shrugged again, and Ava stepped aside and pointed to the kitchen. He smiled and ducked through the doorframe. While he was turned away from her, Ava snuck a better look at him.

His broad shoulders hinted at a man who stayed active, but they weren't gratuitous enough for him to be a gym rat. His wavy brown hair, sun-streaked with blonde like a child's hair in summer, fell in a tousled style that reached his chin. He wore a collared shirt like the first time she'd seen him, though today he had on indigo jeans. She couldn't help but notice they seemed to hug in all the right places.

Suddenly, Ava looked at the floor, a lump of shame forming in her throat. What was she doing? She had her own gorgeous man waiting faithfully in New York. She was tired and emotional and clearly not thinking straight.

Ethan dried his hands on the kitchen towel and turned to face her. "So, I hear you and Macy are cousins," he said. "I thought she was acting awfully weird to a first-timer. Also explains the matching button noses."

Ava laughed. "Yeah, long story. Basically, we haven't seen each other since we were teenagers, and we didn't leave things so great."

"I don't know what she was like back then," Ethan said, his face softening, "but she's a strong, big-hearted woman, and she's been through a lot. Give her a chance to warm up to ya."

"I intend to," Ava said.

"Hey," he said, leaning his hip against the kitchen counter. "I've only lived here a few years myself, but I'm told Cobalt has changed a bit in the last decade. I thought you might need a tour."

"Oh, wow," Ava said, a little flustered. "I'd hate to ask you to do that, especially after you just helped at the barn."

"Nah, it would be my pleasure," said Ethan. "Besides, I don't have anything on the calendar tonight except dinner for one and catching up on my Netflix."

"Well, in that case, that would be great," she said. "Thank you."

"I just need to stop by my place and let my dog out, if you don't mind."

"Sure," said Ava. "Why don't you have a seat for a sec while I freshen up?"

"It's getting dark so much earlier now," he said, settling onto the tiny sofa. "Better bring a warm coat." He gazed out the bay window, a patient smile on his lips.

Ava picked up her fallen pencil, making sure Ethan didn't look her way as she tucked it into her sketchpad, and carried it into the bathroom. She closed the door behind her, sat on the closed toilet seat, and looked again at her list.

1. Find Macy a date.

Who would be better than Ethan? He was kind, almost impossibly handsome, and seemed to have a great connection with Macy. And that comment—dinner for one—made it sound like he might be single. She'd have to find out.

She snapped the book closed and stashed it in the cabinet beneath the sink. She grabbed her powder brush and swirled it around her compact before lightly dusting her nose. She glanced in the mirror, pausing mid-swipe before tossing them both back in her makeup bag. The air was so much drier here; her normally oily skin was barely shiny at all. She dabbed a little rose-colored gloss on her lips, combed her fingers through her tangles, and checked her reflection once more. When she walked out of the bathroom, Ethan stood and zipped his jacket.

She grabbed her phone off the charger and saw a text from Lucas:

Hey babe, miss you. XOXO.

She smiled and tossed the phone into her handbag along with her keys. She'd call him when she got back tonight.

"Ready?" she asked.

Ethan drove a Range Rover that smelled like a mixture of new leather and hay. Ava enjoyed the chance to see the rolling landscape as a passenger. They rode in a comfortable silence as she registered every forest, field, and mountain. It all seemed both achingly familiar and strangely foreign at the same time. She sank into the leather seat, feeling more relaxed than she had in a long time.

She glanced at Ethan, startled to find him watching her with an amused smile.

"What?" Ava asked.

"As my dad always says, you're gonna catch a fly with your mouth open like that," he said, laughing.

"Hey, it's not my fault," she said, playfully whacking his shoulder with the back of her hand. "It's absolutely breathtaking here. These colors? It's hard to believe they're real."

The fall leaves had begun their fashion show in full force. Brilliant yellows, vibrant oranges, and deep velvet reds made the mountainside appear to be on fire. It wasn't like in New York, where the leaves were immediately trampled by millions of feet and tires. This was all Mother Nature; all untouched.

Ava had spent a few autumns here, but the colors had faded in her mind along with the memories. This time, she wanted to memorize them. She knew she might not be back anytime soon.

"Lizzie told me you're an artist," Ethan said. "Painter, right?"

"Yep."

"Do you paint stuff like this?" he asked, nodding to the passing landscape.

"I did, when I was younger," she said. She glanced out the windshield, the endless sky creating an illusion of water on the horizon. "I wish I could capture this with paint. My style is something totally different now."

"How so?"

She shrugged. "It's abstract and very geometric. Lots of grays and blues. . .More industrial colors."

Ethan studied her.

"What?" she asked.

"It's just—and take this for what it's worth, coming from a tax guy—but I thought art was all about breaking rules and doing what you want," he said. "Can't you do both?"

"It's more complicated than that," Ava said. "It's a business. Now, I have to think about 'branding' and 'legacy' and other words that publicists love to throw around. I learned a long time ago that pretty pictures of horses and fields don't sell for much, and many artists are better at that style than I am. I seem to have a knack for the kind of art I'm known for, and, to be frank, it sells."

"You could paint these mountains just for you. . .just because you want to," Ethan said. "I mean, hasn't your success earned you the right to do what you want with your spare time?"

Ava didn't respond. What he said made sense, but it wasn't that simple. She painted to stay sharp, but she didn't have any leftover creative energy to paint for *her*. She felt something cold gnaw at her insides, a feeling that had begun when she saw that wooden carving at Oakenwood & Sons. It felt like envy.

Ethan noticed the shift in her mood. "I'm sorry, Ava," he said. "It's really none of my business."

She shook her head and summoned a small smile. "No, it's fine," she said. "You have a point."

I just don't want to think about art anymore today, she added silently. The dry wind was slapping little pockets of dirt and pebbles against the windshield. Ava saw the Quik Pik in the distance, which meant they were about halfway to town. As they passed the empty parking lot, she noticed a perfect funnel of leaves whirling across the lot. With each new gust of wind, it picked up discarded lottery tickets and plastic soft drink lids as it spun around the blacktop.

"Look!" Ava exclaimed. "It's a leaf tornado."

Ethan followed her gaze and smiled before turning his eyes back to the road.

"They call them wind eddies," he said. "We get them all the time."

"Is it dangerous?"

He chuckled. "No, you can walk right through it. We get so

many weird winds here. It happens when a gust hits a building or a rock. It makes the air spin, like an eddy in the water."

He glanced at her and shrugged when he saw her raised eyebrow. "I watch a lot of Discovery Channel. Maggie likes to have it on in the background."

Maggie. Girlfriend or roommate? Ava would need to clarify that point before she played matchmaker for Macy. She decided to be on the lookout when they stopped at his house to let his dog out.

"So, how did you find Autumn Lantern?" she asked. "It seems like most of Macy's new students are kids."

"A happy accident," he said, his eyes still on the road.

"You're gonna have to do better than that," Ava said.

"Well, I spent about four years doing corporate taxes in Vegas," he said. "Truth be told, I was making a ton, but all I did was work. And I was too drained when I wasn't working to be a real human."

"I know that feeling," Ava said.

He looked at her and smiled. "I needed a change. I started Googling job openings when my brain was too numb to do anything else. I had some ties to Cobalt, so I kept an eye on the area. Then, one sleepless night, I was scrolling ads on my phone and saw one for a local tax firm whose owner was retiring. I put in my two weeks and bought it sight unseen."

Ethan's grip tightened on the wheel. "Anyway, once I got settled in Cobalt, I suddenly had time on my hands and the energy to go with it. Now, I'm the boss. With two other accountants and an office manager that's been there as long as I've been alive, I don't need to spend endless hours behind a desk anymore. I started to explore, going to the local plays, all the festivals. I was at Sky of

Embers a couple years ago when I saw Macy's booth."

"Sounds like the festival is really popular," Ava said.

"That's an understatement. Some local businesses shut down so their employees can all go. I think that's one reason it's only on a weekend—parents would probably let kids skip school if they added Friday."

"What a great place for Macy to advertise."

"Exactly," Ethan said. "It worked for me."

They passed the green *Welcome to Cobalt* sign. As much as Ava had been enjoying some quiet solitude on her first time through, the drive went by much quicker with company.

"When I was a kid, I always wanted to ride a horse," Ethan said. "But my mom was so overprotective. Maybe it was an only child thing... Anyway, when I was ten, I went to a friend's family farm for the weekend. They asked if I could ride; I lied and said yes. I was so desperate to try. Long story less long, I fell; nothing near-death happened, but I sprained my wrist and got a concussion."

"That must have been scary," Ava said.

"Well, it scared the crap out of me, but really terrified my mom. She still likes to remind me of the time I 'almost died,' which is a total exaggeration. Regardless, that experience stayed with me. It felt like unfinished business."

"So, you signed up for lessons?"

"Not quite," Ethan said, laughing, his hazel eyes crinkling at the corners in a way Ava was beginning to recognize. "Remember, I've only been riding a few months. I took a flyer from the booth and after staring at it for weeks, I called. I was sure I'd end up paralyzed on day one. It took me a long time to get confident enough to actually ride, but I picked the right place; Macy totally got me. She was so patient with me, never pushing me until I was ready."

"Yeah, Macy's pretty amazing," Ava said.

"Yes, she is."

"Gorgeous, too," she said.

Ethan looked at her, a curious smile curling his lips.

"I just hadn't seen her in a long time," Ava added quickly. "She grew up to become a beautiful woman, don't you think?"

Ethan's expression was unreadable. "Yeah. Macy is a beautiful woman," he said finally. "Very grounded and honest. I admire those qualities in a person."

He flashed her that pearly grin once more, and Ava couldn't help but smile back.

Handsome, kind, and valued a woman beyond her appearance. Ethan might be exactly the man Macy needed to see that life was still waiting for her.

Ava sat back, watching the warm hues of fall became less of a blur as they slowed. They crossed the ancient railroad tracks that marked where the rural highway became Main Street. She took a deep breath and exhaled slowly. The week was already flying by. But at least now, she had a plan.

The Range Rover slowed to a bumpy stop on a long gravel driveway in the town's historic district. Ava looked up to see a massive red brick Victorian with a wraparound porch and a huge front lawn. She glanced at Ethan, her eyes wide.

"This is where you live?" Ava asked, gaping.

"I'm a sucker for history, so I've been learning to restore this place in my free time," Ethan said. "I learn through YouTube, mostly. Like I told you, all I used to do was work. Once I moved here, I was ready for some hobbies."

She turned back to the house. A large stained-glass window with a colorful geometric floral pattern was centered above the front door. The evening sun created a dappled pattern across the lawn as it filtered through the canopy of mature trees. A meticulously restored gazebo stood in the long shadows, and Ava spied a charming wooden swing beneath the shingled roof.

"It's gorgeous," she said.

"It's a work in progress," said Ethan, his cheeks pink as he spoke. "But you should have seen it a few years ago when I moved in. It's come a long way. I can show you the before-and-after photos sometime if you're interested."

"I'd love to see them," Ava said. Sensing an opportunity, she added, "Seems like a lot of space for someone living alone."

"I'm not living alone," Ethan said, grinning. He climbed the porch steps two at a time and flung open the front door. Ava had noticed that no one seemed to lock their doors in Cobalt, which was absolutely unheard of in New York. A flash of brown and white flew past Ethan and began running circles around Ava's feet. Suddenly, an excited little beagle threw her front paws onto Ava's thighs and began to feverishly lick her hand. Ava laughed.

"Maggie, down!" Ethan said.

So, this was Maggie. Maybe Ethan was single after all.

Maggie sped off and began running laps around the perimeter of the front yard. "I'm sorry about the jumping," he said. "She stopped growing, but she's still got a lot of puppy in her."

"She's sweet," Ava said. "How old is she?"

"About a year and a half," he said. "One of the farmers I prep taxes for had a litter and decided I needed a roommate. She was a gift."

Maggie began to enthusiastically sniff the ground around the gazebo.

"She won't run away?" Ava asked.

"I've got one of those electric fences," Ethan said. "But I doubt she'd go anywhere. We're besties."

Ava laughed. She settled onto the bottom porch step, buttoning her jacket. Ethan sat down a few feet away. It had been a warm day for fall, but the darkening sky ushered a crisp arid wind that Ava had only ever felt in Utah. She could sit here for hours. It was hard to get used to how quiet the town was, but she could feel herself relaxing into its peace.

Eventually, Maggie plopped beneath a tree to chew a rawhide and Ethan called her back inside. His house was only two blocks from the town square, so they decided to walk.

They shared the usual weather niceties and talked about their riding lesson. They compared favorite shows: reruns of *The Office* for him, BBC mysteries for her. He told her he planned to turn his front porch into a mini haunted house for the trick-or-treaters this Halloween and feigned horror when Ava confessed she probably wouldn't celebrate the holiday at all. It was refreshing for Ava to spend time with someone who took life a little less seriously than she did, and she could see Ethan becoming a good friend. He was so sincere and positive and. . .something else.

Present. That was it. She was used to being around people

who were always striving and building and achieving toward the future. Talking to Ethan felt slightly disorienting. . .like stepping off a speeding escalator onto still ground.

Soon, the sky turned dark. They walked through a blanket of leaves along Founders Row. The narrow cobblestone lane boasted the oldest homes in town, all of which faced the narrow river. Ethan proved his claim of being a history buff, telling Ava stories of the town founders: a mix of miners, missionaries, and railroad men. He wiped the brass plaques mounted on the iron fences of the houses with his coat sleeve, announcing the construction dates as he went: 1852, 1850, 1847.

"I never thought about the beginnings of this place," Ava said, smiling as they rounded the corner onto the main drag. "I guess every town has a history. So... What do you do to get into trouble around here?"

"Well, if you feel like getting really wild, this is the old ice cream parlor," he said, nodding to a storefront that looked straight out of the fifties. Through the window, red patent stools lined a long Formica counter. A young family was checking out at a retro metal cash register.

Ava's eyes widened. Bonnie's Ice Cream! It looked exactly as she remembered. Ethan shot her a questioning look.

"Harris brought me and Macy here all the time when we were little," Ava said. "And then when we got older, we'd beg to come here so we could hang out and meet boys."

Ethan laughed. "See, I called it! Trouble."

A few doors down, Ava stopped abruptly in front of a brightly lit building.

"Is that a tattoo shop?" she asked.

"You in the market?" Ethan asked, looking a bit intrigued.

"No," Ava said. "That used to be the second-run movie theatre."

The marquee had been covered with a giant lightbox sign: *Freddy's Ink Art.* The ticket booth was gone, but the tiny blue-and-white-checkered tile floor still stretched across the entrance.

"That's so sad!" Ava said. "Back in the day, you could see a movie for a dollar on Friday and Saturday nights. They always had a Disney movie or a family comedy at seven, then something at nine for the grown-ups. I used to think I'd get a job there one day so I could get free movie posters."

"I'm sad I missed it," Ethan said, looking up at the old marquee.

"I remember seeing Titanic there," Ava said.

"Always a classic," Ethan said. "It was on TV not long ago. The special effects really hold up."

"At age ten, I was much more interested in the romance," Ava said. "But the biggest takeaway for me? How embarrassed I was to see a topless woman while sitting next to my uncle."

"Not as embarrassed as he was, I bet," Ethan said.

They both laughed.

"Never thought of it that way," she said. "I wish you could have seen the theatre in its heyday. It felt like a safe place for a kid to spend the evening. Harris said it had been open since he was a kid and I guess I assumed it would last forever. I'm sure it was a tough business to keep profitable."

"Take it from the tax guy," Ethan said. "Any small business that makes it to the ten-year mark should consider itself successful."

They continued down the street, looking in shop windows as they walked. Some, like the drugstore, hadn't changed a bit since Ava was last here. Other shops from her memories were long gone. The arcade was now a Verizon store; the secondhand bookstore was a day spa. Despite the differences, Cobalt had the same nostalgic, friendly vibe Ava remembered.

As they neared the corner of Main and Second, Ethan pointed to a small building decorated to look like an old Western saloon. "And last but not least on our tour of Main Street, we have—"

"The Country Western Dance Hall!" Ava exclaimed. "Oh my gosh, it's still here?!"

"I take it you're familiar," Ethan teased.

"I totally forgot about this place," she said, tiptoeing to peek inside the neon-lit window. "Macy and I used to come here literally every Thursday for teen night. It's been here long enough that my mom and Harris came when they were younger. We line-danced for hours. . . 'Amos Moses,' 'Boot Scootin' Boogie,' 'Tush Push'—"

"'Tush Push?!'" Ethan said, laughing.

"I'd say I'd teach you, but it's a bit advanced for novices," she replied playfully.

"Excuse me! You haven't seen my moves."

"Fair enough," she said, smiling as she watched an older man in a biker vest push a broom across the wooden floor. "I can't even remember the rest of the dances. We had so many great nights at this place. I wonder what it would take to get Macy to come back here."

Ava felt an ache in her chest. It was hard to imagine ever being that close to Macy again.

"Hey," Ethan said. "I have one more thing I want to show you. Come on."

He walked around the corner. Between his long legs and Ava's three-inch high-heeled boots, she had to walk quickly to keep up. She really should have packed some sensible flats.

She caught up to Ethan as they reached an intersection and crossed to a quieter street. The buildings were spaced further apart here. He stopped in front of an empty lot that had been roped off.

A woman wearing a *Festival Volunteer* shirt was collapsing a folding table. A vinyl banner hung from the fence behind her: *Sky of Embers Fall Festival, Lantern Release Point*. Ava was confused.

"So. . .this is where the festival takes place?" she asked. "It's smaller than I imagined."

"This is just one of the spots where people can release their lanterns," Ethan said, chuckling. He gestured to an open box full of folded white paper objects. "In the week or two leading up to the festival, you can come here to pick up a lantern or buy tickets. You'll find a few other spots around town just like it. The actual festival is outside the city limits, at the old fairgrounds."

"No charge for lanterns!" the volunteer called as she stacked a couple plastic lawn chairs. "Help yourself."

"Thanks!" Ava called back.

The woman stretched a tarp over the table and chairs and Ava got the impression she was planning to leave them there overnight—yet another thing you'd never do in the city.

"It used to be the lantern release was just on Sunday night," Ethan said, "but it became so popular that now they do it on Saturday, too. People come from all over to watch. The radio stations even do a countdown so folks can send their lanterns into the sky at the same time, no matter where they are. And then, a few years ago, they added a firework show afterward."

"That's so cool," Ava said, pulling one of the lanterns out of the box and expanding the thin paper from the metal frame. It was bigger than she expected, almost two feet long. "I wish I could be here to see it."

"You're leaving that soon?" Ethan asked.

"I'm supposed to be. But I'd sure like to see that sky full of lanterns. Sounds beautiful." She carefully refolded the lantern and set it back in the box.

"You want this in your car?" Ethan called to the volunteer, pointing at the lanterns.

"Oh, that would be great! Thanks," the woman responded.

On the ground beside the box, Ava noticed an old pretzel canister labeled "Donations" filled with small bills. She grabbed it and followed Ethan to a Subaru parked on the street where the woman was waiting beside the open hatchback.

"Thanks for the help, you two," the woman said. "I was running the booth with Eddie Lambert, but he got called in."

"I know Eddie," Ethan said. "My tax firm is next to his bakery. He's a volunteer firefighter, right?"

"That's the one," she said, sticking out her hand. "I'm Helen."

They shook hands and introduced themselves, and then, Ava handed Helen the donation jar.

"Bless you, child, I almost forgot," Helen said, laughing and smacking her forehead. She shook the jar. "Good showing today. I started with three boxes."

Helen stared pointedly at their empty hands. "You didn't take a lantern after all?"

"I'll get mine at the festival," Ethan said. Ava said nothing.

"I'm hearing they expect a big crowd this year," Helen said. "I can't wait to see the sky. Do you both know about the meaning of the lanterns?"

This time, it was Ethan who said nothing. He glanced at Ava and she smiled. "Just that it's based on some Chinese tradition, from what my uncle said."

"That's right," Helen said. "It's what the lanterns stand for that brings me to tears every year. I'm not sure how true our festival sticks to the Chinese tradition, but everyone writes a wish on their lantern. When you release it into the sky, it's supposed to tell the universe you're ready and for it to bring you good luck. All those prayers lifted into the heavens at once... Truly something to behold. It's a symbol of new beginnings, or so I've been told."

"New beginnings," Ava said. "I like that."

"Well, I better head home," Helen said. "It was great meeting you two. I'll look for you at the festival."

Ava didn't have the heart to correct her. They said goodbye and Helen climbed into the station wagon, giving a little wave out the window as she drove off.

"Shall we?" Ethan said, gesturing down the block. They walked on, passing the municipal park; the swings and picnic tables were now empty. Ava had once played there, though the metal slides and blacktop had been replaced by a state-of-the-art jungle gym and rubber flooring. Even though it had been a decade, the change still felt jarring. Ava's chest tightened; she was running out of time.

"Ethan," Ava said. "Do you have a girlfriend?"

"Do I, uh, have a girlfriend?" Ethan repeated, his neck turning red as he fumbled.

"Sorry for the bluntness," she said. "I'm not trying to hit on you. I have a boyfriend."

Ethan looked no less confused.

"It's Macy," Ava continued. "I know you didn't know her before, when she had Ben—well, neither did I, but that's not the point. She's not the girl I remember. I think she hides it well, but she has to be lonely. I just thought, maybe if she could spend some time with a nice, charming guy like you, it could help her see that there's more out there, waiting for her. More than just her old memories."

Ava knew her relationship with Lucas needed some maturing before it was on the same level that Macy had with Ben. They needed to figure out a better work-life balance, and someone would have to make some compromises when it came to settling down. Even so, Ava knew she had someone who would always choose her first, who would always have her back. Macy deserved to find that again.

Ethan grew quiet and seemed to be considering. Ava knew she had caught him off guard, but she had no time to waste.

"Macy is amazing," he said finally. "I care about her and hate to think of her not being appreciated, which she definitely should be—"

"And she's beautiful?" Ava interrupted with a sideways smile.

Ethan laughed. "Of course, she's beautiful, anyone can see that," he said. "But she's also my riding teacher, and, I don't know—wouldn't that be weird?"

"I'm not asking you to marry her tomorrow or anything," Ava said. "Just have some fun. Help her see that guys like you are out there. Who knows what might happen?"

Ethan didn't look convinced.

"Tell you what," Ava said. "Harris is meeting us for a drink tomorrow night at the Timber Café. Why don't you come too, and we'll just act like you showing up is a coincidence? Then there's no pressure, and if it seems weird, she'll never know the difference."

She stopped walking and turned to face him. The ancient streetlights cast an amber glow across them both. Though his face was in the shadows, Ava could see he was studying her, his eyes thoughtful.

"Please," she said, a bit softer. "It would mean a lot to me."

Ethan shook his head, a wry smile forming, and Ava knew she had him.

"OK," he said. "I'll be there."

"Thank you," Ava said, smiling as she fastened the buttons on her peacoat.

"Speaking of Harris," Ethan said. "I always wondered...was he ever married? To Macy's mother?"

Ava hesitated for a moment before replying, "My Aunt Anna passed away giving birth to Macy."

"Oh my gosh, I'm so sorry."

Ava shook her head. "I never knew her. Neither did Macy, of course. I'm told she was a lovely, generous woman. But Harris raised Macy all on his own."

Music floated their way from the town square, but this street was quiet except for their footsteps on the sidewalk. Ava exhaled loudly, watching her breath form a foggy cloud in front of her. Though the moon was not yet visible above the trees, the temperature was dropping by the minute.

"Well, I think that's all the Cobalt highlights," Ethan said. He shoved his hands into his pockets as an icy gust whipped by when they reached the corner.

"Thanks for the tour," Ava said. "I sort of surprised Macy when I came back and I'm still not sure it was the right decision. It's nice to feel welcome."

Ethan smiled. "How about a milkshake for the ride back?"

"In this weather?" she asked, squinting at him.

"Absolutely," Ethan said. "Range Rovers have heat, you know."

Ava laughed. "Such technology," she said. "A milkshake to go, it is."

"I miss you too, babe," Ava said. "Goodnight."

Lucas hung up first.

Ava changed into her pajamas and brushed her teeth. As she braided her hair, she thought back on the events of what felt like the longest day in history.

It had been great to see Harris after all this time—to see how little he had changed. Ava could now admit that a part of her had been afraid he'd been angry with her all these years, or worse— had forgotten her altogether. But between the scrapbook and that bone-crushing bear hug, it was clear he still loved her. For the first time since she had arrived, she felt some small sense of belonging.

She had changed since her years here, and so had Cobalt. She had forgotten how still this place could feel. Though most days she loved the joyful noise and frenetic energy of the city, she couldn't help but wish New York had a little more of this slow, community vibe. . .and a little more silence.

It was good to catch up with Lucas, though he hadn't been able to talk for long. Ava had donated one of her pieces to a charity auction and he was going in her place. He'd been understandably distracted, but she still hung up feeling disappointed. She wanted to tell him about all these mixed-up feelings; she wanted him to help her make sense of it all.

Ava was finding a piece of herself she had left behind and she wanted to share that with him. It would be so fun to take a riding lesson with Lucas, get ice cream at Bonnie's, maybe even have a night out at the Country Western Dance Hall.

She chuckled to herself. Lucas line-dancing might be a stretch. But there was something to Cobalt. . .One day, she'd convince him to visit. She knew the town could work its magic on him. How could it not? She'd only been here for two days and she already felt different.

Ava climbed into the loft and turned off the light. She yawned. Maybe Cobalt could be a second home for them, once the gallery and residence were off the ground. Once they didn't have to push quite so hard. She closed her eyes, swirls of burnt orange and deep red dancing across her mind as she drifted into a deep sleep.

Ten

Ava groaned and stretched, pulling the blanket off her face. The sun was already high overhead. She looked at her watch: it was after ten. Ava hadn't slept this late in as long as she could remember. In fact, she was usually up before her alarm, her mental to-do list spurring enough anxiety to wake her.

As she climbed down the narrow stairs to the main level, her hips protested, an obnoxious reminder of her lesson the day before. Still, she had expected worse. She glanced at her charging phone on the counter. She knew she should check in; somewhere, it was a workday.

After unplugging her phone she opened her Gmail app. There were tons of new messages: the usual spam, a few interview requests, collaboration inquiries, and an e-mail chain with both Lucas and Carla that had clearly continued just fine without her—probably about the winter tour they'd been planning before Ava left.

She locked her phone and set it face down on the counter, feeling a delicious disconnection from the chaos of her usual life. Even her inbox couldn't reach her in the same way here.

Ava thought about her plans for the day as she brewed a pot of coffee. She definitely needed to paint; at the rate she was selling, weeks without a new piece was not an option. She padded barefoot to the living area and looked out the front window. In the distance, she could see three riders circling the outdoor arena. Lessons must have started for the day.

She walked back to the kitchen and opened the cupboards, finding only a bit of cereal and a few apples leftover from her trip to the Quik Pik. She'd have to stop by the grocery store in town, but before that, she needed caffeine. As if on cue, she heard the little coffee maker beep.

Twenty minutes later, Ava had dressed and gotten ready for the day. She grabbed an apple from the counter and slipped on a pair of blue rubber muck boots that had been bought for Macy's mother-in-law. Ava wondered what she'd been thinking when she packed heels and those boots that still weren't broken in. Already, that Ava almost seemed like another person.

As she stepped onto the porch, a warm wind blew her hair across her face. She tossed her jacket back inside the cabin and closed the door behind her. As she trudged across the grassy field and entered the barn, she wondered if Cobalt being a mile above sea level was why the sun felt closer here.

Gunner whinnied a hello as Ava approached his stall. She wiped the apple on her sleeve before holding it under his nose. He immediately devoured it, his giant lips leaving a sticky mess on her hand. She scratched his ears, then continued down the aisle toward the open office door.

Lizzie looked up from the computer. "Ava!" she exclaimed. "I was just thinking about you. How ya settling in?"

"Well, considering I just woke up, I'd say not bad," said Ava, with a laugh. "I could get used to that."

"It's about time for me to hit round three of coffee," Lizzie said. "I've got doughnuts too. Can you hang for a few minutes?"

"Well, I just had coffee, but I won't say no to doughnuts," Ava said, sitting in the small vinyl chair opposite Lizzie. "Is it just me or do sweets seem to follow you around?"

"Fair enough," Lizzie said, laughing. "But it's really for Macy. Her students love her, but instead of bringing apples, they tend to favor baked goods."

"Don't be modest," Ava said. "I have a feeling you're just as popular around here."

Lizzie smiled as she passed her the box of doughnuts. Ava took a strawberry-frosted pastry as Lizzie refilled her mug from a stainless-steel carafe.

"I went looking for ya on my way out yesterday to see if you needed anything, but you were driving off with Ethan," Lizzie said.

"He's sweet," Ava said. "He gave me a tour of the town since I've been gone for so long. Have you seen his house? It's gorgeous."

"You know, come to think of it, not once has he invited me to his house," Lizzie said, cocking an eyebrow. "I could think of a couple reasons why."

"Oh! No," Ava said, shaking her head. "It's not like that. He kind of took me under his wing. Trust me, I am not who he's after right now."

"Uh huh," Lizzie said, pursing her lips.

"And I'm in a very serious relationship," Ava continued. "His name is Lucas. He's great."

She pulled out her phone and swiped to a photo of the two of them at the zoo.

"Ooh, girl," said Lizzie, her eyes wide. "Dark, gorgeous, and boy, does he know how to dress. Does he cook?"

"Uh, not really," Ava said. "But he knows a lot of great restaurants."

"Good enough," said Lizzie, giggling.

"I'm trying to get him to come visit," Ava said. "I think he'd love it here—well, once he got used to the lack of cell service. I want him to see for himself how special this place is. And meet everyone too, of course."

Lizzie smiled. "I know what you mean about the ranch. I feel it, too. I came here after getting off that nine-to-five treadmill. . .It's hard to put words on it. But it energizes me. Gives me hope. I feel inspired when I leave here every day."

"Yeah. . .Inspired," Ava said. "I get that."

Lizzie sipped her coffee as they sat in comfortable silence. Ava crumpled her napkin into a ball and tossed it in the trash.

"I feel like you're here way more than twenty hours a week," Ava said. "I understand wanting to stay busy, but I almost wonder if you live here."

Lizzie laughed and shrugged. "I probably would move in if Macy asked. I had great coworkers before, but there's just something different about this place. When my boys moved away, I felt a little lost. Now, I feel needed. Macy is family now and this ranch is my second home. I can't think of a better way to spend my days."

Ava smiled. This place seemed to have that effect.

"Well, as much as I'd rather not, I should go back to the cabin and answer some e-mails," Ava said.

"I'm running to the store later to restock some stuff," Lizzie said. "If you wanna give me a list, I'll grab you some groceries and what-not."

"Thanks, I was just thinking about the store. I don't really know what I need, but my afternoon is wide open. Why don't you tell me the best place to shop and I'll handle it?"

"You are the sweetest!" Lizzie said. "Thank you."

Ava waited as Lizzie jotted down a list. She was happy to help Lizzie, but even happier to do something that felt like pulling her weight.

Back in the cabin, she sat crisscross on the window seat and looked out at the gray craggy mountaintops cutting jagged against the sky.

She unzipped her duffel and grabbed her box of colored pencils. Flipping her sketchbook to a blank page, she began to draw, slowly at first. Soon, her sketching took on a feverish urgency. Under her hand, a landscape began to form. The trees in the foreground appeared, every leaf defined with a pencil stroke. The sky began to blend into a fusion of orange, gray, and blue. At the base of the mountain, Ava sketched Gunner. . .His black, thoughtful eyes, then his graceful, muscular body. Shadowing and scribbling; lining and shading. Minutes, or hours, might have passed. By the time Ava stopped, her pencils dull, it was two in the afternoon. She was thirsty.

She blinked, disoriented. It had been years since her art had overtaken her like that. She looked out the window, then down at the sketch. She smiled. Maybe it was only good enough for a gas station calendar, but it was clearly Autumn Lantern Ranch, and it made her happy.

More than that, it was the colors that resonated deep within her soul: the reds of the leaves just before they fell, the burnt burgundy of the early evening sky, a deep orange she'd only seen on the smokebush around the ranch. It had taken hours to get the shades just right. They were warm, inviting, alive. Ava hadn't realized how much the icy blues and institutional grays that were her trademark also felt a bit like handcuffs. She could no longer remember whose idea those colors had been in the first place.

She stretched her fingers before sharpening each pencil and placing them back in the case. She closed the sketchpad and wrapped the chunky knit throw around her shoulders. She felt full—satiated. She couldn't remember the last time she was truly in the moment. No voices talking at her, no one reminding her to hurry or hustle. And in that quiet stillness, she began to remember what it was like to enjoy her own company.

Ava glanced at the revolving door of the Timber Café, checking her watch for what felt like the millionth time. Macy was seriously late. She drained her water and waved to the waiter.

"One glass of pinot noir, please," Ava said. Might as well enjoy herself while she waited. The server gave a curt nod and walked off.

The Timber Café was bigger than it looked from the outside. A generous dining room opened into a full bar, where every stool was now claimed. She'd had to wait for a table when she arrived, but now the dining room was quiet, all the families long gone. Everywhere Ava looked, she saw wood: the ceilings, floors, tables. Except for the green vinyl cushions, the place clearly lived up to its name.

Earlier, Ava had stopped by the arena after dropping the groceries off with Lizzie. Macy had just finished a lesson, her students a teenage boy and his mom. When Ava had asked what time she should pick her up, Macy's blank face suggested she'd forgotten all about the dinner. She refused Ava's offer to drive them both. Now, Ava was beginning to think she'd been stood up. She glanced at her cell. No messages.

Ava was picking at a biscuit when Macy finally came through the door a few minutes later.

"There you are!" Ava said. "I was about to ask for the check."

"Sorry," Macy said, breathless. "I needed to stop somewhere and it took longer than I thought it would. I should have called."

Yeah, you should have.

"It's not personal," said Macy quickly.

It felt personal. "It's no problem," Ava said, her voice tight.

Still, she was glad Macy had come. In the past few days, Ava had yet to have a single meaningful conversation with her. Based on the increasingly urgent e-mails from Lucas and Carla, she was needed back in New York as soon as possible. She had to get this show on the road.

Macy glanced around the dining room, but the waiter was nowhere to be found.

"I'm gonna grab a drink from the bar," she said. "You want one?"

Ava raised her wine glass, still half full. "I'm good. You go ahead."

"Oh, never mind then," Macy said. "I'll just wait."

They studied their menus in silence. After a very long few minutes, their waiter reappeared.

"Y'all ready to order?" he asked.

Ava smiled at him. "Definitely," she said.

Thankfully, the food came quick, and Ava and Macy eventually found their way to small talk. Macy told Ava a bit about getting the riding school off the ground, how she had to write a business plan to show to the bank to secure the loan. It sounded like a lot of work, and Ava was reminded of her own business plan she'd presented to Carla just a week earlier. When Macy talked about Autumn Lantern, her whole face lifted, and Ava could see glimpses of the girl she used to know. Man, she missed her.

"So, enough about me and Utah," said Macy. "This must all seem pretty small time to you now, huh?"

"Not at all," Ava said. "I love being back."

"Dad tells me you're a big-time artist these days."

Something in Macy's tone felt like more of an accusation than a compliment.

"I've been doing alright," Ava said vaguely.

"I haven't seen any of these world-famous paintings yet. Is it like the stuff you used to do back in the day?"

"No, not exactly," said Ava. She pulled her phone from her purse. "It's more experimental, sort of abstract."

Ava pulled up her website. She tapped an image, zoomed in, and passed her phone to Macy. "This is my most recent sale. . .It's called *Dolphin at Rest #5.*"

"Huh," Macy said, the phone almost touching her nose. "Where are Dolphins at Rest One through Four?"

Ava laughed. "Believe it or not, you're the first person who's asked me that," she said. "The other dolphins don't exist."

Macy looked confused.

"This is the fifth painting in this series," Ava explained, "but it didn't have a name until I finished it. I sat at my easel in Damrosch Park, trying to find the motivation to keep working. Suddenly, this little boy, couldn't have been older than four, walks by. He points at my painting and says, loudly, 'Daddy? Is that a dead dolphin?'"

Ava giggled at the memory. "The dad was mortified and kept apologizing, but I thought it was great. I could totally see it. So, I named it '*Dolphin at Rest.*' Had a better ring to it than '*Dead Dolphin.*'"

"I bet that story alone sold it," Macy said, almost smiling.

"Actually, you're the only one who's heard it. I paint, I sell, and yeah, I get interviewed all the time. . .but no one seems very interested in my true, everyday experience. They like their artists to stay on the mysterious side."

Macy studied the image a moment longer, then passed the phone back to Ava. She said nothing; just took another bite of her tilapia.

"Not your style of art, I take it," Ava said. She didn't know why Macy's opinion mattered to her, but she couldn't help feeling a bit hurt.

Macy set down her fork and wiped her mouth with her napkin. "It's not that," she said. "It's nice. Super artsy. I could never do anything like that. It's just. . .I guess I'm a little surprised. It's so different from what you used to paint. When it was us."

When it was us.

Ava swallowed. "I know it's different," she said, her voice rising slightly. "But people spend a lot of money on these paintings. Anyone could paint those farm pictures I made when we were kids, but no one wants to *buy* them. They want something modern; something original." She stuffed her phone back into her purse.

"I'm sorry, Ava," Macy said. "I'm happy for you. Really. I just hope you paint for yourself, too. . .It always made you so happy. You were like a camera when we were kids, except better; you captured the world on your canvas the way you saw it. Everything became a painting. The fields, those kittens that were born in the loft, the tree house..."

"I remember," Ava said, quieter.

Macy took another bite. Ava downed the last of her wine.

"I almost forgot about the tree house," Ava said. "We spent so much time in that place."

"It was struck by lightning years ago," Macy said, studying her fork. "It burned."

"Oh," Ava said. She twisted a straw wrapper between her fingers. She had always assumed the tree house would stand forever, peeking over the same river from the same treetops, storing their long-forgotten conversations and songs in the gnarled roots of the old sycamores it rested upon.

"Dad told me you invited him for a drink?" Macy asked.

"Oh, yeah, I almost forgot," Ava said. "I hope that's alright."

"Sure," said Macy. "I know he missed you. You were like another daughter to him. And you just. . .Well, you know. You disappeared."

Ava looked at the straw wrapper, now a crumpled ball. "I'm sorry," she said. "Mom always said we'd come back when we got settled in Paris, but then it was art school, and then work. . .I meant to come back. I really did."

Macy said nothing.

"You know, it wasn't just that," Ava continued. "When I was here. . .I mean, you were my best friend, of course, but you were also this gorgeous blonde cowgirl that every guy wanted to ask out. I was your artsy redheaded cousin who got to tag along. In Paris, for the first time, I wasn't weird; I found my people."

Macy looked at her. "I never knew you felt like that," she said softly.

"It's not like it was your fault," Ava said. "And there's more to it than me just being an awkward teenager."

She took a steadying breath before continuing. "Mom had just. . .Well, she ditched me. That's honestly the only way to describe it. But when she came back? She suddenly had all this time for me. She was proud of me. She took me everywhere with her, and I never had had that before. I think I was scared that if I left her, even for a visit, it might all go away."

Ava swallowed. "Anyway, I wish I could go back in time and handle it better. But I want you to know it had nothing to do with you or Harris. I loved you. *Love* you."

Ava's hand shook as she sipped her water. She set her glass down and tucked her hands into her lap. "I can't tell you how much I wish I could have been here when Ben went missing. I never even met him. I thought I had more time."

"We all thought we had more time," Macy said softly. She crossed her arms and rested her elbows on the table. The waiter came by and filled their water glasses before shuffling on to the next table. "You know," she said, stirring her ice with her straw, "you would have gotten along great with Ben. You guys are a lot alike."

Are.

Present tense.

Macy stared pointedly at Ava, as if daring her to correct her.

"I hope you know that I had no idea Ben went missing until last week," Ava said. "I would have been here. I realize I have no idea what you went through—"

"*Going* through," Macy interrupted, slapping her napkin on the table as water sloshed from both their glasses. "What I'm *going* through, Ava. This is my life, okay? Are you gonna be like everyone else and tell me to get over it?"

"No," Ava said, chastened.

"Then why are you here? Really?"

Ava hesitated for only a moment. "For you. Just. . .for you."

Macy chewed her lip. She soaked up the spilled water with her napkin, eyes fixed on the table. "It might sound crazy, but I just can't let him go," she said. "He's still out there, somewhere, trying to come home to me. I feel it in my bones. In my soul."

Ava opened her mouth to speak, then closed it again.

"The truth is, I am mad at you," Macy said. "You missed my wedding, you missed my business. . .and I missed your whole life. We said we'd do everything side by side, only you didn't hold up your end of the bargain."

"I'm here now," Ava said, offering a weak smile.

Macy closed her eyes and pinched the bridge of her nose. After a moment, she rubbed her face and looked at Ava. "The past is the past, right? You coming here says a lot. I should have mentioned that sooner."

Right then, Ava knew she needed to tell Macy what had led to her return. Though parts of it were admittedly selfish, deep down, Carla's ultimatum was the excuse she'd been looking for. This wound had been festering for long enough. Macy would have to understand. "Macy, wait. There's more I should say—"

Macy raised her hand, silencing her.

"I'm not a victim here," Macy said. "When you left, I blotted you out. I was so mad when you never invited me to Paris. . .or even New York, which was just a short plane ride away. I made myself feel better by saying you were this pathological narcissist —that you just used me until I had nothing more to offer. In my heart, I knew it wasn't true and it wasn't fair. It was a two-way street."

Ava's words froze in her mouth. Clearly, now wasn't the time to tell her about the deal. She'd have to try again tomorrow.

Macy sighed and shoved her wispy bangs out of her face. "Besides, we were kids. As the years passed, I realized we were too young to write our futures in cement. I'm really sorry, too, Ava."

"Thank you, Macy," Ava said, her throat dry.

Macy smiled, then drained the last of her wine. "Okay, but

seriously," she said. "Enough about the past. Tell me about this Lucas guy."

Ava smiled. "What do you want to know?"

"Lizzie says it's pretty serious? Come on, you have to tell me. It's been a while since I've gotten to gossip. I miss girl talk."

"Lucas is great," Ava said. "He's also the best publicist in town, which is how we met. He's super protective of me, always making sure the pompous male art collectors are respectful. Plus, he's this gorgeous former soccer player, which I know shouldn't matter. . ."

"But it helps," Macy said.

"It totally does!" Ava said.

They laughed.

"Do you think you guys will get married?" Macy asked.

Ava hesitated. "I mean, I hope it's moving in that direction," she said. "I get burned out with work sometimes, but Lucas is good at keeping me focused. We're both so busy. . .I guess it's not smart to settle down when so much is happening in my career."

"Well, don't leave me hanging," Macy said. "Let's see him!"

Ava pulled up Lucas' Instagram page. She couldn't help feeling a surge of pride as Macy gushed about how handsome he was. It was hard to argue with tall, dark, and chiseled. Macy scrolled through pictures of the couple at galas and dinners. The last post was new: Lucas beaming in his custom-fit tuxedo surrounded by laughing, rich-looking people, some Ava didn't recognize. Her life in New York felt a world away.

The rest of the meal flew by. Ava told Macy about her neighborhood: the street artists, food trucks, and her favorite quirky off-Broadway theatres. Ava mentioned the old Cobalt Cinema and was delighted when Macy was equally horrified that it was now a tattoo parlor. Macy updated her on some of the kids they used to hang out with: Cathy, a sweet neighbor who'd kept a horse on the ranch, was now principal of the elementary. Wild child Derek had become a respected real estate agent. Megan, the eighth-grade busybody, was a news reporter. Macy had lost touch with most of the others, but none had left Utah. It seemed to have a way of holding its people tightly.

Ava had told Macy that she'd never belonged until Paris, but that was only another half-truth. Even in the City of Light, something had been missing. Maybe that nagging in her had nothing to do with the place she lived, but rather with something broken deep inside her.   Nevertheless, it felt cleansing to be where no one saw her as a visionary, or a competitor, or a price tag. She was just another woman out to dinner with a friend. Just then, she couldn't think of anywhere else she'd rather be.

Ava insisted on picking up the check. Macy balked at first but finally agreed if Ava would let her pay the tab at the bar. They decided on one drink and no more. . .Neither were heavyweights and they still had to drive back to the ranch in the dark.

"Do you know where the bathroom is?" Ava asked.

Macy pointed to the back corner.

"I'll meet you at the bar," Ava said before weaving between the tightly clustered tables as she spotted the sign for the restrooms. She twisted the handle to the ladies' room, but the door didn't budge.

"One minute!" called a voice from within.

Ava leaned against the wall and let out a long, slow exhale. She'd missed her cousin and was beginning to feel a lot better about her decision to come back.

She watched from the doorway as Macy stood and threw her purse over her shoulder. Just as suddenly, she sat back down and rested her face on her folded arms. Before Ava could call to her, the waiter rushed by to clear the dishes. Macy sprang back to her feet as if she was perfectly fine. Ava watched her walk toward the bar, her pale face the only indication anything had been wrong.

Just then, the bathroom door swung open. "All yours," a grizzled woman said, holding the door open with her cane.

"Thank you," Ava said, stepping out of her way. She looked once more toward the bar, but Macy was now out of sight. She sighed. Something was clearly bothering Macy. If only she trusted Ava enough to let her help.

"Sorry that took so long," Ava said when she joined Macy at the bar a few minutes later. "I had to return a quick work call." Margo wanted Ava's blessing before approving the retouched photos from last week's shoot. Ava assured her that she honestly didn't care what they looked like, and told Margo to send them to the magazine's editor as she saw fit.

"There are my gals!" Harris' voice called from behind them. Ava shot Macy a quick glance. Color had returned to her cheeks, her face now composed. Whatever had happened, Ava would have to wait to ask her about it.

"Look who I found eating the Prime Rib Special all by his lonesome," Harris said. He had his arm around Ethan, who smiled a bit sheepishly.

"Harris just finished telling me about how the stable used to be an old barn," Ethan said. "He showed me some old photos. It's amazing what you've done with that building, Macy."

"Ooh, I'd like to see those," Ava said.

"It's been a long road," Macy said. "But we really have come a long way."

"This sure is a nice surprise," Ava said, as innocently as she could. "We're just grabbing a drink. Why don't you join us?" She looked at Harris and Macy. "You guys don't mind, right?"

"Of course not!" said Harris, clapping Ethan on the back.

"The more, the merrier," Macy said, but Ava noticed her smile looked worn.

They walked deeper into the bar and snagged a four-top table. Ava shot Ethan a grateful look as they passed around the drink menus. He smiled.

The evening flew by as they wound up emptying a pitcher of Blue Moon, everyone switching to soft drinks for round two. Ava thought they all seemed to be having fun, though Macy was still quieter than she had been at dinner. At least she laughed along as Harris regaled them with yet another tale of his childhood on the ranch.

"Uncle Harris, you really need to write these stories down somewhere," Ava said, giggling. "I cannot get the image out of my head of you, ten years old, riding on the back of a dairy cow."

"But did it work?" Ethan asked. "Did you get the wranglers to let you stay?"

Harris grinned. "Let's just say the next time they rode all the way to Wyoming, I had myself a job," he said. "Made the mistake of not telling my parents ahead of time. But I was a fifth-grade cowboy by then, what did I care?"

He glanced at his watch as they all roared with laughter.

"My goodness, it is clear past my bedtime," he said. "We'll have to save that story for another night."

He winked at them as he threw a few dollars onto the table. "This was fun," he said. "Let's do it again."

They said their goodbyes, and Harris left, whistling the opening to Patsy Cline's "Walkin' After Midnight" as he weaved his way to the door.

"Well, it's getting late. . ." Macy said.

"Yeah, I should probably. . ." Ethan added.

"Wait!" Ava said. They'd gotten so wrapped up in Harris' stories that she'd hardly had time to play matchmaker. "I heard the pie is great here. Do you care if we hang for just a few more minutes?"

"I could do pie," Ethan said.

Macy pressed her lips into a tight line, but said nothing.

"While we wait, maybe Ethan could tell us some more of the town history," Ava said brightly. "You'd never think he was new here. He knows so much about all the old houses on the river. Macy, didn't you say one of the MacDaniel ancestors lived on the river?"

"I'm not sure," Macy said, picking at a peeling spot on the table's veneer. "Dad might know."

Silence.

"Well, I think it's all really fascinating," Ava said. "Have you considered writing a guidebook, Ethan?"

"Uh, not really," Ethan said. "I'm sure someone else knows a lot more about Cobalt than I do."

"I doubt that," Ava said, as cheerily as she could.

Macy just kept picking.

Ava sighed. This wasn't going to be as easy as she'd hoped. She waved the waiter over to their table. "What's your best pie?" Ava asked.

"The pecan is our most popular," he said. "We're usually sold out by now, but we've still got a few slices left."

"Well, you sold me," Ava said. "Three slices, please. Warm, with ice cream if you have it." She smiled at Ethan and Macy. "My treat."

"I'm gonna pop into the ladies' room," Macy said, grabbing her purse.

After Macy had walked out of earshot, Ethan asked, "She always this quiet outside the ranch?"

Ava shrugged. "At this point, you probably know her better than I do. One thing I can say is that Macy was always a tough book to read." She leaned closer to Ethan, pasting what she hoped passed for wide-eyed innocence on her face. "I'd say she sure makes up for it by looking that gorgeous, wouldn't you?"

Ethan laughed. "I think every man in this place was envious tonight, seeing me surrounded by the two of you."

Ava smiled. The combination of good company and draft beer was seriously underrated.

"I have a confession," he said. "I Googled you."

Ava groaned. "Uh oh," she said. "Did you find my extensive

criminal record?"

"I had no idea how talented you were," Ethan said. "I'll be the first to admit, I'm not exactly an expert when it comes to art. But wow, Ava. I stared at one of your paintings for five minutes, no lie. I kept seeing new things in it, even though at first glance it just looked like a bunch of curves and spheres. It reminded me a little of Robert Delaunay ."

"Thank you," Ava said, surprised. "Delaunay, wow. I didn't expect you to be such a modern art fan."

"It was mostly my mom," Ethan said with a little shrug. "She loved museums and art and opera, and Dad had no interest. Being an only child, I got dragged along. At the time, I was less than thrilled; now I'm glad I had that."

Cultured, kind, handsome, successful. Ava was sure Ethan had flaws, but she hadn't found them yet. She couldn't think of anyone more likely to measure up to Macy's standards.

"You know, we have a great art store in town," Ethan said. "I'm sure it's nothing like you have in the Big Apple, but I hear it's pretty well stocked."

"Oakenwood and Sons?" Ava asked.

"You know it?"

"I was just there," she said. "You're right; it's great."

"I used to help out at the high school a bit," Ethan said. "They gave the school a big discount, so I'd grab supplies for the art classes sometimes."

Ethan told her about the fine arts program at Cobalt High. He knew more about art than he let on. When Ethan confessed a love of Rembrandt, Ava squealed in delight. She'd always been fascinated by artists who created such detailed images before the invention of cameras. They were not only painters back then, but historians. Ethan surprised Ava by knowing more about Rembrandt's history than she did. He told her that a Dutch art dealer had discovered a previously-unknown portrait by the master just a few years before, and experts speculated that more unidentified works were likely still out there. Ava couldn't imagine how it would feel to find one of those treasures of light and paint. Before she knew it, the waiter was sliding the pie onto the table.

"Two slices of pecan pie, heated, and à la mode," the waiter said.

"Oh, I'm sorry, it was supposed to be *three* slices," Ava said.

The waiter looked at Ava, confused. "The other woman who was with you—she said to change it to two. She paid the bill just before she left."

Ava looked to the door, then down at her phone. More than fifteen minutes had passed since they'd ordered. Macy must have snuck out while they were talking.

"Sorry, you're right," Ava said. "Just two; my mistake."

"She's gone?" Ethan asked as the waiter walked away.

"Seems so," Ava said, sighing as she tucked a loose strand of hair behind her ear.

"Give her time," Ethan said. "Sounds like just coming out tonight at all might have been a big step for her."

"You're right," she said. "And there's no possible way she didn't enjoy herself. We're obviously the coolest."

Ethan laughed and Ava couldn't help but join in. Tonight *was* fun. Still, her mind reeled as she took a bite of pie. Why hadn't Macy at least told them she was leaving? This certainly wasn't going to be as easy as she'd hoped.

Eleven

Ava's eyes popped open and quickly adjusted to the dark cabin. Though she hadn't gotten back until after midnight, she couldn't sleep any longer. She took her phone off the charger beside the bed. It was five a.m., and still nothing from Macy. Ava had called and texted her several times when they'd gotten home. If she hadn't seen Macy's red pickup truck parked outside the house, Ava would have been tempted to call the police. It seemed Macy just didn't want to talk to her. What had happened between dinner and the bar?

Ava reached over and grabbed the sketchbook from the floor where she'd dropped it the night before. She flipped it open to her list and mindlessly doodled a question mark next to item one— Get Macy To Date. If Ethan wasn't intriguing enough to get Macy to last through pie, Ava couldn't imagine who would be.

She opened her e-mail and saw a message from Lucas. He needed her to sign another release for the editorial photos.

Hadn't Margo already handled that? Ava scanned the rest quickly, stopping on the words *Vanity Fair* in the last paragraph. Lucas wrote that the prestigious magazine wanted to include one shot of her choice along with a blurb about Ava. Apparently, they were running a feature about the rebirth of the New York art scene.

Wow. *Vanity Fair?* That was big.

She sat up and pulled her laptop onto her bed, resting it on her crisscrossed legs. She clicked the folder, and several images filled the screen. Ava's eyes looked back at her own from the computer. She hardly recognized herself. Even she had to admit, she looked stunning. Her rust-colored hair cascaded over her shoulders, the emerald silk of the gown a perfect match for her eye color. But those thick fake lashes? The Spanx that flattened her every curve? It felt just as artificial to Ava as the obvious Photoshopping that each picture had undergone. She noticed her chin pimple was nowhere to be found.

One photo grabbed her attention—it was of both her and Lucas.

He was brushing a loose curl out of her face as she gazed into his eyes. It was tender and intimate. She ached for him and wished he would just show up and surprise her.

A different part of her felt a weariness when she thought of the distance between them. The Ava in that picture had so much clouding her eyes: the stress of deadlines and making Carla happy; the pressure to set life aside and take the art world by storm; the quiet fear that she would never be able to contort herself into the image of the mysterious artist that people seemed to expect her to be. That Ava seemed very far away. Like another woman altogether.

Ava peered over the edge of the loft. The first light of the October sunrise was just beginning to spill across the floor. Her painting was waiting, staring back at her expectantly. Time to get to work.

She climbed down the steps and flipped the switch on the coffee maker before heading into the bathroom to wash her face. While the dark French roast gurgled and dripped, she climbed onto the window seat and tied her hair into a messy bun, studying her painting more closely.

Blue, gray, black. Circle, line, square. She felt a tingle in her brain—an itch.

Orange. She needed orange.

She pulled out her paint. She began mixing and smoothing, adding red until the color was warm and deep, almost like molten lava. *Or the harvest moon*, she thought, looking out the bay window and remembering the sky that had greeted her last night. She smiled and kept mixing, completely forgetting about the waiting pot of coffee.

Ava entered the stable and inhaled the now familiar sweetness of hay and grain. The barn was quieter than usual. She poked her head into the office, but it was empty. She heard a voice as she walked further down the aisle and found Macy grooming a tall bay gelding.

"Morning," Ava said, trying to sound light. "I tried calling you last night. A lot."

Macy wiped her hands on her jeans and turned to Ava. "Yeah. I'm sorry. I started feeling off all of a sudden. I meant to text you, but I fell asleep."

Macy continued brushing the horse's neck, though it already looked spotless. Ava could tell she wasn't going to offer anything more in the way of an explanation.

"Well, I'm sorry to hear that," Ava said. "Glad you're OK."

She leaned against the open stall and watched as Macy tossed her saddle onto the horse's back as if it weighed nothing. Ava was just happy to be able to lift one by herself at all. She couldn't imagine ever making it look easy.

"No students this morning?" Ava asked.

"Nope," Macy said. "I try to limit the number of lessons on the weekends. One of the perks of being my own boss."

"That sounds like a great perk," she said. "So, what are you up to?"

"This is Cash," Macy said, affectionately rubbing the big horse's nose. "He's been a little cooped up this week, so I thought I'd take him out on the trails, let him stretch his legs."

"Do you want some company?" Ava asked.

"Oh," Macy said, looking surprised. "Well, I was going to do Pioneer Loop. It's a long one."

"I remember Pioneer Loop," Ava said. "I can handle it."

After a moment, Macy nodded. "Why not? One less horse to exercise later. Why don't you saddle up Gunner and meet us out back?"

"Perfect," Ava said, smiling. She scratched Cash's whiskery chin, then headed to the tack room. A long trail ride on a beautiful fall morning and a chance to dig deeper with Macy; Ava could think of worse ways to spend a Saturday.

Ava felt a swell of pride in her chest as she led Gunner through the barn. She could now groom and saddle a horse all on her own. She'd been writing everything down when she went back to the cabin each night: how to tie that all-important slipknot, what bit to use, how to make sure the girth was tight enough. Ava wasn't sure if she was simply remembering everything or if it was more of a desperate cramming to save face in front of her cousin. Either way, it was working.

The clopping of Gunner's hooves on the concrete floor created a comforting rhythm. When he looked at her through those thick black lashes, Ava felt seen, right to her soul. Though it had been less than a week, she felt a bond with Gunner unlike she'd ever felt with an animal before.

Though Ava was getting stronger already, she felt muscles twinge that she didn't even know were there. She wondered how she'd managed when she was a kid. She had a feeling it would take months before she no longer felt like goo after a long ride. Maybe she could find a stable to take lessons at when she got back to New York. She couldn't imagine giving all this up.

Ava led Gunner to the clearing between the stable and the open fields. Sunlight washed over them, warming her face. It was the perfect day for a trail ride, even warmer than when she'd left the cabin a half hour earlier. She snapped her helmet's chin strap and checked to make sure the saddle was still tight. Though her left leg protested a bit as she lifted it into the stirrup, she swung herself into the seat easily enough as Gunner stood patiently. She saw Macy astride Cash in the distance.

"Looks like someone has gotten her sea legs back," Macy called as Ava and Gunner approached.

"A lot of things seem to be coming back to me these days," Ava said, smiling.

Macy said nothing. It seemed it was not quite time for the heart-to-heart just yet.

"That's an awfully big horse for a gal your size," Ava said. Cash towered over Gunner. Macy just shrugged.

In her nightly Google sessions, Ava had learned that horses were measured to their withers—the name for the prominent bone that stuck out at the base of their necks. A "hand" was four inches, so at sixteen hands, Gunner was about five foot four at the saddle height, only two inches shorter than Ava. Cash had to be at least seventeen hands.

Macy opened the pasture gate and rode Cash through. She gestured for Ava and Gunner to follow, then closed and latched it behind them, all while horseback. She made everything look so easy.

They rode side by side through the field. Ava felt herself relaxing into the rocking rhythm of Gunner's walk. The creaking of the saddles, the wind rustling through the trees, the distant sounds of the rushing creek... She wished she could bottle it all up and take it back with her to the city.

"Cash was Ben's horse," Macy said, suddenly breaking the silence between them. "That's why he's so tall."

"Oh," Ava replied, unsure what to say.

"If you're over two hundred pounds, you need a bigger mount," Macy continued. "Especially when you're learning and don't quite move with the horse yet. That's why Ethan rides Nikita. . .She's a big girl."

"Was Ben an experienced rider?" Ava asked.

"He pretended to be, to impress me," Macy said, then chuckled softly to herself. "When it came time to actually ride a horse, he confessed his experience was limited to a week at Scout camp as a kid. I can still see the look on his face. . .He was white as a ghost. At the time, I thought he was scared to ride, but later, he told me he thought I might dump him for lying. But by then I was already smitten."

"So, he eventually ended up with his own horse?" Ava asked.

"Oh, yeah," Macy said. "Once his secret was out of the bag, he approached riding with the same military precision he gave to everything he did. Within a month, he was better than most of my beginners. A year later, it was as if he'd been riding his whole life."

They circled the pond, now riding in a line behind the row of pastures. A single duck dozed on a fallen log, not even opening its eyes as they passed.

"I think Cash really misses him," Macy said, her voice catching.

"I'm sure he does," Ava said, reaching down to pat Gunner's neck. "I just got here and I already can't imagine life without my new horse friend."

As they rode along the edge of the field, Ava noticed a new fence where once there was only forest.

"You've really done a great job with the ranch," Ava said. "It's even more beautiful now than when I was here last."

She pointed to two long fields in the distance that ran along the main drive. "Are those the fields Harris used to lease?"

"For cattle," Macy said, nodding. "Good memory."

"And that other field is where Ben grew his famous vegetables?" Ava asked.

Macy shot her a sideways glance.

"Whenever I tell people in town where I'm staying, they always mention two things: the new riding academy and the amazing organic veggies," Ava said. "They were famous around here, it seems."

"They were pretty legendary," Macy agreed, her face relaxing a bit. "In true Ben style, every tomato and cucumber was the biggest and the best."

"He sounds like quite a man," Ava said.

"Yeah," Macy replied, her voice quiet.

Ava waited. Macy seemed more willing to talk out here. Maybe she felt most at home on the back of a horse. Or maybe it was easier to share when they didn't have to look at each other.

"The gardening was more therapy than hobby for Ben, at least at first," Macy said. "He saw some things in his line of work—things that would be hard for anybody to deal with—and he was diagnosed with PTSD more than once. It was during a particularly bad spell that he went to the local nursery to pick up some shrubs for the front gate. On impulse, he got a single pepper plant. He kept it on the porch at first, fawning over it like it was a pet. Once it started to fruit, he was hooked."

"Wow. I assumed he'd grown up doing it," Ava said. "You're telling me he learned all that stuff about crops just in the time you were together?"

Macy nodded, a proud smile tugging on her face. "He told me he liked escaping into a smaller world where things were simpler. I always thought maybe it had something to do with using his hands. It seemed to pull him out of his head." She paused to swat a fly that had landed on Cash's neck. "He was more present after he started gardening. I really believe it healed him more than counseling ever could. More than I ever could."

She tipped her face away from Ava. "I'd be ashamed for him to see what it looks like over there now."

"We could fix it up," Ava said. "I could help you."

Macy laughed. "You? What do you know about farm work?"

"Not a thing," Ava confessed. "But I'm good at following orders, and I'm even better at watching YouTube."

Macy smiled, but it didn't quite reach her eyes. "I don't know, Ava. It seems like too much to tackle. At first, I just couldn't face it. But then it didn't take long for everything to die, and the weeds to take over." She sighed. "I wouldn't even know where to start, and it would take a long time to make any kind of real difference."

"Maybe I'll stay longer," Ava blurted. "I mean, assuming it's okay with you." Until that moment, she hadn't realized just how much she wasn't ready to leave. She had stared at the ceiling last night, feeling the days slip through her fingers. It wasn't enough time. She knew Carla and Lucas wouldn't like it, but how much work could she possibly miss if she stayed for just one more week?

Cash stopped to chew on some grass, and Macy quietly nudged him on.

"I can paint and handle work stuff later in the day," Ava continued, "and you don't usually have morning clients, right? We can start right away."

"Thanks for the offer, Ava," Macy said. "You can stay as long as you want. It's not like anyone uses the cabin. As for the rest. . .Well, I need to think about it."

They approached a worn wooden sign at the trailhead and Ava immediately recognized the childishly-etched letters. "Smugglers' Canyon!" she exclaimed. "I can't believe it's still here!"

"It's a bit dramatic of a name for an old flat trail, but I've always left it for the sake of posterity," Macy said.

Harris had never paid for cable, and as a result, Ava and Macy had watched countless reruns of *Bonanza* and old Westerns one summer. When the girls presented Harris with the handmade sign, he hadn't laughed at them. Instead, he just smiled, tucked it under his arm, and headed out to the trail with his tool belt.

"When I bring students back here for the first time, I have to explain that they'll find no canyon and no smugglers. Just the former playground of two very bored girls."

Ava lengthened Gunner's reins as they followed Macy and Cash down a shallow slope. Soon, they approached the sign for Pioneer Loop. Ava leaned forward as the horses climbed a steep embankment. Once they reached the top, the ground leveled off into a narrow, winding trail.

As they rode on, the horses navigated every rock and fallen branch with graceful precision. Ava's body eased deeper into the saddle as she admired the dense forest; there were carpets of freshly fallen leaves, frantic squirrels scurrying from one tree to the next, and even a few curious deer who came to gaze at them with mild curiosity before scampering off into the hidden depths of the woods. Ava could smell the earthy musk of burning wood. Some nearby farm must have had their fireplace going.

The trail began to slope upward once again, winding its way toward the mountaintop in switchbacks. Soon, they approached the overlook, the highest point of the ride. Cash halted and Ava stopped Gunner beside him. To their right, the entire ranch stretched below. Ahead, the mountains loomed, purple with the shadows of late morning.

"About last night," Ava said. "I'm sorry you got sick, but I had a really great time with you."

"I did too," Macy said. "I'm glad we got to talk."

"Me too. And it was such a nice surprise when Ethan showed up, don't you think? He seems like such a nice guy."

"Yeah, Ethan's the best," Macy said. "He helps out so much around here, even when I tell him to go home."

"What a very generous man," Ava said.

"You know, he's super smart too," Macy added. "People in town are really grateful he took over the tax company from Mr. Lopez."

"I'm glad you like him," Ava said.

Macy eyed her with amusement but said nothing.

"I was thinking you guys could be a great match," Ava continued.

Macy blinked a few times before erupting into roaring laughter. Gunner skittered sideways, enough to make Ava grab the saddle horn. Just as quickly, he settled and began sniffing the dirt.

"What?!" Ava asked. "Why is that so funny?"

"I thought you were asking about Ethan for *you*!" Macy exclaimed.

"Me?!" Ava said. "Oh my gosh, no!"

"Ava," Macy said, leveling her gaze. "The chemistry between you two was so obvious, I bet even the waiter could tell."

Ava fidgeted in the saddle and looked away, cringing inside. She'd been so focused on selling Ethan to Macy that it didn't occur to her it might be misinterpreted as a crush of her own.

"Well, you're wrong," Ava said firmly. "We get along great, but in that brother-sister kind of way. What you saw was me trying to set up my awesome cousin with a great guy."

Macy pursed her lips. "I appreciate your intentions, Ava, but I don't know what to tell you. I consider Ethan a wonderful friend, a valued student, and nothing more. I'd like you to leave it that way." Something brittle in Macy's tone kept Ava from pushing further; she could recognize a dead end when she found one. Ava chewed on her cheek as she watched a large hawk circling over the forest far below them.

"Come on," said Macy, turning Cash back to the trail. "We've got a couple miles left and these horses will need water soon."

Gunner followed Cash automatically. Despite her disappointment in her failed matchmaking, Ava couldn't help marveling at the silent language horses seemed to share, as if they could read each other's minds. Ava could use a bit of that magic right now.

They guided the horses down a steep ridge. Ava gripped the saddle horn tighter as she tried not to focus on the abrupt drop to her left. Gunner's hoof knocked a pebble over the edge. She could hear it clunking against the rocks, faster as it picked up speed; the sound went on forever down the precipitous cliffside.

"Lean back more," Macy called over her shoulder.

After a few moments of terror, Ava relaxed her sweaty grip. Gunner was as sure-footed as he'd been in the flat fields.

Further down the mountain, the path turned sharply to the right and the incline began to diminish. Still, it felt like they continued downhill for hours. Ava wiped her face with her shirt. Her tailbone was sore, and her thighs were starting to shake.

Eventually, the ground leveled off again and the trail widened. Soon, they reached the creek, although "creek" was a bit of an understatement. With the recent rains up north, it was more of a river now. The last mile of the path followed the water until it dumped them onto the main road, the end of the trail. Ava had always liked this last part—the feeling of riding upstream opposite the current.

The dry winds couldn't reach them behind the quiet curtain woven by the thick clusters of pine trees. Gunner's head hung low as he walked, sluggish after the steep ride. Curled leaves and pine needles formed a thin blanket across the trail, untouched like fresh snow. Ava closed her eyes and listened to the soft roar of the stream. She trusted Gunner to know the way home.

"I didn't leave last night because I was sick."

She opened her eyes. Macy had stopped, her eyes fixed on the trail, only nudging Cash on when Ava and Gunner were beside them. Macy's jaw was clenched so tight, Ava almost thought she imagined her speaking altogether. They rode on side by side.

"I left because I couldn't do it," Macy said, after a moment. "I can't do light, fun little things. Not anymore. I tried... I really did. But I can't."

"What do you mean?" Ava asked gently.

"Grabbing drinks, seeing movies, going to concerts," Macy said. "All the things normal people do in their normal lives. All the things I used to do with Ben."

Ava said nothing, afraid of startling Macy back into her shell.

"I just. . .feel so bad, you know?" she continued. "How can I do that stuff when Ben might be out there somewhere, lost? Maybe starving? Scared?"

Macy raised her hand in protest as if Ava had spoken.

"I get it, okay? Time to move on." She finally looked at Ava, her eyes red and glassy. "I know it sounds crazy after two years. That's not news to me. But there's just this little voice I can hear, this little voice that tells me not to move on."

Macy slumped as she turned back to the trail. She looked like a little girl at that moment, her petite body contrasted against Cash's leggy frame.

"I'll never know what it feels like," Ava said. "So, take this for what it's worth: I think, maybe if Ben can't be living his life with you right now... Maybe it could be your job to live for the both of you."

Macy stared at the water.

"Would he want you to shut yourself away from the world?" Ava asked.

Macy sighed. "If there was ever a 'seize the day' kinda guy, it was Ben."

"I promise to only say this once, Macy: you still have your whole life ahead of you. Maybe you don't feel ready to move on because you haven't met the right guy yet. Maybe Ben will nudge him your way. Just don't close yourself off to the possibility."

Macy looked hard at Ava, her blue eyes barely masking a pain unlike any Ava had ever experienced. Her own chest ached in reply, but Ava was glad Macy had finally begun to open up.

Two squirrels burst onto the trail in front of them, startling Ava, but neither horse so much as raised his head. One squirrel chirped as it chased the other in a playful circle before both disappeared into the forest.

"I met Ben at the Timber Café," Macy said.

"What? Why didn't you say something? We could have gone anywhere."

Macy shrugged, her eyes now on the trail. "I think a part of me wanted to see what it felt like. See if I felt him there."

"And did you?" Ava asked, her voice soft.

"No."

"Can you tell me about it?" Ava asked. "About the night you met?"

Macy raised an eyebrow. "You really want to hear about that?"

"I really do," Ava said.

Macy readjusted in her seat and took a deep breath. "It's a very ordinary story, but okay. This was back when I was in school. I always had a hard time focusing on my classes. You probably remember I wasn't exactly a top student, but I like to think I made up for it in determination. I uaually studied at the library where I didn't have any distractions. It was about a week until finals and Comparative Economics was really kicking my butt."

Macy hesitated before her face lifted into a warm smile. Ava was afraid to make a sound—afraid to ruin the moment.

"Anyway, the library closed and I still had hours to go, so I took my books to the Timber Café and ordered food at the bar. At some point, someone calls to me from across the bar, saying 'You know, this isn't the place for party animals. You need to take it down a notch.' When I looked up, I saw this gorgeous man that looked a few years older than me. He had dark eyes that crinkled when he smiled, and I'll never forget the vintage Eagles tee under this open denim shirt that did nothing to hide all those muscles."

Macy laughed, a light sound that nearly disappeared into the roaring creek.

"I must have had quite a look on my face, because he immediately apologized for the bad line and started stuttering a little. I was still recovering from this cheating basketball player I had survived junior year. I figured he was just another guy trying to pick up a lonely girl."

"But it was Ben?" Ava asked as they rode on.

"It was Ben," Macy agreed. "I went back to studying, but a few minutes later, he slid onto the stool next to mine. He introduced himself, and his hand was so rough and warm when I shook it. He smelled like whiskey and mint—I would later find out he ate those little starlight peppermint candies anytime he was in the car. I tried to play it cool, but once he asked me to dance, it was already over."

"Timber Café has a dance floor?" Ava asked.

"Nope," Macy said, and Ava laughed. "He loaded up the jukebox with twenty bucks and dragged me to my feet in front of a half-empty bar. But no one paid us much attention. We must have danced for a good thirty minutes, but I was a goner by the end of the first song. I don't know exactly how I knew. . .but I knew."

"Nothing about that sounds like an ordinary story to me," Ava said, her eyes stinging a little. Macy smiled.

Ava recognized a small wooden footbridge that crossed the creek just ahead. They were close to the end of the trail.

"I know the way back from here," Ava said. "Think I could take the lead?"

"Have at it," Macy replied, offering a tired half-smile.

Ava clicked her tongue, nudging Gunner into a jog. He had

such a smooth gait that she hardly moved at all as he sped up, her body easing instantly into the motion. She glanced back and saw that Macy was following close behind. Waves of sunlight greeted them as the pine trees gave way to the nearly naked skeletons of the Rocky Mountain maples. Once her eyes had adjusted to the brilliant midafternoon light, Ava could make out the ranch in the distance, growing larger as they drew closer. Autumn Lantern Ranch. . .Its name alone stirred longing in her stomach. It felt like home. But then, so did New York.

They slowed as they reached the end of the trail, then crossed the asphalt road to the ranch entrance. They walked along the driveway, the horses preferring the patchy grass on the shoulder to the fickle gravel rocks.

Gunner and Cash began to pick up speed as they neared the stable, tugging gently on their bridles. They were ready to go home.

Back at the barn, the women dismounted and filled buckets for the horses. Ava patted Gunner's neck, stiff with dried sweat, as he lapped the water. She led him into the barn behind Macy and walked him to his stall.

Ava unhooked Gunner's throatlatch and slid the bridle forward, gently pulling the bit from his mouth. After she haltered him, she clipped him to the lead line and secured him to the stall. She unfastened the cinch, then groaned as she lifted off the saddle and wool pad and gently laid them on the floor outside the stall. She began to rub his coat in firm circles with the rubber curry comb, starting on his neck and working her way across his muscular body.

"Hey, Ava?" Macy called.

Ava poked her head out the stall door. Macy was standing by the tack room, grooming caddy in hand, her saddle balanced on her hip.

"I need to go to town tomorrow. . .but can we start the day after?"

"Start what?" Ava asked.

"On the field."

Ava smiled. "Any day you like, boss."

Macy gave a little nod and then ducked into the tack room.

Finally, some progress. Some purpose for Ava to be there.

Ava stumbled through the front door of her cabin, her muscles screaming. The long ride had been exhausting, but she felt a warm swell of contentment as she fell back onto the sofa. When she wiped her sleeve across her gritty face, a brown smear of dirt came away with it. She peeked under her grime-covered jeans: luckily, she hadn't stained the light tan upholstery. Her legs were noodles as she slid to the floor, swiping as much dust off the couch as she could.

She tugged off her boots, then her sweaty socks. Her stiff calves protested as she reluctantly climbed to her feet. After tossing her dusty boots onto the porch, she filled a glass with water from the kitchen sink and downed it.

She found a leftover sub sandwich in the fridge behind the almond milk. She unwrapped it and took a huge bite, not bothering with a plate as she picked up her phone. There were several missed calls from Lucas, the last being a FaceTime. She tapped the little camera icon to call him back.

He picked up right away, his smile filling the screen. "There she is!" Lucas exclaimed. He was dressed in a tux and surrounded by several people all wearing suits and gowns.

"Hi!" Ava said, her mouth still full of roast beef.

Lucas' smile wavered. "You OK there, Ava?"

"Yeah, why?" Ava asked, then saw her face in the tiny square on the top right of the screen. Matted helmet hair plastered to her forehead, mayonnaise on her right cheek, a mustache of brown dirt across her lip. She put down the sandwich and wiped her face with a paper towel.

"Sorry, I was out riding," she said. "I didn't realize you'd be around other people when I called you back."

Lucas laughed tightly, glancing at the faces around him.

"Surely you didn't forget today is the Lucier Gala for the opening of the Pollock exhibit," he said. "I was just telling them how sorry you were to have to miss it."

Ava's mind was blank. "Oh, of course," she replied, forcing a smile. "I guess I lost track of the date."

She could tell Lucas didn't buy it for a second, but the rest of them smiled politely back at her.

"Anyway, I was showing Cora and Brant Lucier some photos of your recent sales, and I thought I'd try to catch you," Lucas said hastily. "Ava, meet the Luciers."

A silver-haired woman in a black velvet gown gave a courteous nod, as did the distinguished-looking bald man to her left. Ava knew all about the Luciers. They owned the most prestigious auction house outside of Christie's, and Lucas had been trying to get her a meeting with them for months. It could have been Ava's imagination, but she thought she saw Cora's lip curl ever so slightly in disgust.

"It's very nice to meet you," Ava said as sweetly as she could. "I've heard many wonderful things about your business."

The Luciers said nothing, just blinked back at her expectantly.

"You know artists," Lucas said, breaking the awkward silence. "Eccentrics, always looking for inspiration in odd places. That's what Ava's doing now."

"I'm sorry, what?" Ava asked.

"I told everyone how you went on your own personal artist retreat to find ideas for your next series. I think it may be the most daring one yet," Lucas said, nodding ever so slightly at her.

Ava could tell he wanted her to go along with it, so she forced a smile. "Yep, that's right," she said, her voice sounding stiff to her own ears. "I'm just being an eccentric artist."

"Well, maybe we can all sit down and discuss some future collaborations when you return," another of the strangers said. He looked exactly like Brant Lucier beside him, only more rotund and a bit less bald.

"This is Thomas, the Luciers' son," said Lucas. "He runs the day-to-day operations."

"Sure, Thomas, let's do that," Ava said. She couldn't wait to get off the phone.

For a moment, no one spoke. Lucas looked pale, his dark eyes unreadable.

She swallowed a lump in her throat, feeling as though she'd failed some test no one had prepared her to take.

"Well, we should probably let you get cleaned up," Lucas said finally.

"Yeah."

"I'll call you later," he said.

She hung up, her face hot. She switched her phone to silent. No more business today. She wished she could separate work Lucas from her Lucas—just cut them right down the middle into two different men.

A few minutes later, Ava stepped gingerly into the hot shower. She watched the dirt swirl down the drain and soaped up a second time. She was used to being inside, desk-bound in a sterile office with central air. Getting this filthy was kind of satisfying, like being a kid all over again.

After she toweled off her hair, she picked up her formerly gray crewneck sweater and black jeans. They'd wash clean, but it was really the only practical outfit she had packed. Her normal clothes were all silk and wool, delicate, and dry-clean only. And her European riding outfit was a joke. What had she been thinking when she packed?

Ava threw on her pajamas and opened her laptop. She'd need to find a store nearby to get a couple more machine-washable outfits.

Her e-mail was already open. She saw one from Carla, the subject: "An exciting new opportunity."

Ava hesitated. She felt a knot of dread in her stomach, then scolded herself. She was an artist. Why wasn't she clicking the message that second? But instead of excitement, she just felt exhaustion. She closed the e-mail app, resolving to look again when she could give it proper attention.

Ava found listings for a couple of stores in town that carried women's clothing and typed the addresses into her phone. The nearest Target was about an hour away, and she knew she could find some things there to tide her over if the local places weren't her style.

The sky had darkened to a jammy indigo, rich and berry-stained. She grabbed her sketchpad and climbed into the window seat. She opened her case, pulled out two purple pencils, and began to sketch. She planned nothing—just watched her hand draw and shade as it pleased. After a few minutes, she set the pad aside and stretched onto her side as she gazed out at the night sky. There was another color up there, one she couldn't quite place, just along the horizon. As she studied it, her eyes began to close. A moment later, she knocked her pad to the floor. But Ava was already so deeply asleep, she didn't hear a thing.

Twelve

The next morning, Ava switched on the coffee maker and mixed a bowl of instant oatmeal. She groaned and stretched. She had promised herself that first thing after breakfast she would deal with the mountain of work e-mails she'd been putting off.

She opened her laptop and watched as messages began to fill her open text app. She glanced at her phone, still charging across the room on the counter. After the embarrassing FaceTime the night before, she had switched it to silent. Once the computer finished loading, she scrolled to the top of her new messages. Lucas had sent her several texts, all timestamped from the night before.

Lucas: Hey babe... I'm sorry I caught you off guard tonight!

At least he had apologized. Something about the way he had looked at Ava had left a bad taste in her mouth.

Then, after a couple more messages, the texts became more agitated. She scrolled toward the end:

Lucas: I shouldn't have to sell your art on my own, you know.

Then, a message sent ten minutes later:

Lucas: I think you need to get your priorities straight, Ava.

Whoa, where had that come from? Ava knew she hadn't been devoting much time to her career since she'd been in Utah, but it hadn't even been a week. And she couldn't recall the last time she'd taken a break. She always did what Lucas asked of her, never questioning his expertise or his devotion to her career. She felt a heavy fatigue that reached down into her bones. She was burnt out.

This wasn't like him. Lucas was almost ten years older than Ava and she'd always thought of him as grounded and mature. Maybe he was feeling neglected. Ava could imagine Lucas might feel like she'd taken off to Utah and forgotten about him. She sighed. She'd have to call him later.

She wrote back:

Sorry. I fell asleep early last night. No worries about the FaceTime. Can we chat later?

She saw the little word "Read" appear below the text and waited for the ellipses that showed he was responding. They didn't come. Her heart thrummed in her chest, but she resisted the urge to write more and forced herself to minimize the app.

She opened her e-mail and saw the usual collaboration inquiries and interview requests. Margo had full access to this account and Ava knew she would respond to those on her behalf. Several other e-mails followed. She opened one from Margo, filling her in on the meetings she'd missed. At the end, she'd attached a photo of the Monstera plant from Ava's living room, which Margo had clearly pruned in her absence. Ava smiled. Margo was such an overachiever. She typed a quick reply, then opened the e-mail from Carla she'd seen the night before:

Ava,

An opportunity of a LIFETIME just fell into your lap. Money, fame. . .all we've been working for! Call me – too much to discuss over e-mail. Sending my love.

Best,

Mom

The next several e-mails were sent through the late hours of the previous night, the urgency growing with each one.

Carla: Where ARE you?????

Margo: Your mom asked me to get ahold of you. Call us back! :)

Several similar messages stacked in the queue after these.

Call us back? Ava grabbed her cell from the kitchen counter. Sure enough, she had several missed calls. Carla never texted when she was in a hurry, so it hadn't shown up on the laptop. No voicemails, though. . .Whatever it was, her mom clearly wanted to deliver the details live.

Ava dialed the New York office.

"MC Enterprise, Ava MacDaniel's office," Margo chirped.

"Hey Margo, it's me," Ava said.

She could hear a relieved sigh on the other end of the line.

"Where have you been, Ava?!" Margo exclaimed before lowering her voice to a whisper. "Your mom has been tearing the place apart trying to talk to you."

"Well, she could have left a message," Ava said. "What's this big opportunity, anyway? Does Lucier want to move some of our pieces?"

"Oh, no, Carla would fire me on the spot if I spilled," Margo said. "But she's in some international investor meeting downtown until later. I'll have her call you."

"Okay," Ava said, reluctantly. She'd just have to wait.

"And please answer!" Margo added. "For my sake, at least."

Ava laughed. "I'll do my best. But leave a message if I don't. There's no service out here, so I only see missed calls when I'm on Wifi."

They chatted for a bit longer. Margo told Ava that the interest list for her pieces had doubled since the *DAR #5* sale, and everyone expected it to explode once the *Vanity Fair* article was published. All the major modern art museums had inquired about displaying her work.

Imagine, thought Ava. *My art in the MET*. It felt like a dream.

Margo told her that Lucas had been prowling the office like a caged lion, his usual confidence and charisma replaced by what Margo deemed "teenage angst." Maybe Lucas was finally realizing how much he cared about Ava outside their work.

After they hung up, Ava clicked through the rest of her messages, but everything urgent had already been responded to by Lucas or Margo. Ava felt detached, as if she was an intern of her own work rather than the artist herself. It didn't bother her; she'd never been interested in the business side of things. Instead, she examined this thought with curiosity. If she never went back, would her career continue forward without her? This was absurd, of course, but it was a lovely daydream. She stashed her laptop back in the case and rinsed her oatmeal bowl.

She unrolled her yoga mat and sat, inhaling deeply as she crossed her legs. She matched her breathing to her movement as she began a sun salutation. The throbbing pain in her legs had faded to a mild ache, and her whole body felt stronger as she flowed through the familiar poses. She'd come to love yoga for the way it stilled her thoughts, grounding her when life felt chaotic. Today, however, her mind was everywhere but on the mat. After a few more stretches, she gave up.

Ava showered and threw on a caramel-colored cashmere turtleneck and high-waisted black slacks. She twisted her wavy hair into a bun and examined her shoe options: all heels except for her muddy boots on the porch. She decided to pick up a pair of flats in town. She slipped on her black leather booties.

Now what? The stores wouldn't open for a few hours. She could work, continuing with her painting or sketching out some new ideas, but she just wasn't in the mood.

She decided to wander over to the barn. Luckily, the morning sun had already dried the dew from the grass, making her chunky-heeled boots manageable. Still, she wobbled on loose stones and kept her eyes on the ground in order to avoid tripping over roots.

Once inside the stable, she stopped by Gunner's stall. "Hey buddy," she said. His ears perked up at the sound of her voice and he stuck his nose through the bars. Ava smiled. He was happy to see her.

Lizzie was typing away on the desktop computer when Ava entered the office a few minutes later.

"Hi, you!" Lizzie said. "Pop a squat."

Ava grabbed a pumpkin-shaped sugar cookie from a bowl at the end of the desk and sunk into the vinyl chair.

"Just one sec while I finish sending these invoices," Lizzie said, her eyes on the screen. "The cookies are good, huh? This time, I made them."

They were good. While Lizzie finished, Ava scanned the walls of the office. Long satin championship ribbons were clustered in colorful bouquets, while horse show photos and trophy plaques covered every other inch of open space. In one photo, Macy perched atop a tall palomino horse, a huge belt buckle in her hands. Harris stood beside her, holding a trophy with a proud smile on his face. *AQHA World Show—American Quarter Horse Association* was engraved in the frame below. She leaned forward to read the smaller print underneath. *Wow, Macy was a world champion?*

"OK, sorry about that," Lizzie said, grabbing herself a cookie. "Always piles up on me mid-month."

"I'm in no hurry," Ava said. "In fact, that's why I came by. Got anything you need help with?"

Lizzie raised a brow, her eyes amused. "Dressed like that?"

"Yeah," Ava said. "I don't mind getting dirty."

"I'm just teasing," Lizzie said. "We're all good around here. You're welcome to hang around or ride. I'll be shackled to this desk all day, so I'm afraid I can't provide much entertainment."

"Maybe I'll head to town," Ava said. "Wander around, do a little shopping. Can I bring you anything?"

"Well, now, there's an idea," Lizzie said. She opened a desk drawer and retrieved a stack of light green papers. She handed them to Ava. *Autumn Lantern Riding Academy* was printed at the top. Just below was a quote attributed to Winston Churchill: *"No hour of life is wasted that is spent in the saddle."* A big photo of Macy teaching a class of riders took up the middle of the page.

"Just got these flyers back from the printer," Lizzie said. "It has our updated hours and such. Could you take a few and tack them up in any businesses you stop by? They all know us, so they won't mind. And just take down any old ones you find."

Ava smiled. "I'll do you one better," she said. "I have nothing but time on my hands. I'll hit as many shops as I can and spread them around the whole town."

"You don't have to do all that," said Lizzie, waving her hand. "Just whatever's easy."

"I want to," Ava said. "I'm putting off some work today myself, so it will give me a good excuse. Plus, I'll get to see more of the town."

"If you say so," Lizzie said. "Thank you. I know Macy will appreciate it, too."

"Is she here?" Ava asked.

"Meeting of some sort in Cobalt. She'll be back soon. Maybe you'll run into her."

Ava didn't think she'd ever tire of the half-hour drive into town. Sure, the trees would soon be stripped, the reds and oranges long gone, but even in winter Utah had a certain magic to it. Its browns and grays were rich and textured, not bleak and sullen like back east. Sloping rocks and jagged, bare December forests could inspire anyone, artist or not. And when it snowed, it looked like a wonderland of ice. Too bad she'd be gone by then, even with the extra week. New York loomed gloomily in her mind.

Ava parked in the public lot in the center of town and searched for a shoe store on Yelp. The first listing was for Tate's Shoes: one block away and with a five-star rating. Perfect. If she was going to walk the entire town, she had better make comfortable footwear her priority. Maybe she'd get some loafers or ballet flats.

She paid the meter and walked west. She couldn't miss the sign for Tate's with its flashing lights and lasso around the "T." Once inside, she scanned the walls where hefty construction boots lined the long wooden shelves. She had a feeling she wouldn't be finding Manolos here. An older man behind the counter raised his head from a newspaper.

"Help ya?" he said.

"Women's?" Ava asked.

He nodded to the back right corner. Ava wandered over and found every kind of work and cowboy boot imaginable. She held up a pretty black pull-on style with intricate designs embroidered on the calf.

"How comfortable are these?" Ava called to the man.

"Those the Ariats or the Justins?" he asked.

She looked at the sole. "Justin."

He nodded and, with surprising dexterity, lifted his boot-clad foot onto the countertop. "Been wearing mine just about every day for more years than I care to admit," he said.

Ava laughed. "Sold! Can I try these in a seven?"

The man introduced himself as "Chuck" and brought her a few different sizes and colors to try. He was right; the Justins felt broken-in and comfortable. Even with her current outfit, she liked the way they looked. She decided on the black.

As Chuck added her total in the ancient register, Ava asked if she could hang one of the flyers. Chuck gestured to a bulletin board near the front. Once he learned she was from Autumn Lantern, he insisted on giving her a discount. It turned out his granddaughter was one of Macy's students. Everybody seemed to know everybody around here.

Ava wore the boots out of the store and walked back to her car to stash her heels. Then, she went inside every business she could find—the bakery, the library, the auto repair shop… The shopkeepers were all so kind, offering her tips about the town and even a free tea at the coffee shop. And everyone was happy to hang a flyer. It seemed the town was really rooting for Macy.

Soon, Ava found herself at Oakenwood & Sons. Kelly was behind the counter yet again, her face lighting up when she saw Ava enter.

"Back for more supplies?" Kelly asked.

Ava passed a flyer across the counter. "Working for my cousin today," she said. "Is it cool if I hang one of these?"

"Oh yeah, go for it," Kelly replied.

As Ava walked over to the bulletin board, the wooden bridge sculpture caught her eye once more.

"This one," Ava said. "I noticed it doesn't have a price. Is it for sale?"

"Oh, gosh, no," Kelly said. "Who would want that? It looks like a toy."

"It's really good," Ava said. "Whoever made it has a great sense of proportion, and the detail is incredible… I can't imagine drawing that with a pencil, let alone carving it with a knife. Do you know the artist?"

Kelly laughed. "I don't know if anyone has ever called me an artist before," she said.

"*You* made this?"

"Yeah, just for fun," Kelly said. "Dad lets me display my stuff up there, kind of like a public refrigerator. But no one has ever asked about it before, much less a famous artist like you."

"May I?" Ava asked, raising her hand over the sculpture. Kelly nodded. Ava gently picked up the carved scene. She rubbed her thumb over the little boy's face, his expression intent as he attempted to reel in a fish still invisible below the creek. It could have been Macy's creek. She turned it over and was delighted to find the back every bit as detailed as the front. It was no bigger than a large snow globe, but Ava had never seen anything like it. She set it back on the shelf, noticing the way the light seemed to reflect off the wooden water.

"Kelly, you are seriously gifted," Ava said. "Would it be okay if I took a picture of it?"

"Not sure why you'd want to, but be my guest," Kelly said, her high cheekbones flushed pink with Ava's praise. Ava pulled out her phone and snapped a quick photo.

"Are you applying to art school?" Ava asked.

"Oh, no, definitely not," Kelly said. She held up her left hand and a small diamond ring glittered in the store light. "My fiancée got a full ride to Brigham Young."

"And what about you?" Ava asked.

"Well, we're getting married after graduation, and then I'll move with him until he gets his Bachelor's," said Kelly. "I might take a couple community college classes in Salt Lake, but I'll be getting a job there to support us. The scholarship doesn't cover living expenses."

"Is that what you want?" Ava asked.

Kelly shrugged. "It's temporary," she said. "Family is really important to me. I love art, and I like school, but if I have to choose, I'll pick Charlie a million times over."

"Too bad you have to choose," Ava said. "For an untrained artist, you're unbelievable. Have you done other pieces?"

Kelly nodded. "Loads. Back in Girl Scouts ages ago, we learned whittling basics. From that first block of wood they handed me, I was hooked. I carve everything I can get my hands on."

Ava couldn't believe what she was hearing. People could spend years in art school and never create anything nearly as intricate as what Kelly had done.

"If you ever change your mind and want to pursue this, call me," Ava said, handing Kelly a business card. "I'd be happy to give you a good reference."

Kelly gaped. She looked from Ava to the card, then back up again.

"I mean it," Ava said firmly.

"I'm just. . .Well," Kelly began, clearly flustered. "No matter what, this is like, the best day of my life. Thank you."

Kelly tucked the card into her jeans pocket, then looked back at Ava with a cautious smile. "So, not to sound like a total spy, but the other day I saw you walking around with Ethan Coleman. Sorry if that's weird to say."

"No, not at all," Ava said. "He's a friend and he was showing me around Cobalt. How do you know him?"

"Well, that's why I mentioned it. We had this really great art teacher at the high school, Ms. Kidd. For a small-town, she was the real deal. She had studied all over the world. Anyway, when she left town, it was kind of a big scandal."

"Involving Ethan?" Ava asked.

"Sort of," Kelly said. "Ms. Kidd took off with Vice Principal Peters, who had been married for like, decades, and had a bunch of kids. The two of them just left, no explanation. But Ethan was Ms. Kidd's boyfriend, and he's so handsome and so nice. He came in here a few times to pick up stuff for her. I just felt so bad for him. I thought for sure he'd go back to wherever he came from once she didn't come back."

Poor Ethan. That explained what he had meant when he said he had ties to Cobalt. He must have moved here for her.

"Is he seeing anyone now?" Ava asked.

Kelly blushed again. "You'd know before I would," she said. "But I haven't seen him out with anyone."

Ava noticed a framed newspaper article hanging behind the counter. Two grinning teenagers stood arm in arm.

"Is that you?" Ava asked, squinting to try to read the text.

Kelly groaned and pulled the frame off the wall, then handed it to Ava. "My dad insisted on hanging it up. It's kind of embarrassing."

It was an engagement announcement. Kelly and Charlie looked even younger in the photo, their beaming faces bright and earnest.

"You guys make a cute couple," Ava said.

"Thanks. You just missed him. He works here part-time, too. He's not an art guy, but he does cleaning and maintenance—that sort of thing."

"Maybe next time," Ava said.

"Yeah, next time."

"Well, I better keep at it," Ava said. "Thanks for hanging the flyer. I'll come by again soon."

Ava continued down the main drag, hanging flyers in the sewing store and the candy shop. She found some cute tops and jeans in Jennifer's, a little boutique run by the store's namesake. She added the bags to the growing pile in her truck. As Ava slammed it closed, her conversation with Kelly replayed in her mind.

Ava wondered how long it had been since this Ms. Kidd ran off, leaving Ethan surely heartbroken. How could anyone treat such a kind man with such cruelty?

And Kelly. . .Ava truly hoped the youngest Oakenwood would find a way to keep her artistic spirit alive, even if she ended up choosing a life as a housewife. She could only imagine how well she'd do in art school if that carving was all raw talent. Ava was tempted to ask to see some more of her work the next time she stopped by. There was something about Kelly that reminded Ava of herself, of the Ava before Paris.

She grabbed a granola bar from the glove compartment and locked the car with her key fob. It was warm out. She was glad she hadn't worn a jacket. The stack in her arms was now thin, but she was determined to hang every flyer before she left. Her cell rang from inside her purse, and she picked it up: Lucas.

"Hello," she said coolly when she answered.

"I'm sorry, I'm an idiot, please forgive me," Lucas said in one breath.

Ava laughed, despite herself.

"I'm not trying to be funny," Lucas said. "I know I behaved like a complete toddler yesterday, especially with that stream of texts I sent. I don't know what got into me—I have never behaved like this, not in business, and certainly not with a woman I care about."

"I suppose I can forgive you," Ava said. "But would you please just talk to me next time? I had no idea you were feeling like I ditched you. That was never what this trip was about. If you remember, I asked you to come with me."

"I know," Lucas said. "I just miss you. I want to wrap my arms around you and smell your apple-scented shampoo. I want to dance all night at McCoy's to whatever wannabe band is playing. You've really done a number on me, Ava."

"The offer stands," Ava said. "You can come here anytime. But I'll be back before you know it."

Ava didn't tell him exactly when that would be. She had to let him know she was staying longer, but she didn't want to upset him all over again. It felt so good to know that they were okay.

They chatted a bit longer before he told her he had to go to a meeting. As Ava hung up, she felt a hollow ache that she recognized as loneliness. She longed to tuck herself into his strong arms; she could imagine it so clearly. His scent a blend of aftershave and minty toothpaste with a hint of that cologne she had bought him. The way his cheek always had a touch of scratchy stubble when she rubbed her thumb along his jaw, the way his eyes crinkled a little at the corners when he saw her. And the things he had said. . .Maybe he was finally coming around to see what truly mattered. They could have real, committed love, maybe eventually a family, and still have plenty of time for business. If only he could see that.

Ava realized she'd been so focused on Lucas she had walked into the residential area of town without realizing it. She looked up. This was Ethan's street.

Flyers in hand, she headed toward his house. Maybe he was home. She could use a glass of water.

As she approached the looming Victorian, she saw Ethan out front, bent over a table saw. She could hear the screeching of wood and the thump of cut pieces being tossed into a pile. She noticed Ethan wasn't wearing a shirt. Sweat glistened on his muscular back as he stood, wiping sawdust from his forehead. Suddenly, he looked up and saw Ava.

"Hey, you," he said and smiled. He removed his safety glasses and threw on a gray sweatshirt. His eyes lingered on her outfit for a moment, but he said nothing. Ava knew this sweater looked good on her; everyone always said it made her red hair pop. Then he noticed her boots. He laughed. "Cowgirl chic?" he asked.

"Straight from the runway," Ava teased.

"What are you doing here?" he asked.

"I've been hanging flyers all over town for the ranch and I somehow managed to wander over here without realizing it," she said. "Any chance I could bother you for some water?"

His eyes were so warm, his face so kind. Ava hated Ms. Kidd.

"I could use a break myself," he said. "Come on in."

The foyer was a circle of warm wood, and the air smelled

of lemon. Ava noticed rays of pink, blue, and yellow across the checkered tile floor, and she looked up to find a stained-glass chandelier hanging from the ceiling.

"It's beautiful," Ava said.

"This, I can't take credit for," Ethan said. "All original. It just needed some dusting and polish."

He led her into the kitchen. Although it had antique cabinets and fixtures, the recessed lighting and appliances were all new.

"This room was my first project," he said. "Grab a stool."

He poured them each a glass of ice water and sat across from her at the wooden island.

"I'm so curious what it looked like before you moved in," Ava said.

"Be careful what you wish for," he said, grinning. "You know, every good weekend warrior takes before-and-after pics."

"Let's see them," Ava said. "I love a good HGTV makeover as much as the next person. "

"I have some on my phone," Ethan said, pulling up his photos as he moved his stool next to hers. His sleeve pressed against her arm as he showed her photo after photo, explaining the months of labor that went into each project. How could Macy not be into him? On top of everything else, there was something undeniably sexy about a man who was handy with tools.

The before-and-after pictures were dramatically different. Yet, all the renovations seemed to honor the turn-of-the-century design seamlessly.

"You're really good at this," Ava said.

"My mom and dad flipped houses before that was even a thing," Ethan said with a nonchalant shrug. "They both loved old homes and felt like restoring them was a way to give back to the community; a way to add to local history. I guess it's in my blood."

He shared more about his childhood, what it was like growing up in Provo. He'd been a decent athlete and a fervent math whiz. He told her he had joined the co-ed softball league when he first moved to Cobalt, and his friend group was still mostly made up of his teammates. *That explains the muscles*, Ava thought.

He confessed that numbers were still like a game to him, which is how he'd ended up in accounting. He talked about how he felt an instant connection to Cobalt's historic small-town charm from his very first visit. Ava hoped he would mention his ex, but she wasn't about to be the one to bring up the situation.

Suddenly, he laughed. "I am so sorry. I swear, I never talk about myself that much."

"I'm glad you did. I hardly know anything about you. And your walls give nothing away."

Ethan looked at her, confused.

"Art nerd, remember? It's a game I play," Ava said. "Whenever I go to someone's house for the first time, I like to look at the art on their walls and see what I can learn about them. Some people obviously choose certain art because it's expensive while knowing nothing about it. They tend to be more focused on keeping up appearances. Some folks have all kinds of funky different things, cheap or pricy, and each piece has a story. These people have a good sense of themselves. And so on and so forth, you get the idea. But you. . .Well, no art, no answers."

Ethan looked at her for a moment, then peered around the kitchen. "I guess I haven't really gotten to the decorating part," he said. "To be honest, I've never bought any real art before. I know what I like, but I don't know of any current artists. Well, except you now, of course."

"In my opinion, you don't need to need to know anything," Ava said. "Unless you're dropping major cash on established artists, it's all a gamble. I've seen incredibly technical art sell for fifty bucks. I've seen a few lines painted by an elephant sell for hundreds of thousands of dollars. The value of art is subjective. If you buy what you like, you'll at least enjoy it. And you never know; maybe one day it could be worth something."

Ethan smiled. "I like that," he said. "And you're the art expert. If you're ever in town when they do the Cobalt Art Walk, maybe you can guide me."

"When's the next one?" Ava asked.

"I think the last one for the year is in two weeks," Ethan said.

"Oh, that's too bad. I'm actually planning to stay a week longer now, but I'll be gone by then."

"Ah," he said. "That *is* too bad. But at least now you'll be here for the festival."

"Oh, that's right!" Ava said. "I forgot that was so soon. I will definitely be there."

"I'm glad," he said.

"Tell you what," said Ava. "I'll make sure you have my number. When you finally art shop, you can text me photos if you're torn and I'll help you decide."

"Deal," Ethan said, holding her gaze. Neither looked away. Ava's heart thudded in her chest. His eyes looked more blue than gray today.

He looked over her shoulder to the clock on the wall. "Didn't you say you needed to paint in daylight?"

"Yeah, why?" Ava asked.

"It's almost five," Ethan said. "I'm sorry, it looks like I stole your whole day."

Ava turned and looked at the clock. How was it four forty-five already? She glanced out the window. Sure enough, the sky was already starting to glow orange. It would be pitch dark by the time she got back to the ranch.

"I guess I lost track of time," Ava said. "Oh well, the world won't stop if I don't work today."

"I'm glad you came by," Ethan said. He was so close to her that Ava could feel his breath on her cheek.

"Me too," Ava said, standing quickly. She set her glass in the dishwasher and collected her purse and flyers. "I should hurry back to the parking lot while I can still see where I'm going."

"Can I give you a ride?" Ethan asked.

"No, it's nice out. I'd like to enjoy it before the drive, but thanks." She didn't add that something about the last couple hours made her think it was a bad idea to be alone in a car with him again. "I appreciate the water," she said.

"You bet."

Oh, that smile.

Once on the sidewalk, Ava glanced back at the house, now awash in the glow of the setting sun. Ethan leaned against the doorframe, watching her go. He gave a little wave. Ava waved back, then hurried toward the town square.

What is wrong with me? She didn't want to leave Ethan's house. She wanted to talk to him all night. If she was being honest with herself, she wanted to do a lot more than talk.

But she had Lucas, and she loved him. She was sure of this, just as sure as her feet wanted to turn around and walk right back to Ethan's door. Whatever these feelings were, she needed to squash them right away. Her life was in New York, with Lucas, with her art. *That's what was causing this*, she thought. She was a fish out of water here, alone, everything she knew thousands of miles away. Ethan was handsome and he was here. And nothing more.

The temperature was dropping fast. She gripped the flyers tightly, realizing she had never finished hanging the rest. She sighed, her breath clouding the dusky air in front of her.

Thirteen

The sun had yet to crest the trees when Ava trudged across the field between the cabin and the main house. She wished she'd brought her parka, but the thin wool peacoat would have to do. The grass was still stiff with overnight frost, but thankfully, the new cowboy boots kept her feet warm.

Before Ava could knock, Macy swung open the front door, bundled in a trapper hat and a thick tan Carhartt coat. She glanced at Ava's boots with an amused smile. "Been doing some shopping?" Macy asked.

"You like?" Ava asked, turning to show them off.

"Much better than those fancy ones you brought," Macy said. "Is that the only jacket you have?"

Ava nodded.

Macy ducked back inside, returning a moment later with another tan coat like the one she was wearing. She handed it to Ava, then closed the door tightly behind her.

"This also belongs to my mother-in-law," she said. "It's heavy, but it should keep the chill off until it warms up in a couple hours."

Macy drove them in her pickup to the storage barn, still the same shade of gray it had been a decade earlier. They loaded a cobwebbed wheelbarrow into the truck bed, as well as buckets of gardening tools and thick black contractor garbage bags.

Macy drove slowly through the back pastures to the overgrown field, then backed the truck up to the gate. She shifted into park but didn't switch off the engine.

"You ready for this?" Ava asked.

"Absolutely," Macy said, a tight smile on her face.

Ava grabbed her hand. "Listen to me," she said. "We've got this. I'm with you every step of the way."

Macy nodded, then glanced at the weed-covered field in the rearview mirror. "Thanks, Ava."

They climbed out and unloaded the truck, filling the wheelbarrow with tools. Macy rolled it over to the gate and removed the heavy chain before swinging the fence open. She stood with her hands on her hips, surveying the field. Ava joined her.

Now that they were closer, Ava could see at least three rows of raised garden beds, spaced about five feet apart. One appeared to hold nothing but dirt and leaves, but the others had toppled wooden trellises, overturned rusty tomato cages, and tangled ropes of dead vines. To their right, long dirt mounds stretched the depth of the field where Ava guessed Ben had planted directly into the ground. The skeletal, sun-bleached remains of crops planted long ago contrasted with the wild winter weeds. One patch of the field was just dirt and rocks.

"So, where do we start, boss?" Ava asked, forcing an optimistic tone.

"Well, the ground's gonna be too cold to do any digging," Macy said, "but come spring, I can deal with that. The raised beds should be a bit easier to turn over."

"What if I start cutting down all the dead stuff with those big scissor things?" Ava asked.

Macy laughed. "Well, it's all dead stuff or weeds, so go for it. I've got my toolbox in the cab, so I'll see about repairing some of the loose boards. Just be careful with those shears—there's little black tubing throughout that's part of our irrigation system. I'm crossing my fingers it's still intact and we don't have to replace it."

"Chop off brown stuff, don't chop black stuff," said Ava. "Got it."

"This is going to take a lot more time than you have, Ava. Let's put in a few hours and we can come back tomorrow."

Ava nodded, then followed Macy as she pushed the wheelbarrow into the center of the field.

Macy handed her a pair of thick calfskin gloves that matched her own. Ava pulled a garbage bag from the wheelbarrow and grabbed the largest pruning shears she could find. She began to snip and tear the dry branches and vines. Once the pile around her feet was waist high, she shoved the debris into the bag and began again. The sun was high above them as Ava finished the first bed. Macy was right; this was going to take a long time. Ava stripped off her jacket and tossed it in the back of the truck, glad she had thought to wear layers. The thin fleece pullover underneath would soon be too warm, as well.

Ava grabbed her water from the front seat. Parched, she

watched Macy work as she gulped the entire contents of her bottle. Despite her own warnings of frozen ground, Macy was wedging a shovel under a stubborn root. Once loose, she tossed the whole plant into a pile twice the size of Ava's bag. Ava thought she was probably the strongest person she'd ever met, male or female. She threw her empty bottle back into the cab and wiped her face on the front of her fleece. Back to work.

They labored on, finding a quiet, comfortable rhythm. Though the field hardly looked as if they'd been there, the six giant bags of rubbish leaning against the truck proved otherwise.

"Hey! You hungry?" Macy called to Ava.

Ava was starving. She looked at her watch. It was after one in the afternoon. "What do you have in mind?" she asked.

Macy smiled. "I packed a nineties-style picnic, for old times' sake."

Ava laughed. When they were little, they'd always had picnics, even indoors when a perfectly good table was available.

Macy retrieved an old wicker picnic basket from the cab, then grabbed a wool blanket from the truck bed. Ava refilled their bottles from the red thermos Macy had packed and followed her through a slim patch of woods to the rushing creek. A long flat rock overlooked the water.

Ava took the blanket from Macy and spread it across the stone. Macy unpacked sandwiches, little bags of chips, and apples. She pulled out a tiny speaker and switched it on, controlling it with her phone.

"That old boom box died years ago, but I have the next best thing," Macy said. Suddenly, the opening notes of "Kiss Me" filled the quiet woods.

"Oh my gosh!" Ava exclaimed. "I forgot about this song. Whatever happened to Sixpence None The Richer? We had that single on CD, remember?"

"Yeah, we put it on repeat until we killed it," Macy said, laughing.

They listened and ate, singing along like they had so many times before. Ava was reminded of the longing ache this song had inspired once, before she'd ever even had a boyfriend. It had all been a beautiful fantasy.

"I really thought this song was everything I needed to know about falling in love," Ava said, sighing as she leaned back on her elbows. "We were so young and naive. Personally, I'm still waiting for the woods to come alive with magic while I slow dance with my Prince Charming."

"I had that," Macy said quietly.

Ava looked at her but said nothing. The song ended and another from Third Eye Blind began. They ate and watched the water flow past.

"I feel like our best work was done during picnics," Macy said. "Do you remember that business idea we came up with?"

"You mean when we were in, what, eighth grade?" Ava asked. "Was this the same rock?"

Macy nodded.

"How could I forget?" Ava said, laughing. "We'd open a vacation dude ranch. You would teach the tourists to ride horses and rope cattle, and I'd paint their pictures as a one-of-a-kind souvenir."

"It's never too late," Macy said, a playful glint in her eyes. She crumpled her napkin and tossed it into the basket. "Well, you saw how my end of the dream turned out. How about yours? What's life like as a professional artist?"

Ava considered. "Most mornings, I wake up early to sneak in a quick yoga class, then paint until eleven or so," she said. "After that, I head into the office to take meetings Carla arranges, or talk to investors on Zoom if they're international. That usually takes up a good chunk of the day, depending on the time zones everyone is in. Lucas schedules interviews or photo shoots in the afternoon for me, and then there's usually some networking dinner. By the time I get back to my apartment, I crash—well, unless there's an opening or some other schmooze-fest I have to attend."

Ava felt like she was describing someone else's life. This past week had given her some much-needed distance from her usual anxiety.

"That sounds. . .exhausting," Macy said.

"It is, but it's just this stage of my career. Hustle, hustle, hustle. I hope that once I get a little more established, I'll be able to take my foot off the gas a bit."

"You think they'll let you?" Macy asked.

Ava didn't respond. She wasn't sure they would.

"So, this is what your dream looks like," Macy said.

"Yes, and no," Ava said. "It's so hard to make a living as an artist. I'm grateful I don't have to have a second job to pay my bills like most creative types. But I thought it would be more actual *art*, I guess. I also thought I'd be the one deciding what I would make. I just didn't know any better. The price of success, as they say."

Macy reached into the basket and pulled out two little chocolates.

"Care for dessert?" she asked with a wink before passing one to her. As Ava unwrapped the foil, she saw a small message printed inside: *Don't settle for a spark... Light a fire instead.* Cute. She popped the chocolate into her mouth and tossed the wrapper back in the basket.

"Can I tell you my real dream?" Ava asked.

"Uh, duh," Macy said, smiling.

"I want to open an artists' residence. Like, with dorms, classrooms, workspaces—you name it." Ava sat up straighter and began gesturing emphatically with her hands. She couldn't talk about this stuff without getting excited. "I'll recruit underrepresented talent from all over the world. They can learn there and have a safe place to live, and then I'll help introduce them to the art world. People don't value art everywhere, and I've been so lucky to have all these opportunities myself. I want to give them the chances I had. Being great at this doesn't automatically mean you get to be successful. I want to find these people and show them to the world."

Ava paused as a deer emerged from the trees. It stretched its long, graceful neck to drink from the creek, before scampering back into the woods when it spotted them.

"It's pretty hippie-dippy, I know," Ava said, turning back to Macy. "Lucas and Carla both think it's not focused enough on profit, and there's liability to consider, of course. . ."

"I think it's a wonderful idea," Macy said. "It sounds just like something the Ava I remember would dream up."

Ava smiled but felt a pang of guilt resurface. She wished Macy knew the whole story. If Ava told her what it would take to get that dream, maybe she'd help. Or maybe Macy would hate her all over again. Either way, she had put it off long enough.

"It's not something I can do right now, at least not financially," Ava said. "Something like that will be really expensive. Even if we create a gallery to help fund it, the initial costs would be insane."

"I know all about that part," Macy said. "You wouldn't believe how much it cost to get the riding academy up and running."

Ava nodded. "Dreams are really expensive, Macy. That's something they don't tell us when we're little. So, to be totally honest. . .there are a few things we really should have talked about before now. Things I've been trying to say since I came back."

Macy looked at her, opening her mouth, then closing it again. "I should have known you'd figure it out," she said finally.

Ava stopped.

Figure what out?

"You're right," Macy continued. "Dreams cost a lot. . .and yes, I am struggling to afford mine. I'm probably going to lose the ranch."

Ava's breath caught in her throat.

Macy cocked her head toward Ava, studying her. "What gave me away?"

"I... I don't know," Ava fumbled. What could she say?

"I guess it doesn't matter," Macy said. "You could always read me better than most people."

"I thought the riding academy was doing really well?" Ava asked.

Macy picked up a pebble and rubbed it between her fingers before tossing it into the water. She shrugged. "For a new business, it's grown pretty steadily," she said. "It's just—I'm still paying on the construction loan, and Ben's produce business wasn't just a hobby. It was bringing in several thousand bucks a month."

"Can't the Army help?" Ava asked.

Macy sighed. "It's complicated. I'm still trying to understand all the spouse benefits myself. When he first went missing, his pay was the same. Then, when they—well, after a certain amount of time, you get a lump sum." She cleared her throat and looked away.

"I'm sorry, Macy," Ava said.

"It has nothing to do with the Army," Macy said. "We knew the riding school would stretch us. Our plan was that the money from Ben's produce would fill in the gap until the school properly got its footing. I know I could never have done it by myself, but I didn't even try. It's like I saw the ship fill with water and just stared at it, bucket in hand."

Ava scooted closer to her. "Don't blame yourself. You were surviving *and* running a new business. You did the best you could, right?" She wanted to hug her, but Macy kept curling herself tighter into a ball.

"Yeah, well, it's all connected," Macy said softly. "It always is. I thought if I kept Ben's disappearance in this tiny little box, maybe I wouldn't lose my mind. Maybe, just that one part of me would be destroyed and everything else could survive, at least. Kinda like letting the weakest in a pack get picked off to save the rest. I just let my heart go. But it didn't matter. His absence has touched everything now. My home. My business. I don't know what I'm going to do."

"Do you have time?" Ava asked. "To get the money together?"

Macy sighed. "That's what I've been trying to figure out," she said. "First, if I can save the place even if I can't come up with the money. That's why I met you in town for dinner last week; I had an appointment at the bank first. Exploring options."

"Here I thought you just didn't want to be stuck in a room alone with me without a getaway car," Ava said.

"Well, that too," Macy said, smiling a little.

"So, have you figured anything out?"

Macy shook her head. "It's not great, no matter how you shake it," she said. "Even if I can scrape together enough for the short term, without that second income, it's only a matter of time before I'm back here again. It's not sustainable. So, I've been meeting with some other stable owners around the area, seeing if anyone wants to merge businesses, or own a part of the school."

"Lizzie told me you were in town yesterday for a meeting," Ava said. "Does she know?"

Macy flipped over on her stomach and propped her chin on her fists. "Lizzie seems to know everything, whether I tell her or not, but I've shared a good bit with her. I met with Brookhaven Stables yesterday. Not sure if you remember, but that's where I took lessons as a kid, and then taught at before I started my own place. They were sympathetic, but it's been a slow year for them. And all the older barns own their land outright, so there's no incentive to them to rent here."

Ava considered. "What if we get the field ready to plant and make a good plan for spring—would that be too late?"

"There's no way I can plant and sell on the level that Ben did," Macy said. "Even if I had the time, what he did was special."

"Couldn't Harris help?"

"Please don't tell him," Macy said quickly. "He'd just worry, and he's in no position to help. This place has been refinanced plenty over the decades, like most farms. He paid for that house he's in now with cash from our buyout and lives mostly off his social security. I'll tell him when there's something concrete to tell."

They sat quietly, both staring at the water. If the rushing creek had the answers, it gave no indication.

"So, what's next?" Ava asked.

"Well, I've thought about what matters most to me here," Macy said. "These hundreds of acres are my home. They're who I am. But I can't keep it all. If I sell off most of the land, I could probably afford to keep the buildings, the barn, the arena, and the pastures by the road. Everything else would have to go."

"Everything?"

"Yep," Macy replied. "The trails. The creek. And Ben's field. It's road-front property. Like anywhere, that's the most valuable part."

"There must be another way," Ava said.

"I've tried everything, Ava," she said, then sighed with controlled patience. "If you can come up with a better way, I'm all ears. At this point, I'm just grateful I'll still have a home to live in."

They heard cracking branches from the direction of the field. Suddenly, Lizzie appeared, her faced flushed with exertion as she picked bits of leaves from her chunky pumpkin-orange sweater. Ethan stepped out from behind her. He wore jeans and a sky-blue cable knit sweater that Ava bet was the same shade as his eyes. There really was something about a man in cowboy boots... Ava's neck burned as she quickly refocused her gaze on Lizzie.

"There you are!" Lizzie exclaimed. "An empty truck next to an empty field wasn't a good find for my blood pressure."

"Sorry," Macy said. "We snuck away to have some lunch." She

looked curiously at Ethan. "What are you guys doing here?"

"Well, I thought I had a makeup lesson at two today, but maybe I got it mixed up," Ethan said.

Macy glanced at her watch, then sprang to her feet. "Oh, shoot! No, you're right. I'm so sorry, Ethan. Here—let me just get organized and we can get started right away. I really am sorry." She quickly fastened the wicker basket, then hoisted it onto her arm. Ava stood, shook the blanket clean, and rolled it up.

"No need to rush on my account," Ethan said, holding up both hands. "Lizzie already rescheduled me."

"When I told him what you gals were up to, he insisted on coming down to help," Lizzie explained, "and with no other students until seven, I wasn't about to miss out on all the fun."

Ava turned to Macy. "If you don't need to hurry off, I can spare a few more hours," she said. "It couldn't hurt to double the manpower."

"You guys. . .Thank you," Macy said, smiling gratefully. "You're the best."

She nodded toward Ethan. "And with those muscles, I have just the shovel for you. Don't worry, the ground's not as frozen as you'd think."

"Sounds like a plan," Ethan said, laughing. He took the basket and blanket from them, then gestured toward the path. "Ladies first."

The foursome hiked back to the field. Ava glanced behind her and caught Ethan's eye. Yep. Same color as the sweater. He winked. She smiled and shook her head. There was just something about that boy.

Fourteen

The sky was fuschia and purple when Ava finally climbed the steps to her cabin. She kicked off her boots and left them on the porch. Once inside, she tossed a white paper sack onto the coffee table and flopped down onto the sofa. Ethan had insisted on picking up food for the crew.

Ava knew she should wash up, but she was ravenous. Harris had always said that good dirt made you stronger and bad dirt made you sick. If ever there was good dirt, it had to be here. She unwrapped the sandwich and found a perfect meatball sub. She took a huge bite, savoring the peppery basil sauce. Delicious. Carla was a culinary snob and Lucas was a vegan. . .Picturing their faces watching her devour these chunks of meat made her giggle. She pulled out a tiny bag of Cheetos and lay back on the couch, popping them into her mouth as she watched the sky thicken to an inky black.

She heard her phone vibrate. She reluctantly climbed to her

feet and grabbed her cell, the screen one notification box after the next: Carla, Carla, and more Carla. Ava called her mother's cell, the last number Carla had called from.

"Where have you been?! I've been calling you nonstop for *days*!"

"I tried calling you back a bunch of times yesterday," Ava said. "But you know how it is out here—no service. Sorry."

"If you weren't coming back so soon, I'd overnight you one of those Wifi anywhere thingies, you know, like the military uses."

Ava didn't bother asking how Carla knew anything about what the military used. "About that, Mom... So I know we had originally decided I'd fly back in a couple of days, but I think I need more time. I'm starting to make some real progress here and —"

"Forget about that, Ava," Carla interrupted. "Things have changed. Something much more important than fixing old family squabbles has presented itself. Something we've been building toward for years. I'd go back in time and bring you home yesterday if I could, but Thursday shouldn't be too late. Not if we can start planning now."

"Whoa, Mom, can you please back up?" Ava asked. "What are you talking about?" Carla was normally so controlled; Ava couldn't remember the last time she'd heard her so agitated.

"Friedrich Shubert—yes, *the* Friedrich Shubert—wants a commission. From you!" Carla exclaimed.

Ava paused. The name was familiar. . .Then suddenly, she placed it. "That patron family?" she asked. The German Shuberts had been responsible for financing some of the world's most famous works of art since the Middle Ages. You didn't need a Shubert patron to immortalize you in the art world, but having one would guarantee it.

"He called for you *himself*," Carla continued. "He wants to commission a mural for his ballroom and he wants *you*. You'll be in residence for at least six months, maybe more, if it goes well. But get this: his initial offer is half a million dollars! And that's not including travel, housing, per diem, etcetera. And I get the impression he is *very* open to negotiating."

Ava couldn't speak. She didn't need Carla to explain that this was a once-in-a-lifetime opportunity. Not only was this her chance to become a permanent name in the halls of art history, but a Shubert endorsement would set her up for a lifetime of commissions. And with that, she'd be rich. Things like this just didn't *happen*. . .And they certainly didn't happen twice.

"But what about Macy?" Ava asked finally. "You said—"

"Ava, Ava, Ava," Carla interrupted in a huff. "This is bigger than Macy. This is bigger than family. It's even bigger than *us*. Surely you can see that. This is your moment, your chance to enter the class of artists that history never forgets."

Ava's heart drummed. It didn't seem real. She still couldn't find words, not that Carla paused long enough to hear them anyway.

"Macy has made it this long on her own," Carla said, diplomatically, though the giddiness in her voice was barely masked. "I'm sure she'll still be there a year from now, sitting on her farm, same as today. Nothing ever changes there. You can always go back."

"You really don't get it, Mom," Ava said. "It's not that simple—"

"Ava, here's what I do get: I know you're gifted, but there's no way you're the only artist on this list. Don't get cocky. You're replaceable."

"Thanks for that confidence boost," Ava said, her voice catching in her throat. "But this is a lot... I need to think about it. Can I call you back?"

Carla half-scoffed, half-laughed, a note of hysteria in her voice. "Ava, you have more than yourself to think about here. Yes, you're the artist, but we are all a part of this brand with you. Me, Lucas, even Margo. Surely after all we've devoted to you, *years* of our lives, you'll make the only right choice."

"I said, I'll think about it, Mom," Ava said tightly. "I mean it."

"Fine, Ava, think about it. But call me back first thing in the morning and start sketching tonight. Shubert won't wait."

Ava said goodbye and hung up. A billion possibilities flooded her mind at once. Just then, she felt like one of those British royals: paraded out for events and to drum up funds, but with no real function or power of her own. She knew that was silly; at the end of the day, it was *her* artwork. Still, Ava wondered when she'd climbed into the backseat of her own career.

Maybe she'd never asked to drive in the first place. Ava remembered all-nighters spent cramming in art school, just as she remembered shapes repainted a hundred times until the image in front of her matched the one in her head. But had she ever spoken up about branding or marketing or any other necessary evil required for a career as a painter?

Ava realized she had been just about Kelly Oakenwood's age when Carla first began managing her work. She had been so desperate for her mother's attention after the years she'd gone without her. A part of her thought that if Carla had insisted she study medicine instead of art, she would have become a nurse without a second thought.

She had never refused Carla. And now, she never refused

Lucas. Not once had she turned down a meet-and-greet he arranged or canceled yet another interview for a college radio station. Ava could no longer tell where her dedication to her art ended and her need to please them began. If she could be the perfect daughter, the perfect client, the perfect artist, the perfect girlfriend—well, then maybe they would need her, too.

And now, she saw a mirrored future for Kelly. That girl had no clue just how talented she was. If something didn't change soon, Kelly would walk down the aisle and dedicate her life to making someone else happy. Only, her future would hold Happy Meal-scented minivans and casseroles for potlucks instead of gallery openings and business trips to Milan. Kelly deserved someone who recognized her gifts—someone who put her first.

That was it: Kelly just needed a chance. Ava tapped her photo app and scrolled to the picture of Kelly's carving. She hurried to the kitchen counter, flipping open her laptop as she slid onto the stool. She smiled when she found Dr. Pierson's contact info in her e-mail. Hopefully, it was still current. She typed out a quick message and sent it before she could change her mind.

She closed her eyes and rubbed her temples, willing her brain to quiet. She swallowed, but the metallic taste remained. Filthy and exhausted, she climbed onto the window seat, tucking her knees into her chest as she pressed her forehead against the cold glass. Either the sky had clouded or the moon was new—all she could see was black. She closed her eyes and saw the same.

She knew she needed to make a decision quickly. Carla was right about at least one thing: a man like Shubert wouldn't wait. But Ava was certain of something else... Neither would Macy.

Ava's phone vibrated against her thigh, waking her a few hours later. She blinked open her eyes and pulled her phone from underneath her outstretched body, squinting as she registered Lucas' name.

She quickly answered. "Babe, you OK?" she asked groggily.

"There you are!" Lucas said. "I tried to reach you earlier but figured you were out. Then, when Carla called tonight and told me the exciting news, I tried again. And again."

"You scared me," Ava said. "It's after one in the morning in New York. You're never up this late."

"That's because *you* scared *me*!" Lucas said. "I had visions of you lying on a pile of rocks in the woods after a herd of giant horses stampeded you."

Despite her sleepy haze, Ava giggled at the ridiculous image. "Well, you didn't need to be worried. I just dozed off. Today was all manual labor." She sat up and stretched, cradling her phone against her shoulder. "Wait, you didn't know about the Germany thing before tonight?"

"Carla said she wasn't sure if I was pro-Utah or, and I quote, 'pro-success,' and didn't want me to get to you first," Lucas said.

"Pro-Utah or pro-success," Ava repeated. That sounded like Carla. "So. . .which are you?"

"How could you even ask that?" Lucas said, his voice husky with the late hour. "I'm pro-Ava. Always. Whatever is best for you, best for your happiness, that's what matters to me."

Ava smiled.

"But let's back up," Lucas said. "Can you believe it? Friedrich Shubert?!"

"I'm still trying to wrap my mind around it," Ava admitted. She probably would be for days. "It sounds like a huge opportunity. And the money? Well, I can't pretend that's not exciting."

"I was surprised you didn't say yes right away, if I'm being honest," Lucas said. "I assume it was a shock."

"We're so close to our dream, Lucas," she said. "Carla mentioned a minimum of six months in Germany—how long will that set us back?"

"Set us back?!" Lucas said, his voice rising. "The publicity will be immense. It will launch your career into the stratosphere! You do realize that, right?"

"I was thinking more of the artists' residence," Ava replied. "And Lucas, you should see Macy. It took some time, but I think I'm finally getting to the heart of it all. She's not—"

"Whoa, wait a second," Lucas interrupted. "You're not thinking of turning this commission down, are you?"

"I thought you said you were pro-Ava!"

"I am," Lucas insisted. "And anyone with half a brain could see that what's good for you is this opportunity of a lifetime. Negotiate anything—more money, a few more days in Utah. But for the love of all that is holy, don't say no."

Ava pursed her lips and tried to steady her words. It was so hard to know her own mind when people kept talking and filling her brain with their ideas. Why had this never bothered her before? Just as quickly as the question entered her mind, she knew the answer: she'd never noticed.

But Lucas had a point. If she cared about her career at all, about her legacy in the art world, there was only one possible answer. But a half a year felt like an eternity to be away from her life. Her relationship with Lucas already seemed like it was moving forward at a snail's pace.

"Would you come with me if I went?" Ava asked.

The line was silent.

"Hello?"

She heard him sigh.

"Ava, you know what you've done to me. Before I met you? Well, you never said so, but I know you heard stories. I was a complete commitment-phobe. And then I met you and I never saw any other woman again. I still don't. I love you, babe. But I'm still me. My career will always come first. Plus, I have my other clients. If I went to Germany with you. . .Well, I'd just be there. Waiting for you. I wouldn't like that Lucas very much. And neither would you."

Ava closed her eyes tightly and tilted her head back, willing hot tears back into her head. She knew he was right. "I understand," she said softly.

"But let's put us aside for a minute, okay? If you don't go, you might never be able to build that dream of yours. Any of it. You really think your mom is going to give you that money if you turn this down? Even if your little adventure out there is a success, you know she'll never forgive you for that. You're not the only one who worked to get you to this place."

He didn't say it, but Ava got the message: *I've worked to get you here too, Ava. Don't let us down.*

"Think of it this way," Lucas continued. "If you decide to go, you'll be rich. Sure, this job alone could easily make you a millionaire, but think of every commission that will just drop into your lap after this. You could sneeze paint and people would mortgage a house to buy it. Who cares if you build the artists' residence or not? You'll have made your mark already. People will learn your name in art school."

"Who cares?!" Ava repeated, her voice shrill, even to her own ears. "I thought this was your dream too?"

All those late nights together, drafting proposals, crunching numbers, Googling artists from tiny countries whose names they couldn't pronounce—Ava knew he couldn't fake the excitement he'd shown when they'd created their dream roster of the first five residents. Lucas had wanted this too. She curled her legs under her, wrapping herself in the throw blanket.

"My dad was a musician," Lucas said. "You know the story; I don't need to rehash it. But I saw him bleed and sweat every minute for his dream. I wouldn't call him a starving artist, but he was usually just one day away from busking in the subway. I watched my mom stay up late trying to make the numbers add up, always afraid of being evicted or worse. I won't ever end up like that. Or put someone I love in that state of constant anxiety."

But you also aren't an artist, Ava thought. No one chose this life because it guaranteed security; they chose it because it was in the fiber of their being. Ava knew she had been so fortunate to make a living as an artist. But even if she was only ever selling her pieces at the Brooklyn Flea, scraping together her rent each month, she couldn't imagine doing anything else.

"My dream, Ava?" Lucas continued, pulling her away from her thoughts. "My dream is of comfortable success. Space to breathe. A week ago, that looked like a little artists' retreat with a gallery that had real potential to turn a profit. It was a great idea, noble, even. But this commission is a guarantee. A sure thing. Let's just say my dream is where the sure bets are."

"I'm considering it, Lucas," Ava said. "I really am. I just have some things I need to figure out first."

"Well, do it fast," he said. "I'll see you soon, right?"

"Soon. Right."

What choice did she have?

Fifteen

Ava sipped her fourth cup of coffee as she stared at her blank sketchpad. It had taken her a long time to fall back to sleep the night before. She had Googled the Shuberts, then gone down a rabbit hole clicking links about Friedrich. More recent photos showed a man in his sixties or so, always photographed with an amused smile. She could see why he had reached out to her; from what she could find online, his personal collection was icy and bare. Cold, linear, and very similar to the work she was becoming known for. It looked as though his entire collection had been acquisitions, and most of the artists had been prominent decades ago. An art connoisseur with unlimited funds like Friedrich needed a commission. Her piece would be the central gem in his already glittering crown.

Once Ava had finally fallen asleep, she had never drifted past the surface, waking in fits what felt like every hour. By the time the first yellows crept into the sky, she had given up and started drinking coffee.

She flipped open her sketchpad and read her list with a new lens:

1. Find Macy a date.
2. Take back the field.
3. Get Macy to have fun with friends again.
4. Help Macy accept that Ben is gone.

She felt ashamed of how simple she'd tried to make everything. This was Macy's life. And what did Ava know about a soulmate? She couldn't even get Lucas to take a trip with her, let alone make a commitment. Still, Ava's presence and enthusiasm had seemed to help Macy, at least a little. But there was so much more yet to be done.

She flipped to a fresh sheet and pulled out her pencils. She smoothly sketched a few lines, then some curves. The triangles that adorned the facades of traditional German homes. The rounded arches of the portico that framed the house in Munich where she had stayed during a semester abroad. Her memories of Germany were filled with images of strength and beauty, but she'd have to do better than that. She needed to dig deep, but her heart just wasn't in it this morning.

She swallowed the grainy dregs of her coffee, then threw on her peacoat. With her sketchpad and pencils under one arm, she stepped out onto her frigid porch and slipped on her borrowed muck boots. She was glad she'd bought new jeans. As the temperatures dropped with each passing day, Ava became aware of just how much time she spent indoors in New York. It never mattered what she was wearing during the thirty seconds she was outside between the car and yet another revolving glass door.

Her breath fogged in front of her as she crunched across the frosty grass behind the cabin. She stood under the bay window and absorbed the view, this time without glass in the way. The mountains stretched the horizon, the snowcapped peaks the only indication of just how far away they truly were. Between Ava and the skyline, the fiery autumn trees danced in the crisp wind while the pastures stretched sleepily below. She simply breathed, allowing all of her senses to be consumed by this tableau. It was Mother Nature at her fullest. Harsh and jagged, warm and safe. Alive and dying. Nature wasn't just one or the other. Why did her art need to be? Was it because she always did as she was told?

Ava shook the thought from her mind before awkwardly climbing a cluster of low boulders. Her boots nearly slid off her feet several times and her palms became numb as they gripped the damp stone. Still, she climbed on. When she reached the top of the tallest rock, she sat, the cold wind penetrating her thin clothing. She felt alert and alive. This was better than coffee.

She carefully balanced her pencil box beside her, then flipped her sketchpad to a blank sheet. Her eyes on the horizon, she began to draw. Soon, the flow took over and her fingers could barely keep up with the images burning her mind. Pencil after pencil dulled until she knew she'd need to sharpen the lot before she could draw anymore. She held up the sketch in front of her to compare it to the real thing. The same craggy mountain lined the top. The same swirls of shedding trees. The same zigzags and angles of the fields below. It was beautiful, and it almost captured the magic in front of her. Almost.

Ava blinked as she entered the stable. Her eyes took a moment to adjust, the skylights offering less illumination than usual on this cloudy afternoon. Carrots in one hand and a sketch in the other, she peeked into the office but found it empty. She looked at the drawing she carried. It wasn't quite realistic—it still featured her trademark ambiguous shapes—but it was clearly the mountains above Cobalt. And the colors. . .It had taken hours to get them just right, but she knew she had nailed the blood orange, the burnt red, and the steel gray of the distant peaks. Once she'd finished, she decided she wanted Macy to have it.

She could make out soft voices down the aisle, just past Cash's stall. As she drew closer, she heard a hushed giggle.

"Macy?" Ava called.

No reply.

Cash's stall was empty. Then she heard the voices again, coming from the open tack room. She found Ethan huddled with a stunning girl, who couldn't be older than nineteen. Ava couldn't help noticing her supermodel-long legs or the jet-black hair that cascaded to her waist. Or the fact that she was watching Ethan like a cat that had found a bowl of cream.

"Ava, hey," Ethan said, backing up a few steps as soon as he saw her.

"I'm sorry," Ava said, getting the message from Legs' death stare that she was interrupting a private conversation. "I was looking for Macy. Have you seen her?"

"Not this morning," Ethan said, then looked from Ava to Legs.

"Ava, this is Shelly. Shelly, Ava."

"Oh, *you're* Ava the art girl!" Legs-now-called-Shelly squealed. "I hear you're famous. Ethan told me about you. He didn't say you were hot though."

She giggled and nudged Ethan with her elbow in an inside-joke kind of way. Ethan studied his feet.

Ava lamely raised her fistful of carrots. "I just brought these for Gunner. Sorry again to interrupt your. . .well, whatever. If you see Macy, please tell her I'm looking for her."

She hurried out the door, blood draining from her face. She heard footsteps behind her.

"Hold on, Ava," Ethan said. She turned and saw Shelly standing close behind him. "You wanna hit a trail with us? Shelly just asked me to show her the—"

"Oh my *gawd*, let me see that!" Shelly squealed, ripping Ava's sketch from her hand. "Did you draw this? Is that an Ava-the-art-girl orig?"

Orig. *Not a word*, thought Ava, but she nodded politely. Shelly stared at the sketch.

"Totally adorable," Shelly decided before looping her arm around Ethan's own. "Ethan, look how adorable. This could totally be one of those posters you win at the festival, right?"

Ava's smile felt like it would crack.

Ethan looked bemused. "You need any help, Ava?"

"I think I can handle a few carrots," she said. "But thanks anyway. Nice to meet you, Shelly."

Ava walked straight past Gunner's stall, not even stopping to pat his nose. She'd come back with the carrots later.

Sixteen

Ava had been at her easel all morning. She twisted a piece of hair with her fingertips as she studied her sketch, the red diffusing to the color of muted clay as she continued to blend with her other hand. After the embarrassing encounter with Ethan and Shelly the day before, Ava had retreated to her cabin. To her surprised delight, her fingers itched to get back to drawing.

Before the sun had disappeared behind the mountain skyline, Ava had drawn six more landscapes, each capturing a different angle of the ranch. The rooftop of the stable, the rock above the creek, the barn owl's view of the arena below. . .She could have drawn all night, but eventually dark shadows splayed across the paper. She knew the natural light was worth waiting for. Exhausted, she'd heated a frozen pizza, eaten the entire thing, and collapsed without brushing her teeth or putting on pajamas.

That morning, she had awakened at dawn. She'd placed each finished sketch along the kitchen counter, and then against the windowsills as she ran out of room. She wanted to translate each one into paint, but her mind was flooded with other images that needed to be birthed first. Her fingers were becoming blistered, but she didn't care. In fact, she hardly noticed as the cabin filled with new drawings, and her pencils grew shorter with each sharpening.

Ava picked up her most recent sketch. She ran her thumb over the graphite lines, blurring the edges ever so slightly. Abstract could spark the imagination, sure, but there was something about realism that held its own power. A muscular gray quarter horse with warm eyes and a proud stance stared back at her.

She smiled as she set the drawing against the little window over the kitchen sink. Gunner had become a frequent player in her artwork this week, but this was his first solo portrait. She glanced at the clock on the microwave.

"Oh, shoot!" she exclaimed. How could it be nine-thirty already? There was no point in calling; she knew no one would have service at the field.

She ripped off her day-old clothes and threw on high-waisted jeans and her newly-purchased pink hoodie. She quickly brushed her teeth, sprayed her scalp with dry shampoo, and ran her fingers through her hair before throwing it back into a loose braid.

Before running out the door, she glanced in the mirror. She was no Shelly, but it would have to do. She ran outside, slamming the door behind her.

Ava half-ran, half-waddled to the field in her borrowed muck boots. Her black Justins had been comfy to work in the last time, but she had already grown too attached to them to get them any muddier than they already were. She spotted the red truck and Range Rover parked just outside the fence. Lizzie, Ethan, and Macy looked up as she approached.

"Well, look what the cat drug in!" Lizzie teased. "Don't let us interrupt your beauty sleep."

"You should have come by and knocked!" Ava said. "I've been up since six. I was drawing and I just. . .Well, I'm sorry. I lost track of time." She spotted her calfskin gloves and grabbed them. "What can I do?"

"Don't worry, we knew you'd jump in when you could," Macy said kindly. "If we hadn't heard from ya by lunch, we decided we'd come knock down the door."

Ava glanced at Ethan, who gave her a little smile. She gave him a polite nod but avoided his gaze as she grabbed a bucket of tools and joined Macy.

"Wanna walk the irrigation line with me and see if we can find any leaks?" Macy asked.

"I only understand about sixty percent of those words, but I'll follow your lead," Ava said.

Macy laughed. "Perfect. Basically, I'll turn on the water, and you tell me when it sprays in weird directions where no plant would grow."

"Sounds like a plan," Ava said.

They walked to the end of the field. Ava noticed everything already looked more tended. The progress was beginning to show much faster with four of them working. If she concentrated, she could picture the entire field alive with vibrant tomatoes and winding vines of cucumbers. They had a ways to go, but they were definitely getting there.

Macy bent down and twisted a spigot. Down the row, Ava saw water spray into the air.

"I don't think anything grows up there," Ava said.

"See? You're an expert already," Macy said, laughing. She turned the water off and looped black tape around the hole. "Were you working on something for Carla?"

"Not exactly, though I should have been," Ava replied. "It's hard to explain. But I was working on something more like what I used to do, back when I lived here."

"I'm glad to hear it," Macy said, with a little smile. "Fair warning: This is going to take forever. But at least with the two of us, it'll be a lot more fun."

Macy called instructions and Ava did her best to follow them. It was tedious but easy work. Ava marked the leaks and then, when the water was off, they glued them with a sort of adhesive she had never seen before. She did her best not to look at Ethan as she waited for Macy to turn on the water again, but she could feel his presence across the field. The pull was electric, but she focused on the task in front of her.

He has Shelly, and I have Lucas. And that's the end of that.

Lunch was savory fried chicken, mustard potato salad, and homemade cornbread, courtesy of Lizzie. Ava refilled their water bottles from the thermos in Macy's pickup.

"Well, I definitely got my steps in today," Lizzie said, glancing at her watch. "Fifteen thousand and counting! I better get back and finish the newsletter."

"I'll drive you," Macy said. "I know if I don't, I'll probably forget my three o'clock altogether." She turned to Ava. "I'd say you more than made up for joining us late. Want a ride back?"

"You know, I think I'll keep going a bit longer," Ava said. "Now that you showed me what to do, I kind of want to keep patching these leaks. It's meditative, in a weird way."

Macy smiled. "I won't say no to free labor. Don't have too much fun without me." She stood and walked toward the truck. After loading her tools into the bed, she turned back to Ava. "Do you want to come over for dinner tonight?" she asked. "I don't cook well enough to feed people I like, but there's a Chinese place that actually delivers all the way out here. If you don't have plans already."

"You know I don't have plans," Ava said, laughing. "That sounds great."

"Should we say seven?" Macy asked. "Gives me a chance to shower after lessons and open a good bottle of pinot."

"Sounds glorious," Ava said.

Macy looked at Ethan. "You headed back too?"

"It's pretty slow in the office this week," he said. "I think I'll keep going. I can be of more use here." He didn't look at Ava.

"You don't need to—" Ava began.

"Awesome idea," Macy interrupted. "Ava, it would be really hard for you to run the water and mark leaks by yourself. Thanks, Ethan."

She watched Macy and Lizzie drive off, the truck disappearing around the edge of the trees. Now, it was just the two of them.

"Hi," Ethan said as the engine faded out of earshot.

"Hi?"

He just shrugged and smiled.

Those perfect teeth. Ava found herself wondering if he'd had braces. Her stomach wobbled. She took a deep breath and straightened her shoulders.

"We doing this or what?" she asked.

They worked for hours. Ethan turned the water on and off at her command, and Ava marked and dried the leaks. Every so often, they switched jobs. Beyond simple orders, they didn't talk much.

"Leak!" Ava called, as a particularly forceful stream of water spurted from the line. Suddenly, the hose jerked from her hand, blasting her in the face. "Off!" she shrieked.

"What?!" Ethan called from across the field.

"I said, TURN IT OFF!" Ava wailed, but the water kept spraying. Suddenly, Ethan was beside her.

He burst into laughter when he saw her doused bangs matted against her face. "Oops," he said. "I couldn't hear you."

"Oh, you think that's funny, do you?" Ava said, her clothes dripping onto the dead grass. She grabbed the line and turned it onto Ethan, spraying him. He coughed and sputtered as the stream hit his face. Then he wrestled the tubing out of Ava's hands, the water shooting into the sky as he aimed it upward.

"At first I couldn't hear you, but now I'd say you deserve it!" Ethan said, turning the water back onto her.

She shrieked and lunged at him, knowing she'd never get

it back now. He wrapped his arms around her wet body to restrain her, and although she continued to fight, a part of her surrendered into his grip. Her stomach clenched as his hard chest pressed against her back. He laughed, and as she spun around to face him, his eyes gave him away. He wanted her. Ava knew that if she leaned closer right that second, Ethan would kiss her. She held his gaze. After a moment, she yanked away from his grip, then jogged over to the spigot and turned the water off.

Ava rubbed her cheek against the hood of the BYU sweatshirt Ethan had found for her in his trunk. They sat on the rock by the creek, both drying in the dappled afternoon sun. Luckily, the day had warmed, and Ava's teeth no longer chattered.

Ethan sat a few feet away. She couldn't resist studying him as he stared at the rushing water. Up close, she could see little lines around the corners of his eyes. Not surprising for a man who smiled as much as he did. He had thick, long lashes that curled to his brows. Lashes like that were always wasted on boys.

He passed her the box of Cracker Jacks he'd found in his car. They'd been sitting here for at least an hour now, drying and talking. About riding, about art. . .about everything easy and nothing too personal. At some point, they'd fallen into a comfortable silence, neither seeming to want to be the one to end this respite.

"Ethan," Ava said, breaking the quiet. "Why did you stay? In Cobalt?"

Ethan looked up at her. "You know about Jess," he said simply.

Ava shrugged, embarrassed. So, her name was Jess. Jess Kidd. It sounded like a name out of the Wild West. "I heard in town," she explained. "I'm sorry about what happened. I'm surprised you didn't leave after. . .but I'm glad you didn't."

Ethan stretched onto his side, propping himself on one elbow. His shirt rode up a little and Ava tried not to look at the inch of his toned stomach that was now exposed. "It worked out," he said.

"Did it?" Ava asked.

Ethan smiled, but his eyes were pained. "I thought I was coming to Cobalt because I'd found my person. At the time, that's all I could see." He picked up a twig and began to peel the bark off with a fingernail, avoiding Ava's gaze. "When she left, I realized it wasn't her I missed. Not once the shock wore off." He shrugged. "I missed having a person. I missed the idea of forever. I think we both knew deep down that we weren't right for each other." He tossed the stick into the water, but his fingers still twisted restlessly.

"I was angry and humiliated," he admitted. "But if it wasn't for her, I might still be in Vegas, hating my job. No matter how great my year looked on paper, I wasn't okay working every waking moment. I needed to slow down and build a life on my own, one that made me happy. I have. The house, my firm, this town. Plus Maggie, of course."

"I'm sorry she did that to you," Ava said. "I kind of hate her for it."

He looked at her again, this time studying her face as if really seeing her for the first time. "I've forgiven Jess, for what she did," he said finally. "At least in my heart. I wish it hadn't happened that way, but I'm glad she left me."

Ava tucked her knees against her chest, the huge hoodie like a dress on her. "You make it all sound so simple," she said. "Moving on, following your destiny. For every person who tells me to focus on what matters, there's another who says to seize the day and hustle. How did you know who to listen to?"

"I listen to myself," he said simply. Ethan looked at her, and Ava saw a barely-masked longing in his eyes. He scooted closer. "Once I started to make choices with my gut, the other voices got quieter," he said, softly. "I realized no one really knows what they're talking about anyway. I won't lie. At first, I was terrified. But it was the right move and deep down, I knew."

Ava nodded. Her head felt like an entire press conference of voices sometimes. She wasn't sure her own voice was even among them. Something didn't feel right in her life.

This time, it was her who scooted closer. If she reached out her arm, she'd be touching him. She tucked her hands into her lap.

"What if you listen to this inner voice and follow it, but then you lose everything anyway?" Ava asked, as much to herself as to Ethan.

"You mean like Macy might be doing?" Ethan asked. Ava studied him. She'd been so wrapped up in her own problems, she hadn't realized what was right in front of her. Ethan had created his path and it had bought him freedom; Macy had created hers and she might lose everything. Ava didn't know what she was supposed to take away from that. And how had Ethan even known about Macy's situation?

"She told me about everything this morning," he explained, as if reading her mind.

"I guess I meant it in a more general sense," Ava said, "but Macy's financial situation is really scary. I wish she had told me sooner. I only just found out myself." She pulled the band from her hair, unwrapping her tangled mane from its loose braid. She ran her fingers through it self-consciously: she didn't need a mirror to know she must still look like a drowned rat. Oh well. The last thing she should be trying to do was impress Ethan.

"I asked her what she was receiving from the military, but she was a little vague," Ethan said. "She did say it wasn't enough, that she needed the farmers' market income, too. I didn't want to push her. It's not really my business."

"She was kind of evasive when I asked her, too," Ava said. "I think I know why. I tried to Google how much spouses get when a soldier goes missing, and I think it's the usual pay. But Macy mentioned a lump sum she got and the only thing I could find about that was in death benefits."

Ethan cocked his head. "Meaning what, exactly?"

"Meaning they had enough reason to designate Ben as killed in action, not missing in action."

They sat quietly for a few moments, the weight of it all leaving no room for other words. If the military knew Ben was dead, then Macy was truly alone in her resolution. Ava remembered watching a documentary about climbers who died on Everest, how no one could safely retrieve their bodies, so they had to stay there in the ice and snow. She wondered if it was kind of like that.

"I don't think it helps that no one knows Macy's in trouble," Ava continued. "I never would have guessed if she hadn't told me, though she seemed to think it was obvious."

"I had no idea either," Ethan said. "Not that she'd run around telling her students. But in my line of work, I'm used to getting a good read on businesses."

"Well, how can people help if they don't know?" Ava asked. "I mean, *we* know, but what can we do?"

"You *are* helping," Ethan said. "Look around—I think there are more ways to lend a hand than just passing out money. I didn't know Macy before she lost her husband, but I've never seen her so hopeful. I don't know if I'd ever seen her laugh at all before this past week. Even with all she's dealing with, she seems lighter since you came."

"I'm sorry for trying to set you up with her," Ava said. "You were a really good sport to go along with it." She hesitated for a moment before adding, "For the record, I never would have suggested it if I had known about Shelly." She stared at the water, avoiding his eyes.

"Wait, what?" Ethan asked. "Shelly, like barn Shelly?"

"Barn Shelly, supermodel Shelly, call her what you want, but yes, that Shelly," Ava said.

Ethan scrunched up his face in confusion. "I'm not with her," he said.

"Anyone could see she's enamored with you," Ava said. "You can't tell me you just let any random woman hang all over you."

He shrugged. "I can't say I noticed."

"You expect me to believe that there's a girl who looks like that and worships the ground you walk on. . .and you're not interested?" Ava said, raising an eyebrow.

"I'm not blind," Ethan said. "I know she's attractive. If she has a crush on me, then I'm flattered. But she's a kid, and I'm not looking for the same kind of woman I did during my frat years.

She's not my type."

"Well, what is your type, if not gorgeous and interested?"

"I know her when I see her," Ethan said, holding her gaze.

Heat rushed through her stomach. She swallowed. After a beat, it was Ava who looked away first. "Well, it's none of my business," she said quietly. They sat in silence again, the only sounds the cawing of a distant bird, the water rushing past, and the light breeze whispering through the woods.

"You know, I worked in a lender's office for a few years right out of undergrad," Ethan said. "I don't know how much good it would do, but I could look over Macy's loan, see if anything jumps out at me."

"Thanks, Ethan," Ava said gratefully. Suddenly, her vision blurred with hot, unexpected tears. She tipped her face away from him and tried to hold her voice steady. "Unless we find someone to invest in the riding academy, she's going to lose the soul of this place," she said. "All the land will be gone, after a century." She took a steadying breath. "I just feel like, if I'd come sooner or had been there for Macy, this might never have happened. The butterfly effect and all that. If I had never deserted her in the first place, *everything* could be different." She blinked and the tears spilled down her cheeks.

"You're right," Ethan said, his voice hardly above a whisper. "Everything would be different. But maybe then, she never would have even met Ben. And maybe I wouldn't be sitting here with you now. The butterfly effect and all that."

He touched her cheek, turning her face towards his. He gently wiped her tear-streaked face with his thumbs, his rough fingertips electrifying her. Her mouth was dry as she looked up at him, and as their eyes met, she felt a hunger intensify deep from within.

It was hard to say who leaned in first. But when their lips met, their bodies seemed to melt together automatically. His lips brushed against hers softly at first, then urgently. She wrapped her arms around his neck, pressing him even closer. He ran his fingers through her hair and wound it around his hand, pulling her head even tighter to his. Ava's body vibrated with need.

Suddenly, Lucas' smiling face flashed across Ava's mind. She tore herself from Ethan's embrace and leaped to her feet. "What am I doing?" she said, her voice high-pitched.

"Are you okay?" Ethan asked. He stood and reached for her, his fingertips brushing her shoulder. She jerked away and started to frantically tug her borrowed sweatshirt over her head. "Keep it, you'll freeze."

She darted back to the field, Ethan close behind.

"You want to head back?" he called.

She said nothing.

"Ava!" he yelled. A slight quiver in his voice made her stop. She turned back.

"I don't know what just happened back there," he said, closing the distance as he spoke. "But you can't pretend it wasn't—well, it wasn't *something*. I know you feel it too." He stopped beside her but kept his arms safely by his side. "I've never met someone like you, Ava. That's not some line. If you want to pretend that nothing just happened, go for it. But I can't."

His eyes searched hers. Ava looked away. She said nothing, just continued walking.

She walked past the SUV, past the stable, never stopping until she reached her cabin. She tucked her face deep inside the hood so anyone she passed wouldn't see the endless tears still streaming down her face.

Ava closed the door softly behind her and pulled off Ethan's sweatshirt. She dropped it into her laundry pile in the corner of the cabin and groaned, burying her face in her hands.

What had she done? She kissed Ethan, and even worse, she had wanted to do so much more. His soft lips pressing needfully against hers had lit up Ava's entire body. But that wasn't hers to feel. It was a horrible mistake. Poor, devoted Lucas. Ava had never cheated on any boyfriend in her entire life. Should she tell him? Did she have to?

Ava bit her lip until it hurt. She knew better. Lucas was her life, her home—not to mention, her publicist. Sure, sometimes it didn't feel like they were on the same page lately, but how could it when they weren't even in the same time zone? Soon enough, she'd be back in the city, back to work, and back beside Lucas. Assuming he forgave her.

She couldn't deny there was something magnetic about Ethan. Every time he entered the room, her heart drummed faster. She wanted to be close to him, her face burning anytime he looked at her. But even she knew that was kid stuff—a crush, an infatuation. That wasn't real. And it didn't last.

And even if it did, what then? Ethan made it very clear city life was not for him. And Ava certainly wasn't about to give up her career because of some fall fling. And again, there was Lucas.

She couldn't breathe. She couldn't think. She felt numb and

frozen all at the same time, and she couldn't come up with a single person she could talk to about any of it.

She turned on the shower and let the steam fill the tiny bathroom before stepping in. She twisted the faucet even hotter, letting the scalding deluge rush over her head. The water drowned out all sound, all thought. Even after she'd scrubbed her body twice, she still didn't feel clean.

Ava blasted a "Best of Queen" playlist from her phone on full volume, then wrapped herself in the terry robe she'd found in the small closet on her first night in the cabin. She took her time blow-drying her hair, then curling it into smooth waves. She had no reason to give herself the full glam treatment, but she needed to stay mindlessly busy.

Ava glanced at the clock as she walked back into the living area. It was barely two; there were still five hours to kill before she was due at Macy's for dinner. She knew there was no point trying to work right then. Her mind felt like a pinball machine, pinging in different directions every few seconds.

She checked her e-mail, ignoring anything that looked remotely work-related. A message from Dr. Erik Pierson caught her eye. She quickly skimmed his note and smiled. She grabbed her purse and flew out the door to the rental car.

She had found a mission. She would go to town and visit the art store. Plus, she could grab something from the market to take with her to Macy's house that evening. Anything to keep her mind off men.

Kelly looked up, her professional expression dissolving into a huge grin when Ava entered Oakenwood & Sons an hour later. Ava gave her a little nod, then waited for her to finish with her customer, a wiry older man in a battered driving cap.

"See, most people suggest basswood as the best wood for beginners," Kelly said to him, gesturing enthusiastically to an open book on the counter. "But I really like white beech as a starting point. You can't usually get the Australian kind, but I stock it because I like it for my own work. It has more color variation than basswood, which I think is good to get used to manipulating as early as possible. Plus, it's just prettier."

The man shook his head and smiled.

"I knew I came to the right place," he said. "At that uppity shop in Salt Lake? That guy was three times your age and not nearly as smart. White beech it is!"

"Excellent choice, Mr. Collins," Kelly said warmly. "You won't regret it—you just have to promise to stop by and show me your progress."

Kelly rang up his purchase, then turned to Ava once he'd gone. "I thought you'd be back in New York by now!"

"You know family business," Ava said with a shrug. "It's like a cat. You think you're in charge, but it's gonna do what it wants no matter what you say."

Kelly laughed. "I'm more of a dog person myself," she said.

Ava reached into her bag and pulled out the stack of papers she had printed at the office supply store. She set them in front of Kelly, who looked back at her with a confused smile.

"What is this?" Kelly asked.

"An application for the New York Fine Arts Conservatory," Ava said.

"Wow, okay... But, um, why did you give it to me?" Her round eyes blinked innocently back at Ava; she looked younger than seventeen.

"The application process is by invitation only," Ava said. "I hope you don't mind, but I snuck a picture of your carving into the e-mail of the enrollment committee."

"But that piece is my worst one!" Kelly exclaimed.

"That's your *worst* one?" Ava asked. She couldn't imagine what could be more beautiful and intricate than that little boy fishing on the bridge.

"That's not the point," Kelly said, taking a small step back from the counter. "I can't go even if I did somehow get in."

Ava had expected this response. "I know conservatory programs are crazy overpriced, and they take up too much time to be able to work a part-time job," she said. "That's why I put out a feeler to Dr. Pierson, one of the school's board members and an old teacher of mine. He said with your raw talent, he thinks you'd be a shoo-in for a scholarship, which includes tuition, room and board, and a stipend."

Kelly's eyes widened, her mouth gaping open and then quickly closing. After a moment, she shook her head. "I'm grateful," she said. "I really am. But I'm getting married. Soon. I can't ask my husband to live thousands of miles away from me for years while I take some art classes."

"*Some art classes?*" Ava repeated. "Kelly, this conservatory only has a two-percent acceptance rate, and that's after every applicant has been *invited*. If you graduate from there, scholarship or not, you're guaranteed to have doors open to you before you even finish."

"It sounds amazing," Kelly said, pressing her hands together against her chest. "Truly. And I'm honored! Especially that someone like you thinks I'm even worth the trouble. If you'd told me about this when I was fifteen, I'd be over the moon. But things have changed since then, and I want this life. I can't be selfish. I just. . .That's just not me."

Ava blinked as her excitement deflated. Couldn't Kelly see how incredible of an opportunity this was?

"Tell you what," Ava said. "I'll just leave the papers with you. Would you look it over and check out the website? Just see what it has to offer?"

Kelly nodded. "That's the least I could do," she said. "I'm sorry you went to all this trouble."

"I believe in your work, Kelly. I just hope you do too."

Kelly looked as if she might say something, but instead just pressed her lips into a tiny smile. She studied the paper again.

"I wrote my number on the back," Ava said, as she turned to leave. "And you know where to find me."

"Okay—Hey," Kelly said, interrupting herself. "Charlie and I are gonna get dinner. Do you want to come? He's got a list of projects from my dad to work on in the shop, so we thought we'd try that new Mexican place after we close up. He's dying to meet you. At the risk of sounding super lame, I sort of gushed about you."

"I already have dinner plans tonight, but rain check?"

"Definitely rain check," Kelly said.

Ava headed for the front, turning back as she reached the

door. "I hope Charlie knows how lucky he is," she said.

Kelly smiled. "We're both the luckiest. Thanks, Ava."

Seventeen

Ava knocked on Macy's door, a bottle of wine in one hand and a small envelope in the other. It felt good to be an invited guest for a change. The crisp air stung her nose as she waited, a hint of the barren winter just weeks away. Only the humming wind interrupted the absolute silence. She walked to the edge of the front porch and leaned over the railing. The moon was nowhere to be found, but the black sky was speckled with thousands of shimmering pinpricks.

The door swung open behind her. Ava turned to find Macy grinning at her.

"Never gets old, does it?" Macy asked, nodding toward the sky.

"I wouldn't know," Ava said. "But I can't imagine it does."

"Should we eat out here?" Macy asked.

Ava hesitated before shrugging with what she hoped passed as casual indifference.

Macy laughed. "Kidding," she said. "It's forty degrees! Come in."

Ava followed her into the foyer and handed Macy the bottle of wine. "Brought this: 19 Crimes. Nothing fancy, but it's a favorite. I'm not sure what pairs well with Chinese food."

"It's perfect," Macy said. "Plus, I just drink what I like no matter what's on the menu."

"Me too!" Ava said. "I swear, food never tastes any different no matter what I'm drinking."

"It's that famous MacDaniel palate, or lack thereof," Macy said, laughing, her eyes glittering, playfully. "Remember that time your mom visited—"

"And Harris dumped that bottle she brought because he said it was too sweet! Oh my gosh, yes!"

"I can't believe Aunt Carla paid eight hundred dollars for one bottle," Macy said, shaking her head. "Maybe the gene is recessive, and she knows something we don't."

"Nah," Ava said. "She just looks to other people to tell her what to like. We have our own taste."

"I've got a whole wall of wine and I never have anyone to drink it with," Macy said. "So how about we call this one an appetizer and get to it?"

"Sounds like a plan," Ava said, then handed her the envelope she'd brought. "Almost forgot."

Macy opened it, eyeing her with curiosity. She pulled out three packets of tomato seeds and laughed. "What's this?" she asked.

"My contribution to dinner!" Ava said. "Well, future dinner. I know they'll take some time to grow, but I guess I'll have to come back to find out, won't I?"

Macy studied the little packets in her hand but said nothing.

"I won't say it's time to start over," Ava continued, "or time for a new beginning... But I think it's time to plant the seeds for the next chapter. At least sixty seeds' worth, anyway."

Macy's eyes shone as she looked up at Ava and smiled.

"Thank you, Ava," she said, finally. "This is so thoughtful. . .and these are good ones, too. Early Girl was a favorite of Ben's. It fruits early in the season and he's—well, he was so impatient." She tucked the packets back into the envelope and cleared her throat. "But not yet. It's not time yet."

"Oh. Okay, yeah," Ava sputtered. "Of course. It's totally your call."

"...Because tomatoes get planted in the spring," Macy said, flashing Ava a mischievous smile.

"You are so mean!" Ava said, and they both erupted into laughter. It felt good. It felt like old times. "Glad to see you haven't lost your charming sense of humor."

"Sometimes you make it too easy, city girl," Macy said. "But actually, I pulled out a couple of Ben's books this morning that have winter crops for this zone. You were right. It's time."

Ava followed her into the living room, her chest tightening with every step. This had been her home once. At first glance, it looked just like it had when she was a girl; upon closer inspection, she realized it had been updated seamlessly. The entire house boasted new windows and high-end appliances. The wall bordering the dining room had been removed, creating a huge, open space with sliding doors to a back deck that Ava imagined would offer stunning views of the woods in the daylight.

"Wow, Mace, the place looks ridiculously amazing," she said. "I feel like people either remodel or they restore. . .but somehow you've done both. It's perfect."

Macy smiled. "We did it together, Ben and I. His dad was a contractor and Ben's first job had been as his assistant. I have no real building skills myself, but I picked everything out and did all the shopping. And I spent a lot of time researching the history of old farmhouses like this. I didn't want it to change too much."

"Sounds like you guys could have had your own HGTV show," Ava said.

"Seriously!" Macy said, laughing. "You should have heard us argue. He always wanted to save money and keep stuff simple and practical, and then I'd come in with my Pinterest boards and a Craigslist ad for a thousand-dollar vintage staircase railing. Would have made for some juicy TV!"

"I would totally watch that show," Ava said.

"Me too," Macy said, taking in the dining room as if seeing it for the first time.

"You know, Ethan is really into restoration, too," Ava said. "You should see what he's done to his place so far."

"You've been to his house?" Macy asked, raising an eyebrow.

Ava gave a quick, awkward shrug. "What can I do to help?" she asked, desperate to change the subject.

"Oh, the food! Thank you for reminding me!" Macy said. She took Ava's coat and hung it in the foyer. "I'll send the order through—I wanted to wait until you got here. There's a bar cart over there with glasses and an opener... Wanna pour the first round?"

Ava found a corkscrew and opened the wine. She grabbed two glasses from the cart, noticing only one was free of a fine layer of dust. She wiped the other with her shirt and poured two generous servings. She carried the wine to the dining room, where she found Macy with her laptop open on the table in front of her.

"Cheers," Ava said, handing a glass to Macy.

"To chapters yet unwritten," she replied.

"I'll drink to that," said Ava, as they clinked glasses.

"I need to respond to a quick e-mail from a student, so why don't you relax in the living room and I'll be right there?" Macy said.

"Sure I can't do anything?"

Macy shook her head. "The table's set and the food is on its way."

"Okay, well, holler if you need a refill," Ava said.

"Holler?" Macy repeated. "That didn't take long. You almost sound like you belong here."

Ava smiled. "Who says I don't?"

She walked back to the living area and noticed a gallery wall of photos. The first was a faded photo of Macy, probably six or seven, bleach-blonde tangled curls almost obscuring her face. She looked tiny on top of an old blue four-wheeler that Ava remembered. Harris stood next to her, playfully feigning terror.

This must have been Macy's birthday, the year Harris had given that four-wheeler to her as a present. Ava suddenly realized she must have been the one to take that picture.

The next photo was of Ava and Macy, not much older than in the first, perched on the tire swing that used to hang from the towering oak out front. Ava was suspended on her belly through the rubber opening, arms spread wide. Macy stood on top, flashing the camera a defiant smile while holding the rope with only one arm. They sported matching Grand Canyon t-shirts and missing front teeth.

Then, sixteen-year-old Macy behind the wheel of Harris' old F-150, with Ava perched on the edge of the truck bed. All they had cared about was passing their driver's tests and the freedom it was sure to bring. Life had been so much simpler back then. Ava smiled. This was a timeline of her life, too.

Until it wasn't. Soon, the photos became unfamiliar, and the clothing and faces began to change. Harris gradually got a bit thicker and a bit grayer. Macy transformed from a teenager that was all sharp angles and elbows into a softer version of herself. A woman.

Ava stepped back, taking in the rest of the gallery wall as if she was ripping off a Band-Aid. High school graduation. Harris' fiftieth birthday barbeque. Macy, horseback, holding a giant belt buckle at the state fair.

Then, there he was: Ben. Ava realized that although she'd never seen him before, he somehow looked just as she had imagined: broad-shouldered and tall, with dark brown eyes, hair, and skin. Handsome as hell, as Ava knew he would be. And his eyes. . .Even in photos, Ava could tell they were full of kindness and that playful twinkle that always meant a good sense of humor. Macy's soulmate. And Ava had missed it all.

She could see now that the wall was arranged chronologically. A photo booth strip showed Ben and Macy in their dating days, just another happy young couple making silly faces and kissing, their infatuation oozing from the squares.

Macy's college graduation: Harris with his arm around her, Ben proudly holding her diploma toward the lens.

Their wedding day: Ben in full Green Beret uniform and

Macy. . .Wow. She was beautiful, wearing a classic form-fitting lace gown with long sleeves, her blonde curls pinned around her face like a character from *Downton Abbey*. The couple stood hand in hand, the stony mountains contrasting the green of the ranch, spring flowers in full bloom. Ben had his head tipped down at Macy, his eyes intense and passionate. Just looking at the two of them made Ava breathless.

Did Lucas look at her like that? She didn't really think Lucas was particularly romantic, but he probably looked at Ava as thoughtfully as he looked at anyone. Had Ethan looked at Jess Kidd like that? She swallowed and shook her head, clearing his image from her mind.

She looked at the photo again, this time focusing on Macy's expression. Ava had never seen her look so bright and full of joy. A scratchy lump of regret throbbed at the back of Ava's throat.

The rest of the photos blurred by: Ben and Harris on the fishing boat, proudly hoisting their catch. Ben in uniform shaking hands with an important-looking military figure. In another, all three grinned under a "Grand Opening" banner strung beneath the riding academy sign. Next to it was a picture of Ben and Macy posing on the counter of a produce booth at a festival.

Last, not a photo, but a small painting. Ava recognized it immediately: two girls perched in an out-of-proportion treehouse, their cartoonishly long legs dangling over the edge as two horses waited on the ground below. In the bottom right corner was a childlike scrawl: *by Ava*.

"I could use a new trailer," Macy said from behind her, making her jump. She nodded at the little painting. "Think it's worth big money now?"

Ava turned. "Probably at least fifty bucks," she said.

Macy laughed. Until tonight, she had forgotten this part of Macy—the playful part. The part that was two steps ahead of Ava, but always fun, never malicious. Ava realized that although she had found Macy MacDaniel-Paxton when she got here, she was only just now finding her old best friend. She had missed her.

Soon, the food arrived, and they carried the bags to the dining room. The table was easily big enough to seat eight, but she suspected it hadn't held more than Macy and Harris for some time now. The thick carpet from Ava's childhood had been removed, revealing original hardwood that gleamed. The bright white paint made the room seem larger, and the chair rail molding fit perfectly with the farmhouse style. Ava remembered the very nineties floral wallpaper that had been in that room when they were kids. Macy and Ben had done such a great job.

The Chinese was just as good as any New York takeout, and Ava was relieved to find the conversation pouring as easily as the wine. Macy told her about dealing with the academy parents who seemed to be trying to train their kids for the Olympics. Ava told her more about the nightlife in New York—free Shakespeare plays in the park and the bookstore you could visit at midnight. Macy couldn't believe Ava could have pizza or Thai food delivered twenty-four hours a day, even on Christmas. She said she couldn't imagine not having a car, and Ava told her how much she loved the camaraderie and energy of the subway anytime she slipped out and evaded her driver. As Macy uncorked a second bottle of wine, Ava began to truly relax. But even as she focused on Macy's words, Ethan's face kept dancing across her mind. The hungry look in his eyes as she pulled away from his kiss, his wet clothes plastereed to his frame after the water fight.

"So, how's Aunt Carla these days?" Macy asked, pulling Ava back into the room.

"Same old, same old," she said. "Well, different than you remember in some ways, I guess. I see her every day. That's probably surprising to you."

"I'm glad to hear it," Macy said with a slight edge. Long ago, Ava had forgiven the loneliness her mother had caused, but maybe Macy never had.

"My mom has really tried to make up for lost time. Sometimes, I wish she gave me *more* space. But she works hard to support me. Actually, I just found out she got me an incredible job offer in Germany."

"That's great!" Macy said. "When do you go?"

"I don't know... It's complicated."

Ava set her chopsticks on her plate and wiped her napkin across her mouth. She was stuffed. She looked up and saw Macy watching her expectantly.

"What?" Ava asked.

"That's all you're gonna tell me?" Macy asked. "This sounds huge! I want details."

Ava sighed. "I've been thinking about it nonstop. But tonight, I don't need to. Don't take it personally, it's just stressful. Let's talk about something fun instead. Like crops!"

"Never thought I'd hear those words come out of your mouth," Macy said, laughing.

"I'm a complicated woman," Ava teased.

"It's looking like the ranch I remember," Macy said. "I love it out there, Ava. With the field cleared, it's all taking shape. I'll be the first to admit that I've been lost in my head for a long while now. I forgot how beautiful Utah was until I stopped and, well, looked, I guess."

They shared a quiet smile. Ava had thought Macy seemed less troubled, but hearing her say it lifted her soul. Maybe she wasn't in Macy's way after all; maybe she was needed here. Macy looked as if she wanted to say more, but instead, she just shoved the remains of her fried rice around her plate with one chopstick. Ava waited, draining her wine glass and watching as the old wooden cuckoo clock chirped on the half hour.

"You know," Macy said, finally, "everyone sees the two years Ben has been gone. . .That's the hurt that's easy to see. But it's more complicated than that."

She sighed. Ava grabbed the open cabernet and filled Macy's empty glass first, then her own.

"No one really knows this, but we were hoping to start a family. Before Ben left," Macy continued. She closed the food containers as she spoke and shoved the napkins into the paper restaurant bag. "I had gotten pregnant a year before but miscarried before we'd told anyone."

Ava's hand flew to her mouth, an icy heaviness settling on her chest. "Oh, Macy! I had no idea."

"It was completely devastating," Macy said. "Somehow, we got through it and we tried again." She pressed her lips into a tight line and began to fiddle with a button on her blouse. "It wasn't so easy the second time, but I got a positive test about two weeks after Ben shipped out. I didn't tell him right away; I wanted to wait until after my first doctor's appointment. But then, they were on a mission, so I had to wait. Then I lost her. The baby. I lost her right there in the middle of Ben's field while I was picking strawberries. And I never got to tell him." She closed her eyes and exhaled.

"I'm so sorry, Macy." Macy had always loved babies and playing house had been one of her favorite games when they were little. After being happily married for a few years, a baby would be a logical next step. Ava could have kicked herself for not asking sooner.

"I've never felt more alone," Macy said. "And then when Ben disappeared, I just. . .Well, I just didn't know how to go on. No one could help, even if they wanted to. No one even knew the whole story." She dug around in the paper bag. "Fortune cookie?" she asked weakly.

"Uncle Harris didn't know?" Ava asked as she took one.

Macy shook her head as she tore open the wrapper, then cracked open the shell and tossed half the cookie into her mouth. "No one knew," she said, chewing. "And then I got mad. At everything and everyone. At this place. At that field. It made me forget all the good that was here. All the beautiful things that filled my life. In order to lose that much, you need to have a lot to begin with, right?" She blinked a few times at Ava before turning her gaze out the dark window. "I guess I forgot that part. I lost my baby in that field, but it's also where Ben proposed to me. This ranch is my soul, the good parts and the bad."

She absentmindedly twisted the little white fortune around her finger. Then, she inhaled deeply, straightening her shoulders as she looked back at Ava.

"I want to live the rest of my life here. Whether that means I need to sell off most of the property or not, it won't change the fact that this house is my family, as much as Harris, or Ben, or. . .well, you. Thank you for helping me see that."

"Me?" Ava asked.

Macy smiled weakly. "I wallowed. That's the only word I can think of to describe it. I guess I needed to for a bit, but I got cozy in my wallow and never wanted to come out. But then, you came. I still have so much..." Her voice cracked as she looked toward the ceiling. "God, I have so much." She sniffed and wiped her eye with her sleeve before clearing her throat. "Now I can see that. Call it grace, or gratitude, or getting my head out of my ass. Either way, you did that for me even though I've been nothing but awful to you. Just because. It's one of the most generous things anyone has ever done for me."

"I'm glad, Macy," Ava said, hoping her face didn't betray her growing guilt. "I wish I had been here for you a long time ago."

"You're here now," Macy said. "It still counts."

Ava smiled and bit into her cookie. "What's your fortune say?"

"Oops!" Macy said, reaching into the bag. "I was so busy yakking your ear off, I tossed it in with my food. What's yours say?"

"*A lifetime of happiness lies ahead of you*," Ava read. "Generic, but I'll take it."

Macy unfolded her little paper and smoothed it with the heel of her hand. "Well, apparently, *an unexpected event will bring me riches*," she said, tossing her fortune to Ava. "Do you think they offer a thirty-day guarantee on these things?" She chuckled half-heartedly.

"There has to be a way to get the money you need," Ava said. "You know, Ethan told me he used to work in real estate finance. He said he'd be happy to look at your loan. Maybe there's something there you haven't seen?"

"Yeah. . .Maybe I'll take him up on that," Macy said, before narrowing her eyes at Ava. "Speaking of Ethan, how did the rest of the morning go?"

Ava shrugged. "We finished, I went to town, and here I am," she said, keeping her face even as she pretended to study the label on the wine bottle. "I've been shopping at the art store a lot. The owner's daughter is an incredibly talented artist."

"Uh-huh, that's great, love the Oakenwoods," Macy said, waving her hand dismissively. "But I think you know what I'm really asking."

Ava looked up and met Macy's patient stare. She clearly wasn't giving in.

Ava sighed. "He's great, OK? Ethan is attentive and funny and sensitive and smart and absolutely gorgeous. So what?" She shoved her hair behind her ears. "He'll be perfect for someone. I mean, I tried you, but you weren't interested. Hopefully, it will be someone great. It better be."

"But not you?" Macy asked. Her face had softened, and Ava could tell she wasn't teasing any longer.

"He's a friend and will never be anything more," Ava said, her voice firm. "Maybe in a different life, one where I never left Utah, one where my world was here. But it's not. I know it has its highs and lows, but I do love my job. I'm not giving that up. What would be the point of trying something long-distance if neither of us would ever end up where the other lives?"

Macy didn't reply. Even though it was a rhetorical question, even though Ava had tried to untangle all of this in her mind a thousand times, a less rational part of her had hoped Macy would point out some obvious black-and-white solution. Ava picked at a lint ball on her sleeve as her head began to pound.

"I know by now you probably think I don't care about Lucas," Ava said. The anger in her voice dulled into something more resigned. "The thing is, I do. It's just more complicated with him. Sometimes he's my publicist; sometimes he's my boyfriend. It's hard to separate the two. One day, I'll be ignoring his work calls, but then the next, I'm begging him for *more* attention."

She wiped her mouth with her napkin, noticing a little berry-colored stain before shoving it in with the rest of the trash. She had a feeling her teeth were stained to match. Whatever. She took another sip.

"Have you talked to Lucas about all this?" Macy asked.

"No, not exactly," Ava said. "It doesn't seem to bother him. I know he loves me, and I've pictured a future with him for years now. And he's here. Well, not *here*, Utah, but here in my life as it is, you know? And maybe I'm not thinking about him as much because I don't see him every day like I normally would. Maybe he's not ready to settle down yet, but it's only a matter of time. He'll realize that he can have his business and a wife and a family and that it will make all the success worth it. I don't know anyone who couldn't see that, and he's not an idiot, so it has to happen, right? It just has to happen!"

Ava realized she was yelling, but Macy just kept watching her with patient eyes.

"I'm sorry," Ava said, her vision blurring with tears. What was she thinking, complaining about not seeing her boyfriend for a week when Macy hadn't seen Ben in two years?

"I have a lot on my mind."

"Don't apologize," Macy said. She rested her hand over Ava's clenched fist. "That's what cousins are for."

Ava tried to smile, but instead, her face crumpled. Frustrated sobs poured out, loud and forceful. Macy scooted her chair around the table and rested her head against Ava's shoulder, tenderly rubbing her back.

Ava had everything figured out before she came here. Her life wasn't perfect, but it was good enough and it was certain. Utah was seriously messing with her head.

After a few minutes, she took a deep shuddering breath. Her head pounded a little, but she felt better. Macy passed her a napkin from the takeout bag, then stood.

"I'll grab the dessert," Macy said, squeezing Ava's shoulder. "Then I think we might need another refill."

Ava laughed, despite herself.

Macy shrugged. "At least no one's driving," she said, smiling as walked into the kitchen.

Good job, Ava. You come here to help your cousin cheer up and then you sob into her nice tablecloth. Still, she felt a bit better.

Ava heard her phone vibrate loudly from the foyer. She wiped her face on her napkin before crossing the room and grabbing it from her coat pocket. A Delta flight notification blinked back at her: *"It's time to check in for your flight to New York!"* She stared at it for a moment before shoving it back inside the pocket and returning to the dining room. With everything going on, she had never changed her flight. And now, she had no idea if she should. Her mother could definitely be dramatic, but even Lucas had insisted Ava needed to get back as soon as possible or risk losing Shubert's interest.

Macy reentered with a box of tissues and a lemon tart. Ava's mouth fell open. It was the same dessert Ava had requested on every birthday she had ever spent on the ranch.

Ava grinned as she snatched a tissue and blew her nose. "Thanks, Macy."

"I'm glad you're here, Ava. I missed you. We're both going to be okay. I believe that."

Macy refilled their glasses one last time, the second wine bottle now empty. With every fiber of her being, Ava hoped Macy was right.

Eighteen

It was still dark when Ava lumbered down from the loft to refill her water glass. Her body was stiff, her mouth chalky. More than tipsy, she had stayed up late talking to Lucas, insisting he stay on the phone. She thought it was partly the wine, partly to assuage her guilt, and partly because she was lonely.

For his part, Lucas seemed to enjoy her drunken rambling. They talked for two hours, though not about much of substance. They had laughed and teased each other, reminisced and made plans for a date night when she returned. Ava couldn't remember a call like that since their early days of dating, when she'd survived on not much more than coffee after late nights chatting with him about everything and nothing. Even so, when they'd finally hung up, Ava had felt the warmth drain from her and an empty ache replace it. And in that cold darkness, she made a decision.

She was leaving today after all. She would fly home to meet Friedrich Shubert. Whether or not she took the job, she'd fly back to Utah after a few days. She needed to see Lucas, see how she felt in his presence again. And she needed to get away from Ethan, just long enough to clear her head. Something about being here was clouding her judgment and she was afraid of what she might lose if she stayed. She was afraid of herself.

Ava looked out the window toward Macy's house. The lights were still out. Ava needed to talk to her before she left and explain her plan. She knew Macy would understand and the work in the field could continue without her, at least for a few days.

Ava padded over to the kitchen and heated a bowl of oatmeal, too distracted to add her usual raisins and walnuts. She forced herself to eat half, though her nervous stomach resisted every bite. She brushed her teeth and began to pack.

After tucking away her clothes and toiletries, she took stock of her artwork. She had worried about finding motivation while she was here, and yet nearly every inch of counter space was covered with a sketch or painting. Something about packing them felt strangely final. She wasn't sure if it was worth the bother at all; she would be shocked if Carla or Lucas saw any prospect in the pieces. Still, she felt an urge to hold them in her apartment. She wanted to remember this person she'd rediscovered and remind herself to come back. She stacked the drawings and zipped them into the front pocket of her suitcase. The large linen canvases would have to stay for now.

As Ava shoved her sketchbook into her carry-on, a paper fluttered to the floor. Her hand hovered over it as she recognized the sketch of the ranch skyline she had made for Macy. She must have forgotten to give it to her after that run-in with Ethan and Shelly. Setting it aside, she glanced out the window once more and saw that Macy's house was still dark. She zipped her suitcase closed and glanced at the clock. It was only five-thirty.

Now what?

Ava threw the heavy Carhartt over her pajamas and pulled her sketchpad and pencils out once more. She stuck them in a plastic grocery bag she found under the sink, along with a granola bar and a bottle of water.

As she stepped outside into the crisp morning air, her nostrils were filled with the musk of burning wood. Thin gray smoke rose from Macy's chimney; she must be awake. Ava would give her time to have her coffee, then she'd go explain herself. She stepped into her Justin boots as the icy remains of night nipped at her cheeks. From the east, the pink hues of morning were just beginning to light up the landscape around her. A fat raccoon wobbled out from under her car as she stepped off the porch, blinking at Ava before sniffing the ground at her feet. She shooed him away and walked around the corner.

The huge jumble of boulders cast a long shadow that completely engulfed this side of the cabin. She swung the plastic bag over one shoulder and climbed to the top. The cold penetrated her thin cotton pants as she sat on the flat edge. She opened her sketchpad, retrieved a freshly sharpened pencil, faced the sky... And waited. She pressed the pencil tip to the paper, but the nudge that had driven her outside had disappeared. She put the pencil away and ate her granola bar.

The sound of silence filled her ears. She wondered if she'd ever be able to ignore blaring sirens again.

Should I just stay forever?

The idea was delicious. She closed her eyes, trying to picture it, but the image was incomplete. She couldn't permanently vacation, and she had worked so hard to get this far in her career. She had a feeling press junkets and benefit auctions were few and far between way out here.

And then, she realized that in this blurry vision, she would be alone. The idea of Lucas moving here was laughable, and even if he somehow gave in, she knew he'd be miserable.

There would never be an artists' retreat. She would never build her dream. There would be unknown masters whose work the world would never know.

So, then I go?

She could have her old life. Without Macy, without Utah... Without Ethan.

She opened her eyes and swallowed, the cold air amplifying the ache deep inside her chest. There was no right answer, but at least she could finally hear herself think.

She tossed the bar wrapper into the bag. The itch to create had her fingers clenched once more, but it was calling from somewhere else. She climbed back down to the brown grass below and turned toward the field behind the cabin. Without thinking, she hurried toward the tree line until the woods enveloped her, blotting out her churning thoughts along with the growing sunlight.

She walked with purpose but without plan, her feet following a trail first forged by ancient people long before any road existed here. She walked and walked until she met the creek, which began to move alongside her as the path turned. Soon, the trail swerved left, but she moved right, stepping onto a lesser-used trail, one first beaten down by two young girls decades before.

Eventually, she reached a clearing and looked up. Suspended

between two trees was the treehouse. Ava blinked, but it was still there.

Macy had told her that it'd been struck by lightning and burned down. Why had she lied to her? She gave the bottom rung of the ladder a shake and realized that not only was the treehouse still there, but it had also been completely rebuilt. A steel ladder had replaced the rickety wooden one and handrails now paralleled the rungs. She began to climb.

When she reached the platform, she saw that the floor was still wood, but it was much newer than the uneven redwood she remembered. The chicken wire that had stretched between the railing and the treehouse floor had been replaced with neat wooden slats. She looked over the edge and her stomach clenched. It seemed higher than she remembered. Ava suddenly realized that as the trees grew, so would the treehouse.

She laid on her back on the cold wooden floor, cradling her head in her crossed arms. She supposed tree "house" might not be the right term, since it had no roof and no real walls. Still, this was better. If the view of the canopy above had changed since she'd been here last, she couldn't tell. The sky was now a lazy gray, not quite full morning, but no longer pink.

Ava's mind flooded with memories of the treehouse. Of precious childhood secrets and pretend worlds; of ghost stories, of promises of intertwined futures, of tears for lost mothers; and of visions of strong, beautiful men with eyes full of love and words of utter devotion that only a child could conjure. And just as a colorful image filled her mind of sitting cross-legged in that very spot, knotting a friendship bracelet while Macy braided her hair, she fell asleep.

"Ava?"

Ava blinked and opened her eyes. Macy's bemused face stared down at her. The sky behind her was now fully blue. Ava sat up and stretched her stiff neck.

"What are you doing here?" Ava asked.

"I was gonna ask you the same thing," Macy said, glancing at Ava's pajama pants as she sat across from her.

They both looked up at the rustling treetops. It was a wonder there were any leaves left; with each gust, crisp leaves of every color rained down around them.

"Why did you tell me the treehouse was struck by lightning?" Ava asked, raising an eyebrow.

"Because it was," Macy said.

Ava narrowed her gaze.

"I didn't lie to you," Macy said, holding up her hands in defense. "Look."

She pointed to a large branch that stretched low over their heads. The underside was covered in thick black patches that Ava hadn't noticed before. Under the scab-like lesions, the branch was smooth and white as bone.

"You can see places where fire spread if you look closely," Macy added when Ava's eyes widened. "There's a long fissure somewhere on the other side where the lightning struck it."

Ava crossed her arms and frowned at Macy.

"What?" Macy asked. "You didn't ask me what happened next."

"That's lame and you know it," Ava said.

Macy shrugged and laughed. "I was mad at you," she said.

"But you're not anymore?"

"No," Macy said, simply.

Ava looked over the edge, trying to picture the structure engulfed in flames. It was lucky the treehouse was in the center of a clearing, which must have kept the fire from spreading to the rest of the forest. Still, how were both trees still alive?

"The will to survive is an incredible thing," Macy said, as if hearing her thoughts. "When it first happened, I was sure both trees were dead. But just months later, new branches emerged, and these patchy shoots of leaves grew from some of the old ones."

Ava stood and ran her hand along the charred limb, marveling at the tree's tenacity.

"The treehouse was already ancient, and nothing was left except a few ladder rungs," Macy continued. "But Ben. . .Well, I guess he gathered from my stories that it was a pretty special place for me. You may not believe this, but he also knew how much *you* meant to me."

Ava raised an eyebrow but said nothing.

"Anyway, for our first wedding anniversary, we had a picnic at the creek. Then, he walked me back here." Macy's eyes glittered at the memory. "He had totally rebuilt the whole thing without telling me. I don't know how he hid it, but I was clueless. He went through old photos to try to match it and talked to Harris and, well, here we are."

"Here we are," Ava echoed. "I'm so glad I got to see it."

Macy's smile slowly wilted. After a moment, she pulled an

opened envelope from her back pocket and passed it to Ava without a word.

"You want me to read it?" Ava asked, glancing from the envelope to Macy's pensive face.

Macy shrugged. Ava sat back down beside her.

"I'll give you the gist," Macy said. "It came with a more official-looking letter I haven't opened yet, but I don't really think I need to. This one is from Darren Willoughby's mom."

"Darren Willoughby?" Ava asked.

Macy took a ragged breath. "The other soldier," she said. "With Ben."

Ava's insides turned to ice as she waited for Macy to finish.

"They found him," Macy said. "Darren. A couple miles from the crash. They found his remains."

"And they're. . .?"

"Sure it's him, yes. He still had his dog tags," Macy said evenly.

"I see," Ava said. Because what else could she say? She took Macy's hand and sandwiched it between her own.

Macy leaned her head against Ava's shoulder. "Now it's just Ben," she said.

They sat like that for a long time, until they were both stiff and hungry—both thinking about what it all meant.

Words began to pour from both Ava and Macy on the long walk back to the house. This was something different than the friendship Ava remembered; it was rawer and deeper. Macy shared things she'd kept locked tightly inside her for the last two years. How she mourned their child that would never be—how deep down, she mourned Ben too. She told Ava she knew she was living with a shadow; she just didn't know how to let go. Not yet.

For Ava's part, she said things aloud she hadn't even admitted to herself. She had pictured a life with Lucas for so long; a life that included busy careers, but also marriage and children. Had they both changed? Or had she always ignored the things she didn't want to see? Ava confessed that on many nights, she had prayed for him to want the domestic picture she craved so badly. She admitted to Macy that, deep down, she didn't think it would ever happen.

She didn't say much about Ethan. It wasn't because she was hiding anything from Macy, but because she didn't know what to say; her feelings were tangled, and she told Macy as much. Why push something that would be doomed from the start? There was a new fear that was whispering to Ava, too:

What if I'm just destined to be alone?

Sure, that was fine for some people, if that's what they wanted. But Ava knew with more certainty than she had in any other area of her life that she wanted to build a family. Not pieced together and *sometimes*, but grounded and *always*. Not like the unnamed father who never claimed her. . .and not like Carla. She knew in her heart that she could do better.

As they broke from the woods into the warm sun, Ava spotted a sleek, black SUV idling a few hundred yards away in front of her cabin. She froze.

"Who the heck is that?" Macy asked.

Ava had completely forgotten about her flight. She glanced at her watch: it was later than she thought. Carla must have sent a driver to ensure Ava wouldn't change her mind.

"Uh, you know what?" Ava mumbled. "I think it's. . .Well, I'll handle it. You go on ahead, okay?"

Macy looked as if she'd like to ask more questions, but Ava was grateful when she didn't. Macy simply nodded and walked off in the direction of the stable.

Ava approached the driver's side door. The dark-tinted window rolled down, revealing a bald man with aviator sunglasses.

"Ava MacDaniel?" he asked.

She nodded.

"I was supposed to see that you were on the road a half-hour ago," he said.

"Sorry."

He blinked at her.

"I just need my stuff," she said, weakly.

"Want a hand?" he asked.

She shook her head.

"Well, how about you bring it to the porch, and I'll load it from there?" he said.

"Sounds good," she said. She headed for the cabin, then turned back. "On our way out, I'd like to stop by the stable and say a quick goodbye, if that's OK?"

He nodded and rolled up the window. Ava could hear muffled music radiate through the Navigator.

Her heart pounded as she rushed into the cabin. Why hadn't she explained her plan to Macy when they saw the car waiting? There would be no saying goodbye to Ethan, but that was just as well. Her stomach felt like it was eating itself.

She quickly changed, stuffed her pajamas into her bulging suitcase, and dragged it to the door. A tiny painting propped on the kitchen counter caught her eye. Had she missed one while she was packing?

She balanced the suitcase and picked up the little picture. The clumsily drawn figures of two girls smiled back at her, their horses waiting below the treehouse where they sat. It was the same painting Ava had seen hanging in the ranch house living room.

Macy.

She must have left it there before she found Ava in the woods. That whole morning, Macy must have known she was leaving. As Ava's fingers moved over the rough paint, emotion tightened her throat. A sudden memory flooded her mind: Macy's gap-toothed grin when she'd unwrapped the painting on her tenth birthday. Ava tenderly sat the image back on the counter and walked outside to the idling SUV.

The driver rolled his window down, then made a show of lowering his sunglasses and looking from her to the empty porch, then back again.

"Ready to go?" he asked, flatly.

"No, actually," Ava said. "I think I'm going to stay."

The driver squinted at her. "Well, I only get paid for completed trips," he said.

"One minute," she said. She ran back inside, retrieved her wallet, then hurried back to the SUV.

"How much was she going to pay you?" Ava asked, out of breath.

"Five hundred," he said.

Her eyes widened.

"Long drive," he added with a shrug.

"I'm sure you're well worth it," Ava said, gritting her teeth. She peeled five hundred-dollar bills from her wallet.

"Tips not included," he said.

She sighed and gave him the last bill from her now empty wallet, glad she'd brought her credit cards. She had a feeling Carla was going to draw the line on her reimbursements now.

The driver pushed his aviators back up his nose, gave her a nod, and rolled up his window. Ava watched the Navigator back up onto the gravel, turn around, then slowly disappear down the drive until the trees swallowed it up.

She climbed the steps into the cabin again, this time slowly. Once inside, she slumped onto the window seat and stared out the window. She pulled her phone from her back pocket and sent a text to Lucas:

I'm sorry. I'm not ready to come back. Please tell Carla.

Then she powered off her phone, watching the little white apple flash on the screen before it went black. She tucked it into a kitchen drawer, then fell back onto the window seat, waiting for the tears to come. But this time, they didn't.

Nineteen

Ava looked at her suitcase, still standing at attention. She could unpack later.

She grabbed her chunky cardigan and walked outside. The sun was warm, but the breeze had a chilly bite. She slipped on her boots and headed toward the ranch house. She found Macy standing in the doorway.

"Oh! Hi," Ava said, doing her best to sound casual.

"You're still here," Macy said.

"You knew," Ava replied, as much a statement as it was a question.

"I suspected there was something you weren't telling me," Macy said, "but then when I came over this morning to give you that painting, I saw your suitcase. Seemed ironic when I found you in the treehouse."

"Macy, I'm so sorry," Ava began, "I was going to come right back, I should have explained—"

"Don't be," Macy said, raising a hand to silence her. "You don't owe me an explanation. You've done more than enough. I just hope you're finally making a choice for you."

"I am," Ava said. "That's why I'm staying."

"What?! You are?"

Ava nodded, a smile finally breaking through the cloud of anxiety. Saying it out loud, she knew it was the right decision.

"At least until I can figure out my next move," she said, taking in the quiet land as she spoke. "Maybe it will be right back in the swing of things in New York, maybe not. But I'm finally starting to figure out what's important to me. I owe it to myself to listen. I just feel like I'm not finished here." She flashed Macy a smile. "Whether you actually do need me or not, you're not getting rid of me yet."

Macy grinned. "I support you no matter what, obviously," she said, "but I'm so glad you're not leaving!"

"So, maybe we can celebrate," Ava said. "What are you doing today?"

"I've got my usual lessons, and then I told Lori Kersker she could use the ranch this afternoon; she's the photographer who does the high school senior pictures every year. I don't need to do much, just make sure no one sets the horses free."

"Got plans after?"

Macy laughed. "Do I ever?"

"Well, you do now," Ava said. "Get dressed for a night out once lessons are over. I'll meet you here around eight."

"What are you up to?" Macy asked. "You know I'm not a big 'going out' person."

"Just trust me," Ava said, an impish glint in her eye. "It will be a night for the books." And with that, she headed for the barn, wanting nothing more than to nuzzle the sweet, soft face of her friend Gunner.

Tap, tap, tap. Ava glanced up from her canvas and saw Kelly's round eyes smiling at her through the front window. Ava grinned. "It's open!" she called as she waved her in.

"Look at you!" she exclaimed as Kelly stepped through the door in a polka-dotted lavender sundress. "You look beautiful!"

The dress had a cowl neckline and a tea-length skirt that ruffled against Kelly's long legs. Her usual work ponytail was nowhere to be found, her long black hair instead pinned up halfway and curled.

"It's nice to lose that polo shirt and khakis for once," Kelly said, her cheeks flushing at the compliment. "My sister-in-law did my hair and makeup."

"Oh! Macy mentioned senior pictures were happening today," Ava said. "How's it going?"

"I'm all finished. Lori showed me a couple of the shots," Kelly said, her face glowing. "There's one of me leaning against the fence with all these horses behind me—I swear, someone would think I was a country singer or something! She got some of Charlie and me together too, so we can use them for our Save the Dates. I'll send you one when I get them."

"I'd be honored," Ava said. "Can you stay for a few minutes?"

"I don't want to disturb your work," Kelly said, nodding to the easel. "I told Charlie to meet me here when his pictures were finished, but I thought I might wait on the swing, if you don't mind."

"Nonsense!" Ava said. "I could use a break and some iced tea. Chatting with you will be a treat. Can I pour you some?"

"Sure! Thanks." Kelly kept stealing little glances at the back of the canvas.

Ava laughed. "You can look at it, if you want."

"Really?" Kelly's eyes widened.

Ava nodded. "Go for it. It's still in the early stages, but you'll get the basic idea."

Ava smiled as she watched Kelly gape at the painting. "Sugar?" she asked.

"Please," Kelly replied, never looking up.

Ava placed the two glasses on the coffee table. Kelly joined her on the couch, reluctantly tearing her eyes from the canvas.

"The design is really cool," Kelly said, after taking a sip. "I was surprised the paint is flat. Not that I've seen your work in person, but in pictures, it always looked kinda textured."

"This one will too, eventually," Ava said. "All that depth comes from layers and layers of paint. I like to say my work stretches first and then it starts to stand up."

Kelly laughed. "I like that."

"That's the kind of stuff they'll teach you in art school," Ava said. "You can focus on whatever you want, but you'll learn to work with all kinds of media."

Kelly smiled but began to study the ice cubes in her glass.

"You okay?" Ava asked.

"I'm fine," Kelly said. "I just... Well, I wanted to let you know I decided not to apply to the school after all."

"Oh," Ava said, more disappointed than she would have expected. "I had hoped you'd be convinced after you had time to look into it."

"It's nothing to do with the program," Kelly said quickly, twisting her skirt in her fingers before looking at up Ava. "I would love to do something like that. I want you to know, I thought really hard about it. But Charlie needs me in Salt Lake City. He's never been on his own and his mom still does everything for him. And I promised."

"Kelly," Ava began, choosing her words carefully. "I think it's wonderful how devoted you are to him. But don't you deserve the same? I can't believe he doesn't see what this could mean for you."

"I didn't tell him about it," Kelly said, her voice small.

"What?! Kelly, why not?"

"Because I know how much he loves me," Kelly said simply. "It would make him feel guilty about his scholarship, and there's no point in telling him, anyway. There's nothing to be done."

Ava sighed. "I know what it's like to shape a life based on what someone else tells you matters," she said. "I also know that after listening to someone else for long enough, your own voice stops talking. If you don't put your dreams first, who will?"

"That's what I'm trying to tell you, Ava," Kelly said, setting her glass on the coaster. "These *are* my dreams. All I've ever wanted was to have my own little family. I used to fantasize about this mystery man who would come along and commit his life to mine; I knew Charlie was that man from the moment I met him freshman year in homeroom. Yeah, I might have to sacrifice a little, but it will be worth it to belong to him."

Ava wanted to remind her that women could be so much

more than just a foundation for men to build upon. She wanted to show Kelly what carvings had sold for that were nowhere near as special as hers. She wanted to shake Kelly and tell her she must be confused; there was no way being a wife without an education was better than realizing her own potential. But before she could say anything, a knock on the door startled them both.

"That'll be Charlie," Kelly said, a bit apologetic as she went to the door. "Please don't say anything to him."

"I won't," Ava said. "But promise me you will. If he loves you as much as you say he does, he'll be hurt if you keep this from him."

Kelly considered for a moment before giving a resigned nod. Ava stood as Charlie entered, and she immediately recognized the lanky boy from the engagement announcement she'd seen hanging in the store.

"So, this is Charlie," Ava said, offering him a welcoming smile.

He grinned and shook Ava's hand. He had a square, open face with boyish dimples and tan skin that hinted at a summer working outdoors. Ava could tell he was still growing into himself, but he would be a very handsome man when he did.

"It's so nice to finally meet you," he said, with puppy-like enthusiasm. "Kelly won't stop talking about you."

Kelly elbowed him.

Ava laughed. "I was just about to say the same about you."

Ava watched her breath form a hazy cloud as she leaned against the cold metal of the Range Rover in front of Macy's house. October had both feet in fall now, and it was full dark. She pulled her coat more tightly around her, but there was nothing to be done for her bare legs. *Worth it*, she thought, adjusting her denim mini skirt. *Totally worth it.*

Macy threw her a little wave, then jogged down the steps to join her. She gave Ava's bejeweled cowboy hat a double take but said nothing. Macy was wearing black skinny jeans, a form-fitting button-down, and her nicest pair of black cowboy boots.

Perfect.

Just then, the SUV doors opened, and out climbed Lizzie and Ethan. Ava smiled as Macy gaped at the three of them—her smile was still there, but a look of trepidation had crept into her eyes.

"Didn't realize this was a class field trip," Macy said.

"To be fair, ya didn't ask," Ava replied lightly.

"What's with the skirt and bling-covered hat?" Macy asked. "Is there a dress code?"

"Nah," Ava said. "You know me. I'm from New York—I dress like a weirdo."

Macy glanced at Lizzie and Ethan and seemed to relax when she saw noticed their usual puffer coats and jeans.

"You're dressed perfectly, Macy," Ava said. "You're just missing one thing."

Ava uncrumpled a red bandanna from her jacket pocket and quickly folded it into a flat band. "You can tie this yourself, or I can do it for you," she said, holding it up to Macy's eyes.

"Uh, excuse me, you think I'm going to let you blindfold me?!"

"Three against one," Lizzie said, crossing her arms.

"The hard way or the easy way," added Ethan, also crossing his arms for good measure.

Ava just shrugged and smiled as innocently as she could.

Macy groaned, but her eyes crinkled with amusement. "Fine," she said. "But if you're going to abandon me in a field somewhere, at least let me get a warmer coat first."

"You really watch too much true crime TV," Ava said, laughing.

Macy rolled her eyes, but turned and gamely let Ava tie the bandanna at the back of her head. As she tightened the knot, Ava glanced up and saw Ethan watching her. She looked away, hoping he couldn't see her cheeks flush pink in the darkness.

"All set!" Ava said to Macy. "Now it's off to a night of adventure with your devoted fan club."

Lizzie opened the passenger door and bowed. "Madam, your chariot awaits," she said theatrically as Ava led Macy to the car.

"Cool," Macy said, laughing. "Can't see a thing."

Ava helped Macy climb inside and fastened her seatbelt around her. Then, she and Lizzie climbed into the backseat. Once Ethan had settled into the driver's seat, he turned back to Lizzie and Ava. He pointed at his head and mouthed: *Now?*

Ava nodded. Lizzie reached into a bag on the floor and withdrew three cowboy hats. She set one aside, then handed one to Ethan and they both put them on.

Ava grinned. Everything was going just as she'd planned. They drove away from the house as Garth Brooks' rich voice crooned to them from the speakers. Ava may not exactly be a country queen, but everyone knew Garth.

"Turn it up!" she said as the opening notes of the next song began. "Aint Goin' Down ('Til the Sun Comes Up)" filled the cab. Ava leaned over and glanced in the passenger-side mirror.

Sure enough, there was a blindfolded Macy, singing along at

the top of her lungs and grinning ear to ear, just as she had any time this song had played on the radio many years before.

A half hour later, the quartet walked down Main Street, a still-blindfolded Macy tucked between Ethan and Ava. Ava glanced behind her and smiled when she saw that Lizzie had remembered to grab the last cowboy hat, the cream-colored felt Stetson tucked under her arm. When Lizzie saw Ava's grin, she winked.

"Step!" Ava ordered Macy as they reached the curb where Main met Ward.

The shops were dark, but downtown Cobalt was still bustling, full of families out for a weekend dinner and young couples on dates. The group got lots of curious looks and a few giggles.

As they passed a middle-aged man in a Raiders hat and denim trucker jacket, his eyes widened. "Ma'am," he said to Macy, stepping in front of the group. "You okay?"

Macy smiled, but didn't move her blindfold. She was proving to be a good sport. "As far as I know, this is supposedly some kind of surprise, but thank you for looking out for me!"

The man nodded and walked on, tossing a slightly suspicious look at Ethan as he passed.

"It's good to know chivalry isn't totally dead," Macy said.

"I don't know what you're talking about," Ethan said, smiling playfully at Ava and Lizzie. "What's more courteous than a trio of bodyguards?"

The distant thrums of honky-tonk grew louder as they walked

on. Soon, the chorus of "Coal Miner's Daughter" became louder and then deafening as they came to a stop.

"I hear Loretta!" Macy said.

"Hush, or we'll lock you back in the Range Rover!" Ava hissed. She noticed a bouncer perched on a metal stool a few feet away, eyeing her with wary interest.

"Totally kidding!"

His gaze narrowed.

"It's an inside joke," Ava said, trying again. She caught Ethan's eye, but he just shrugged.

"Lou!" Lizzie pushed through the group and dove right into a bear hug with the previously stone-faced bouncer.

His face broke into a toothy grin. "Evenin', Miss Lizzie!" he said.

"Lou went to Cobalt High with my nephew," Lizzie explained to the group.

"She okay?" Lou said, cocking his head toward Macy.

"I'll be better when I can see what these people are doing to me!" Macy said.

Lizzie leaned toward Lou and whispered something. Ava could make out the words "private party."

Lou nodded and the foursome stepped inside as the music engulfed them. Macy jumped as Lizzie plunked the white hat she'd been carrying onto her yellow-blonde curls. Loretta Lynn had been replaced by Tim McGraw's "Don't Take The Girl," a song Ava remembered well. Harris loved his Greatest Hits cassette, and the girls would sing it at the top of their lungs from the truck bed anytime it came on.

Ava pulled Macy's bandanna down around her neck, unrolling

the tail end so it looked like a cowboy's neckerchief. Macy blinked as her eyes adjusted to the low light of the nearly empty Country Western Dance Hall.

"Ta-dah!" Ava said, opening her arms wide.

Macy's mouth dropped open. She whirled around to face the trio, then started laughing. Lizzie had taken off her parka and was a bedazzled wonder in a turquoise blouse fit for the rodeo. She had really come through, styling Ava and Ethan from her own wardrobe and borrowing the rest from friends. Ethan looked handsome, though slightly uncomfortable, in a light blue shirt with pearl buttons from Lizzie's next-door neighbor. Ava noticed the sleeves strained over his muscular biceps. He caught her eye. She quickly looked at Macy who was now marveling at the winking disco ball and the framed posters of state fair country concerts dating back to the seventies.

"What did you do?!" Macy said, shaking her head. "And where did you get that shirt?"

Ava twirled in her own rhinestone-covered blouse, hers a deep burgundy. "Don't be jealous," she said. "Remember this place?"

Macy laughed. "I think we both know I could never forget," she said. "But why the blindfold?"

"Would you actually have come line dancing with me if I'd asked?"

"Heck no!" Macy said. "But just because I'm here doesn't mean you can make me dance."

Lizzie snorted. Ava stuck out her bottom lip in a dramatic pout.

Macy rolled her eyes. "I'll think about it," she said.

"I'll take what I can get," Ava said, glancing over her shoulder toward the empty dance floor where the band was setting up their instruments. "I'm gonna go see what they have in store for us tonight."

"I'll grab a pitcher!" Lizzie said. "Four glasses?"

Ava leaned against the massive speaker near the stage as Morris, the bandleader, flipped through his binder of country songs. The group was called Southern Wonders and they certainly lived up to their name, covering everything from the oldies of Woody Guthrie and Patsy Cline, to classics from Kenny Chesney and Alan Jackson, and even songs from newer groups like Dan + Shay. Ava chose a mix of crowd-pleasing favorites, some of them for actual line dancing, and some just to sing and bounce along with.

While Morris wrote down Ava's list, she glanced at the others, noticing Ethan tugging Macy's elbow toward the dance floor. Ava laughed and shook her head as she watched Macy twist away and cross her arms defiantly. Ethan held up his hands in mock surrender.

"Well, what are you waiting for, Macy?" Ethan coaxed. "Are we gonna show this place how it's done, or what?!"

He stuck out his hand once more, but Macy just flashed him a stubborn smile.

"If you think I'm about to make a fool of myself in front of a bunch of strangers without even so much as one beer in me, you don't know me at all, Ethan Coleman."

He chuckled, then winked at Ava when he saw her watching.

"Look around, Macy!" he said. "Who's gonna see you?"

Macy dramatically gestured toward the bar, her arm freezing in place when she saw the empty stools. She threw Ethan a quizzical look; the place was empty except for the staff and the four of them.

"That's weird—where is everybody?" Macy asked him, wide-eyed, and Ava couldn't help but giggle. "This place is always hopping when I drive by."

"Ava told me how you two used to tear up teen night here," Ethan said. "Apparently, that ended several years ago. . .probably just as well. As youthful and lovely as you both might be, we might not have been too welcome in the seventeen-and-under crowd. So, Ava rented the whole shebang for two hours. It's all ours. . . Well, and Harris' too, of course."

He nodded to the dance floor where a two-stepping Harris was now working his way to the center. The jukebox music quieted as Morris signaled the Southern Wonders to grab their instruments, but Harris didn't seem to notice.

Macy laughed and Ava took that as her cue to rejoin them. Macy looked from Ethan to Ava, shaking her head slightly. "Ava... You did this for me?"

Ava nodded.

"Why?"

Ava shrugged. "Maybe part of it was selfish. . . It's been a long time since I got to share my moves anywhere outside my bedroom mirror. But mostly, it's because I want you to remember where you started."

Macy's eyes shined as Ava wrapped an arm around her shoulder. Ethan politely walked a few feet away, giving them privacy.

"Macy—you've always been this whole amazing person, even before Ben came along. It's time to stop beating yourself up. Have some fun... Do it for both of you." Ava squeezed her tighter as a tear snuck down Macy's cheek before she could wipe it away. "Remember," she continued, "the world has love in all kinds of places, even dimly-lit dive bars."

Macy laughed, then groaned as she wiped her nose on her sleeve. "There goes my makeup," she said.

"Nah, you still look great," Ava said. "A natural beauty."

Just then, Morris signaled the band and the opening bars of "Forever and Ever, Amen" filled the dance hall. While no one could argue with the quality of the Randy Travis version, the Southern Wonders were no chumps. Morris, who was also the lead singer, had a deep booming voice. The band played the original keyboard and guitar parts, but the addition of a fiddle gave their sound a unique flavor.

Macy sighed, then looked over at Ethan. "Alright, Twinkle-toes, let's do this," she called over the music.

Ethan smiled, then crooked both of his elbows in their direction. As both Ava and Macy hooked their arms through his, Ava's body tensed. She could smell his aftershave. She felt the heat of his body through his thin sleeve and she wondered if he could feel her racing pulse. Ethan led them to the dance floor where Harris was now doing the twist.

"Hey, Dad!" Macy shouted. Harris turned, his eye alight with glee.

"I haven't been dancing in ages!" he said. "But I still got it."

Ethan sidled over to Ava. He whispered as he leaned toward her, his voice barely audible above the music, "Confession: I have never line-danced in my life. Help."

Ava laughed. As she tiptoed to whisper back, he moved, her

lips accidentally brushing his ear.

"Oh, sorry!" she said. Where was Lizzie with the beer? Ava could use one.

"I requested an easy song first," she said, struggling to steady her voice. "It's been a long time for me, so I thought we should take it back to the basics. Here, before it starts, I'll show you."

Ava stepped a few feet away and put her hands on her hips. "It's very simple. You just put your right heel forward, then back." She waved her hand at him, indicating he should follow along. She repeated the step once more and he mimicked it exactly, if not with a bit of awkwardness. "Great!" she said. "Now, switch feet. . .and do that one once more... Yeah! That's exactly it!"

Ethan shot her a look: *Yeah, right.*

"Now, you're going to do a grapevine," she said.

"A what now?" Ethan said, his eyebrows raised.

"A grapevine," she repeated. "It's just where you go step, cross, step, together."

He scrunched up his face.

"Here, I'll show you," she said, laughing and stepping quickly to the music. Her body recognized the long-forgotten rhythm, much like when she'd started riding again. "Now you try!"

Ethan moved slowly, waddling like a confused penguin: Step. Cross. Step. Together.

"There you go!" she encouraged. "Only in the next song, the grapevine turns a little."

A moment later, the song ended and the band began to strum the opening of "Amos Moses."

Ava smiled. "Time to give it a shot!"

Ethan laughed and dramatically threw his face into his hands.

"By the end of the song, you'll be a pro," she insisted, but he shook his head. He couldn't hear her over the music.

She began to dance just as Lizzie came over with a stack of five glasses and a pitcher with the Blue Moon logo on the side.

"You guys want this here?" she shouted.

"Heck yeah!" Ava said. "There's no jumping in this dance. . .I'll take mine right now!"

Ethan took the pitcher from Lizzie and filled each glass, leaning it so only a thin layer of foam skimmed the top. "Bartender in a past life," he said, smiling when he noticed Ava watching. He passed her the first glass.

She swallowed the cold, crisp ale. Drinking mass-produced beer in cowboy boots was about the furthest she could get from her usual New York nightlife, and she was loving every minute of it.

Beers in hand, they stepped and crisscrossed through the song, Harris singing every word at the top of his lungs. Ethan was always one count behind, but if he felt at all self-conscious, he hid it well.

"You know, this song came out when I was in high school!" Harris shouted over them. "Classics never age!"

"Just like you, Harris!" Lizzie said with a wink, and they all laughed. Harris set his beer on the wooden counter and spun Lizzie around the group, not graceful in the slightest, but with all the pizazz and enthusiasm he could muster. They all clapped as the band segued into "Achy Breaky Heart" by Billy Ray Cyrus.

Macy looked right at Ava, eyes wide, and they both shrieked. Harris burst into a hearty belly laugh.

"Did I miss something?" Ethan called to Harris.

Harris shrugged, then shouted back, "The girls thought Billy Ray was a dreamboat! Never saw it myself... That strange mullet, you know."

Ethan laughed and glanced at Ava, an unreadable look in his eyes.

She flushed. "Come on!" she said to him. "I'll show you this one too!"

Ava deftly moved through the crisscrossing steps, then walked backward, hitching her left knee into the air. "Try it!" she called.

He did his best to mimic her steps. At least he was starting to get the hang of the grapevine.

"You're doing it!" she called.

He smiled. He stared at her feet as they walked forward, crossing one foot over, then tapping the other out to the side. Lizzie and Macy joined her line; Harris did too, though he was definitely improvising.

Ethan was starting to keep up and he was being such a good sport. She wondered where she could find good line dancing in New York. Her body shifted to autopilot as she moved through the steps, her thoughts drifting to Lucas. Would he be game to try something like this? She doubted it. He was a naturally good dancer, but he was not a fan of making a fool of himself.

Suddenly, Ethan's left foot caught behind the heel of his right, and he pitched sideways, knocking Ava hard to the floor.

"Oh my gosh, Ava, I'm so sorry!" he said, squatting down beside her.

She turned to him with a grin, raising her glass. "Didn't spill a drop," she said.

He laughed and pulled her to her feet. They set their drinks on the counter.

"OK, I'm all in," he said. He stood at her shoulder as they danced, moving side to side in rhythm with Lizzie, Macy, and Harris.

As one song flowed into the next, one dance into another, Ava felt light and free. These people, this place—it felt like home. But then, a little voice whispered: *Just enjoy it while it lasts.*

She closed her eyes for a moment and soaked in the smell of fried food and beer, the sound of honky-tonk and laughter, feeling sweat begin to bead her forehead. She *would* enjoy it while it lasted. . .but she would make sure she didn't get too attached.

Winded and sweaty, Ava plopped down on the red vinyl booth across from Ethan and Harris. She snatched a glass filled with ice water and slurped it down. She could hardly catch her breath. She glanced at her watch. No wonder! It was past eleven. She'd been dancing nonstop for over two hours.

Ava's private rental had ended at ten-thirty and the dance hall had begun to fill with a hodgepodge of Cobalt faces. Ethan and Harris were intently watching the back corner of the room, and she wondered if they'd even noticed her sit down.

"Am I interrupting?" Ava teased.

"Not at all; you're just in time," Ethan said, grinning as he finally looked at her.

"Time for what?" she asked.

"Come sit over here, Ava," Harris said, nodding to the space on the booth beside Ethan.

Ava slid out and squeezed into the other side. She had no choice but to touch Ethan, their arms pressing together. She suddenly became aware that she was covered in perspiration. She ducked her head to sneak a whiff of herself. Thankfully, she just smelled deodorant.

She followed their gaze and burst into laughter. There, surrounded by Lizzie, Lou the bouncer, and a growing crowd of western-clad locals, was Macy. She was arm-wrestling a man at least twice her size—and she was holding her own.

Everyone was cheering and heckling, but Lizzie could be heard bellowing above the crowd, "You go, girl! That's my boss! She's a beast!"

"I can say with confidence that I have never seen this side of Macy before," Ethan said.

Ava felt light-headed. She could smell the beer on his breath. "You finally get to meet the old Macy," she said, beaming.

Ethan looked at her, his face only inches from hers. Her heart jackhammered and she felt lightheaded. She tore her gaze away and watched Macy take a sip of water without losing her hold whatsoever. She really was a beast.

"I haven't seen Macy like this in. . .Well, you know," Harris said, a dreamy smile on his face. Ava had almost forgotten he was beside them. He leaned forward and looked at her over Ethan. Now, Ava could see that his eyes were brimming with tears.

"Thank you, Ava," Harris said. "You brought her back to me. Whether it's forever, or it's for a little while. . .now I know it's possible. She's still in there."

Ava's swiped at her own eyes with the back of her hand and

laughed. "Okay, Uncle, crying was *not* on the agenda tonight," she said, reaching over and squeezing his hand. "I don't know what finally reached Macy, but it most certainly was not just me. I missed her too. I had no idea how much."

Just then, a wave of shouting and laughter erupted from the corner. Lizzie pumped Macy's hand into the air and shouted, "All hail the queen!" Her opponent's buddies were clapping him on the back and teasing him.

Ava saw the man drop his head in defeat, but he was smiling. He leaned over to Macy and said something. Now that she could see his face more clearly, Ava thought he resembled a younger Hugh Jackman with his thick, chestnut hair and wide, toothy grin. Macy smiled, took his hand, and followed him to the dance floor. The crowd cheered.

"Okay, break over," Ethan said to Harris and Ava. "Did we come here to dance or what?"

Ava laughed and scooted out of the booth, Ethan close behind.

Harris didn't budge. "I think I got my dancing in for today, kids," he said with a chuckle. "You go on. I'll hold down the fort."

Ava felt an urge to grab Ethan's arm as they walked to the dance floor, but she shoved her hand into her back pocket instead. She glanced back at Harris and saw a wistful look on his face as he watched Macy and Hugh Jackman dance. This was a good night.

Lonestar's "Amazed" began to play. The lines of dancers started to pair off and spread out, and Ava saw Macy spin out of sight with Hugh until they were blocked by the crowd. Ethan grabbed her hand. She looked at him, trying to cover her surprise. He just smiled, and she wondered if he could see straight into her jumbled-up mind. She hoped he couldn't sense the storm that thundered in her every time he touched her.

"May I have this dance to the cheesiest country song in existence?" Ethan asked.

"It's sweet," she said. "I happen to like it."

"It's growing on me," he said, flashing her that warm, charming smile as he pulled her close to him, his free hand wrapping around her waist. Ava gently placed her left hand on his shoulder, warmth spreading through her entire body. He was a confident slow dancer, guiding them gracefully across the floor with ease. He might have line-danced like a flightless bird, but someone had made sure this boy knew how to move. Here and there, other dancers glanced their way and smiled. Ava looked up at Ethan and tried to imagine what they must look like to an outsider: a happy young couple, not a care in the world, madly in love. It was fun to play pretend, at least for one song.

She leaned her head against him and could hear his heart beating. His shirt stuck to his chest with sweat, but she didn't mind. Surely, one dance couldn't hurt. If she didn't let things go further, what was the harm?

She surrendered to the music. None of it was real. Soon enough, it would just be that one autumn in Utah.

"Amazed" ended and the band signaled they were taking a break as a recording began of some song Ava didn't recognize. The lights went up and several folks left the floor, likely to get another round or hit the restrooms. But as the song droned on, Ethan pressed her body tighter against his own, and she forgot anyone else was around. In fact, it wasn't until about halfway through the song that Ava realized there was no one else on the dance floor at all.

Ava and Macy huddled together on the curb outside the Country Western Dance Hall while Ethan went to get the car. It was cold. Harris had taken off just before midnight mumbling about needing a weekend to recover but otherwise looked as happy as Ava had ever seen him.

Ava watched as Lizzie and Lou added each other as Facebook friends and promised to catch up more often. Lizzie was a constant stream of "Oh my word" and "Just the most perfect" and "Isn't she a doll?" as Lou scrolled through a photo album on his phone from his recent wedding.

Ava glanced at Macy. She was glowing. Yes, she looked happier, but it was more than that: she looked younger, the hard tension of her face more relaxed. A sadness still lingered behind her eyes, but a sunny spark was now keeping it company.

Ava nudged her with her shoulder.

"What?" Macy asked.

"So, that was fun," Ava said.

"Really fun. As much as it pains me to say," Macy said, but she was still smiling.

"You sure seemed to be hitting it off with that arm-wrestling guy," Ava said, raising an eyebrow.

"Mark?" Macy asked.

"Ah, so he has a name," Ava said. "Mark" fit better than "Hugh."

Macy said nothing, but Ava wasn't about to let it go. "Mark seemed like quite the dancer," Ava said. "What's his story?"

"He's nice," Macy said simply. "Really nice. I can see him becoming a good friend."

"Just a friend?"

"And maybe a client," Macy said. "He has a daughter from a previous marriage who's about to turn nine. He asked about getting her riding lessons as a birthday present."

"Uh-huh," Ava said, grinning. "Sounds like there could be plenty of opportunities in the future to get to know Mark even better."

Macy sighed and turned to her. "Ava, I know it's time for me to move on. But you can sleep easy—I *am* moving on. I feel like myself again for the first time in years."

Ava felt a shred of guilt. She didn't want Macy to feel nagged, but she also couldn't ignore how much fun she had seemed to be having with a handsome divorcée.

"I'm excited for the future of my riding academy. I'm excited for the future, period," Macy continued. "I'm even remembering what it feels like to have fun, and I have friends again." She paused, seeming to choose her next words with care. "When it comes to Ben... I'm not ready. Not now and maybe not ever. I don't care if it sounds cheesy, or even crazy, but what I had with him was absolutely magical. Like straight out of a fairy tale."

She shoved her hands in her pockets, her breath misting in the cold night air as she gazed at the sky.

"I know he might be gone," Macy continued. "He probably *is* gone. But I've found peace knowing that I had one great love. I'm not going to search around for someone to just fill that spot. I'm okay. And it wouldn't be fair to some lovely guy who deserves better."

Ava nodded but said nothing. Maybe Macy really was okay. Ava felt an ache carving itself deep inside her chest. She wondered if what Macy described was how love was supposed to be, like something made of magic. She could see headlights waiting at the intersection and wondered if Ethan was looking back at them.

Macy reached out and hooked her elbow around Ava's own. "There's a reason people keep writing songs about it," Macy said, gently. "I hope one day you'll feel love like that. With Lucas. . .or someone else."

The headlights grew closer. Ethan's Range Rover pulled up to the curb and he quickly hopped out to open the doors. Lizzie said goodbye to Lou and climbed into the back. Macy jumped in beside her before Ava could follow.

"I need to catch up with Lizzie," Macy said, with a little too much innocence in her voice.

Ava rolled her eyes, but Macy was already closing the door. She climbed into the passenger seat, her fingers trembling as she fastened her seatbelt. She looked out the window as the blasting heat numbed her chilled face. The Garth channel was now serenading them with the dangers of wild affairs on stormy nights. She could feel Ethan glance at her from time to time on the dark drive back to the ranch, but she kept her face turned safely away.

Ava felt used up and exhausted, her head and her heart in a million different places. She needed to shower and sleep and wake up with a clear mind. She tried to focus on the bubbly chatter of Lizzie and Macy in the backseat.

After what felt like hours, she felt the bumpy pops of the gravel drive and saw the iron ranch sign loom ahead. She peeked at Ethan; he was watching the road intently. Only his clenched jaw made her wonder if his mind was also somewhere else.

Ethan parked in front of Macy's house, and they all climbed out. Ava stretched, her calves burning from the hours of dancing. She took a deep breath, the chilly night air rousing her after the long drive.

"Not to be rude, but I am dead on my feet," Lizzie said, turning to Macy. "Where do you want me?"

"Guest room is all ready for ya," Macy said. Lizzie gave them a little wave as she disappeared into the house.

"Lizzie doesn't usually work Fridays, right?" Ava asked when the door closed.

"Oh, she's off tomorrow, but I'd put money on her working anyway," Macy said, giving Ava a look. "She can't help herself."

"Must be a lot of loose ends with the festival this weekend," Ethan said. "Do you guys need a hand tomorrow? I'll be here anyway."

"You know, I just might take you up on that," Macy said. "We could use some extra muscle to load the truck if you really don't mind."

"It would be my pleasure," Ethan said, and Ava's throat tightened as he flashed them both that gorgeous grin.

"You sure I can't tempt you to take the pullout?" Macy asked him. "It's comfier than it looks."

"Thanks, but no," he said. "I better rest up for our lesson."

"Well, I don't think Lizzie knows where I moved the guest towels," Macy said, shooting a tiny smile in Ava's direction. "I better get in there. See you two bright and early."

She stopped at the top of the steps and turned back. "And

don't expect me to go easy on you guys just because you gave me the best night ever."

Ava smiled. It *had* been the best night ever. Macy closed the door and disappeared from view. Ava crossed her arms and looked down, kicking a piece of gravel into the grass. She wondered why Ethan wasn't leaving, but just as quickly realized she didn't want him to go. She turned to him with her best attempt at looking casual. He was leaning against the SUV, watching her with a naked longing in his eyes.

Her breath caught in her throat and she felt fire inside her whole body. She averted her eyes and abruptly walked away from the glow of the porch lights into the clear darkness. She looked up. Thousands of stars filled her view, too many to absorb all at once. She knew it was the same sky that stretched over her Upper East Side apartment, but it didn't feel that way. The city, the office, the job in Germany. . .It all felt very far away. And it just didn't seem to matter that much. She closed her eyes and exhaled, a gust of raw wind sweeping her breath away before rattling the nearby trees.

After a moment, she heard Ethan approach. She didn't open her eyes, but she could feel him beside her.

"Tonight was really something," Ethan said, "but all it takes is one look at that sky and everything just feels small. Not in a bad way. Just in a, I don't know, we're-all-little-pieces-of-a-big-puzzle kind of way."

She opened her eyes and looked at him.

"That was cheesy," he said, smiling.

"Different words," she said, nodding, "but that's pretty much what I was thinking too."

They stood in silence, watching the sky. Ava knew it was getting colder by the minute, but she wasn't ready to go inside just yet.

"Ethan," she said. "I'm sorry for how I handled things at the creek the other day, when. . .Well, you know."

"When I kissed you," Ethan said simply.

"Yeah. That." Ava's voice felt thick. She wanted to say more but couldn't find the right words.

"You don't have anything to apologize for," Ethan said. "I do. I'm not the kind of guy who goes around kissing women who aren't into me—believe me—and I guess I just misread the situation."

"No!" Ava exclaimed, her insistence startling them both. She cringed. But Lord, the way the corners of his eyes wrinkled when he smiled—not his polite smile that he wore for everyone, but that electric smile he was giving her right then. It turned her insides to fire. She could tell he was waiting for her to say more.

"I wanted you to kiss me, and we both know I kissed you back."

"That's not what I expected you to say," Ethan said.

"Yeah," she said. "Me neither."

He laughed.

"I'll be honest with you," Ava said. "I do have feelings for you. Real feelings. I have no idea what they mean, or what I'm supposed to do about it." She hesitated before adding, "Or even if you want me to do anything about it."

Ethan opened his mouth to speak, but Ava silenced him. "No. Please," she said. "Don't say anything. I realized I don't listen to myself very often. Not like you. I need some time to figure this out. And if you told me, right now, that you wanted me. . .Well, I don't know if I could hold myself back."

Her chest burned.

Ethan held her gaze for a moment, his expression unreadable. "Okay."

Ava had a sudden urge to press her mouth against his. She wanted to pull him into her cabin right then. Every cell in her body craved him, demanding to revisit the fury of that kiss by the creek—to just forget about tomorrow, or the next step, and just give in to that night. But she knew it wouldn't be right. And she knew it would only hurt in the end.

"In the meantime, could we still be friends?" she asked, after a moment.

"Friends," he said, trying on the word. "Yeah... We can definitely be friends." He stuck his hands in his pockets and shrugged. "Besides," he added, his eyes crinkling again. "It's probably not the best idea to date women who already have boyfriends."

Ava laughed a little, but inside, her stomach twisted. He was right. Ethan Coleman was the total package. He deserved the best of everything.

"I'll see you tomorrow," she said.

He nodded. "See you tomorrow, Ava."

He continued to stand there, and Ava realized he was waiting for her to leave.

"You think I'm gonna get kidnapped on the walk across the field?" she asked, raising an eyebrow.

"I'm not taking my chances," Ethan said with a little smile.

Ava scoffed, but she couldn't deny feeling flattered by his chivalry. She began the short walk across the field to her cabin, her feet feeling as heavy as lead with each step. She could feel

Ethan's eyes burning into her back the whole way. She had a feeling she wouldn't be sleeping much that night. She turned back once she reached the low porch. He waved and she wiggled her fingers in response.

She went inside and threw her boots onto the porch before she closed the door. She plopped down onto the little couch and felt her sketchpad poke into her thigh. Her mind somewhere else, she flipped it open. She smiled as it automatically fell open to the list she had written what felt like a lifetime ago.

Her eyes scanned it, stopping on the third line.

Get Macy to have fun with friends again.

She grabbed a pen and drew a big blue checkmark next to it. Then, she read the line below it for the thousandth time:

Help Macy accept that Ben is gone.

She traced the words with her finger. Though Macy seemed to now accept a life without Ben, it certainly wasn't how Ava would have planned it. She remembered the plane ride from New York, picturing some hot cowboy who would kiss away Macy's tears and show her how to love again. Maybe they would have had a couple of kids and named one Ben and put flowers on an honorary gravestone as a family every year. But Macy had decided on a different future for herself, one she had chosen on her own.

Ava washed her face and crawled into bed. She didn't think to turn on her phone or check her e-mails. In fact, to her relief, her mind felt empty and unburdened.

She dreamt of riding alone on a spotted Appaloosa through the streets of New York, free to weave between the Ubers and taxis and crowds of tourists and businessmen. She waved to everyone she passed, and they all greeted her by name. She galloped through Central Park, stopping to buy an ice cream cone and sit in the tidy grass, not a care in the world.

Twenty

Ava felt buoyant as she crossed the field to the barn the next morning, frost still blanketing the grass. She wiggled her toes; her riding boots were finally broken in. She inhaled deeply, relishing the smell of wet leaves and still-smoldering fireplaces.

When she woke, she'd been ravenous, but also something else: she felt at peace. She was done looking ahead, trying to predict the next move. It felt like trying to win a game of chess and never really knowing who she was playing—or even how to play, for that matter. For now, Ava was just going to be here and be alive.

Gunner greeted her with a whinny when Ava approached with the grooming bucket. She had come to love the meditative rhythm of the curry comb, the way that Gunner now opened his mouth for the bit when she brought the bridle near his head.

After she saddled him, Ava led the big gray horse to the outdoor arena. The sun had just broken the mountaintops, and she felt the draft of the stable evaporate. She could tell today would be beautiful. Ava thought she might go for a trail ride this afternoon. She could invite Macy. . .or Ethan.

And just like that, there he was, waiting for her next to the arena with Nikita. He tipped his helmet to her as if it was a cowboy hat.

"Mornin', ma'am," he said.

Ava laughed. "You seem to have recovered nicely," she said.

"Don't let this pretty face fool you," he replied. "I couldn't sleep." He held her gaze.

Ava's heart thudded.

"You two planning to actually ride these horses?" Macy called playfully from the stable, walking over to join them.

"Morning, Macy," Ava said, hoping she wasn't blushing.

Macy unwrapped the chain and swung open the gate. Ethan stepped aside, waving Ava through first. She walked to the center of the arena and mounted Gunner with ease.

When she'd climbed into the saddle during that first lesson, it had felt like trying to survive an earthquake. Now, her body instantly molded to Gunner as one synchronized unit. Macy had suggested she try bareback soon. Ava couldn't wait.

They began their lesson with the usual warm-ups, walking the whole of the arena, then practicing backing and sidestepping. Macy had arranged a set of poles across the center, and Ava and Ethan took turns jogging over them. The horses were patient, the riders were confident, and everyone was in good spirits. At the end of the lesson, Macy had them lope around three barrels that formed a large triangle in the arena, a beginner's version of barrel racing.

"What do you think, Macy?" Ethan called. "Am I ready for the

Sky of Embers rodeo?"

Macy laughed. "Ooh, I think it's probably too late to enter this year," she said. "Maybe next year?"

"Good point," he said. "I wouldn't want to scare off the competition this close to the show."

"Scaring them off is right!" Ava said, and they all laughed.

Ava noticed Ethan's cheeks were flushed. He had a couple days' worth of scruff, casting a masculine contrast to his boyish smile. Ava couldn't stop herself from staring at him.

What is going on with me?

Ava glanced at her watch and realized their hour was almost up. As if on cue, Macy shouted for them to lope their horses one last time. As hard as Ava tried to focus on her seat, she was consumed by thoughts of Ethan. He felt like a magnet across the arena and Ava was acutely aware of his every movement. Her stomach knotted and the peace of the morning shifted to a wistful ache.

"Amazing work today, guys!" Macy called as they lined up their horses in the center of the arena. "Ethan, I didn't have to tell you to put those heels down once!"

"I'm glad you noticed," Ethan said. "I've been practicing."

He winked at Ava. She smiled.

"You're both making incredible progress," Macy said, her voice tinged with pride. "Ava, at this rate, you'll be passing up your teenage self in a few weeks."

"Thanks, Macy," Ava said. "I think my muscles finally caught up. And it doesn't hurt that I'm learning from the best."

"I second that," Ethan said. "We're lucky to have you."

Macy's face flushed. "OK, you two, flattery isn't going to cool these horses off. You know the drill. I'll meet you both inside."

"Thanks, boss," said Ava.

Macy smiled and hopped off the fence, then headed for the barn.

"Shall we?" Ethan said to Ava.

She nodded and guided Gunner to the arena perimeter, his head hanging low as she loosened the reins. They rode in silence, the only sounds the occasional huffing of the horses and the calls of birds in the nearby woods.

Ava glanced toward Ethan and he looked away quickly, a sheepish smile on his face. He'd been watching her. She wondered if it was possible that he felt half as drawn to her as she did to him. Come to think of it, she wasn't sure which was more terrifying—if he felt the same way or if he didn't. She reminded herself that she was the one who asked him not to tell her what he was thinking. She swallowed, and her dry throat felt tight.

"I hope I didn't make you look bad today," Ethan said, a playful glint in his eye. "You heard Macy. I was on fire."

"I don't think those were her exact words," Ava said, laughing.

"I call it 'reading between the lines,'" he said.

"Well, in that case—reading between the lines—I'd say my riding ability speaks for itself. Macy said so in the subtext," she teased.

"Oh, now she's fancy! Using big words like 'subtext' to put me in my place!"

Ava snorted, causing Gunner to jump, bringing on a new fit of laughter from them both. Ethan rode up next to Ava, their legs only a couple of feet from touching. That dazzling grin seemed permanently etched on his face now, and Ava couldn't help but mirror it right back.

"You look like you belong up there, Ava," he said, cocking his head toward her. "I love watching you ride."

"The feeling is mutual," she said, softly.

"Ava!"

Ava's smile fell into her stomach. She turned. Lucas walked into the arena, shielding his wayfarer sunglasses with one hand as he beamed up at her.

"Lucas?!" Ava exclaimed, her voice suddenly high-pitched. Ethan shot Ava a confused look. She threw him a little shrug that she hoped carried an apology, then turned back to Lucas.

Even here, he was dressed in a tailored navy Tom Ford suit. His black hair was perfectly swooped up in the front. He couldn't look more out of place, and yet, he still managed to be as handsome as ever.

Ava dismounted, gathering Gunner's reins as she removed her helmet. "What are you doing here?" she squeaked.

Lucas eyed Gunner suspiciously as he walked a wide berth around him. He wrapped both arms around Ava, pressing her tightly against his chest for several seconds before letting her go. Ava glanced at Ethan, who was unfastening his helmet. He kept his eyes fixed on the ground.

"When I got your text, I thought something might have happened to you!" Lucas said, his eyes full of concern. "It was so unlike you to be hard to reach, but then when your phone was turned off? Well, I panicked! I assumed the worst. I was sick with worry and Carla thought—"

Lucas cocked his head toward Ethan as if noticing him for the first time. "Who's this?" he asked Ava.

Ava took a small step back from Lucas and straightened her twisted sweater. "Lucas, this is Ethan Coleman. Ethan, Lucas Dawson."

Ethan stuck out his hand. Lucas stared at it for a moment, then gave him a clipped nod.

Ethan's lips pressed into a tight smile. "How's it going, Lucas? Heard a lot about you."

"Ethan," Lucas said. "Sure wish I could say the same."

Ethan's hand still hung in the air. Finally, to Ava's relief, Lucas extended his own. Ava saw their knuckles turn white as they shook.

"So, what exactly is going on here, Ava?" Lucas said, laughing tightly as he turned back to her. "You're not getting brainwashed out here in the boonies, are you?"

Ava's smile turned sour, but she didn't know what to say. Ethan still wouldn't look at her.

"I should go," Ethan said. "Ava, want me to take Gunner in for you?"

She nodded. "Thanks, Ethan." As she passed him Gunner's reins, their fingers touched. He quickly pulled away.

"See ya, buddy!" Lucas called after Ethan as he walked both horses out of the arena.

Ava could feel her pulse in her forehead. The ground felt unsteady beneath her, and a wave of nausea flooded her throat. She winced. Lucas wasn't known for his tact, but he wasn't usually downright rude. She tucked her helmet under her arm and ran stiff fingers through her matted hair.

Lucas turned to her and tenderly placed his cool, rough hands on either side of her sweaty face. "Ava, I will only ask this one time," he said quietly. "Is he the reason you didn't come back?"

Ava shook her head and sighed. "Lucas, there's so much more to me than that." She watched the horizon tilt and suddenly felt like she might faint. "Can we—can we sit down?"

Lucas nodded and followed her outside the area. They sat side by side on the small bleachers, the metal warm through Ava's jeans. A dry gust of wind blew Ava's loose waves across her face. Lucas smoothed her hair before she could, a tender gesture he'd performed countless times in the wind tunnels of New York's skyscrapers. Ava studied the familiar lines in his forehead. They looked deeper than she remembered and his jaw was clenched.

"I've been doing a lot of thinking," she said. "About my career, my home. . .my whole *life*, really."

Her voice caught and he pressed her hand between his own.

"Lucas," she said. She met his gaze. "I've tried to tell you what I want and you wouldn't listen. No one does. So, *I'm* trying to listen. I'm trying to figure out how to connect my life in New York with my dreams, and with you, and where I want to be headed. It hurts that you would chalk all this up to some romantic whim."

"I'm sorry, Ava," Lucas said. "I got jealous. No woman has ever had this effect on me and it's terrifying, to be honest." He chuckled nervously. "Now that we're so close to getting everything we've worked so hard for. . .I guess I just freaked."

"I'm sorry too, Lucas. For the way I handled everything. You deserve better. And based on that, I think maybe we need to talk about some things."

"Ava, wait," Lucas said, squeezing her hand tighter. "Before you say more, I want you to hear me out. I'm glad this happened. I took you for granted. I'll be the first to admit that... But this made me see what life would be like without you. I was like a ghost when I got your text saying you weren't coming back; ask Carla."

He let go of her hand and climbed off the bleachers, spreading his fingers as he pressed both his hands against his chest. "Ava," he said, an intensity in his voice. "I am so afraid of losing you. And of what might be happening to you here without me."

He took a deep breath and stretched his arm toward her. She took his hand and let him pull her to her feet beside him. He brushed her hair from her face once more and stared deeply into her eyes.

"I thought I could have you on my terms, with no compromise," Lucas said. "That was selfish and stupid. I'm so sorry. It was unfair to expect you to just follow me. I'm ready to follow you for a change."

Lucas knelt in the clay-colored dirt, Tom Ford suit and all. He reached into his breast pocket and pulled out a small light blue box. Ava gasped.

He opened the box and a huge pear-cut diamond ring glittered in the morning sun.

"Lucas," Ava said, her voice barely a whisper.

"I've been doing a lot of thinking," Lucas said. "Compromise is a good thing. I know you want a traditional family. You need marriage, and kids, and a house that isn't forty floors up. I believe in our future." He smiled up at her, his face open and hopeful. "I know we don't always agree, but we overlap where it matters. I'll give you those things. Because I love you and that's all that really matters. I want to marry you, Ava."

Lucas waited, the box outstretched, but Ava couldn't speak. She took a deep steadying breath and saw Ethan standing in the doorway to the stable. Her heart tightened as he turned and disappeared into the dark building.

She looked back at Lucas and saw a childlike fear flash across his eyes. She tried to offer a reassuring smile, but her face was frozen.

Finally, Lucas stood and dusted his pants, then pressed the ring box gently into her hand. "I know this is a lot," he said, his voice small and uncertain. "Don't give me an answer now. Think it over, OK?"

She managed a small nod.

He reached out and stroked her cheek softly with his thumb. "This fixes everything. And I'll go to Germany with you, if you'll have me." His eyes searched hers. "We can start our life together. Everything you ever wanted."

Ava glanced at the open box, the ring casting colored beams in every direction as it reflected the sunlight. It was exquisite. She was sure it had cost a small fortune. She gently closed the box and reached for Lucas' hand. It was trembling. She had never seen him nervous.

She squeezed it and smiled at him. "I'll think about it, Lucas," she said. "I'm a little overwhelmed right now and I just. . .I need to think. But you coming here to see me. . .and all this? It means a lot. So, thank you."

Lucas smiled and exhaled loudly as if he'd been holding his breath. "Good," he said. "I'm glad. Just please don't leave me hanging too long. I don't think I can bear it."

"I won't," Ava reassured him. Her stomach was doing flips. She needed to be alone.

Ava closed the arena gate and latched the chain. So much had changed since Macy had opened it only an hour before. She led Lucas around the barn rather than through it; she didn't want to see Ethan just yet. Maybe she could ask Lizzie to give Lucas a tour, buying her some time to breathe.

Ava stopped as a familiar French twist backed away from a spotless black Escalade. The driver raised his hand in greeting and Ava recognized him as the same man who had come to take her to the airport. Ava shot a questioning glance at Lucas, who simply shrugged.

"I didn't have a chance to mention it," he said, still looking pale.

At the sound of Lucas' voice, Carla spun around, and her wild eyes landed on Ava. "My dear, sweet girl! Thank goodness you're okay!" Carla shouted, charging Ava, her stilettos wobbling across the gravel drive. She wrapped Ava in a tight hug. Ava inhaled the familiar vanilla notes of her perfume, clocking Carla's off-white wool pantsuit as she released her from her grip. Lucas had always been a city dweller, but Carla should know better. It seemed to Ava like a statement: *I am here, but I am not of this place.*

"Hi, Mom," Ava said, forcing a smile. "Never thought I'd see the day you stepped foot in Utah again."

As much as they could butt heads, Ava was touched to see her. She didn't know exactly what it had cost Carla to come back here after all these years, but she knew it couldn't have been easy.

"I've been so worried. I'm sure Lucas told you—we were both just sick," Carla sputtered. "I know I was pushing you to get home, but you could have talked to me. Above all, I'm your mother, Ava."

"Aunt Carla?" Macy called, stepping out of the shadows of the stable.

Carla turned. "Is that my little niece?!" she exclaimed, her mouth dropping open. "Oh my goodness! Look at you!"

"And this must be the infamous Lucas," Macy said as she joined them.

"Guilty as charged," Lucas said. He seemed to have regained some of his composure. "I bet that makes you the country cousin."

Macy smiled. "Something like that," she said.

"You've done some amazing things with this old place," Carla said to Macy. "It certainly doesn't look like the patch of dirt I left behind."

Carla gave a little laugh, but Macy said nothing.

"Is that brother of mine around?" Carla asked.

"He's at his house in town, but I'm sure he'll come when I tell him you're here," Macy said. "Why don't you all come for dinner at my place tonight? Carla, I have a guest room you're more than welcome to use. And Lucas. . ." Macy shot a questioning look to Ava.

"I'll stay with Ava," Lucas said quickly, before leaning toward her and adding in a low voice, "If that's alright?"

"Of course," Ava said weakly. So much for alone time.

"Carla, let me help you get those bags inside," Lucas said as the driver finished unloading the back of the SUV. Lucas handed him a crisp hundred-dollar bill then grabbed the larger of the two suitcases. Carla grabbed her carry-on and followed him toward the big white farmhouse.

"Where should I put this?" Lucas called from the bottom of the steps.

"Second floor, the room at the end of the hall," Macy said. "Help yourselves to anything in there. I have some iced tea in the fridge. I'll be right in."

As Carla and Lucas disappeared into the house, Macy gripped Ava's arm. "Okay, was so not expecting that!" she whispered. "Did you know they were coming?"

Ava shook her head, a numbness now replacing the nausea.

"Are you alright?" Macy asked.

"Me?" Ava asked, forcing a smile. "Fine."

She could tell Macy didn't buy it. Macy gave her arm a gentle squeeze, then walked off toward her house.

Ava tipped her head back, squeezing her eyes shut. She wrapped her arms tightly across her thin sweater. The dusty breeze had picked up, making the day feel much colder.

Here was her alone time, these next five minutes. Here was her time to think. But Ava's mind was a cacophony.

Why didn't I just say yes?

This was what she wanted. She had dreamed of a marriage to an amazing man who only wanted her. She could have a family of her own. She'd been waiting for Lucas to catch up for years, and now that he had, she was caught off guard.

Ethan's hurt expression flashed across her mind. Sure, she had a little crush, but that's all it was. She loved Lucas. Now, nothing stood between them. She needed to lie down.

She headed to the cabin, figuring Macy would point Lucas in the right direction. She would shower and drink some water and by then, maybe her brain would start functioning again.

Twenty-One

"So, Ava tells me about a job in Germany," Harris said between bites of pulled pork. "Sounds like a big deal."

"I'm surprised she told you," Carla said. "She sure didn't show any excitement when I told her about it. I'm curious... Did she also mention she was supposed to return to New York yesterday? One can only hope Mr. Shubert will wait."

"I'm sure he will," Macy said cheerily as she cut into her barbecue chicken. "From what I hear, Ava's work is one-of-a-kind."

"Oh, I see you've found time to become an art expert on top of all your farming duties," Carla said, smirking at Macy.

Macy reddened but said nothing.

Harris chuckled. "You don't need to be an art expert to look for the best in people, Carla. If this Shubert fellow is that fickle, then good riddance, I say."

Ava downed the rest of her chardonnay and hoped her

efforts at a polite smile were still convincing. She glanced at her watch. How had they only been sitting here for twenty minutes? Thankfully, although Ava seemed to be the focus of conversation, no one except Lucas was paying much attention to her.

Watching Carla instigate a quiet standoff against Harris and Macy was nothing short of excruciating. Carla seemed to be out for blood, while Harris maintained his good-natured sense of humor. Meanwhile, Lucas seemed oblivious, too focused on Ava's every need. Right on cue, he filled her wine glass once more.

Ava sighed. She felt like she was watching her life being decided for her, as if she wasn't even there. Ava had become a pro at listening with detached interest, a tethered balloon on a ten-foot string. She shoved a forkful of pulled pork into her mouth, savoring the smoky flavor. At least the food was good. Harris had brought Owen's BBQ, a Cobalt favorite.

"Adam Dixon of *The New York Times* called Ava a 'millennial Picasso,'" Lucas said, nodding proudly at her.

"That's the fella who painted the messed-up faces, right?" Harris asked. "Good for you, Ava, that sounds like a nice compliment."

Ava noticed Lucas hadn't touched his sandwich or his wine. She wondered if he was upset about earlier or if he simply found the quality beneath him.

"Ava's art exudes this cool confidence that is really in demand right now," Carla said.

Cool confidence. Ava had heard that exact line recited to her during every interview in the past year, and she still wasn't exactly sure what it meant.

"How funny," Macy said, her voice flat. "And here, I always

admired Ava's warm approachability."

"Yes, well, a week in the city and we'll get rid of that," Lucas said, chuckling. "Won't we, Ava?"

Ava looked up, caught off guard at being included in the conversation.

"I'm kidding," Lucas said quickly, seeming to interpret her silence as offense.

"You know, Macy's riding academy has really taken off," Ava said, eager for a change of topic. "Her students seem to love her and she's an incredibly skilled teacher. I can't believe how much I've learned."

She turned to Lucas and flashed him a smile. "I thought maybe you could share some publicity ideas with her. Maybe some ways to get the word out?"

Lucas smiled politely at Macy. "What's your most recent ad campaign look like?" he asked.

"Ad campaign?" Macy asked, twisting her wedding ring. "I mean, we have a Facebook page, where we post photos from horse shows. And we have this new flyer Lizzie made. Thanks to Ava, it's now in almost every shop in town. Oh! And we always have a booth at the Sky of Embers Festival. People come from as far as Weber County, and we usually get tons of new students after that. It starts tomorrow, funny enough. The festival is a really good time if you want to stop by."

Lucas' smile tightened. "That all sounds very charming," he said, ignoring the invitation. "Unfortunately, I think my contacts are at a bit of a different level, if you know what I mean."

Macy's cheeks burned pink as she stared at her plate.

Ava gripped her fork. "Mom, do you remember the Country

Western Dance Hall?" she asked.

"Unfortunately," Carla said dryly.

"Well, it's still there," Ava said. "They've updated in some ways, like remodeling the bathrooms, but other than that it's exactly like I remember."

"Your mom and I used to bring down the house whenever 'Louisiana Saturday Night' came on," Harris said, throwing Carla a wink.

"How could one forget?" Carla asked through clenched teeth.

"I can't tell you how thankful I am to have had Ava here," Macy said. She nudged Ava's foot under the table. "I really let some things get away from me around the ranch, and for a city girl, she sure can wield a pitchfork."

"That might be a bit of an exaggeration," Ava said, but the compliment made her smile.

"No, I mean it," Macy said. "A month ago, I couldn't even look at Ben's field, and now it's ready to plant. That never would have happened without you, Ava."

"Well, speaking of the Dance Hall, let's not forget my biggest achievement," Ava said. "Getting you out there on the dance floor." She turned to Carla. "Not only did she give those regulars a run for their money, but I believe she is the current undefeated arm-wrestling champion."

"By that she means I beat one guy," Macy said, laughing.

"Only because no one dared to mess with you once they saw Mark go down," Ava said.

Now, even Lucas and Carla joined in the laughter. Ava felt the tension in her body start to ease. Carla and Harris might not ever be the best of friends, but maybe they would finally act like they shared blood. The dinner could definitely be worse.

"So, let's see," Carla said. "Fun with friends, fixing up the farm. . .It sounds like Ava has been checking off those little boxes left and right."

Warning bells rang in Ava's head.

"Boxes?" Macy asked.

Ava's stomach dropped.

"So, what's left?" Carla asked Ava, ignoring Macy's question. "Dating?" She turned to Macy. "Did she find you a nice guy?"

Macy's brow furrowed as she laughed tightly. "Did I miss something?"

"I'm sorry, Macy," Harris said before Ava could respond. "I didn't want to tell you this, because I knew you'd try to change my mind. But I asked for Ava's help. I asked her to come to Utah."

"Oh. I see," Macy said, her expression unreadable. Ava tried to meet her eyes, but Macy just stared at her fork.

Lucas, seeming to sense the tension, began refilling everyone's wine glasses, pointedly skipping his own, which was still full.

"To be fair, Harris, you can't take all the credit on this one," Carla said loudly.

Mom, please stop talking, please stop talking.

How many glasses was that for Carla? She had belligerently criticized more than one auction house over the years when an open bar had been involved. Ava knew once her mom was tipsy, no secret was safe. Carla took a big gulp of her fresh glass. Ava caught Lucas' eye and gestured toward her neck: *Cut her off.* He nodded.

"Ava never would have come if I hadn't dangled her dream in front of her," Carla continued. Ava's blood felt like ice. "So, I'll ask again, Macy: Are you seeing anyone?"

"No," Macy answered, her voice stony.

"Too bad," Carla muttered. "For you and her. Ava had just one item left on her list and all that money would have been hers." She turned to Ava, her eyes glazed. "Sorry, my dear, but you gave it the old college try. At least you can make that money back in Germany!" Carla hiccupped and laughed, the only sounds in the frozen room.

Macy set her glass down and stood. "Well, it seems I missed the memo," she said, her voice thundering across the small dining room. "You came here to win some bet with your mom? That's why you came?!"

"Macy, it didn't come out right, but I can explain!" Ava scrambled to her feet, rushing around the table. She grabbed Macy's arm, but Macy roughly jerked it away.

"Don't touch me," Macy hissed, tears filling her eyes.

"Did I say something wrong?" Carla asked, looking innocently from Macy to Harris. Ava couldn't believe it; Carla actually had no idea what she had done. Ava couldn't stand to look at her mother.

Macy charged towards the stairs.

"Honey!" Harris called, rising to his feet.

"Macy!" Ava yelled, running after her. "Wait, just give me five minutes, please—"

Macy stopped on the landing and spun to face her. She was shaking, hurt and fury permeating her entire body. "Don't even think about following me!" she spat. "You know that saying, 'When someone shows you who they are, believe them the first time?' Well, it's my own damn fault for forgetting. I've known who you are for *years*. You need to leave. You have no business being here." Macy stormed up the steps and a door slammed a moment later.

Ava turned slowly. Harris, Carla, and Lucas stood, each looking unsure what to do next.

Ava glared at Carla. "Mom, this was low, even for you," she said. "How could you? Can't you see what you just did?!"

Ava grabbed her coat and burst through the front door into the cold night air. Before she ran off the porch, she realized her purse was still inside. She cursed as hot tears spilled down her cheeks. She felt guilty and rotten and defeated. She turned the corner of the wraparound porch and leaned against the railing, her head in her hands.

Ava was furious with her mother's tactless behavior, but she knew it wasn't all Carla's fault. Ava had ignored countless opportunities to tell Macy the whole truth, but she hadn't. Did she really think Macy would never find out?

Ava had soaked up Macy's newfound affection, and she had known she risked losing it by telling her the whole story. She'd been afraid of Macy hating her all over again. But now, the truth had come out even worse than she'd feared. She drew in an icy breath, shaking as she exhaled.

She heard the front door close quietly and looked up. Harris walked toward her, holding out her handbag. Ava took it, grateful as she wiped her face with her sleeve. He stopped a few feet away, politely gazing over the darkened fields instead of at her tear-streaked face.

"I'm so sorry," Ava finally said.

Harris shoved his hands in his pockets. "You don't owe me anything, Ava," he said. "I can see how it looks. But even if that story your mama told is what got you here in the first place, I know it's not what made you stay."

Ava looked at him, the kindness in his eyes conjuring a fresh wave of tears. "You think Macy will ever forgive me?" Ava asked.

"Probably," Harris said.

Ava raised her eyebrows.

"Maybe," he admitted. "You women are complex creatures."

Ava laughed, despite herself. "Thanks, I think," she said.

They both turned toward the field, the remaining grass a sea of white in the moonlight, and a comfortable silence settled between them.

"Uncle Harris?" Ava asked.

He turned.

"Do you know why Mom took me with her when she did?" she asked. "Before, I mean. The last time?"

Carla had plopped her on the ranch for a week or two so many times that Ava had lost count. It usually happened when Carla was chasing a hot investment tip in some far-flung country. But when Carla had left her for the final time, she'd mumbled some reason about how teenagers needed to stay in school. When Ava asked how long she'd be staying, Carla wouldn't give her an answer, and Ava knew something was different. But as the months turned to years, Ava's tears dried, and she built a life with Harris and Macy. Carla had rarely called, but she'd usually visited for a few days at Christmas and Ava's birthday, passing out lavish gifts before rushing back to her work.

The last visit had started just like all the others. The first night, they'd had Jimmy's pizza and watched *10 Things I Hate About You* on VHS. Carla, long-distance calling card in hand, had been on the house phone the entire time. But the next morning, she'd shaken Ava awake and made her pack her bags. When Ava had begged for an explanation, Carla just said it was time to go.

Harris closed his eyes and sighed. "I suppose I might know," he said. "That last time you stayed. . .Well, it wasn't like the other times, Ava. At first, you were withdrawn, a shell of the spunky, creative niece I knew. She had abandoned you and you knew it."

His shoulders slumped slightly as he leaned against the railing and the light of the moon shadowed the creases in his face. Ava could see glimpses of the old man he was becoming. "I always saw you as a daughter, and your mom leaving you dang near broke my heart. It wasn't right. I was angry. Then, as you got settled here, you really took root. You were growing up so fast. . .but all that felt fragile, you know? Like your happiness was up to the whims of my sister. I'd been chewing on it for a long time and had kept it to myself, but I must have had a few extra beers that night. Seems loose lips and booze run in the genes. It's possible that after you girls went to bed, I said a thing or two she didn't much like."

"What did you say?" Ava asked.

"Well, it's been a long time," Harris said. "But I believe my words were something along the lines of 'It's a shame two girls have to grow up without a mother when one doesn't have to.'"

Ava stared at the peeling white paint on the porch railing, now gray in the dark.

"Ouch," she said.

"Yeah," Harris replied. "I was seeing red, but I'll be the first to admit it wasn't fair of me to say. She's my sister and I love her. It's not for me to pass judgment on her parenting." He cleared his throat. "I expect she was doing the best she knew how, just like

I have for Macy. I did apologize, more than once, but she wasn't having it. Couldn't blame her, I suppose."

He tenderly squeezed Ava's shoulder. "Looks like she proved me wrong," he said. "From what I gather, she hasn't let you out of her sight since."

Ava half-laughed, half-sniffled. "That's an understatement," she said.

"You know, you're lucky to have a mama who loves you so much," Harris said.

Ava nodded. She knew. She wiped her face for what felt like the hundredth time, took a deep breath, and walked to the top of the steps.

"Ava?"

She turned back.

"You know you always have a home with me," he said. "Uncle, father, however you see me—family is family."

Ava squinched her eyes to keep a fresh wave of tears at bay. She nodded.

"Thank you," she said, then hesitated before adding, "Do you still miss Aunt Anna?"

He smiled and gazed out over the fields. "I miss her for myself, but I'm used to that," he said. "She's been gone for twice as many years as I knew her for. It's hard to picture her any older than she was when she passed, but I still see her, in Macy. I wish she'd been able to know her."

"She would be proud, Uncle. You've been everything for Macy." Ava reached out and placed her hand over his. "Not just her," she said. "For so many years, you were everything for me, too. You really are a father to me. I hope you know that."

Harris opened his mouth to speak but closed it again before finding any words. It could have been the light, but Ava thought his eyes were shining now too.

"It's an honor, Ava," he said, finally, his voice thick. "No matter what. . .please don't disappear again."

She smiled. "Never again."

He nodded. "Night, Ava."

"Night," she said.

Ava walked down the creaky wooden steps and across the field, the porch light from the cabin guiding her. Once she reached her stoop, she turned back and saw the distant figure of Harris, silently watching. She gave a little wave. He waved back. She let herself inside, then remembered Lucas would be coming back soon. She left the door unlocked and climbed into the loft without so much as turning on a light.

Twenty-Two

Ava brushed mascara onto her long lashes, then stepped back to examine her reflection in the small bathroom mirror. She looked a little silly all done up and still wearing her pajamas, but she hadn't wanted to wake Lucas by getting into the closet. She sighed. No amount of makeup could cover the dark circles that betrayed her sleepless night.

She swallowed the dregs of her second cup of coffee, replaying the night before in her mind. Lucas had entered the cabin just minutes after Ava, but the tiny house was already dark and quiet. Ava had curled up in the loft bed, her face to the wall. She heard Lucas silently climb the ladder. After a few moments, he sighed, then she heard him climb back down. He had fallen asleep under a quilt on the small couch, his legs hanging over the edge.

She woke several times in the night, never feeling like she drifted below the surface of unconsciousness. She gave up and got out of bed once the first of the morning light had entered the cabin. Lucas slept on as she tiptoed to the shower, welcoming the solitude.

After finishing the last touches of her makeup, Ava walked out of the bathroom and saw Lucas through the window sitting on the porch swing. She filled her mug a third time and went outside, throwing her jacket on over her pajamas. He looked up, smiled, and made room for her on the swing. She sat beside him and they both sipped their coffees in silence.

Ava heard a door slam and looked across the field to see Lizzie and Macy stretching bungee cords across the top of the truck bed. Lizzie looked up and waved. Ava waved back.

Macy followed Lizzie's gaze, then looked away when she saw Ava. She hurried around to the driver's side and climbed in. A moment later, Lizzie joined her, and they drove off without a backward glance. Ava's stomach clenched. *There she goes*, she thought. *Gone from my life again.*

She looked up, fighting the tears that were forming in the corners of her eyes. She thought she'd cried more in the past week than she had in her entire life. Lucas didn't seem to notice.

"Wonder where they're going with all that stuff," Lucas said.

"The lantern festival," Ava said.

"The what?"

"Lantern festival," Ava repeated impatiently. "Macy told you about it last night, remember? It's called Sky of Embers. It starts today."

"Huh. Cute," he said, his voice dripping with sarcasm. "Bet you're super bummed to be missing that."

"I am, actually," Ava said quietly. She stared down the road where the only lingering sign of the truck was a thin swirl of dust.

"I would have loved to go."

"Another time," Lucas said, but she doubted he meant it. "Are you packed?"

"No," Ava said. "Should I be?"

"Well, our flight isn't until after dinner, but I say the sooner we get to Salt Lake, the better. Pretty sure I had nightmares about that barbeque from last night."

Ava's throat felt dry as she set her mug on the railing. Lucas wrapped his arm around her waist and pulled her up and onto his lap. He kissed her cheek.

"Don't you want to see this place?" Ava asked. "I could give you a tour, show you my old stomping grounds. I can't see being invited back anytime soon."

"I would, babe, but I didn't exactly bring the right clothes to hike around a farm," Lucas said. "Let's do a little loop in the car on our way out."

"Well, I'd like to at least visit Gunner one last time," she said. "And I don't want to leave without saying bye to Harris. We could have lunch in town. Cobalt has some great spots."

"I guess we don't have to rush out that quickly," Lucas said. "Lord knows Carla is probably still dead to the world."

He pressed his face into her hair, then kissed her ear. "No one is here...Maybe we don't need to rush anywhere." His lips trailed her neck. "Have you thought any more about it?" he murmured.

He didn't have to clarify what 'it' was.

She stood, pulling away from his grip. "I'm still processing. I better go ahead and pack," she said, ignoring the disappointed look on his face.

She went inside and pulled out her phone, then found Ethan's number in her contacts. Her thumb hovered over his name. Finally, she wrote a text:

Sorry about yesterday. Can we talk soon?

She waited a moment, but he didn't reply. She sighed and stuffed her phone into her jacket pocket. The ring box was still there, undisturbed since the afternoon before when Lucas had given it to her.

Ava packed, then went for one last walk of the property. Lucas had been reading on his phone when she left, but she found him asleep on the couch when she returned. She quietly closed the door and settled onto the porch swing. She pulled out her phone. Still no reply from Ethan.

"Good morning, dear," Carla called. Ava looked up as her mother tiptoed across the field as if she was wading through a pit of snakes. No one would ever guess that woman grew up there.

"It's one p.m.," Ava said.

"Cheap wine always does that to me," Carla said, laughing a little too hard. She looked at the swing, but Ava didn't move.

"Listen," Carla began, "I owe you an apology..."

Ava waited.

"I think I was a bit dehydrated after the flight and things are a tad blurry," Carla continued, "but I remember enough. I should have kept my big mouth shut. I hope I didn't mess things up too badly for you."

Ava looked at her mother, timid and sallow. Her shoulders were slumped, uncharacteristic for a tidy woman who prided herself on perfect posture. Carla's eyes were glassy, and Ava thought she could detect a hint of fear in them. Ava sighed, then scooted over. She patted the swing beside her, and Carla gingerly sat.

"You caused quite a show last night, Mom," Ava said. "And the worst part was that you didn't seem to care who it hurt."

"I'm sorry, Ava," she said, her voice small. "I care now. I think I should lay off the wine for a bit."

"You can't just blame the booze," Ava said, her eyes narrowing as she shook her head. Carla blinked back at her with wide eyes. Ava rubbed her face and sighed. "I'll never forget the way Macy looked at me last night. I don't think she'll ever forgive me. Still... I'm just as much at fault as you. It's hard to blame you for telling the truth."

Carla hesitantly patted Ava's thigh. After a moment, Ava covered her mother's hand with her own.

"How did I get such a wise daughter?"

"I honestly don't know," Ava said.

They both laughed, and Ava felt the space between them thaw as they rocked back and forth on the big wooden swing. The spindly tree in front of the cabin was now bare, its branches somehow blown clean before the others nearby. Ava watched as a crimson bird landed on the highest limb, its vibrant feathers stark against the gray bark. Cardinals were everywhere in Central Park, but Ava had never seen one in Utah. Its black eyes seemed to stare right at her before it pushed off and disappeared into the forest.

"Shall we grab some food then get on the road?" Carla asked. "I figure your rental car will suffice for the three of us."

A sleepy-eyed Lucas walked out onto the porch, his suitcase in one hand. "Hey, Carla," he said. "Are you both packed?"

Ava nodded.

"My bags are on Macy's porch," Carla said.

"I'll drive over and grab them, then circle back for you ladies," said Lucas.

After he drove off, Carla suddenly wrapped her arms around Ava's neck.

"I've missed you, my dear," she whispered, her voice insistent.

Ava smiled. "I've missed you too, Mom."

Ava went inside and dragged her suitcase onto the porch. She watched as Lucas parked in the gravel outside Macy's house. Carla was gazing out at the horizon, a funny look on her face.

"You really don't miss it at all?" Ava asked.

"What, this place?" Carla asked. "Heavens, no. But it's nothing against Utah. We were simply never a good match."

"Did you ever see the treehouse?" Ava asked.

"I remember you mentioning it," Carla said, "but Harris built that thing long after my hiking days were over."

"I can show you on the way out," Ava said. "There's a place to park right beside the path."

"That sounds nice," Carla said, her eyes still fixed on the mountaintop. "I'm glad this place became something special for you, Ava."

"Well, it doesn't matter now," Ava said. "I can't imagine I'll be welcome here anymore."

Carla waved her hand distractedly. "Emotions pass, dear," she said.

Ava wanted to believe her. As she watched her mother swing, she wondered what she had been like as a child. It was hard to picture a girl with skinned knees and sun-kissed cheeks, though she must have been that way once.

"Do you care if we stop to say goodbye to Harris?" Ava asked.

"Sure, let's invite him to lunch," Carla said cheerily.

Ava glanced sideways at her. "Do you like him again?" she asked. "Did I miss something?"

"I've always liked him," Carla said. Ava narrowed her eyes at her. "Okay, fine, loved him, anyway. He is my brother, after all. We may not agree on everything, but I think after last night, I can at least understand him a bit better. We had a little chat after you left. I had so many things I planned say to him one day, but given the chance, we're both too old and tired. Once you reach a certain age, you look around and notice the blazing fires of your past suddenly seem to do nothing more than smolder."

Lucas pulled up and popped the trunk, then hurried to the porch to grab their bags.

"We're grabbing lunch in town," Carla told him.

"Great," he replied, without enthusiasm.

They loaded into the car and drove away without fanfare. Ava felt empty, her chest scraped clean. She watched the forest blur as Lucas sped down the road, gravel clanging against the car's underside.

"Lucas, slow down," Ava said, touching his arm. She nodded to the clearing up ahead. "Will you stop up there, on the right?"

He said nothing, but pulled over and put the car in park.

"Anyone else want to see the treehouse?" she asked.

"Is there mud?" Lucas asked, scrunching his nose.

"Never mind," she said.

"Honey, why don't you take a picture of it and show me?" Carla said brightly. "Then you can keep it forever."

Ava sighed and stepped out of the car, slamming the door harder than she intended. They probably wouldn't appreciate it anyway. But it wasn't a bad idea to take a picture.

She walked up the grassy embankment into the forest. It was windy today and the rustling of the trees sounded almost like rain. She remembered the way, but the trail was well worn and easy to follow, anyway. She wondered what had been there before the treehouse. It was hard to imagine this place ever belonging to anyone other than her and Macy.

Ava walked into the clearing and looked up. She pulled out her phone and took a photo. Ethan still hadn't responded to her message, or at least not before her phone had left the Wi-Fi.

She walked under the larger of the two trees, running her hands along the smooth wood of the ladder rungs. Her throat ached as she swallowed.

Out of the corner of her eye, she saw a flash of white. She bent down; it was a paper lantern, deflated and empty, just like the ones she had seen in town with Ethan. She picked it up and gently flipped it over.

I wish for another chance.

Ava looked around. She didn't recognize the handwriting, more formal than Macy's girlish round scrawl. She left the lantern on the ground where she'd found it, but the words were tattooed onto her brain.

Another chance.

She heard footsteps approaching and turned. Lucas stepped into the clearing and smiled.

"There you are," he said. He chuckled as he looked up at the treehouse. "That's what you wanted to see one last time?"

His smile faded as he noticed her shallow breathing. "You okay?" he asked.

She steadied herself and reached out her hand. He walked to her and took it, massaging her palm with his thumb like he had done a thousand times in the past six years.

"Lucas, you know I've loved you for a long time," she began. "I knew I would fall for you the first time you walked into MC Enterprise. I'm sorry if it feels like I've been avoiding you lately. I've had a lot on my mind."

He studied her, listening patiently, his brown eyes warm and open.

"Coming here. . .Well, I kind of felt like Alice in Wonderland," she continued. "Suddenly, everything felt upside down and I just—well, the point is, I can see clearly now. For the first time in a long time, I know what I want."

"I'm glad to hear you say that," he said, smiling. He stroked her cheek tenderly and bent to kiss her. She pushed her hand against his chest and stepped back. His arm still reached to where her face had been, his eyes confused.

"Lucas. . ." Ava faltered. She couldn't speak the words that would break his heart, but he seemed to hear them, anyway. He cleared his throat and looked away. Ava had never seen him cry. She felt sick.

After a moment, he wiped his face on his sleeve and turned back to her. As if watching herself, Ava pulled the ring box from her jacket and pressed it into his hand.

"Is this something you don't want now?" he asked, his voice barely above a whisper. He cleared his throat again. "Or ever?"

"Lucas, I'm so grateful for what we had," she said. "You were my first real love. It's thanks to you that I know the kind of partnership I want. I learned that from *us*. We've been a pretty great team."

His face crumpled as the reality of her words hit him. A part of her longed to take him into her arms and comfort him, but she thought that might just make it harder.

Her vision blurred. She blinked, hot tears spilling down her cheeks. It was hard to believe she had any left.

"I know you'll be an amazing match for someone," she continued, "but neither of us should have to sacrifice that much to make another person happy. We deserve better." She pulled a crumpled tissue from her pocket and wiped her nose. "I'll always appreciate that you were willing to give up so much. For me."

"You're sure?" Lucas asked.

She nodded.

He managed a small smile, but it stopped short of his eyes. "I know what we could have achieved together," he said. "We could have been the ultimate power couple."

"I know," she said. "But you'll find the person who wants to be the other half of that. I just want to be me."

He looked as though all the air had been sucked out of him.

"So, what now?" he asked, his voice hollow.

Ava blinked. It wouldn't be like Lucas to just turn around and walk away, although Ava found herself almost wishing he would.

"I guess this is pretty complicated, huh?" she said.

Lucas shrugged. She had never felt this awkward around him before. "I don't want to hurt you or your business. At least we both know you never charged me enough." She smiled weakly, but the joke landed flat on the ground.

"I do have other clients, you know," Lucas said coldly.

Ava nodded. "Of course."

Lucas just stared at her, his jaw clenched, his eyes unreadable.

"So, we'll need to talk soon," Ava said quickly. "And we should probably include Carla in that conversation. But you have a flight to catch, and I think we could both use a chance to think things through."

Lucas still said nothing, but his jaw had loosened. Now, he just looked sad. Ava hated what she was doing to him. She glanced at the little discarded lantern once more, looking as feeble and empty as she felt. She sighed and tried to arrange her face into a more confident expression before looking at him once more.

"You guys can take my car to the airport," she said. "But there's somewhere I'd like you to drop me off along the way, if that's okay."

And as she closed her eyes to clear the last of her tears, it was Ethan's face that flashed in her mind. She wouldn't lie to herself another moment. She heard the voice loud and clear: *Ethan. It's Ethan.*

Maybe she was too late. Maybe she had muddied things too much for him to trust her again. Either way, she was done waiting around for other people to paint her life for her.

Twenty-Three

The little white sedan pulled to a stop in a dirt lot just outside the town limits. Ava climbed out, followed by Carla and Lucas. Lucas pulled Ava into a tight embrace, burying his face in her hair. Ava let him hold her for as long as he wanted, though inside, she had already let go. Finally, he pulled away.

"Thank you," she said.

"You promise to call?" he asked. Ava hated that defeated look in his eyes and hated even more that she had caused it.

"I will," she agreed.

"I don't just mean about figuring out where we go from here professionally," he said. "I want to make sure you're okay."

She nodded.

"Goodbye, Ava," he said. He took one last long look at her before walking back to the driver's side.

Ava turned to her mother.

"You're sure about this?" Carla asked.

Ava let out a deep exhale. "I'm sure that it's time for me to make decisions for myself," she said. "For now, that's enough."

"You're a brave girl."

"Woman, Mom," Ava said.

"Right, political correctness and all that," Carla said, waving her hand dismissively. "Listen, I know you're not ready to leave, but I could also tell a few things went unsaid in the car. I can read between the lines enough to realize that man has a broken heart." She nodded toward the car, then raised her hand to stop Ava before she could explain. "You don't have to tell me anything. I only wish I had stepped back and let you lead the way sooner. We both might have a thing or two to learn from you. But if you want to talk—mother to daughter—I'm here, okay?"

Ava smiled, grateful. "OK. Sorry to put you in an awkward situation with Lucas," she said.

"Oh, I'm sure he has too much pride to spill his guts to me," Carla said. "But it's a long flight, and if he needs an ear, I'm happy to listen. I care about you both. As for business... I think it can wait."

"You guys better go," Ava said. "The last thing you need is to miss your flight."

"Be sure to give Harris my love," Carla said. "Tell him I'll see him next time."

"Next time?" Ava asked, raising an eyebrow.

"It's not so bad around here, I suppose," Carla said, giving a little shrug. She looked at the metal turnstiles at the front of the fairgrounds, where a line of people was growing. "At one point it bothered me that I didn't belong here," she said. "But then I realized that if I had fought it, if I had found a way to just make myself fit, I never would have found my home. The city speaks to me. . .The shows, the people, the nightlife—that's where I belong." She sighed and pinned a loose strand of hair back into her icy blonde bun. "But you? You belong in two very different places. I'm not sure which is better."

Carla kissed Ava forcefully on the forehead, then gave her a quick squeeze.

"I just hope Macy will hear me out," Ava said.

Carla chuckled. "Well, you both received the full serving of MacDaniel stubbornness, but she knows you love her. I believe in that."

"Thanks, Mom," Ava said.

"So long, my dear," Carla said. Ava watched her climb into the passenger seat. Lucas gave a little nod as they drove off, and soon, all that was left of the little white car was a fading cloud of dust.

Ava turned and joined the line under a black vinyl banner welcoming all to the Sky of Embers Fall Festival. She watched a cluster of children play tag while their parents waited in the queue. A pimpled teenage boy was reloading a giant cardboard tray with candied apples from an open van. A man unloaded two stout ponies from a trailer.

They all fit. They all belonged. In that moment, Ava felt like an intruder. Carla had told her she belonged in two places, but what if the truth was that she belonged nowhere? She took a shaky, tense breath. What was she doing here?

"Ava?"

She turned to find Kelly and Charlie holding hands just behind her in line. Kelly wore a trendy yellow turtleneck tucked into skinny jeans, a bright smile on that always-open face. Charlie's bootcut Wranglers were a tad too long and his thick-heeled Ariats made his gangly frame look even leggier, but Ava could see how Kelly had fallen for that boyish, dimpled grin.

"Hey, guys!" Ava said, shoving her anxiety underneath a smile. "What a nice surprise."

"I was hoping I'd run into you here," Kelly said. "I thought you'd already be at the Autumn Lantern booth."

"Yeah, I, um, I had some stuff to sort out this morning, so I'm getting here a little late," Ava said.

"Well, lucky me, I guess!" Kelly said.

"Did you enter the art competition?" Ava asked. "I saw that mentioned on the festival website."

Kelly shook her head. "It's for ages sixteen and under. But they let the seniors help judge! I have to come in for that tomorrow morning."

"Probably for the best," Ava said with a little laugh. "You'd sweep all the prizes. I can't imagine Cobalt has seen someone quite like you before."

"I feel the same way," Charlie said, his face shining with devotion as he looked at Kelly.

"I'm glad you think so, too," Ava said. "I hope you know how rare it is to have that kind of natural talent."

Charlie's face lit up. "I always tell her that!" he said. "Granted, I don't know anything about art, but anyone could see she's incredible. Maybe now that you've said it, she'll finally believe it."

"It's not just me," Ava said. "Some of the top voices in the art world are already blown away by her work."

Kelly opened her mouth, then closed it again, her face turning red as a tomato.

Ava's hands flew to her mouth. "I'm so sorry!" she said. How could she have forgotten? Kelly had explicitly asked her not to mention the school.

Charlie tilted his head quizzically toward Kelly, who took a deep breath and straightened her shoulders.

"It's okay, Ava. It was silly to keep it a secret." She gave Ava a little smile, then turned to Charlie, taking both his hands in her own. "It's just this art program. I didn't want to bother you with it, you know, and make things complicated for us. It's all the way in New York, which is obviously out of the question."

"Complicated for us?" he repeated, his eyes widening. "Here, I thought you tossed that application because you thought you wouldn't get in."

"Wait—you knew about it?!" Kelly asked.

Charlie glanced from Kelly to Ava, suddenly looking guilty. "If you didn't want me to see it, you probably should have gotten rid of it somewhere other than in the store trash," he said.

"Oh," Kelly said simply.

Charlie tenderly touched her cheek. "I'm on your side," he said. "If we're going to get married, we should be able to tell each other anything."

"I really am sorry," Kelly said. "I don't want us to keep stuff from each other."

"I'm glad you say that," Charlie said, "because I have something I need to confess, as well."

He scratched the back of his head, his eyes on his shoes.

"What is it?" Kelly asked, her voice small.

"I sent it in," he said. "The application."

"What?!" Kelly exclaimed. "What do you mean, you sent it in?"

"I mean, I filled it out. And I mailed it," he said, raising his hands in front on his chest.

But Kelly was frozen. Ava was, too. She felt like she should give them privacy, but at this point, it would probably be more awkward if she stepped out of line.

"But what if I get in?"

Kelly had spoken so quietly, Ava almost wondered if she'd imagined it.

Charlie brought Kelly's hand to his mouth, gently brushing his lips against her fingers. The look in his eyes wasn't one of puppy love; it was serious and determined. "Then you'll go," he said.

"Go?!" Kelly asked. "What about us?"

"We'll love each other wherever we are," he said. "We have our whole lives, Kell. It's not love if I want to lock you away just for me. I want everything for you. I remember when we took those classes at church... A marriage is supposed to be fifty-fifty, right? We'll make it work."

He pulled Kelly close, cradling her head on his shoulder. They breathed that way, as he held her, his grip patient and devoted. Ava wondered if she'd ever be held like that. If anyone would ever need her that much.

She could see now that she'd never had that kind of love with Lucas. They were both good people; they just weren't good for each other. But clearly something more was out there. It wasn't just a fairy tale, or the stuff dreamed up by two girls in a treehouse. These two high school seniors might not be much more than kids themselves, but they had found something that transcended them all.

Ava looked away as Kelly and Charlie shared a sweet kiss—not that it mattered to them. In that moment, she could tell that no one else in the world existed.

Ava finished her hot dog and tossed the paper wrapper into a big steel trashcan. After talking with Kelly and Charlie, she'd grabbed cash from the ATM and then quickly gotten lost. She had found a massive maze of tents with not a map in sight. The festival was bigger than she had expected it would be and already packed.

After her conversation with Lucas, lunch in town had gone out the window, so she had started with food. True, she was famished, but she knew she was also stalling. She grabbed her Diet Coke and walked toward the furthest aisle of tents. She figured she could start there and just work her way across until she found Macy's booth.

After passing a fortuneteller, a glassblower, and an old Western-themed photo booth, Ava walked under a banner proclaiming *Farmers' Market Alley*. One tent after the next was full of colorful vegetables, fresh eggs, and jams of every flavor. She could smell the booth boasting fresh-cut flowers before she even saw it, and she wondered where they grew them this time of year.

"Interest ya in a sample?"

Ava looked up to see a portly woman with warm eyes and a *Fair Weather Farm* t-shirt holding out a tray with apple slices. "Thank you," Ava said as she took one. When she bit into it, she gasped: it was juicy and tart and like nothing she'd ever tasted from a grocery store.

"Sorry," Ava said, laughing. "I didn't know apples could taste like that."

"Happens to me all the time," the woman said with a shrug, her face as shiny as the rows of fresh, organic produce. "That's what good fruit can do! Have one or two more, if you like."

"Thanks," she said, snatching another. "I'm Ava."

"Jean," the woman said. "Who ya with?"

"Hm?"

"I assume you're here with a booth," Jean said. "I can't imagine a woman dressed so nicely would be wandering the fair by herself otherwise."

"Oh!" Ava said, feeling self-conscious as she glanced down at her maroon cashmere cardigan. "I'm with Autumn Lantern Riding Academy."

"You don't say!" Jean exclaimed, and Ava was filled with immediate regret. "Let me put together a bag of my best, on the house. My nephew Chance is one of your students. He's really come out of his shell, thanks to those horses."

"Oh, that's really not necessary..." Ava began.

"I insist," Jean said, interrupting her as she packed a plastic bag full of apples and pears. "I was going to do this earlier when the owner stopped by, but she seemed distracted. I didn't want to bother her."

"Macy was here?"

"Oh, Macy MacDaniel, that's right," Jean said. "She came by earlier, but she looked a bit. . .preoccupied. Can't blame her. She and her husband used to have that booth right over there." Jean nodded to a larger booth advertising *Vernon's Veggies*. "Such a sweet couple they were. Well, Vernon always had his eye on that booth. His veggies are nowhere near as delicious as, uh...?"

"Ben," Ava supplied.

"Right, Ben," Jean said. "Even this time of year, he managed to have plenty, sometimes even after a freeze. Don't know how he did it."

"Do you know where the booth is? For the riding academy?" Ava asked.

Jean eyed her strangely.

"I just got a bit lost," Ava added quickly.

"Head to the end, hang a left—ya can't miss it," Jean said as she handed the bag to Ava.

"Thanks, Jean," she said, setting the fruit in her handbag. Jean gave her a nod but was already moving toward a group of gray-haired women who had entered the tent.

Ava weaved her way through a group of teenagers, following Jean's instructions. She heard Lizzie's voice carry over the crowd and she knew she'd found Autumn Lantern before she could even see the sign. No wonder Jean had looked at Ava funny: the booth was only a few hundred feet away.

"Oh, you will just love lessons!" Lizzie was proclaiming to a family, the child with them an elementary-aged girl. "Come try us out!" As she handed them a flyer, she saw Ava and her eyes widened in delight. Once Lizzie had answered their questions, the family moved on, and Lizzie ran from behind the booth to hug her.

"I thought you were leaving!" she squealed.

"So did I," Ava said. "It's been one hell of a day. Is Macy around?"

"She's helping a couple students settle their horses in the

stables before the show in the morning," Lizzie said. "She should be back anytime."

"How's it going over here?" Ava asked.

"Couldn't be better," Lizzie said, thrusting the Autumn Lantern interest list at Ava. "Check it out."

The first page was full. She flipped to the second page, then the third. . .All full. Ava looked at her, eyes wide.

Lizzie beamed. "You haven't even flipped it over to the back!" she exclaimed.

More names, each packed into every available space.

"Not only that," Lizzie continued. "We had six students register on the spot!"

"Is the booth normally this successful?" Ava asked.

Lizzie shook her head. "It's only day one and this is already double from the whole weekend last year."

"What did you do?" Ava asked, smiling.

"Well, I'd like to take full credit, but I'm just the closer here," Lizzie said with a laugh. "Several folks said they've heard about Autumn Lantern from word-of-mouth, or that they wanted to know more after seeing that flyer around town. But Ethan's the real muscle. He's been handing flyers to every man, woman, and child since before I even had the booth ready. He must think he works here."

Ava laughed and shook her head. "Macy sure lucked out with the two of you," she said.

"Luck had nothing to do with it," Lizzie said. "We know a good thing when we see it. And Macy is the best." Her face lit up as she looked over Ava's shoulder. Ava turned and found Macy, who was trying unsuccessfully to mask her surprise.

"Hi," Ava said, lifting her hand in a small wave.

"Aren't you supposed to be on a plane by now?" Macy asked, crossing her arms tightly over her chest.

Lizzie shook her head at the two of them and grabbed her wallet. "Since you all are here, I'm gonna go grab a cider before they run out of the fresh stuff," she said. "Anyone want one?"

"No thanks," Ava said. Macy shook her head. After Lizzie walked away, neither woman spoke for several seconds.

Finally, it was Macy who broke the silence. "You didn't answer my question," she said. "Why are you here?"

"We left things unfinished last night," Ava said. "It's not right. I want to talk to you."

Macy sighed. "So? Talk."

"First of all, I'm sorry," Ava said. "I know I screwed up big time."

"Very original," Macy said, studying the interest sheet. "But now that you've gotten that off your chest, you can leave with a clear conscience."

"No, Macy, I'm not leaving like this," Ava said. "I did that once and I was a dumb kid back then; I won't do it again. I am completely in the wrong, and I know you're not just going to forgive me overnight. But you at least have to hear me out."

Ava searched Macy's face, but she wouldn't meet her eyes.

"My mom was right, Macy. It was a bribe that got me here to begin with, or at least, that was part of it. But that's not what made me stay. If I had only come for the money, I would have left as soon as I got that job offer for the German mural commission."

"Hi, Miss Macy!"

Ava watched Macy force a smile as a boy with a group of other kids waved at her. Macy greeted him, her smile dropping as he walked off.

"I came here thinking you needed me to come, that I needed to save you, or something," Ava continued. "I didn't even know what a mess my own life was before I came. Macy. . .You saved *me*. I've been running on autopilot for years, but you changed that."

Despite the fall breeze, sweat beaded on Ava's forehead and she swiped at it with a shaking hand. "You always listen to yourself, even when it seems like everyone else is against you. I admire that, and I want to become someone who has that confidence. I've been running from so many things—the memories of this place, the kind of art that makes me feel excited, even my feelings about Lucas. Thanks to you, I'm done running." She took a deep, steadying breath. "I don't know if you really ever needed me at all, Macy. But I needed you. I still do."

Finally, Macy looked up. "Is that it?" she asked.

Ava sighed. "Yeah. That's it."

Macy looked her square in the face. "You should have told me, Ava," she said.

"I know," Ava said. "If I could do it all over, I would, but. . ."

"But, you can't," Macy finished.

Ava nodded.

"I was completely humiliated last night. You have no idea what that felt like," Macy said. "I'm so mad at you."

"I deserve that," Ava said. Shame flooded her body as she remembered Macy's pale, crumpled face looking down at her from the staircase landing.

Suddenly, Macy wrapped her arms around Ava, squeezing her tightly. "I'll find a way to forgive you," Macy whispered. She released Ava quickly, then wiped her palms on her jeans.

"You will?" Ava asked, blinking back at her as relief washed over her.

Macy shrugged, but she was smiling. "Maybe not overnight, but I spent a decade being mad at you. I've lost too many people I love. I think you're worth fighting for."

Hot tears stung Ava's eyes and all she could do was nod.

"Did you leave Aunt Carla and Lucas in the car or what?" Macy asked.

"Oh," Ava said, clearing her throat. "Actually. . .They left. I— well, I ended things with Lucas."

"You did?" Macy asked, her eyes widening in surprise.

"Yeah," Ava said softly. "It was for the best."

"Oh, Ava, I'm so sorry. I know that couldn't have been easy." Macy reached out and squeezed her hand. "Do you want to talk about it?"

"Maybe later. . .I've thought about it enough for today." Ava tried to smile, but she doubted it looked convincing. "But an important order of business—I was hoping for a ride back tonight. I'm not ready to leave, and I sort of gave them my rental car."

Macy laughed. "That I can do," she said.

Just then, Lizzie came back, cider in hand, looking relieved to find the two women in a better mood than when she'd left. "I saw folks starting to head over for tonight's lantern launch," she said. "I know it's cheesy, but I just love it. Okay with you if I head over, Macy?"

"Let's close it down for the night," Macy said. "I don't want to miss it either."

"I thought Harris was going to be here today?" Lizzie asked.

Macy shrugged. "You know him. He probably ran into some old buddies. If I don't run into him at the lantern launch, I'll give him a call before we head home."

Macy and Lizzie packed up their bags, while Ava put all the pens, stickers, and flyers into a plastic container. Once they'd finished, Lizzie pulled out a lantern from a black duffel.

"Locked and loaded," she said.

Macy pulled a crumpled lantern from her own bag and smoothed it against her leg.

"Did either of you lose a lantern?" Ava asked. "I found one by the treehouse, which I thought was a weird place for it." Her question was met with blank stares. "I thought I might bring it just in case, but... Well, I had a lot going on."

Lizzie and Macy looked at each other and shrugged.

"Wasn't me," Macy said.

"Probably just something the breeze picked up," Lizzie said. "You've been here long enough to see how unpredictable this Utah wind can be."

"Yeah," Ava said, remembering the swirling wind eddies she'd seen when she first arrived. "I guess so."

"Come on," Macy said. "Let's go find you a lantern of your own."

The three women linked arms and weaved their way through the crowd. The midway lights had kicked on, casting a warm yellow glow on their faces. Macy led them to a row of tables manned by several people wearing shirts that read "*Festival Volunteer*" in big black lettering.

She dropped a folded bill into a basket labeled "*Donations.*" The teenage girl behind the table smiled, then slid across a blank lantern and a permanent marker. Macy nudged Ava, so she stepped forward and took it.

Macy and Lizzie waited as she walked over to a nearby picnic table and scribbled down her wish. She knew exactly what she wanted to write.

"Ava, care to share with the class?" Lizzie asked when she'd rejoined them.

Ava turned her lantern so they could see. "I wish to make my own happiness from now on," she read aloud. Macy raised her hand and Ava gave her a high five.

" 'Atta girl," Lizzie said.

"How about you guys?" Ava asked.

"Well, night one, I'm going big," Lizzie said. "I wished for the Utah Jazz to win it all this season."

They laughed.

"Your turn, Macy," Lizzie said.

"Well, I tossed around a couple ideas," Macy said, "but I finally settled on this: I wish for love to keep finding me."

Ava smiled. "I can't think of anyone who deserves that more than you."

"That is just lovely, Macy," Lizzie said, dabbing the corner of her eye.

Just then, Ava spotted that familiar tousled hair a full head above the rest of the crowd. *Ethan.* As soon as she saw him, she realized a little part of her had been looking for him ever since she'd walked away from her rental car hours earlier. He was wearing a green-checkered flannel, unbuttoned at the top. Her heart raced, and she knew her face must be bright red. Lizzie and Macy were still chattering away, the sky just dark enough for them not to have noticed Ava's pitiful state.

She wiped her palms on her jeans and clutched the lantern tightly to her chest. Ethan was weaving his way between picnic blankets in the opposite direction. If there was ever a time for Ava to put this whole, brave "I'm in charge of my own life" thing into practice, it was right then. She took a deep breath and pieced together a confident smile.

"Hey! Ethan!" she yelled.

He turned. When his eyes locked with hers, a cool stare quickly replaced his startled expression. Ethan might have no interest in seeing her after watching Lucas propose, but in that moment, Ava didn't care. She had wasted enough time worrying about what other people were thinking. She was here now, and whether it was that night or next year, Ava would make it up to him.

He headed towards the women, forcing a smile as he kept his eyes on Lizzie and Macy.

"I was looking for you guys, but my cell service is a little spotty back here. Word on the street is that Autumn Lantern is the hottest ticket in town. Congrats, ladies."

"Don't be modest," Macy said. "Lizzie told me all about your guerilla campaign. I really don't have words to thank you, Ethan."

"Nah, it's nothing," he said. "I'm happy to do it. I don't know where I'd be without your ranch, and I want the whole world to know about it. I owe you."

"Agree to disagree," Macy said, smiling. "Well, my legs are screaming from standing all day." She gestured to a spot in the field not yet covered by lawn chairs and glow stick-wielding children. "I'm gonna go snag that rock before someone else does. "

"Right behind ya," Lizzie said, giving Ava a subtle nudge with her elbow as she followed.

Ethan watched them go but didn't follow. People began to fill in around them as the sky grew darker. He folded his lantern under his arm and shoved his hands into his pockets, looking anywhere but at Ava.

"So," he began after an infinitely long moment. "Where's that fiancé of yours?" His voice was ashen and flat, all of his usual warmth extinguished. "Congrats, by the way."

"Ethan, I'm sorry," Ava said. "Lucas isn't normally that awful. He got jealous seeing us together and—"

"You really don't need to defend him to me, Ava," Ethan interrupted. "It's none of my business. It never was."

"I ended it," Ava said. "Lucas and I... We're over."

Ethan finally looked at her, holding her gaze for a long moment. Ava's stomach twisted. But he said nothing—just turned his eyes to the purple sky.

"We wanted different things. I can see that now," Ava continued, unsure if she should. "Every year, our lives were tugging us in completely opposite directions. I couldn't see it, or maybe I didn't want to. But when I came here, I started to think about what I want. And I found this—well, this *feeling* here that I've never felt in my whole life."

Ethan looked at her, and Ava's stomach somersaulted yet again. She was regretting that hot dog.

"I'm glad for you, Ava," he said, simply. "I truly am. I want you to be happy."

"It's you, Ethan," she said, her throat dry. "I won't pretend any longer. I'm falling in love with you."

She reached for him, slowly weaving her fingers through his.

He didn't pull away. His palms were smooth, but the ridges of skin above them were rough and calloused. Ava's small hands disappeared completely inside his grip. People were no more than a few feet away in any direction, but she didn't care. He pulled her closer, and she could feel his shallow breath on her forehead, feel the heat of his broad torso through the soft flannel. They stood like that for a long moment, neither moving, Ava's body electrified.

Suddenly, Ethan stepped back and crossed his arms over his chest. Ava searched his face, but he wouldn't look at her.

"I can't do this, Ava," he said, his voice husky. "I care about you; there's no denying that. But how can I forget what you said to me? What happened to needing time to figure out who you are? I can't believe that's changed in a matter of days."

Ava's eyes stung and she willed herself not to cry for the millionth time that day. Ethan sighed, and his gaze softened as his eyes finally met hers.

"Do you really think starting a relationship now is a good idea?" he asked.

Ava said nothing. She had nothing *to* say.

"I meant it when I agreed to be your friend," he said. "That's not a line. I want you in my life; I just need to be more than the next man in line."

Ava found a strained smile. She nodded. "You deserve someone who gives you their all."

"We both do," he said. He gestured to Lizzie and Macy. "We should probably get over there, don't you think?"

Ava noticed the two women suddenly appeared to be very interested in their cell phones.

"Yeah," she replied. "We should."

They stepped around chairs and blankets, and Ethan offered his hand to Ava to help her onto the towering rock.

"OK, gang!" Lizzie called to them as they climbed to the top. "According to my phone, we've got three minutes until we light them. Ethan, you got a lantern?"

"Sure do," he said. "I'm wishing for the courage to enter the student show this year."

Macy laughed. "I'll be holding you to that," she said.

"I grabbed fuel cells for all of us," Lizzie said. She passed them each a little square and Ava followed her lead as they attached them to their lanterns.

Then, Lizzie smiled—it was time. She held the ring of her lantern, pressing the flame against it until it caught. Then, she gave her lighter to Ava who did the same. Ethan and Macy lit theirs as well.

Ava turned her lantern over, holding the paper at the top with the flame at the bottom. She noticed everyone around them was doing the same. The last light of day was quickly losing the fight against the dark plum night. After a couple minutes, Ava felt her lantern fill with air and start to tug skyward.

"This is crazy!" Ava said, laughing.

They held their lanterns tightly, watching as the paper cylinders wrestled for freedom. Ava noticed that a few people had already released theirs, and a splatter of white dots littered the sky above.

"Here we go!" Macy called. "One. . .two. . .THREE!"

They let go. The lanterns rose slowly, more slowly than Ava would have expected. There was almost something ballet-like about their movement, a graceful hovering as they climbed toward the stars.

They watched the lanterns in silence. Hundreds more joined theirs, until Ava could no longer tell which was hers. It didn't matter. She could feel the strength of this collective prayer all around her. Hundreds of wishes, all joined together, moving their written whispers to a shout. She looked around. Macy's cheeks glowed, illuminated in the lantern light. Lizzie was dancing silently, a grin stretched across her face. Ethan had both hands tucked in his pockets, his eyes unreadable. In the soft glow of the firelight, Ava could have watched him for hours.

It was the first still moment Ava had found all day, and a wave of loose thoughts threatened to drown her peace. She had so many decisions to make about her future; so many choices about where to land next. But that anxiety was sharing space with growing excitement. She had an idea—a big idea—and she had been watching the blocks of it click together all day. She knew she had more details to figure out, but all of that could wait until tomorrow.

Ava tilted her head back and tried to memorize the image of the illuminated heavens above. It was hard to tell if the tiniest orbs were skyward lanterns or stars that had burned long ago. There was real power in this ritual, symbolic or not. She wrapped her arms around herself and closed her eyes. She could still see it all, etched like a tattoo in her mind. That voice inside her spoke again, this time louder:

You're going to be just fine.

After the last lanterns disappeared from the sky, the volunteers guided everyone out of the field with flashlights. Ethan had been quiet as they followed the crush of people through the carnival midway, throwing only an occasional one-word response into Macy and Lizzie's chatter. Near the entrance, he said a quick goodbye when he recognized one of his accountants with her husband and toddler daughter. Ava felt a sudden urge to run after him, to beg him to talk to her again, but she knew she'd said everything she could.

Ava watched an endless snake of headlights weave through the entire lot as she followed Lizzie and Macy single file through the rows and rows of parked cars. They certainly weren't getting on the road any time soon. They fell in step alongside one another as the clusters of parked cars began to spread further apart. The back section of the lot was reserved for people renting booths or entering animals in the 4-H show, since they were usually among the first to arrive and the last to leave.

"Imagine if tomorrow is anything like today!" Lizzie said, a bit breathless. "Autumn Lantern might need a waiting list."

"Let's not get ahead of ourselves," Macy scolded, but she was grinning. "We're just lucky to have Ethan as our unofficial mascot." At the mention of Ethan's name, Macy threw Ava a sideways glance, but Ava pretended not to notice.

"We never did see Harris," Lizzie said.

"I tried calling him, but I just got his voicemail," Macy said. "If you all don't mind, I'll drive by his house when we pass through town. Make sure his truck's there."

"He probably got carried away in the karaoke tent," Lizzie suggested.

Macy laughed. "I forgot about that. I never saw a group of old men excited to sing Journey before."

"Uncle Harris is into karaoke?!" Ava asked.

"Well, he sure was at last year's festival," Lizzie said. "He claimed he just wanted to support the Future Farmers of America, but that man really appeared to be in his element."

"Thanks for offering to pitch in at the booth tomorrow, Ava," Macy said. "With so many of our students at the horse show, we're a little understaffed."

"It's the least I could do," Ava said. "Which reminds me— would you mind dropping me at Enterprise on your way here in the morning?"

"Of course," Macy said.

"So, you'll be here long enough to need another rental car?" Lizzie asked, raising an eyebrow.

"Definitely," Ava said. "As far as exactly how long... Well, we've got a long drive back to the ranch." She looked at Macy. "I have an idea I'd like to run by you."

"I can't wait to hear it," Macy said, smiling.

"Are you sure you know where we parked?" Lizzie asked. "I don't see the truck anywhere."

"Trust me, I paid attention," Macy said. "See that tree over there? We're just behind it."

Sure enough, as they passed the scraggly pine, Macy clicked her key fob and a set of headlights flashed twice in their direction. It was a good thing, too; the fairground lights barely reached this corner of the lot. Ava could think of better ways to spend the rest of the evening than trying to find a truck in the dark.

She suddenly became aware of how isolated they were back here. Most of the vehicles they passed pulled horse trailers or food trucks, undoubtedly parked for the whole weekend and standing empty at this hour. She had a feeling the Cobalt Fairgrounds boasted a low crime rate, but the New Yorker in her had been preparing to be mugged since she was a teenager.

As they approached, Ava could make out two figures leaning against the truck in the shadows. She grabbed Macy's arm. Macy threw her a confused look, then followed her gaze, her eyes widening.

"Lizzie, stop!" Macy hissed quietly. The three women drew closer together as the dark shapes approached, and Ava could tell they were both men.

Macy staggered sideways, grabbing Ava's shoulder forcefully as she steadied herself.

"Macy, are you okay?!" Ava asked.

The men neared the glow of the floodlights, and suddenly, Ava recognized the shorter one as Harris. Right behind him was a tall, dark man dressed in fatigues.

"Ben?" Macy asked, her voice barely above a whisper. "*Ben!*" she screamed, primal now.

The man knelt and she ran, folding herself into his arms as they collided. Ava didn't dare breathe as quiet tears streamed down her cheeks. They stood that way for a long time, Ava, Harris, and Lizzie—a triangle of witnesses holding a silent vigil only broken by the couple's sobs.

Finally, Macy pulled her face away from his and touched it

with her fingertips.

"You're alive," she croaked.

"I came as soon as I could," Ben said.

"No one called me," Macy sputtered. "Why didn't they call me?"

Ava suddenly knew this conversation was not for her. A silent look passed between her and Harris, then Lizzie. They followed Ava to the pine trees. Even out of earshot, no one spoke at first. Ava just couldn't find the words that could hold this. Lizzie kept shaking her head at the sky, then wiping her eyes with her sleeve. Finally, it was Harris that broke the silence.

"She knew. Didn't she?"

"How?" It was all Ava could ask.

"Well, now, I don't know the half of it," Harris said. "But I'll tell you what I can. He's been in a village. Simple folks with old ways, living off the grid; no phones, no English, but humanity is universal, it seems. They saved him. Sounds like he was pretty touch-and-go for a long time after they found him. Eventually, they helped him get to a city."

"It's a miracle," Lizzie whispered. "There's no other word for it."

"But why didn't they call?" Ava asked. "How long ago was he found?"

Harris shrugged. "I suspect he'll share more than I know with Macy, but it didn't seem right to ask. It's a burden of his calling to carry so much inside him. All I know is he asked to be taken to the ranch, but he called me after he found it empty. When I picked up the phone and heard him..." Harris' voice cracked as his eyes filled with tears that glinted in the moonlight. Ava wrapped her uncle in her arms, rubbing his back as he buried his face into her shoulder.

The moon was high above the mountains now, its bittersweet brilliance illuminating the sky. Ava smiled: the real autumn lantern. Deep down, she knew it was always there; only her view of it changed. But in that moment, it had come to testify, burning orange for the soldier who had returned to his love. Burning orange for the girl who had finally found home.

Epilogue

ONE YEAR LATER

Ava slowed as she approached the turnoff for the ranch, her heart thudding in her chest. Though the trees shone the same burnt tones as when she'd been here the last time, she was anxious to see what had changed. Without her.

The gravel clattered against the underbelly of her little sedan, this time a hunter green. Her flight had been early, and she knew Macy wasn't expecting her for another hour. A part of her was terrified she'd made a mistake by leaving again, terrified they'd all greet her as a stranger. A stranger who had left yet again. Ava parked her car in the lot, packed with minivans, SUVs, and a few construction vehicles. She tossed her keys and phone into her purse and took a deep breath. She felt more nervous than she had expected, now that she was back. *Well, no time like the present,* she thought.

As Ava locked the car behind her, Lizzie burst through the stable door. "You're here!" she squealed, crushing Ava in a bear hug.

"Hey, Lizzie!"

"I'm so glad you're back," Lizzie said, releasing her.

Ava smiled. Though the last year had handed her plenty of loneliness, memories of friends like Lizzie had kept her company. "How's Gunner?" she asked.

"Well, go see for yourself," Lizzie said. "He's in his stall, waiting for you. He wanted to make a card, but apparently he has no fingers."

Ava laughed, then turned to the stable. She couldn't believe she was finally here. Suddenly, she realized they were being watched.

"Uh, Lizzie..." Ava said, raising an eyebrow as she nodded toward the family standing in the doorway.

"Oh, shoot!" Lizzie said. "I got so excited when I saw you pull up, I plum forgot I was in the middle of a tour!"

Ava laughed.

"I'll be done in thirty," Lizzie said as she stepped back inside the stable. She spread her arms wide. "Then, I'm coming back for round two!"

As Ava turned to the farmhouse, she saw Harris mowing the lawn on the old tractor. He grinned and lifted his hand in greeting. She waved back.

She walked between the stable and the old storage shed, carefully stepping between feed bins and neat stacks of empty buckets. As she continued behind the wash stalls, she offered a quick hello to two teenagers cooling down their horses. When she finally reached the clearing, she gasped.

A modern two-story building stood where an empty patch of scraggly grass had been only a year before. The front was almost entirely glass, and several wooden rocking chairs lined the low front porch. She watched a man drill a hanging planter into the porch awning. He looked up and smiled.

It was Ben. He was heavier and more muscular than when Ava had seen him last. A lightness had returned to his eyes, a playful glint that Ava had only seen in photos. He wiped the sweat from his forehead as he watched her approach.

"There's my favorite cousin-in-law!" Ben said.

"How many do you have?" Ava teased.

"Just the one, but I really only need one," he replied.

She laughed. She shook her head as she stepped back and took in the building once more.

"I can't believe it's real," she said. "It's even more beautiful in person. How are you so far ahead of schedule?"

Ben shrugged, but she saw pride in his smile. "We've got a great crew," he said. "And that big down payment let us hire a few extra hands."

"Thank goodness Friedrich agreed to the advance," Ava said.

"Well, look at you. On a first-name basis now," he said.

"After eleven months in his manor, I'm basically family," Ava said.

Ben was so vibrant, so alive. It was as if he'd always been at Autumn Lantern. Ava still didn't understand much about how the Army worked, but Macy had told her Ben would no longer be deployed. He only had a few more years until he could retire, and they'd offered him an assignment in recruiting. Macy said he'd cover all of Utah, but even then, it would mostly be day trips. He was here to stay. Macy had her happy ending.

Ava felt a familiar ache in her chest. Her choices this past year had led her to many places. Some had been wonderful; some had been strange—but they had all been her doing. In many ways, these choices had also left her alone.

Not a night had passed that Ethan's face didn't fill her mind before she drifted off to sleep. After conjuring the smell of his cologne a thousand times, and remembering the way his stubble scratched her face as they pulled apart from that kiss, Ava had never truly accepted that Ethan wasn't hers.

They had only spoken a few times over the past year, when Macy had passed him the phone or as Lizzie surprised her with a group FaceTime. For several months, Ava had e-mailed Ethan at least once a week, hoping for him to give her some hint about his feelings for her. But while he always wrote back, he never responded with anything more than short, polite messages. As Ava's work hours increased, supervising six other artists to complete the massive murals, she had hardly written at all. It didn't have anything to do with her feelings for Ethan—she simply didn't have time. He had only written a few more times after that, each e-mail as brief and impersonal as the last. Ava suspected he'd met someone. She couldn't blame him. She hadn't fully given herself to him, and then she'd left. He deserved better.

"Earth to Ava," Ben said.

Ava smiled. "Sorry," she said. "Jet lag. Well, the good news is that now that the murals are finished and Friedrich is happy, we can finish construction."

"We're starting on the driveway next week," Ben said, flashing her a grin. "Maybe you can run the cement truck."

Ava laughed. "I think after a good night's sleep, I'll be up for anything."

"Ava?"

The smile froze on her face. She turned, and there he was.

Ethan.

Just as gorgeous as she remembered. He smiled, but underneath it, he looked as flustered as Ava felt. His faded blue Henley fit snug against his body and Ava couldn't help but notice his biceps as he readjusted his grip on a bale of hay.

"Hi," she said, finally.

"I have something to show you," he said. He tossed the bale onto a pile of several others and disappeared behind the barn. Ava looked at Ben. He just shrugged and smiled.

When Ethan returned, he carried a long wooden plank. He turned it around to face her. Burned deeply into the impeccably stained wood were the words "Autumn Lantern Artists' Residence." On the right, a vivid flame inside a cylindrical lantern almost appeared to be dancing in the wood.

Ava's hands flew to her mouth. It was an exquisite work of art, even more beautiful than the sketched plans. She closed her eyes as she traced her fingers over the smooth lettering. It was real. All of it.

"It's perfect," Ava said, her voice thick with emotion.

Ethan smiled.

"Kelly told me the signs were her first-ever commission," Ava said. "I had to laugh...that girl is going to blow us all away. Her work is being included in the spring show, even though it's usually only for seniors."

"I'm glad to hear she's doing well," he said. "Did you drive through town? Harris already hung the sign at the gallery."

Ava shook her head. "I'll stop by tomorrow."

Ethan gently stood the sign against the porch. "We were waiting to hang it until you arrived. Wouldn't be right to christen it without you."

He held her gaze, the first time in a year she had truly looked at him. Something pulsed through her and her legs felt wobbly, but she fought to keep her expression as even as possible.

"It seems everything went perfectly while I was gone," Ava said quietly. She was grateful, of course. She just hoped there was room for her now that she was back.

"It wasn't anything close to perfect without you here," he said, stepping closer to her. Her heart drummed so ferociously she thought her ribcage might burst.

"So, you convinced old Shubert to bring some more color into his home, I hear," Ben called as he hung a second copper planter, clearly oblivious to the tension between Ethan and Ava.

Ethan swallowed and looked away.

Ava cleared her throat. "Well, I think I've really begun to find my voice as a painter," she said. "I won't bore you with the technical stuff, but someone wise once told me that a true artist should be able to create whatever she wants."

She looked at Ethan. The corners of his mouth curled into a small smile.

"Once I got all the noise out of my head," she continued, "I realized I actually loved a lot about abstract art. But I wanted more color, more ambiguity. Friedrich was very open to my suggestions, and now the mural is going to be featured on the December cover of *ARTnews Magazine*."

"That sounds huge!" Ben said, climbing off the stepladder.

"Congrats, Ava," Ethan said, his warm smile reaching down to her core.

"Thanks," she said. "It feels good to finally create something that other people respond to, but also makes me happy. From now on, I paint what *I* want... But first, I want to get my hands dirty. How was the crop this year, Ben?"

"It's gonna take a few seasons before I'm back at my peak, but I can't wait to show you everything," Ben said, his face lighting up like a kid talking about Christmas. "I've got plenty ready for my booth at the festival. Macy's been staying up making labels and brochures. Our dining room table looks like a QVC set. I keep trying to get her to slow down a little, but you know Macy. Has she seen you yet?"

"No!" Ava said. "Where is she?"

"She'll be in the arena a bit longer," Ben said, glancing at his watch. "It's been crazy around here. We've got a waitlist for new students! You better go say hi."

"I don't want to interrupt her lessons," Ava said.

"She's going to be furious enough that I saw you first," Ben replied. "Get down there and keep me out of the doghouse."

Ava laughed. "Well, in that case, I suppose I will," she said.

"When does the other boss arrive?" Ben asked.

"VP of Publicity," Ava corrected. "And her name is Margo. She'll be here next month, just before the first artists arrive. You guys will love her."

"If you do, I do," Ben said. "Hey, Ethan? I've got four more of these to hang. You mind giving me a hand?"

"Of course not," Ethan said, not looking at Ava as he climbed the porch and grabbed the drill.

Ava walked toward the arena, her neck burning. She tried to steady her shallow breathing, but she was already dizzy. After all this time, seeing Ethan had shaken her in ways she hadn't expected. It had taken every bit of self-control not to press her body against his and bury her face into his broad chest. Suddenly, seeing him now, she wanted him with every cell of her being.

What had he meant when he said things weren't perfect while she was gone? Maybe he was just commenting on the construction progress, but she couldn't help wishing it had something to do with her absence. But then again, she *had* poured a small fortune into the property... Maybe he was just trying to be nice. At least he was alone, although he probably wouldn't bring a girlfriend to the barn. She tried to push him from her mind, but she knew it was pointless.

A shriek of delight brought her back to the present. Macy climbed between the slats of the arena fence and ran to meet Ava. They hugged and laughed, and they were ten once again—just two best friends reunited.

Even though they had talked several times a week on the phone, Ava had missed her fiercely. She pulled her tighter, but stepped back when she felt something hard press into her stomach.

"No!" Ava said.

Macy beamed and pulled back her jacket, turning to the side revealing a taut, round little belly. "Oh yes!" she said.

Ava whacked her on the shoulder. "How could you not tell me?!" she exclaimed.

"I wanted to surprise you," Macy said. "I mean, at first we

didn't tell anyone. Especially after—well—after the other times. And then, once you told me when you'd be back, I swore Ben and Dad to secrecy."

"I thought you said no more secrets!" Ava said.

"Are you mad, Auntie Ava?" Macy asked.

"Not terribly," Ava said, and they both laughed. "How far along are you?"

"Five months," Macy said.

"Five months?!"

"It's been a long five months!" Macy said, rubbing her stomach.

"I'm so happy for you, Macy."

"I'm just so glad you're finally here!" Macy exclaimed.

"Don't you need to go back and teach?" Ava asked, looking at the arena where two riders walked their horses.

"They're just cooling down," Macy said.

"I can't believe how busy you've been," Ava said.

"I know! I'll probably have to bring on more staff soon."

"Look at you," Ava said. "You've really done it."

"We've really done it," Macy said. "Look around. Everything we always wanted—it's here."

Ava smiled. She had grown up believing she had to choose between this place and her real life. But Macy was right—it was all right here.

"Not to be a total pregnant cliché, but I'm famished," Macy said. "Let's go chat in my kitchen."

"I'll meet you there," Ava said. "There's someone I haven't said hello to yet."

Macy raised an eyebrow as Ava followed her into the barn. "I'll be in here wrapping up a few things," Macy said as she ducked into the office.

Before Ava could even see his stall, Gunner let out a high-pitched whinny. As Ava rounded the corner, she saw his nose pressed through the bars, snorting the air frantically.

She laughed. "It's me, Gunner! I'm home!" She scratched his favorite spot between his eyes before letting herself into his stall. He pressed his long velvet face against her chest and heaved a deep sigh. She wrapped her arms around his neck and buried her nose in his mane, inhaling his scent: a mix of horse shampoo and dust.

"I had a feeling I'd find you here."

She turned. Ethan stepped into the dim stall, his arm brushing hers as he leaned forward to pat Gunner.

"Do you have a minute?" he asked.

She nodded. How many times had she imagined the first moment they would be alone, coming up with the perfect things to say to him? But right then, her mind was utterly blank.

He stood close. The stall was small and Gunner was huge, leaving only a slim corner for the two of them. They could have stepped into the aisle to talk, but Ava didn't want to move. She wanted to be even closer to him. She watched his chest rise and fall, too ruffled to meet his eyes. She was afraid to hear what he had to say.

He dug his hands into his pockets. "I don't know how to say this, Ava," he said finally. "I tried a million times to think it up, but I can't. I can't sleep, I can't eat. . .Well, I mean, I eat, but you know what I mean. This isn't coming out right. Will you look at me, Ava?"

He tipped her face towards his own, and there were those

piercing, warm hazel eyes. "I can't stop thinking about you," he said.

Ava bit her lip as she shook her head. "I don't understand—you hardly talked to me. I've hardly spoken to you this entire time. Don't you have a girlfriend by now?"

"Girlfriend?" Ethan repeated, as if the word were foreign to him. "Ava, no. I wanted to give you the space you needed. I knew you were figuring things out for yourself, not to mention working around the clock. Holding back from you was one of the hardest things I've ever had to do, but I had to make sure I didn't screw this up."

He tenderly tucked a strand of her auburn hair behind her ear.

"I want you. I want all of you. If you're ready for this, then I am, too. If you're not, well, it won't be easy, but I'll wait for you. If you want me to. I love you."

His fingers burned into her cheek as Ava just stared, her heart thundering. "Say something," he pleaded.

She took his hand off her face and turned her body toward his. She ran her hand along the back of his head, her arm trembling as her fingers weaved into his thick golden-brown hair. She stood on her tiptoes and pulled his face closer. When he was inches away, she stopped, feeling his hot breath on hers. Thousands of times she had played back that first kiss by the water, rewriting it to a version that didn't end with her pulling away. She pressed her mouth against his, and he groaned. His lips were warm and just as soft as she remembered. After a moment, she let him go, the cold air in the stall a sharp contrast to the heat that clenched her whole body.

Ethan's cheeks were flushed, his breathing now ragged.

"Are you sure about this?" she asked him.

"I've never been more sure of anything in my entire life," he said.

This time, it was his hand that grasped her hair. He thrust her body against the wall of the stall and his mouth found hers once more. He was kissing her, then again, his strong arms holding her body so closely that it felt as if they would melt into one. She surrendered, her body limp as he held her as if she weighed nothing. It could have been five minutes, it could have been an hour, their fingers exploring each other with urgent need. Ava never wanted to stop, but she knew Macy must be waiting. And she knew where this would go next.

Breathless, she broke away. Gunner nickered softly beside them. Ava giggled.

"I forgot he was here," she said, giving his haunch a tender pat. "We better go out there. I don't know if I can stop myself if we don't."

"Then we're definitely staying," Ethan said, a devilish grin spreading across his face.

Sunlight spilled down the length of the aisle as the stable door slid open. They looked at each other, ducking back into the shadows.

"We know you're in there!" Macy called from outside.

Ethan and Ava stepped into the aisle, a few seconds apart, looking as casual as they possibly could. Ava watched him straighten his shirt and blood rushed to her face as she remembered touching the firm stomach beneath. They walked into the glow of the late afternoon sun and were greeted by enthusiastic applause. Ben whooped.

"About damn time!" Macy said.

Ava blushed and covered her face, any attempt at nonchalance now pointless.

"Real mature, you guys," Ethan said. His face was tomato red, but he walked over to Ava and looped his arm around her waist, pressing his hip against hers.

"You know we're just teasing," Ben said, smiling. "We love you guys."

"Okay, well, you can only make me wait so long for a sandwich," Macy said. "Come on in when you're ready."

Macy and Ben walked toward the farmhouse. Ava saw Harris waiting on the porch, a content smile on his face.

"We'll be right there!" Ava called. Once they'd gone, she turned to Ethan, tracing her fingers along his collarbone. He smiled and closed his eyes, a low sigh escaping his lips. She wanted to know every inch of him, hear every story that turned him into this man. And now, she could. They had time.

He kissed her once more, this time gentle and slow as his mouth searched hers. He pulled away, breathless, and they walked toward the house, neither in a hurry to share the other.

She inhaled the crisp scent of the wood-burning fireplace and looked up. The sky was a swirl of pink and orange, the shades darkening by the second. The moon pressed the edge of the horizon, too impatient for the sun to finish. She closed her eyes, knowing the colors were already burned deep into her soul. And they were hers, every year for the rest of her life. This was all hers.

Ava didn't know what her life would look like when it was all colored in, but it would unfold exactly as it should. Exactly as it was always meant to. She'd travel, of course, following her work to every corner of the world. But it would be on her terms, and she would always come back.

Ethan stopped Ava as they approached the porch steps. He smiled and brushed a piece of hay from her hair. "Ava MacDaniel," he said. "I plan to fall more in love with you every day for the rest of my life."

He reached out his hand. She took it.

"Welcome home," he said.

Acknowledgments

This novel stewed within me for years, then ripped out in a fury over a matter of mere months. As I'm going to believe in my future as a writer, I'll refrain from thanking everyone who has contributed to my life in general and keep it specific to this story. I have many more tales to tell and many more acknowledgements to write. I'm confident you'll all get the public embarrassment you've so rightly earned.

First off, back to the beginning: I don't remember a time in my life without a book in my hand. I have my parents to thank for that. My dad, William Frederic Stineman, was the first writer I ever knew and the inspiration for my pen name. He was the smartest human I've met and his unwavering faith in me was a cornerstone of my faith in myself. My mom, Peggy Putthoff, has been referring to me a writer since the third grade, and she has never stopped pushing me to use my voice. She even offered me cash to hire a sitter for my sons so I could find more hours to write! I promise to stop arguing with you now, Mom. You were right, I am a writer.

To my husband Kevin Joy: this book never would have happened without him. The hours of solo childcare and constant encouragement he gave me could never be repaid. When I doubted myself, he was always the first to help me back to my feet and make me a sandwich. I'm the luckiest woman to be living a real-life romance story. To my sons Atticus and Sawyer: I would probably still only be writing in my head if it wasn't for you. I once told Atticus I'd like to write a book and he simply blinked at me and replied, "So, why don't you?" I've spent my entire life making matters too complicated, thinking I wasn't good enough to be a writer. Seeing myself through the eyes of my child left me with no excuse. I hope seeing their mother work so hard for something she's been passionate about for so long inspires them to do the same.

To the amazing team at Di Angelo Publications: without Sequoia Schmidt, there would be no novel. When I asked a few timid questions about the industry, she told me to write a book. She trusted me, believed in my writing, and made this whole thing possible. Her ferociousness in this industry is infinitely inspiring. All the thanks I can muster to my editor Ashley Crantas—HOLY CRAP, how did I get so lucky?! She has been my coconspirator, my teacher, and my Sherpa. Her encouragement, generosity, and patience has truly transformed not only this story, but also my craft. A big thank you to Stephanie Yoxen for your insightful edits and making me sound like a literate human. So much gratitude to Savina Deianova for translating my vision of Ava and Utah to the most beautiful cover I could dream up. It's perfect.

I could not have made it through the editing process without my amazing in-laws, Ken and Liz Joy. On two different weekends they took my kids overnight so I could revise this manuscript in marathon chunks. I'm eternally grateful for all their support in everything I do. I hit the jackpot with you guys!A big shout out goes to Danielle C. Ryan, the inspiration for Macy. This book began as an Instagram conversation about a film that we could star in together, and transformed into something entirely different. Dani was so generous with her insight about life in rural Utah and all that goes with it. Her voice and essence are in every part of Macy. I hope one day, we get to make that movie.

I owe such tremendous thanks to author RaeAnne Thayne. Her own work in this genre has entertained me for years and, more recently, served as a guidepost in my own writing. Months ago, I contacted her through her website as a complete stranger. She immediately replied and offered to read *Autumn Sky*. I'll never forget her generosity and encouragement. I promise to pay this forward if I am ever fortunate enough to be in a position to do so.

A huge shout out to the Fancy Ladies Book Club: Bailey, Mahaley, Elizabeth, Marissa, Flynn, Zarah, Caitlin, Amy, Alli, Rachel, Marshall, Deborah—thank you for cheering me on and being my tribe. Here's to the next hundred book choices!

A note of gratitude is owed to Dr. Russ Proctor, one of my college professors and a mentor. The right words at the right time can change someone's life and your confidence in me changed mine.

I can't go without thanking Stephen King. I doubt this is his genre of choice, but his work has been inspiring me since my childhood. Years ago, his story about the "pink medicine" in *On Writing* gave me a resurgence of grit to continue as an artist when I was close to giving up.

To all novelists, past and future: I salute you. Apologies for any one-star GoodReads reviews I gave prior to seeing behind the curtain. The process of writing and editing a novel is more momentous than I ever could have imagined. In light of this knowledge, I promise never to rate you below two stars again.

To everyone reading this book: I wish I could hug you. I can't thank you enough for taking a chance on a first-time author like me. Whether you know me personally, you know my work as an actor, or you simply picked up my book because it spoke to you. . .it is because of you that my dreams are being realized. Thank you.

About the Author

Willa Frederic is a pseudonym for Galadriel Stineman. In addition to writing novels, Galadriel is an award-winning TV and film actor, screenwriter, and acting teacher. She lives in Los Angeles with her husband and two children.

9 781955 690041